Since 1941, *The Best American Short Stories* has annually laid to rest all predictions that the form was dying. Innovation abounds, emphases change, but year in and year out, this volume testifies to the brilliance of the many writers who continue to work within the short story's demanding limits—and to the liveliness of the magazines, "little" and big, that publish them.

For most of its history, the editor of this collection has been Martha Foley, a tart-tongued, opinionated, dedicated, and thoroughly delightful lady who, year after year, culls the dozens upon dozens of magazines that publish short stories. This year, her twenty selections demonstrate, as always, peerless taste and admirable catholicity.

THE
BEST AMERICAN
SHORT STORIES
1973

The Yearbook of The American Short Story

Edited by
Martha Foley

BALLANTINE BOOKS • NEW YORK

"A City of Churches" by Donald Barthelme. First published in
The New Yorker. Reprinted by permission of Farrar, Straus &
Giroux, Inc., from the book *Sadness* by Donald Barthelme. Copy-
right © 1972 by Donald Barthelme.

"The Slightest Distance" by Henry Bromell. First published in
The New Yorker. Copyright © 1972 by The New Yorker Magazine, Inc.

"The Jewels of the Cabots" by John Cheever. First published in
Playboy. Copyright © 1972 by John Cheever.

"Cambridge is Sinking!" by John J. Clayton. First published in
The Massachusetts Review. Copyright © 1972 by The Massachusetts Review, Inc.

"Old Men Dream Dreams, Young Men See Visions" by John
William Corrington. First published in the *Sewanee Review*, Vol.
LXXX, No. 1 (Winter 1972). Reprinted by permission of the
publisher. Copyright © 1972 by The University of the South.

"Robot" by Guy Davenport. First published in *The Hudson Review*, Vol. XXV, No. 3 (Autumn 1972). Reprinted by permission
of the publisher. Copyright © 1972 by The Hudson Review, Inc.

"The Death of the Sun" by William Eastlake. First published in
Cosmopolitan. Copyright © 1972 by William Eastlake.

"The Real Meaning of the Faust Legend" by Alvin Greenberg.
First published in the *New American Review*. Copyright © 1972
by Simon and Schuster, Inc.

"In the Words Of" by Julie Hayden. First published in *The New*

TO
THE EDITORS
OF THE
LITERARY MAGAZINES
OF AMERICA

Acknowledgments

GRATEFUL ACKNOWLEDGMENT for permission to reprint the stories in this volume is made to the following:

The editors of *The Atlantic Monthly, Cosmopolitan, Esquire, The Hudson Review, The Kansas Quarterly, The Malahat Review, The Massachusetts Review, McCall's, The New Yorker, The North American Review, The Paris Review, Playboy, Sewanee Review, The South Dakota Review;* and to Donald Barthelme, Henry Bromell, John Cheever, John J. Clayton, John William Corrington, Guy Davenport, William Eastlake, Julie Hayden, George V. Higgins, James S. Kenary, Wallace E. Knight, Konstantinos Lardas, James Alan McPherson, Bernard Malamud, Joyce Carol Oates, The Estate of Sylvia Plath, Erik Sandberg-Diment, David Shetzline, Jr., Tennessee Williams.

Foreword

A FACULTY COLLEAGUE with whom I shared an office when I was teaching at Columbia University let out an agonized yell one day. I looked around to see the source of his pain. He was holding up his hand, pierced by a fish hook. On the desk before him lay a student's manuscript. "Dear Professor," a note with the manuscript read, "you told the class a writer should always start a short story with a hook to intrigue the reader so I am enclosing one."

The professor was intrigued all right. So was the campus doctor who had to cut the hook out of his hand. Whether the student was intrigued by the mark he received at the end of the course I never knew, although I often wondered how objective the professor managed to be when he gave it. The episode is a wonderful demonstration of how absurd are all generalities about literature, particularly that division of it called fiction.

Oracular pronouncements on the short story have been more numerous than usual in the past year. There are elegists who base their laments over its alleged decline on the one or two eastern seaboard magazines they read, which use one or two short stories as filling for the pages of lavish advertising for which Madison Avenue pays. There are the literary necrophiliacs trying to exhume the famous dead with thousands of words of pedantic "explication," thereby burying still deeper fine old writers who, if alive today, would ask only to be read and enjoyed. Then there are the "Cubes," a label which some of my younger friends tell me has succeeded "Squares," since the Cubes are denser. They profess themselves baffled by something they call "the New Fiction." Then there are the self-styled innovators who would level whole forests to provide paper for their infatuation with graphics and typography and to hell with words.

There are also, thank "whatever gods may be," several hundred excellent writers and many excellent aspiring writers too busy actually writing to be distracted for long by such diversionary tactics. For when you come right down to it, a good story is neither traditional nor "new." It is ageless. Nor are good stories to be divided into such categories as "a man's story," "a woman's story," or "a child's story." As only one example, how many adults of both sexes revel in that "child's story," *Alice in Wonderland?*

Arnold Gingrich, the founding editor of *Esquire,* which ever since its inception forty years ago has published many of the most "modern" stories of the period by authors considered daringly "experimental," now declares himself worried by what he, too, terms "the New Fiction." And Arnold, of all people, resurrects the moldy cliché about how a story should have "a beginning, a middle, and an end." It was that deadly old scholastic Aristotle who promulgated this theory, and I have always liked what the father of one of my students told her: "Remember, after Aristotle there was no more Greek literature."

The "beginning, middle, and end" edict stems from the once rigid structure of a drama and its requirement of at least three acts. Today not many playwrights worry about such stringencies, even if a few directors and producers may. Many plays are written first as short stories. Eugene O'Neill said his original intention was to write short stories. Tennessee Williams, whose latest short story is included in this book, first writes his plays as short stories. If Ingmar Bergman had not been ineligible for an anthology limited to American authors, I would have liked to have included his "Cries and Whispers." It is a beautiful short story which *The New Yorker* published and which is the basis of his film with the same title.

After bemoaning the loss of b., m., and e., Mr. Gingrich

goes on in a racist and sexist way to say, apropos an argument he has been having, "the only thing we find harder to understand than the New Fiction is our fiction editor's explanation of it, so we read [the stories] with the comforting realization that while they may not come with an ending, at least they come to an end like everything else. It also helps to bear in mind the Chinese father's advice to his daughter on the subject of rape—when you see it is inevitable, try to relax and enjoy it."

Has women's liberation had an effect on the stories published in magazines this year? Not a large one. While the women's magazines have finally become aware of their readers as people, publishing countless articles on the subject and columns by such feminists as Betty Freidan, their stories are about the same as usual. There is, however, growing interest in the rediscovery of earlier stories by American women, some dating as far back as the early nineteenth century, which reveal a strong feminine consciousness. To me one of the most impressive of these women's stories is *Life in the Iron Mills,* a novella by Rebecca Harding Davis, the mother of Richard Harding Davis. It was published as a book by The Feminist Press at the Stony Brook, Long Island, branch of New York University and has a biography and critical comment by Tillie Olsen, herself a splendid short story writer. When recalling the strong feminine characters in the works of Willa Cather, Dorothy Canfield Fisher, Mary Wilkins Freeman, Sarah Orne Jewett, and numerous others of years past, one wonders what happened to neutralize women in our more recent fiction.

Another contrast with the past is to be found in stories about the poverty-stricken. The social consciousness that inflamed Dickens and Hugo and Frank Norris in the nineteenth century and the "proletarian" writers of the thirties has been replaced by ethnicity. The horrors of race prejudice are emphasized and the suffering of all oppressed people is forgotten. The other extreme seems to have disappeared as well. Except for those by Louis Auchincloss, I have read no good stories about the rich for a long time. There are no Edith Whartons, no Henry Jameses to chronicle them.

Spy stories and crime documentaries have been replacing

the detective story, though Sherlock Holmes's constant demand, "Quick, Watson, the needle!" is still with us in other guises. Drug-taking is almost omnipresent in stories of every genre. The casual way in which characters are described as "sharing a joint," swallowing "uppers" or "downers," "tripping" on LSD, or "freaking out" is startling. If you think a "roach" is an insect, you are far, far behind the times. Such expressions are so common that when one writer stated a man was "stoned," he added, "I mean stones were thrown at him."

Most science fiction stories appear to lack the roundedness of those by Bradbury and Vonnegut. For this particular reader they do not bestow the enchantment Jules Verne cast on my childhood days with *Twenty Thousand Leagues Under the Sea, The Mysterious Island,* and the fascinating Captain Nemo. Science fiction short stories have machines for characters and lack the kind of human ambience in weird circumstances that Verne established. Based on mechanical achievements, the people in today's Science Fiction stories are too often robots calling, "Look, Ma, no hands!"

We are beginning to get powerful stories out of the Vietnam War. Probably they will be with us for a long time to come as the stories are implying that the war is a turning point in American history and in the outlook of the American people.

In the matter of styles, there seems to be great emphasis on fragmentation. Chapter divisions are logical and welcome in book-length narratives, but to fracture brief stories into minute units often destroys coherence. When those small sections have pompous Roman numerals imposed on them, I find it ridiculous.

American readers have had slight opportunity to enjoy stories written below the Rio Grande. All through Central and South America prodigious writing is going on which is better recognized in Europe than in the United States. Now a magazine devoted to this literature and printed in English is being published for American readers in this country. It is called *Americas* and its office is in Washington, D.C. Another note about new magazine developments—the *Saturday Evening Post* is with us again. This time it costs a dollar instead of a nickel, but nostalgic readers recalling the Victorian language of its early days need not mourn. Norman Rockwell is still its star contributor and illustrator. Newest of new magazines is *Ms.*, a saucily stimulating feminist publication.

I am dedicating this year's volume of *The Best American Short Stories* to the unsung heroes of American literature, the editors of our literary magazines. These publications are often called "little," although their pages may number more than a hundred and their contents are far from little in quality. The majority of our important writers have first emerged in their pages and they have been the bulwark of short story writing in this country. Even so, they are all but ignored by critics in New York (the alleged capital of publishing) who are so ignorant of countrywide developments in literature that they blindly keep lamenting the "decline" of the short story. These magazines have no circulation departments with big budgets to enable them to reach readers who would enjoy them. They are edited by hardworking brilliant men and women, often unpaid, at a sacrifice of their time and energy. All of us who love good writing are in their debt.

I am grateful to all the editors who have kept this anthology supplied with copies of their magazines and to their authors for generously granting reprint rights. The editor of any new magazine is urged to send copies to me.

The editors and staff of Houghton Mifflin are entitled to gratitude for their help. Finally tribute is paid to the memory of Edward J. O'Brien, who founded this anthology.

Martha Foley
New Canaan, Connecticut

CONTENTS

THE
BEST AMERICAN
SHORT STORIES
1973

DONALD BARTHELME

A City of Churches

(FROM THE NEW YORKER)

"YES," MR. PHILLIPS SAID, "ours is a city of churches all right."

Cecelia nodded, following his pointing hand. Both sides of the street were solidly lined with churches, standing shoulder to shoulder in a variety of architectural styles. The Bethel Baptist stood next to the Holy Messiah Free Baptist, Saint Paul's Episcopal next to Grace Evangelical Covenant. Then came the First Christian Science, the Church of God, All Souls, Our Lady of Victory, the Society of Friends, the Assembly of God, and the Church of the Holy Apostles. The spires and steeples of the traditional buildings were jammed in next to the broad imaginative flights of the "contemporary" designs.

"Everyone here takes a great interest in church matters," Mr. Phillips said.

Will I fit in, Cecelia wondered. She had come to Prester to open a branch office of a car-rental concern.

"I'm not especially religious," she said to Mr. Phillips, who was in the real-estate business.

"Not *now*," he answered. "Not *yet*. But we have many fine young people here. You'll get integrated into the community soon enough. The immediate problem is where you are to live? Most people," he said, "live in the church of their choice. All of our churches have many extra rooms. I have a few belfry apartments that I can show you. What price range were you thinking of?"

1

They turned a corner and were confronted with more churches. They passed Saint Luke's, the Church of the Epiphany, All Saints Ukrainian Orthodox, Saint Clement's, Fountain Baptist, Union Congregational, Saint Anargyri's, Temple Emanuel, the First Church of Christ Reformed. The mouths of all the churches were gaping open. Inside, lights could be seen dimly.

"I can go up to a hundred and ten," Cecelia said. "Do you have any buildings here that are *not* churches?"

"None," said Mr. Phillips. "Of course, many of our fine church structures also do double duty as something else." He indicated a handsome Georgian façade. "That one," he said, "houses the United Methodist and the Board of Education. The one next to it, which is the Antioch Pentecostal, has the barbershop."

It was true. A red-and-white striped barber pole was attached inconspicuously to the front of the Antioch Pentecostal.

"Do many people rent cars here?" Cecelia asked. "Or would they, if there was a handy place to rent them?"

"Oh, I don't know," said Mr. Phillips. "Renting a car implies that you want to go somewhere. Most people are pretty content right here. We have a lot of activities. I don't think I'd pick the car-rental business if I was just starting out in Prester. But you'll do fine." He showed her a small, extremely modern building with a severe brick, steel, and glass front. "That's Saint Barnabas. Nice bunch of people over there. Wonderful spaghetti suppers."

Cecelia could see a number of heads looking out of the windows. But when they saw that she was staring at them, the heads disappeared.

"Do you think it's healthy for so many churches to be gathered together in one place?" she asked her guide. "It doesn't seem . . . *balanced,* if you know what I mean."

"We are famous for our churches," Mr. Phillips replied. "They are harmless. Here we are now."

He opened a door and they began climbing many flights of dusty stairs. At the end of the climb they entered a good-sized room, square, with windows on all four sides. There was a bed, a table and two chairs, lamps, a rug. Four very large brass bells hung in the exact center of the room.

"What a view!" Mr. Phillips exclaimed. "Come here and look."

"Do they actually ring these bells?" Cecelia asked.

"Three times a day." Mr. Phillips said, smiling. "Morning, noon, and night. Of course when they're rung you have to be pretty quick at getting out of the way. You get hit in the head by one of these babies and that's all she wrote."

"God Almighty," said Cecelia involuntarily. Then she said, "Nobody lives in the belfry apartments. That's why they're empty."

"You think so?" Mr. Phillips said.

"You can only rent them to new people in town," she said accusingly.

"I wouldn't do that," Mr. Phillips said. "It would go against the spirit of Christian fellowship."

"This town is a little creepy, you know that?"

"That may be, but it's not for you to say, is it? I mean, you're new here. You should walk cautiously, for a while. If you don't want an upper apartment, I have a basement over at Central Presbyterian. You'd have to share it. There are two women in there now."

"I don't want to share," Cecelia said. "I want a place of my own."

"Why?" the real-estate man asked curiously. "For what purpose?"

"Purpose?" asked Cecelia. "There is no particular purpose. I just want—"

"That's not usual here. Most people live with other people. Husbands and wives. Sons with their mothers. People have roommates. That's the usual pattern."

"Still, I prefer a place of my own."

"It's very unusual."

"Do you have any such places? Besides bell towers, I mean?"

"I guess there are a few," Mr. Phillips said, with clear reluctance. "I can show you one or two, I suppose."

He paused for a moment.

"It's just that we have different values, maybe, from some

of the surrounding communities," he explained. "We've been written up a lot. We had four minutes on the 'CBS Evening News' one time. Three or four years ago. 'A City of Churches,' it was called."

"Yes, a place of my own is essential," Cecelia said, "if I am to survive here."

"That's kind of a funny attitude to take," Mr. Phillips said. "What denomination are you?"

Cecelia was silent. The truth was, she wasn't anything.

"I said, what denomination are you?" Mr. Phillips repeated.

"I can will my dreams," Cecelia said. "I can dream whatever I want. If I want to dream that I'm having a good time, in Paris or some other city, all I have to do is go to sleep and I will dream that dream. I can dream whatever I want."

"What do you dream, then, mostly?" Mr. Phillips said, looking at her closely.

"Mostly sexual things," she said. She was not afraid of him.

"Prester is not that kind of a town," Mr. Phillips said, looking away.

The doors of the churches were opening, on both sides of the street. Small groups of people came out and stood there, in front of the churches, gazing at Cecelia and Mr. Phillips.

A young man stepped forward and shouted, *"Everyone in this town already has a car! There is no one in this town who doesn't have a car!"*

"Is that true?" Cecelia asked Mr. Phillips.

"Yes," he said. "It's true. No one would rent a car here. Not in a hundred years."

"Then I won't stay," she said. "I'll go somewhere else."

"You must stay," he said. "There is already a car-rental office for you. In Mount Moriah Baptist, on the lobby floor. There is a counter and a telephone and a rack of car keys. And a calendar."

"I won't stay," she said. "Not if there's not any sound business reason for staying."

"We want you," said Mr. Phillips. "We want you standing

behind the counter of the car-rental agency, during regular business hours. It will make the town complete."

"I won't," she said. "Not me."

"You must. It's essential."

"I'll dream," she said. "Things you won't like."

"We are discontented," said Mr. Phillips. "Terribly, terribly discontented. Something is wrong."

"I'll dream the Secret," she said. "You'll be sorry."

"We are like other towns, except that we are perfect," he said. "Our discontent can only be held in check by perfection. We need a car-rental girl. Someone must stand behind the counter."

"I'll dream the life you are most afraid of," Cecelia threatened.

"You are ours," he said, gripping her arm. "Our car-rental girl. Be nice. There is nothing you can do."

"Wait and see," Cecelia said.

HENRY BROMELL

The Slightest Distance

(FROM THE NEW YORKER)

THE SUN MADE HER FEEL so heavy she did not believe she had the energy to rise and walk to the water. A drop of sweat snagged on her sunglasses, tickling her cheek. She brushed it away and looked up from her book.

Matthew, her middle child, sat next to her on the beach, also reading, his nose covered with Noxzema. Scobie lay beyond him, and beyond Scobie lay Quentin, her youngest son.

"Anyone for a swim?" she asked.

Matthew shook his head. "No, thanks."

"What time do we leave tonight?" Scobie asked, not opening his eyes.

"Four-thirty. Tomorrow *morning*."

"You're kidding."

"No," she said, then laughed. "So take a long nap after lunch."

Scobie groaned and rolled over onto his stomach.

Matthew's face, and Scobie's back, and Quentin's shoulder formed, in receding perspective, a single motionless statue.

Mrs. Richardson blinked and returned to her book. Not reading, she thought of Scobie, her oldest son; in the six months between last Christmas vacation and this summer he had changed. He had arrived in June too pale, too harried to be anything but unhappy. For six weeks he had said very little. Of course, this had happened before, but never before had she felt such a need to hear him speak. On past occa-

6

sions she had simply waited, counting on his age, his growth, his changing personality to explain. But this time the situation seemed different. Maybe because he was eighteen, maybe because he was about to enter college, maybe because his reticence seemed more nearly permanent—whatever the reason, his silence now was painful.

She closed her book, picked up one of the boys' swimming masks, and quickly waded into the cold water.

The spoon lay at the bottom of the sea, a spark of silver swarming with fish. Fanning the water with her arms, she peered down through her mask at the specks of swirling light and for a second imagined that she was part of the sea, a flash of sponge or scale. Mysterious, diaphanous cells darted before her eyes. It seemed inconceivable that men plunged to the bottom in search of gold, plunged down to where even the light disappeared, down into that maze of rocks. She feared the cold layers of shadow. She feared drowning.

She lifted her face out of the water and pushed off her mask.

Her three sons were still on the beach. To their left, a fisherman sat mending his nets. Heat, quivering above the rocks, rose, the way the water descended, in layers. On the mountain, a donkey brayed. Matthew looked up from his book, saw her, and waved.

She waved back, and then, suddenly, without thought, she pulled the mask over her eyes, sucked in a lungful of air, and dove, kicking her way down toward the seaweed and sand. As she sank, the fear of drowning returned. She clawed for the spoon, but swirls of sand rose and obscured it from view. She kicked harder, forcing her body down, reaching in among the swaying silt and seaweed until she felt the metal touch her fingers. She grabbed but missed. Her lungs ached. Her arms moved slowly. Snapping her legs, she pressed herself down onto the bottom and dug for the spoon. Again she found it, and this time she held on, pulling it away from the rocks and up against her chest.

They were waiting for her on the beach, blankets and books under their arms.

"Look what I found."

"A spoon?" Scobie asked, leaning forward and staring.

"Yes."

"From where?"

"The bottom," she said.

"That's very interesting, Mom. A real find."

Matthew and Quentin laughed.

"*You* used to collect them," she said. "In Italy, remember?"

Scobie grinned. "Yes," he said. "I remember. Ice-cream spoons."

"That's right. So don't be so snooty."

"Mom, *hurry*," Quentin said. "It's lunchtime. I'm starving."

She pulled a white terry-cloth dress over her bathing suit, picked up her beach bag, and followed her sons toward the dock.

"Can you believe your father's finally coming?"

"No," Scobie said. "I can't. My theory is that we'll never see him again. He's disappeared for good. Up the Nile."

They walked along the edge of the water, where the sand was cool, until they came to the concrete steps leading up to the taverna—a two-story, whitewashed building that occupied a small section of rock jutting out into the harbor.

There was a terrace running along two sides of the taverna, covered with wooden chairs and tables and shaded by a green awning. The Richardsons moved toward a table in the corner nearest the sea. A small boy in faded gray shorts and T-shirt was waiting for them.

"Hello, Yorgo," Mrs. Richardson said in Greek.

"Hello." He smiled.

"I think we'll have salad and fish today," she said. "And beer."

Yorgo disappeared into the building, his bare, brown feet slapping across the terrace.

Mrs. Richardson lit a cigarette and laid the silver spoon in the middle of the table.

"Remember when we used to dive for pebbles?" Scobie asked, picking up the spoon. "We thought they were pieces of gold. Remember?"

"Yes," Matthew said. "At Nana's."

"We used to dive for them the way you dove for this," Scobie told his mother.

The salad and beer arrived. They thanked Yorgo and started eating.

"You sure Dad will be there?" Scobie asked.

"He'll be there," she said. "Even he knows he needs a vacation."

The village of Mymeros was organized around the base of a
mountain, rising to an ancient church and Venetian fort at
the top. The sun reflected off the small, whitewashed houses
as Mrs. Richardson and her sons, arm in arm, slowly climbed
the slope. Occasionally an old Greek woman, shrouded in
black, would peer from the shadowy interior of a house and
wave.

Halfway up the mountain, facing the harbor, a green metal
gate gave way to a series of stone steps that led down to the
main floor of their house. A red-and-white tile terrace
stretched along the front. Below the terrace were two levels
of garden, then a wall. The view was of the sea, a few brown
islands in the distance.

Mrs. Richardson crossed the terrace and walked into the
front room. The shutters were drawn, and the room was
shady and cool. She dropped her beach bag onto the floor,
pulled off her dress and wet bathing suit, wrapped herself in
a summer bathrobe, and lay down on her cot. She could hear
her sons outside on the terrace, arguing about which tape to
play on Quentin's tape recorder. From the harbor rose the
gentle *put-put* of the island generator.

She could not sleep. She imagined that her sons had
grown, that she had lost her children. When she was Scobie's
age, she had fallen in love with his father. Now her son's and
husband's voices were so similar she sometimes jumped when
Scobie spoke. It was as if, at the age of forty-five, she were
able to see her husband at eighteen—at any rate, see the
body he had occupied. Staring at the intricate swirls of
shadow on the ceiling, Mrs. Richardson wondered what it
would be like when, years from now, she would visit Scobie's
family, his wife and children, his house, his living room
filled with books. It would happen, she knew; it was only a
matter of time.

Her sons were quiet on the terrace. They had fallen asleep.

The tape recorder was playing a song by the Beatles—"Here, There and Everywhere."

Two months ago the Egyptians had attacked the Israelis—or the Israelis had attacked the Egyptians—and she and Quentin had been put on a train, along with several hundred other Americans and Europeans, and taken to Alexandria. Her husband had stayed behind, part of a small Embassy staff that remained in Cairo. From Alexandria she and Quentin had traveled by boat to Greece, where Scobie and Matthew, on vacation from boarding school, had joined them. They had rented an apartment with a view of the Parthenon, high on Lykabettos; at night they could hear music from the Hilton rooftop night club. And then ten days ago they had come here, to this tiny island in the Aegean. For ten days they had been working on the house—painting the kitchen, clearing the garden, covering the outside walls with a fresh coat of whitewash. Tomorrow they would meet Mr. Richardson in Rhodes.

One of the boys turned off the tape recorder and went back to sleep.

Mrs. Richardson tried to imagine what her husband was doing at this moment. If he had already arrived in Rhodes, he was probably napping, too. She could see him clearly, lying in bed reading *Motor Sport* or *Yachting*. She could see him showering, dressing in khakis and cotton shirt, and descending to the hotel bar with a book (*A History of the British Frigate*) in his hand. Of course, he could still be in Egypt; that had happened before. But she doubted it. She felt quite sure he would be there tomorrow. He would meet them at the dock. And then maybe *he* could talk to Scobie.

Like certain kinds of demonic music, the curve of Scobie's gaze, his bewildered resentment, bore into her and hurt. Scobie had never been prepared for life, though he had done more and seen more than most people his age. He dreamed too much. She sensed this dream but could not glimpse its contents. It had something to do with pride, a refusal to follow orders; though he denied it, he believed himself self-sufficient. Yet he looked at her as if to say, "Why *aren't* I self-sufficient?" And he was so romantic—like her, perhaps, he really did believe in the perfectibility of his future. Believed, but knew better, and so, caught between two perceptions, blamed her for the confusion. Life had not been like this when he was a child. Now—purposely, she suspected—he made things difficult for himself. He had never worked at school and so had been constantly threatened by expulsion, no college, a curtailed career. He seemed, despite himself, to thrive on threat.

Still, she would not have wished to change his life. At least he felt the pain—there was that. At least he was aware.

Slowly, bodies from a dream, the three boys rose and stood with her on the terrace, watching twilight deepen across the water. The white houses glowed in the sun. Here and there a dark figure moved through a doorway, crossed the beach, called a name, and waved. The rocks of the island were red—luminous and shifting, as if dangling from a mobile.

Matthew spoke first. "I'm going for a swim."

"It's too cold," Scobie said.

"No, it's not. Quentin?"

Quentin nodded and stood; he and Matthew disappeared into the house to change.

Scobie and his mother remained on the terrace, sitting in green canvas chairs and gazing at the sunset.

"It's kind of spooky, this time of day," Scobie said.

"That's what your father thinks."

"He does?"

"Yes. He says it depresses him."

Matthew and Quentin crossed the terrace on their way to the gate, both in bathing suits and sweaters.

"Don't be long," Mrs. Richardson said.

"We won't."

The gate clanged shut behind them.

She looked down at the harbor and saw the first fishing boat pull into shore, the sun reflecting off its cabin windows.

"Mom."

"Yes?"

"Has Dad been in any danger?"

"A little."

Scobie rubbed his hands across his shoulders. "Is he mad at me?"

"For what?"

"For, I don't know, school—all that."

"No. He's sorry you're not happy, that's all."

"I'm happy."

"You are?"

"Yes. I feel like I'm missing something, but that's not un-happiness."

"What do you feel you're missing?"

"I don't know." He shrugged.

"I mean, a person, or a . . . thought, or what?"

"A person, I guess. Maybe a thought. A *clearness*."

"To see?"

"Yes. And hear, taste, touch, smell. The works." He paused.

"I feel very distant," he said.

"Distant?"

"Yes. From myself."

It seemed to her that his words ballooned out and allowed her to see, for the first time that summer, something of his dream. "You think of yourself as 'he'?" she asked.

"Yes," he answered, surprised. "That's right."

"You *are* like your father."

"I am?"

"In many ways. Sometimes I think he still feels distant from himself."

"He doesn't act it."

"Oh, you don't know." She watched Scobie light a ciga-rette. "He thinks a great deal of you," she said.

Scobie was silent, staring off to sea. She noticed a thin line above his lip; he was growing a mustache.

"He'll be glad to see you," she said.

"He doesn't talk much."

"No. Neither do you."

He looked at her. "Is that true?"

"What?"

"That I don't talk much?"

She laughed. "Yes, my dear. You are the silent type. The brooding poet."

He laughed, too, shyly revealing his large, bright teeth.

She borrowed his cigarette and lit one of her own.

"Do we have to go to this party tonight?" he asked.

"Yes. It would be impolite not to. Anyway, it will be fun."

"They're celebrating a saint?"

"Yes." She picked a piece of tobacco off her lip. "I remember years ago when we lived in Athens, your father and I went to a wedding on Mykonos. It was very funny. For a long time everybody just sat around on very stiff chairs, the women on one side of the room, the men on the other. But when the wedding was over, the entire island celebrated for twelve hours. I can barely remember myself swaying on the back of a donkey, in the middle of a long line of donkeys winding their way down a mountain path. It was night. Before me and behind me spread a beautiful flickering—dozens of candles. Each rider of each donkey held a candle in his hand. I was quite drunk."

"Look."

She followed his pointing hand and saw her other two sons on the beach below. The sand was in shadow and the water was gray-red and still. Matthew and Quentin were racing, their hair flying out behind them. Every few yards they pushed each other and laughed. The shaking sound of their laughter carried up to the terrace where she and Scobie sat watching.

Mrs. Richardson and her sons reached the top of the mountain just as the sun disappeared into the sea. Strings of electric light bulbs hung in canopies above the open square. Most of the villagers had already arrived. Their voices excited her; she felt the contagious spirit of a festival and clapped her hands. Scobie grinned. Matthew and Quentin, walking ahead, turned and urged them on.

"Dionysus," Scobie said, pointing to a well-muscled young man leaning against the side of the church. He was dark from the sun and dressed in gray cotton trousers and a starched white shirt. He stood perfectly still.

"Where do we go?" Matthew asked.

"I don't know," she said. "Over there, by the wall."

A ring of wooden chairs had been set up with their backs

to the view, facing the square. The four of them nudged through the crowd and sat down.

A tall fisherman approached with glasses of retsina in his hands.

"For us?"

"Yes," he said, his dark mustache bobbing above his smile. "For you."

They each took a glass and saluted him. He bowed, smiling, and vanished into the crowd.

"Cheers," Scobie said.

The musicians tuned their bouzoukis and began to play. Immediately the square was filled with the young men of the village, dancing together in a circle. The older men and women and children stood back, watching and clapping. Bottles of retsina passed from mouth to mouth. Soon the young men were in a frenzy, leaping and slapping the ground, clapping their hands, then springing and kicking into the air like acrobats.

Beyond the perimeter of electric lights it was dark. Mrs. Richardson drew her sweater up closer around her neck and took a swallow of wine. Scobie, his elbows on his knees, was watching the dancing. Matthew, twisted sideways on his chair, was watching the thin horizon streak and diminish. Quentin was also watching the dancing, his glasses halfway down his nose.

She looked at Scobie, then away, embarrassed. This was a man sitting beside her. *Her son.* So much time, and all of it invested in this body—was it a crime to waste youth on youth? Sometimes she thought so. Sometimes she resented Scobie for being her son, just as he surely resented her for being his mother. Soon Matthew would be a man. Then Quentin. Three sons, three departures.

The dancers were waving at her—no, at her sons; they were beckoning her sons into action.

"Go on," she said. "Dance."

Reluctantly, they rose and walked onto the square. Shoulders parted, large brown hands pulled them in, and the music resumed, her sons—flying, bewildered, self-conscious, out of step—joining the dancers.

Mrs. Richardson sipped her retsina. Nostalgia plagued Scobie, she knew, as much as it plagued her. But why? Because he traveled so much? Because each moment of his life, a fragment, was too brief to be real, therefore always beauti-ful? With her it was simply an awareness of all that had gone before, all that she had already passed through—every scent and gesture caught forever. Perhaps it was the same for him. Perhaps the "something" he missed had already come and gone. She didn't know. She could only guess, and it made her sad to think such mysteries permanently mysterious, perhaps deceiving, perhaps—this was the worst—unsolvable.

"Missis?"

She looked up into the dark, smiling face of the young man she had seen earlier—Dionysus. "Yes?"

"Please . . ." He made a loose, uncertain gesture of his hands, smiled, and waited.

"Of course," she said.

He sat down.

She pulled a cigarette from her pack and immediately the young man had his lighter out and sparking.

"Thank you."

"Welcome."

They sat back and stared at one another. He looked about twenty-four, handsome, competent at something—carpentry or fishing. She offered him a cigarette.

"Win-ston," he said, smiling and flicking his lighter. "Very good."

"What is your name?" she asked.

"Kosta."

"Do you live on this island?"

He shook his head, and pointed toward the sea. "Cos." Then, puffing deeply on his Winston, he asked, "What is your name?"

"Laura Richardson."

"Rich-ard-son." He repeated the name.

"Those are my sons," she said, nodding at the dancers.

"Very nice sons," Kosta said. "Very wonderful boys, Mrs. Rich-ard-son."

"You speak good English," she said.

He beamed. "Thank you very much."

A bottle of retsina came their way. Kosta poured some

into her glass, took a swallow from the bottle, then passed it on. He wiped his mouth with a clean white handkerchief.

"You have no . . . husband?" he asked.

His nonchalance betrayed him; he *was* flirting.

"Yes," she said, firmly. "I'm going to see him tomorrow."

Kosta looked at her sadly, his beautiful brown face shimmering beneath the swaying electric lights. She smiled.

"Ch-*rist*." Scobie collapsed into his chair.

"Welcome back," she said.

"Mother, I swear to God, I think I'm dying."

She laughed. "You're getting flabby."

"I beg your pardon, but those guys are freaks. They've got springs instead of legs."

Matthew and Quentin jumped from the circle and returned to their seats. Quentin's glasses were misty and askew.

"My sons," she said.

"How do you do." Kosta rose and shook their hands. "Very nice to meet you."

"Your name?"

"Kosta."

"Hi, I'm Scobie. That's Matthew, and Quentin."

"Sco-bie. Mat-hew. Ken-ton."

Scobie grabbed another passing bottle of wine and they all took a long swallow.

"Mom, you should dance," Matthew said.

"Women don't dance."

"Sure they do."

"Your mother, she is an excellent dancer?" Kosta asked, smiling.

"Fantastic. Just terrific. Incredible."

"Oh, Scobie, stop."

"Hey," Matthew said. "Something's happening."

She looked into the square and saw that all but an old man in blue jacket and baggy brown trousers had drawn back from the circle. His feet were bare and flat, his hair thick, white. Slowly he crouched, his arms spread at his sides, and began to dance. The musicians caught the tempo and played along. He snapped his fingers and sprang straight up, magically tall, then came down in a lower crouch, his feet shooting out before him, his heels slapping the stone, and danced as if, with age and speed, he could spin the entire island out to sea.

"Mom?" It was Scobie, still awake on the terrace.

"Yes?" Mrs. Richardson paused in the doorway.

"Was that guy flirting with you?"

"Yes."

"I thought so."

"Go to sleep," she said. "In four hours you have to get up."

"It's almost not worth it."

"Every little bit helps."

"Mom?"

"What?"

"Did you like him?"

"Who?"

"That guy, Kosta."

"Very much," she exclaimed, surprised at herself. "Very much."

She awoke with the alarm clock in her hands. It was still dark. The only sound was the island generator and a few isolated waves at the mouth of the harbor. She sat up, reached for the light, turned it on. The sudden brightness made her blink. She pulled on her bathrobe and walked out onto the terrace. "Boys."

They didn't move.

"Time to get up. Scobie, arise. You're just in time for dawn."

"Mother, for Godsake . . ."

"It's time to get up."

Like a robot, Matthew suddenly jerked to a sitting position, snorted, and stood. "Good morning," he said.

The light was now gray. They could see each other. Quentin was still zipped into his sleeping bag, a small breathing hole the only sign of life. Scobie slowly propped himself up on his elbow and watched with her and Matthew as the distant edge of the sea grew to a faint, faint red.

"How long do we have?" Scobie whispered.

"Half an hour. Wake your brother and let's get ready."

She returned to the front room and opened her suitcase. She packed her nightgown and bathrobe, the alarm clock, and the book by the cot. Then, dressed, she carried her suitcase out to the terrace. *"Quentin!"*

The lump shook, gasped, and a hand came poking through the air hole, fingers groping for the zipper. The bag opened. Quentin sat up and stared at his knees.

"Get dressed," she said.

She left him sitting on his cot and walked to the outhouse, a small stone building by the garden wall. The door was blocked by Scobie, who was swearing.

"What's wrong?"

"The damn thing won't flush."

"Oh, Scobie, please."

"Mother, it just won't *flush*. It's not my fault."

He straightened and stepped out.

"What shall we do?" she asked.

He pointed to the garden.

"No, I mean, we can't just leave it like that."

"We'll have to."

"Scobie, we cannot just leave it like that."

"We'll tell the mayor. He's awake for every boat. We'll tell him at the dock."

"All right."

Matthew and Quentin were dressed and waiting on the terrace.

"Everybody ready?"

"Should I bring my tape recorder?" Quentin asked.

"Yes," Scobie said. "O.K.?"

"O.K. Let's go."

They picked up their suitcases, closed the gate behind them, and began the walk down the mountain. It was almost daylight, yet she could not see the sun. Roosters crowed all across the island. A single dog barked. Mrs. Richardson and her three sons, forming a single, silent line, wound their way between the ice-blue houses.

At the bottom of the mountain they found a small group, including the mayor, sitting at a table on the taverna terrace, waiting for the ship.

The Richardsons nodded hello and sat down.

A sleepy Yorgo brought them small glasses of hot tea and biscuits.

"Mr. Mayor?"

The mayor turned and smiled. He was a large, round man with a bald head and anxious, startled eyes. He owned the only grocery store on the island. "Yes, Mrs. Rich-ard-son?"

"Our toilet."

"Toilet?"

"Doesn't work."

"Doesn't work. Does-ant work." He shook his head, staring at the table. "Doesn't work?"

"Is broken," Scobie said.

"Ah, *broken.*"

"Yes," she said.

"No worry, have *no* fear. Everything will be fixed." He smiled.

Silently, they sipped their tea and waited for the ship. The sky was beginning to turn the color of mother-of-pearl. Some fishermen appeared and ate their breakfast, then began loading their nets into their caïques. Rooswers crowed through the village.

"There it is," Quentin said.

What looked like a string of floating electric lights appeared around the edge of the harbor. Gradually, the ship itself materialized—a long, white phantom. A whistle blasted and then the anchors splashed into the water, chains rattling loudly in the still dawn.

"Let's go," Scobie said.

They picked up their suitcases and followed the small crowd down to the dock.

One of the fisherman had his caïque ready to take them out to the ship. Scobie jumped aboard, then helped his mother. Matthew and Quentin handed him the suitcases and climbed aboard themselves. The only other passengers were an old man and woman sitting on either side of their wicker suitcase, waving good-bye to somebody on the dock.

"Don't worry, Mrs. Rich-ard-son!" the mayor called, a hat covering his baldness. "Everything is fixed."

She waved. "Thank you."

The caïque pulled away from the dock.

"Don't worry, Mrs. Rich-ard-son!" the mayor screamed. "Everything is O.K.!"

She turned and faced the nearing ship. Warm, salty air blew across her face. When the giant hull was only twenty yards away she swiveled and looked back at the island, the village spread across the mountain, and the sun—there it was—exploding in the sky. At the top of the mountain the dome of the old church caught the first rays and turned pink.

The sky was high and blue, the sea calm. Mrs. Richardson sat in a deck chair on the port side of the ship, watching the islands slide across the horizon; it seemed they were moving, not the ship. In her left hand, resting on her knee, was a glass of tea. She was smoking a cigarette. Matthew sat in the deck chair next to hers, reading. Three seagulls squawked and circled above the wake of the ship.

"Do you realize that Ulysses might have seen this view?" she said.

Matthew looked up from his book. "I know," he said, squinting at the sea. "He probably did."

She looked at him. "What are you reading?"

"Seferis," he said.

She sipped her tea. "He won't write anymore," she said.

"Why not?"

"Because of the government, the colonels. It's his way of protesting."

"I'm sure the colonels could almost give a damn."

"They do, I bet. Bad publicity hurts."

"Maybe."

A Greek in a tight gray suit passed them, nodding and smiling, and disappeared down the steps to the lower deck.

"Where's Quentin?" she asked.

"Asleep," Matthew said.

"And Scobie?"

"Trying not to be sick."

They both laughed.

"Where?"

"In the bar, I think," Matthew said. "Writing."

"He's the only one of you who still gets seasick." She laughed again.

"Mom, why is he so irritable all the time?"

"He's not irritable *all* the time."

"But you know what I mean."

"Yes."

"Why?"

She shrugged. "He's eighteen. He's about to go away to college. He's independent."

"I don't understand."

"I don't either, honey." She stood. "I'm going to find him."

He was in the bar, at a small table near a window. Before him was an open notebook and an empty coffee cup. He looked up as she approached. "Hello, Mother."

"Hello." She sat down next to him. "How are you feeling?"

"O.K. But I'll feel a lot better when I get off this boat." He lit a cigarette and looked out the window.

"Are you excited about seeing Dad?" she asked.

"Yes."

"Me, too."

"I just hope he's there."

"He'll be there."

Scobie smiled. "You have such faith, Mother."

"He'll be there," she said.

They each ordered a cup of coffee—Nescafé—and then sat waiting as it cooled.

"What are you writing?" she asked.

"A story," he said, closing the notebook.

"About what?"

"Nothing."

Scobie turned and looked at her; his mustache was already heavier, thicker.

"Remember what I said about missing something?" he asked. "Well, it's the same with writing. It's never quite right."

"You're young."

"Yeah."

"Don't be impatient."

He lit another cigarette, gently placing the cold match in the saucer of his coffee cup. "Mom, tell me about Dad."

"What do you want to know?"

"What he was like when he was young—my age."

She leaned back and stared across the bar. There was a

young woman by the opposite window, holding a crying baby.

"He was like all of you," she said.

"All of us?"

"Yes. I can see something of him in each one of you."

"When Matthew and I used to visit Nana, she would tell us all about him. One time she drove us to his old high school and showed us the field where he played football. She said she used to come to pick him up after school, and she could always tell it was him because she could hear him whistling."

"That was before I knew him."

"And when you knew him?"

"He still whistled. He didn't play football, but he still whistled."

"He wanted to paint, didn't he?"

"He did paint."

"Why did he stop?"

"He still paints," she said.

"Not seriously."

"I don't know," she said. "He still paints very well."

"But not all the time, Mother. He's not a *painter*. He's a diplomat. Why?"

"Maybe he didn't think he was good enough, or maybe he just didn't think he could support himself painting."

"O.K. That's what I want to know. I mean, could it be that he wanted to fill his life with events—you know, things happening, rather than watching, painting?"

"Yes," she said. "That could be."

"Maybe painting depressed him in a way. Like twilight. Maybe he *cured* himself, you see, by refusing to paint."

"He didn't cure himself," she said.

Matthew tapped on the window, waving them outside. They left the bar and walked onto the deck. Quentin was there, sitting in a canvas chair listening to his tape recorder:

> *Cellophane flowers of yellow and green,*
> *Towering over your head.*
> *Look for the girl with the sun in her eyes,*
> *And she's gone.*

Rhodes was nearing, a sharp blaze of stone and beige soil, olive trees and crumbling walls. Mrs. Richardson and Matthew and Scobie stood at the railing and watched as the island slipped closer and closer. Their ship rounded a peninsula of rock and the city came into view—white houses brilliant in the sunshine. Entering the mouth of the harbor, the ship's whistle gave a startling shriek. Mrs. Richardson pressed closer against the railing, searching the dock for her husband.

"Do you see him?" she asked.

Scobie shook his head.

She looked back at the dock. It was crowded with people and carts. The confusion was intoxicating. She felt herself clapping again, like a child. Voices called out in Greek, laughed and shouted. Then she saw him. He was standing by a coil of rope, dressed in khakis, sandals, and pale-blue shirt. As she watched, his forefinger nudged his glasses back up his nose. He had lost weight. He was skinny. She waved, but his eyes could not pick her out among all the other passengers. He was staring right at her but he could not see her. She waved again, then suddenly felt herself crying. At the same moment Scobie, clear and tall in the sunlight, stood on his toes, smiled, and waved.

"Mom, look. I see him."

JOHN CHEEVER

The Jewels of the Cabots

(FROM PLAYBOY)

FUNERAL SERVICES for the murdered man were held in the Unitarian church in the little village of St. Botolphs. The architecture of the church was Bulfinch with columns and one of those ethereal spires that must have dominated the landscape a century ago. The service was a random collection of Biblical quotations closing with a verse. "Amos Cabot, rest in peace/Now your mortal trials have ceased . . ." The church was full. Mr. Cabot had been an outstanding member of the community. He had once run for Governor. For a month or so, during his campaign, one saw his picture on barns, walls, buildings and telephone poles. I don't suppose the sense of walking through a shifting mirror—he found himself at every turn—unsettled him as it would have unsettled me. Once, for example, when I was in an elevator in Paris, I noticed a woman carrying a book of mine. There was a photograph on the jacket and one image of me looked over her arm at another. I wanted the picture, wanted, I suppose, to destroy it. That she should walk away with my face under her arm seemed to threaten my self-esteem. She left the elevator at the fourth floor and the parting of these two images was confusing. I wanted to follow her, but how could I explain in French—or in any other language—what I felt? Amos Cabot was not at all like this. He seemed to enjoy seeing himself and when he lost the election and his face vanished (except for a few barns in the back country, where it peeled for a month or so), he seemed not perturbed.

24

There are, of course, the wrong Lowells, the wrong Hallowells, the wrong Eliots, Cheevers, Codmans and Englishes, but today we will deal with the wrong Cabots. Amos came from the South Shore and may never have heard of the North Shore branch of the family. His father had been an auctioneer, which meant in those days an entertainer, horse trader and sometime crook. Amos owned real estate, the hardware store, the public utilities and was a director of the bank. He had an office in the Cartwright Block, opposite the green. His wife came from Connecticut, which was, for us at that time, a distant wilderness on whose eastern borders stood the city of New York. New York was populated by harried, nervous, avaricious foreigners who lacked the character to bathe in cold water at six in the morning and to live, with composure, lives of grueling boredom. Mrs. Cabot, when I knew her, was probably in her early forties. She was a short woman with the bright red face of an alcoholic, although she was a vigorous temperance worker. Her hair was as white as snow. Her back and her front were prominent and there was a memorable curve to her spine that could have been caused by a cruel corset or the beginning of lordosis. No one quite knew why Mr. Cabot had married this eccentric from faraway Connecticut—it was, after all, no one's business—but she did own most of the frame tenements on the East Bank of the river, where the workers in the table-silver factory lived. Her tenements were profitable, but it would have been an unwarranted simplification to conclude that he had married for real estate. She collected the rents herself. I expect that she did her own housework and she dressed simply, but she wore on her right hand seven large diamond rings. She had evidently read somewhere that diamonds were a sound investment and the blazing stones were about as glamorous as a passbook. There were round diamonds, square diamonds, rectangular diamonds, and some of those diamonds that are set in prongs. On Thursday afternoon, she would wash her diamonds in some jeweler's solution and hang them out to dry in the clothesyard. She never explained this, but the incidence of eccentricity in the village ran so high that her conduct was not thought unusual.

Mrs. Cabot spoke once or twice a year at the St. Botolphs

Academy, where many of us went to school. She had three subjects: "My Trip to Alaska" (slides), "The Evils of Drink" and "The Evils of Tobacco." Drink was for her so unthinkable a vice that she could not attack it with much vehemence, but the thought of tobacco made her choleric. Could one imagine Christ on the Cross, smoking a cigarette? she would ask us. Could one imagine the Virgin Mary *smoking?* A drop of nicotine fed to a pig by trained laboratory technicians had killed the beast. Et cetera. She made smoking irresistible and if I die of lung cancer, I shall blame Mrs. Cabot. These performances took place in what we called the Great Study Hall. This was a large room on the second floor that could hold us all. The academy had been built in the 1850s and had the lofty, spacious and beautiful windows of that period in American architecture. In the spring and in the autumn, the building seemed gracefully suspended in its grounds, but in the winter, a glacial cold fell off the large windowlights. In the Great Study Hall, we were allowed to wear coats, hats and gloves. This situation was heightened by the fact that my great-aunt Anna had bought in Athens a large collection of plaster casts, so that we shivered and memorized the donative verbs in the company of at least a dozen buck-naked gods and goddesses. So it was to Hermes and Venus as well as to us that Mrs. Cabot railed against the poisons of tobacco. She was a woman of vehement and ugly prejudice and I suppose she would have been happy to include the blacks and Jews, but there was only one black and one Jewish family in the village and they were exemplary. The possibility of intolerance in the village did not occur to me until much later, when my mother came to our house in Westchester for Thanksgiving.

This was some years ago, when the New England highways had not been completed and the trip from New York or Westchester took over four hours. I left quite early in the morning and drove first to Haverhill, where I stopped at Miss Peacock's School and picked up my niece. I then went on to St. Botolphs, where I found Mother sitting in the hallway in an acolyte's chair. The chair had a steepled back, topped with a wooden fleur-de-lis. From what rain-damp church had this object been stolen? She wore a coat and her bag was at her feet.

"I'm ready," she said. She must have been ready for a week. She seemed terribly lonely. "Would you like a drink?" she asked. I knew enough not to take this bait. Had I said yes, she would have gone into the pantry and returned, smiling sadly, to say: "You brother has drunk all the whiskey." So we started back for Westchester. It was a cold, overcast day and I found the drive tiring, although I think fatigue had nothing to do with what followed. I left my niece at my brother's house in Connecticut and drove on to my place. It was after dark when the trip ended. My wife had made all the preparations that were customary for my mother's arrival. There was an open fire, a vase of roses on the piano and tea with anchovy-paste sandwiches. "How lovely to have flowers," said Mother. "I so love flowers. I can't live without them. Should I suffer some financial reverses and have to choose between flowers and groceries, I believe I would choose flowers . . ."

I do not want to give the impression of an elegant old lady, because there were lapses in her performance. I bring up, with powerful unwillingness, a fact that was told to me by her sister after Mother's death. It seems that at one time, she applied for a position with the Boston police force. She had plenty of money at the time and I have no idea why she did this. I suppose that she wanted to be a policewoman. I don't know what branch of the force she planned to join, but I've always imagined her in a dark-blue uniform with a ring of keys at her waist and a billy club in her right hand. My grandmother dissuaded her from this course, but the image of a policewoman was some part of the figure she cut, sipping tea by our fire. She meant this evening to be what she called aristocratic. In this connection, she often said: "There must be at least a drop of plebeian blood in the family. How else can one account for your taste in torn and shabby clothing? You've always had plenty of clothes, but you've always chosen rags."

I mixed a drink and said how much I had enjoyed seeing my niece.

"Miss Peacock's has changed," Mother said sadly.

"I didn't know," I said. "What do you mean?"

"They've let down the bars."

"I don't understand."

"They're letting in Jews," she said. She fired out the last word.

"Can we change the subject?" I asked.

"I don't see why," she said. "You brought it up."

"My wife is Jewish, Mother," I said. My wife was in the kitchen.

"That is not possible," my mother said. "Her father is Italian."

"Her father," I said, "is a Polish Jew."

"Well," Mother said, "I come from old Massachusetts stock and I'm not ashamed of it, although I don't like being called Yankee."

"There's a difference."

"Your father said that the only good Jew was a dead Jew, although I did think Justice Brandeis charming."

"I think it's going to rain," I said. It was one of our staple conversational switch-offs used to express anger, hunger, love and the fear of death.

My wife joined us and Mother picked up the routine. "It's nearly cold enough for snow," she said. "When you were a boy, you used to pray for snow or ice. It depended upon whether you wanted to skate or ski. You were very particular. You would kneel by your bed and loudly ask God to manipulate the elements. You never prayed for anything else. I never once heard you ask for a blessing on your parents. In the summer you didn't pray at all."

The Cabots had two daughters—Geneva and Molly. Geneva was the older and thought to be the more beautiful. Molly was my girl for a year or so. She was a lovely young woman with a sleepy look that was quickly dispelled by a brilliant smile. Her hair was pale brown and held the light. When she was tired or excited, sweat formed on her upper lip. In the evenings, I would walk to their house and sit with her in the parlor under the most intense surveillance. Mrs. Cabot, of course, regarded sex with utter panic. She watched us from the dining room. From upstairs there were loud and regular

thumping sounds. This was Amos Cabot's rowing machine.
We were sometimes allowed to take walks together if we
kept to the main streets, and when I was old enough to drive,
I took her to the dances at the club. I was intensely—mor-
bidly—jealous and when she seemed to be enjoying herself
with someone else, I would stand in the corner, thinking of
suicide. I remember driving her back one night to the house
on Shore Road.

At the turn of the century, someone decided that St. Botolphs might have a future as a resort and five mansions complete with follies were built at the end of Shore Road. The
Cabots lived in one of these. All the mansions had towers.
These were round with conical roofs, rising a story or so
above the rest of the frame buildings. The towers were strik-
ingly unmilitary and so I suppose they were meant to express
romance. What did they contain? Dens, I guess, maids'
rooms, broken furniture, trunks, and they must have been the
favorite of hornets. I parked my car in front of the Cabots'
and turned off the lights. The house above us was dark.

It was long ago, so long ago that the foliage of elm trees
was part of the summer night. (It was so long ago that when
you wanted to make a left turn, you cranked down the car
window and *pointed* in that direction. Otherwise, you were
not allowed to point. Don't point, you were told. I can't
imagine why, unless the gesture was thought to be erotic.)
The dances—the assemblies—were formal and I would be
wearing a tuxedo handed down from my father to my
brother and from my brother to me, like some escutcheon or
sumptuary torch. I took Molly in my arms. She was completely responsive. I am not a tall man (I am sometimes
inclined to stoop), but the conviction that I am loved and
loving affects me like a military bracing. Up goes my head.
My back is straight. I am six foot seven and sustained by
some clamorous emotional uproar. Sometimes my ears ring. It
can happen anywhere—in a Keisang house in Seoul, for example—but it happened that night in front of the Cabots'
house on Shore Road. Molly said then that she had to go. Her
mother would be watching from a window. She asked me not
to come up to the house. I mustn't have heard. I went with
her up the walk and the stairs to the porch, where she tried

the door and found it locked. She asked me again to go, but I couldn't abandon her there, could I? Then a light went on and the door was opened by a dwarf. He was exhaustively misshapen. The head was hydrocephalic, the features were swollen, the legs were thick and cruelly bowed. I thought of the circus. The lovely young woman began to cry. She stepped into the house and closed the door and I was left with the summer night, the elms, the taste of an east wind. After this, she avoided me for a week or so and I was told the facts by Maggie, our old cook.

But other facts first. It was in the summer, and in the summer most of us went to a camp on the Cape run by the headmaster of the St. Botolphs Academy. The months were so feckless, so blue, that I can't remember them at all. I slept next to a boy named DeVarennes, whom I had known all my life. We were together most of the time. We played marbles together, slept together, played together on the same backfield and once together took a ten-day canoe trip during which we nearly drowned together. My brother claimed that we had begun to look alike. It was the most gratifying and unself-conscious relationship I had known. (He still calls me once or twice a year from San Francisco, where he lives unhappily with his wife and three unmarried daughters. He sounds drunk. "We were happy, weren't we?" he asks.) One day another boy, a stranger named Wallace, asked if I wanted to swim across the lake. I might claim that I knew nothing about Wallace, and I knew very little, but I did know or sense that he was lonely. It was as conspicuous as, more conspicuous than, any of his features. He did what was expected of him. He played ball, made his bed, took sailing lessons and got his lifesaving certificate, but this seemed more like a careful imposture than any sort of participation. He was miserable, he was lonely, and sooner or later, rain or shine, he would say so and, in the act of confession, make an impossible claim on one's loyalty. One knew all this, but one pretended not to. We got permission from the swimming instructor and swam across the lake. We used a clumsy side stroke that still seems to me more serviceable than the overhand that is obligatory these days in those swimming pools where I spend most of my time. The side stroke is lower-class.

I've seen it once in a swimming pool and when I asked who the swimmer was, I was told he was the butler. When the ship sinks, when the plane ditches, I will try to reach the life raft with an overhand and drown stylishly, whereas if I had used a lower-class side stroke, I would live forever.

We swam the lake, resting in the sun—no confidences— and swam home. When I went up to our cabin, DeVarennes took me aside. "Don't ever let me see you with Wallace again," he said. I asked why. He told me. "Wallace is Amos Cabot's bastard. His mother is a whore. They live in one of the tenements across the river."

The next day was hot and brilliant and Wallace asked if I wanted to swim the lake again. I said sure, and we did. When we went back to camp, DeVarennes wouldn't speak to me. That night a northeaster blew up and it rained for three days. DeVarennes seems to have forgiven me and I don't recall having crossed the lake with Wallace again. As for the dwarf, Maggie told me he was a son of Mrs. Cabot's from an earlier marriage. He worked at the table-silver factory, but he went to work early in the morning and didn't return until after dark. His existence was meant to be kept a secret. This was unusual but not—at the time of which I'm writing—unprecedented. The Trumbulls kept Mrs. Trumbull's crazy sister hidden in the attic and Uncle Peepee Marshmallow—an exhibitionist—was often hidden for months.

It was a winter afternoon, an early winter afternoon. Mrs. Cabot washed her diamonds and hung them out to dry. She then went upstairs to take a nap. She claimed that she had never taken a nap in her life and the sounder she slept, the more vehement were her claims that she didn't sleep. This was not so much an eccentricity on her part as it was a crabwise way of presenting the facts that was prevalent in that part of the world. She woke at four and went down to gather her stones. They were gone. She called Geneva, but there was no answer. She got a rake and scored the stubble under the clothesline. There was nothing. She called the police.

As I say, it was a winter afternoon and the winters there were very cold. We counted for heat—sometimes for survival—on wood fires and large coal-burning furnaces that sometimes got out of hand. A winter night was a threatening fact and this may have partly accounted for the sentiment with which we watched—in late November and December—the light burn out in the west. (My father's journals, for example, were full of descriptions of winter twilights, not because he was at all crepuscular but because the coming of the night might mean danger and pain.) Geneva had packed a bag, gathered the diamonds and taken the last train out of town—the 4:47. How thrilling it must have been. The diamonds were meant to be stolen. They were a flagrant snare and she did what she was meant to do. She took the train to New York that night and sailed three days later for Alexandria on a Cunarder—the S.S. *Serapis*. She took a boat from Alexandria to Luxor, where, in the space of two months, she joined the Moslem faith and married the khedive.

I read about the theft the next day in the evening paper. I delivered papers. I had begun my route on foot, moved on to a bicycle and was assigned, when I was sixteen, to an old Ford truck. I was a truck driver! I hung around the linotype room until the papers were printed and then drove around to the four neighboring villages, tossing out bundles at the doors of the candy and stationery stores. During the World Series, a second edition with box scores was brought out and, after dark, I would make the trip again to Travertine and the other places along the shore.

The roads were dark, there was very little traffic and leaf burning had not been forbidden, so that the air was tannic, melancholy and exciting. One can attach a mysterious and inordinate amount of importance to some simple journey and this second trip with the box scores made me very happy. I dreaded the end of the World Series as one dreads the end of any pleasure and, had I been younger, I would have prayed. CABOT JEWELS STOLEN was the headline and the incident was never again mentioned in the paper. It was not mentioned at all in our house, but this was not unusual. When Mr. Abbott hanged himself from the pear tree next door, this was never mentioned.

Molly and I took a walk on the beach at Travertine that Sunday afternoon. I was troubled, but Molly's troubles were much graver. It did not disturb her that Geneva had stolen the diamonds. She only wanted to know what had become of her sister and she was not to find out for another six weeks. However, something had happened at the house two nights before. There had been a scene between her parents and her father had left. She described this to me. We were walking barefoot. She was crying. I would like to have forgotten the scene as soon as she finished her description.

Children drown, beautiful women are mangled in automobile accidents, cruise ships founder and men die lingering deaths in mines and submarines, but you will find none of this in my accounts. In the last chapter, the ship comes home to port, the children are saved, the miners will be rescued. Is this an infirmity of the genteel or a conviction that there are discernible moral truths? Mr. X defecated in his wife's top drawer. This is a fact, but I claim that it is not a truth. In describing St. Botolphs, I would sooner stay on the West Bank of the river, where the houses were white and where the church bells rang, but over the bridge there was the table-silver factory, the tenements (owned by Mrs. Cabot) and the Commercial Hotel. At low tide, one could smell the sea gas from the inlets at Travertine. The headlines in the afternoon paper dealt with a trunk murder. The women on the streets were ugly. Even the dummies in the one store window seemed stooped, depressed and dressed in clothing that neither fitted nor became them. Even the bride in her splendor seemed to have gotten some bad news. The politics were neofascist, the factory was nonunion, the food was unpalatable and the night wind was bitter. This was a provincial and a traditional world enjoying few of the rewards of smallness and traditionalism, and when I speak of the blessedness of all small places, I speak of the West Bank. On the East Bank was the Commercial Hotel, the demesne of Doris, a male prostitute who worked as a supervisor in the factory during the day and hustled the bar at night, exploiting the extraordinary moral lassitude of the place. Everybody knew Doris and many of the customers had used him at one time or another. There was no scandal and no delight involved. Doris would charge a traveling salesman whatever he could get, but he did it with the regulars for nothing. This seemed less like tolerance than like hapless indifference, the absence of vision, moral stamina, the splendid ambitiousness of romantic love. On fight night, Doris drifts down the bar. Buy him a drink and he'll put his hand on your arm, your shoulder, your waist, and move a fraction of an inch in his direction and he'll reach for the cake. The steamfitter buys him a drink, the high-school dropout, the watch repairman. (Once a stranger shouted to the bartender: "Tell that son of a bitch to take his tongue out of my ear"—but he was a stranger.) This is not a transient world, these are not drifters: more than half of these men will never live in any other place, and yet this seems to be the essence of spiritual nomadism. The telephone rings and the bartender beckons to Doris. There's a customer in room eight. Why would I sooner be on the West Bank, where my parents are playing bridge with Mr. and Mrs. Eliot Pinkham in the golden light of a great gas chandelier?

I'll blame it on the roast, the roast, the Sunday roast bought from a butcher who wore a straw boater with a pheasant wing in the hatband. I suppose the roast entered our house, wrapped in bloody paper, on Thursday or Friday, traveling on the back of a bicycle. It would be a gross exaggeration to say that the meat had the detonative force of a land mine that could savage your eyes and your genitals, but its powers were disproportionate. We sat down to dinner after church. (My brother was living in Omaha at that time, so we were only three.) My father would hone the carving knife and make a cut in the meat. My father was very adroit with an ax and a crosscut saw and could bring down a large tree with dispatch, but the Sunday roast was something else. After he had made the first cut, my mother would sigh. This was an extraordinary performance, so loud, so profound that it seemed as if her life were in danger. It seemed as if her very soul might come unhinged and drift out of her open mouth. "Will you never learn, Leander, that lamb must be carved against the grain?" she would ask. Once the battle of the roast had begun, the exchanges were so swift, predictable and tedious that there would be no point in reporting them.

After five or six wounding remarks, my father would wave the carving knife in the air and shout: "Will you kindly mind your own business, will you kindly shut up?"

She would sigh once more and put her hand to her heart.
Surely this was her last breath. Then, studying the air above
the table, she would say: "Feel that refreshing breeze."

There was, of course, seldom a breeze. It could be airless,
midwinter, rainy, anything. The remark was one for all seasons. Was it a commendable metaphor for hope, for the
serenity of love (which I think she had never experienced)?
Was it nostalgia for some summer evening when, loving and
understanding, we sat contentedly on the lawn above the
river? Was it no better or no worse than the sort of smile
thrown at the evening star by a man who is in utter despair?
Was it a prophecy of that generation to come who would be
so drilled in evasiveness that they would be denied forever
the splendors of a passionate confrontation?

The scene changes to Rome. It is spring, when the canny
swallows flock into the city to avoid the wing shots in Ostia.
The noise the birds make seems like light as the light of the
day loses its brilliance. Then one hears, across the courtyard,
the voice of an American woman. She is screaming. "You're
a goddamned, fucked-up no-good insane piece of shit. You
can't make a nickel, you don't have a friend in the world and
in bed you stink . . ." There is no reply and one wonders if
she is railing at the dark. Then you hear a man cough. That's
all you will hear from him. "Oh, I know I've lived with you
for eight years, but if you ever thought I liked it, any of it,
it's only because you're such a chump you wouldn't know the
real thing if you had it. When I really come, the pictures *fall*
off the walls. With you it's always an act . . ." The high-low
bells that ring in Rome at that time of day have begun to
chime. I smile at this sound, although it has no bearing on
my life, my faith, no true harmony, nothing like the revela-
tions in the voice across the court. Why would I sooner de-
scribe church bells and flocks of swallows? Is this puerile, a
sort of greeting-card mentality, a whimsical and effeminate
refusal to look at facts? On and on she goes, but I will follow
her no longer. She attacks his hair, his brain and his spirit,
while I observe that a light rain has begun to fall and that
the effect of this is to louden the noise of traffic on the *corso*.
Now she is hysterical—her voice is breaking—and I think
that at the height of her malediction, perhaps, she will begin

to cry and ask his forgiveness. She will not, of course. She will go after him with a carving knife and he will end up in the emergency ward of the *policlinica,* claiming to have wounded himself; but as I go out for dinner, smiling at beggars, fountains, children and the first stars of evening, I assure myself that everything will work out for the best. Feel that refreshing breeze!

My recollections of the Cabots are only a footnote to my principal work and I go to work early these winter mornings. It is still dark. Here and there, standing on street corners, waiting for buses, are women dressed in white. They wear white shoes and white stockings and white uniforms can be seen below their winter coats. Are they nurses, beauty-parlor operators, dentists' helpers? I'll never know. They usually carry brown paper bags, holding, I guess, a ham on rye and a thermos of buttermilk. Traffic is light at this time of day. A laundry truck delivers uniforms to the Fried Chicken Shack and in Asburn Place there is a milk truck—the last of that generation. It will be half an hour before the yellow school buses start their rounds.

I work in an apartment house called the Prestwick. It is seven stories high and dates, I guess, from the late twenties. It is of a Tudor persuasion. The bricks are irregular, there is a parapet on the roof, and the sign, advertising vacancies, is literally a shingle that hangs from iron chains and creaks romantically in the wind. On the right side of the door, there is a list of perhaps twenty-five doctors' names, but these are not gentle healers with stethoscopes and rubber hammers, these are psychiatrists and this is the country of the plastic chair and the full ashtray. I don't know why they should have chosen this place, but they outnumber the other tenants. Now and then you see, waiting for the elevator, a woman with a grocery wagon and a child, but you mostly see the sometimes harried faces of men and women with trouble. They sometimes smile; they sometimes talk to themselves. Business seems slow these days and the doctor whose office is next to mine often stands in the hallway, staring out the window. What does a psychiatrist think? Does he wonder what has become of those patients who gave up, who refused group therapy, who disregarded his warnings and admonitions? He will know their secrets. I tried to murder my husband. I tried to murder my wife. Three years ago, I took an overdose of sleeping pills. The year before that, I cut my wrists. My mother wanted me to be a girl. My mother wanted me to be a boy. My mother wanted me to be a homosexual. Where had they gone, what were they doing? Were they still married, quarreling at the dinner table, decorating the Christmas tree? Had they divorced, remarried, jumped off bridges, taken Seconal, struck some kind of truce, turned homosexual or moved to a farm in Vermont, where they planned to raise strawberries and lead a simple life? The doctor sometimes stands by the window for an hour.

My real work these days is to write an edition of the *New York Times* that will bring gladness to the hearts of men. How better could I occupy myself? The *Times* is a critical if rusty link in my ties to reality, but in these last years, its tidings have been monotonous. The prophets of doom are out of work. All one can do is to pick up the pieces. The lead story is this: PRESIDENT'S HEART TRANSPLANT DEEMED SUCCESSFUL. There is this box on the lower left: COST OF J. EDGAR HOOVER MEMORIAL CHALLENGED. "The subcommittee on memorials threatened today to halve the $7,000,000 appropriated to commemorate the late J. Edgar Hoover with a Temple of Justice ..." Column three: CONTROVERSIAL LEGISLATION REPEALED BY SENATE. "The recently enacted bill, making it a felony to have wicked thoughts about the Administration, was repealed this afternoon by a stand-up vote of 43 to 7." On and on it goes. There are robust and heartening editorials, thrilling sports news, and the weather, of course, is always sunny and warm, unless we need rain. Then we have rain. The air-pollutant gradient is zero and even in Tokyo, fewer and fewer people are wearing surgical masks. All highways, throughways, freeways and expressways will be closed for the holiday weekend. Joy to the world!

But to get back to the Cabots. The scene that I would like to overlook or forget took place the night after Geneva had stolen the diamonds. It involves plumbing. Most of the houses in the village had relatively little plumbing. There was usually a water closet in the basement for the cook and the ashman and a single bathroom on the second floor for the rest of the household. Some of these rooms were quite large and the Endicotts had a fireplace in their bathroom. Somewhere along the line, Mrs. Cabot decided that the bathroom was her demesne. She had a locksmith come and secure the door. Mr. Cabot was allowed to take his sponge bath every morning, but after this the bathroom door was locked and Mrs. Cabot kept the key in her pocket. Mr. Cabot was obliged to use a chamber pot, but since he came from the South Shore, I don't suppose this was much of a hardship. It may even have been nostalgic. He was using the chamber pot late that night when Mrs. Cabot went to the door of his room. (They slept in separate rooms.) "Will you close the door?" she screamed. "Will you close the door? Do I have to listen to that horrible noise for the rest of my life?" They would both be in nightgowns, her snow-white hair in braids. She picked up the chamber pot and threw its contents at him. He kicked down the door of the locked bathroom, washed, dressed, packed a bag and walked over the bridge to Mrs. Wallace's place on the East Bank.

He stayed there for three days and then returned. He was worried about Molly and, in such a small place, there were appearances to be considered—Mrs. Wallace's as well as his own. He divided his time between the East and the West banks of the river until a week or so later, when he was taken ill. He felt languid. He stayed in bed until noon. Then he dressed and went to his office and returned after an hour or so. The doctor examined him and found nothing wrong.

One evening Mrs. Wallace saw Mrs. Cabot coming out of the drugstore on the East Bank. She watched her rival cross the bridge and then went into the drugstore and asked the clerk if Mrs. Cabot was a regular customer. "I've been wondering about that myself," the clerk said. "Of course, she comes over here to collect her rents, but I always thought she used the other drugstore. She comes in here to buy ant poison—arsenic, that is. She says they have these terrible ants in the house on Shore Road and arsenic is the only way of getting rid of them. From the way she buys arsenic, the ants must be terrible." Mrs. Wallace might have warned Mr. Cabot, but she never saw him again.

She went after the funeral to Judge Simmons and said that she wanted to charge Mrs. Cabot with murder. The drug clerk would have a record of her purchases of arsenic that would be incriminating. "He may have it," the judge said, "but he won't give it to you. What you are asking for is an exhumation of the body and a long trial in Barnstable and you have neither the money nor the reputation to support this. You were his friend, I know, for sixteen years. He was a splendid man and why don't you console yourself with the thought of how many years it was that you knew him? And another thing. He's left you and Wallace a substantial legacy. If Mrs. Cabot were provoked to contest the will, you could lose this."

I went out to Luxor to see Geneva. I flew to London in a 747. There were only three passengers; but, as I say, the prophets of doom are out of work. I went from Cairo up the Nile in a low-flying two-motor prop. The sameness of wind erosion and water erosion makes the Sahara there seem to have been gutted by floods, rivers, courses, streams and brooks, the thrust of a natural search. The scorings are watery and arboreal and, as a false stream bed spreads out, it takes the shape of a tree, striving for light. It was freezing in Cairo when we left before dawn. Luxor, where Geneva met me at the airport, was hot.

I was very happy to see her, so happy I was unobservant, but I did notice that she had gotten fat. I don't mean that she was heavy; I mean that she weighed about 300 pounds. She was a fat woman. Her hair, once a coarse yellow, was now golden, but her Massachusetts accent was as strong as ever. It sounded like music to me on the upper Nile. Her husband—now a colonel—was a slender, middle-aged man, a relative of the last king. He owned a restaurant at the edge of the city and they lived in a pleasant apartment over the dining room. The colonel was humorous, intelligent—a rake, I guess—and a heavy drinker. When we went to the temple at Karnak, our dragoman carried ice, tonic and gin. I spent a week with them, mostly in temples and graves. We spent the evenings in his bar. War was threatening—the air was full of

Russian planes—and the only other tourist was an English-
man who sat at the bar, reading his passport. On the last day,
I swam in the Nile—overhand—and they drove me to the
airport, where I kissed Geneva—and the Cabots—good-bye.

JOHN J. CLAYTON

Cambridge Is Sinking!

(FROM THE MASSACHUSETTS REVIEW)

THE SUNDAY NIGHT TELEPHONE CALL from Steve's parents: his mother sorrowed that such an educated boy couldn't find a job. She suggested kelp and brewer's yeast. His father told him, "What kind of economics did you study, so when I ask for the names of some stocks, which ones should I buy, you can't tell me?"

"It's true, Dad."

George rolled a joint and handed it to Steve. Steve shook his head. "But thanks anyway," he said to George, hand covering the phone.

"Man, you're becoming a Puritan," George said.

"Stevie, you're getting to be practically a vagrant." His father sighed.

Susan kissed him in a rush on the way out to her support meeting. Where was *his* support meeting? He closed his eyes and floated downstream. "Good-bye, baby."

A one-eyed cat pounced from cushion to cushion along the floor. He hooked his claws into the Indian bedspreads that were the flowing walls of the living room. The cat floated, purring, until Steve yelled:

"Che! For Christsakes!" and Che leaped off a gold flower into the lifeboat. It wasn't a lifeboat; really an inflated surplus raft of rubberized canvas; it floated in the lagoon of a Cambridge living room. It was Steve who nicknamed it "the Lifeboat" and christened it with a quart of beer.

41

Steve scratched the cat's ears and seduced him into his lap under Section 4 of the Sunday *New York Times:* The Week in Review. Burrowing underneath, Che bulged out Nixon's smiling face into a mask. Che made a rough sea out of Wages and Prices, Law and Order, Education. Steve stopped trying to read.

The *Times* on a Sunday! Travel and Resorts. *Voilà!* "A guide to Gold in the Hills of France." Arts and Leisure. Business and Finance. Sports. Remember sports? My God. It was clear something was over.

All these years the *New York Times* was going on, not just a thing to clip articles from for a movement newspaper, but a thing people read. Truly, there were people who went to Broadway shows on the advice of Clive Barnes and Walter Kerr, who examined the rise and fall of mutual funds, who attended and supported the college and church of their choice, who visited Bermuda on an eight-day package plan, who discussed cybernetics and school architecture. People who had never had a second-hand millennial notion of where we were heading—only a vague anger and uneasiness.

Steve tried to telepathize all this to Che under the newspaper blanket: Che, it's over. Hey. John is making films, Fred lives with eight other people on a farm. But it isn't a *commune,* whatever that was. The experiment is over.

Look. When Nancy cleared out of the apartment with her stash of acid and peyote and speed and hash after being released from Mass Mental, cleared out and went home to Connecticut; when trippy Phil decided to campaign for George McGovern and nobody laughed; when the *Rolling Stone* subscription ran out; when Steve himself stopped buying the *Liberated Guardian* or worrying about its differences from the regular *Guardian;* when George—when *George*—stopped doing acid and got into a heavy wordless depression that he dulled with bottle after bottle of Tavola—and said he'd stop drinking "soon—and maybe get into yoga or a school thing"—something was finished, over.

Che purred.

The lifeboat floated like a bright orange H.M.S. *Queen Elizabeth* sofa in the middle of the sunset floor. Steve sat in the lifeboat on one of the inflated cushions, reading Arts and

Leisure and listening to Ray Charles through the wall of George's room. As long as it was Ray Charles he didn't bother to drown it out with the living room stereo. As if he had the energy. He sipped cranberry juice out of an Ocean Spray bottle and looked through this newspaper of strange science fiction planet aha.

Ray Charles whined to dead stop in midsong. George stood in the doorway and stood there with something to say and stood there and waited.

"Come aboard. I'm liking this old boat better and better."

George: hippo body, leonine face with a wild red mane. He ignored the boat. "Steve, I'm going back to school."

"School? To do what?"

"Get a masters."

"What in?"

"I haven't got that far yet. I'll let you know." The door closed. Ray Charles started up from where he left off.

Steve smiled. He stretched out in the lifeboat and let it float him downstream. They came to a rapids, he and Che and the *New York Times,* and he began negotiating the white water. George. George: school? Well, why not.

George. One day last year when George was tripping he found his Harvard diploma in the trunk under his bed: he ripped it into a lot of pieces and burned—or began to burn—the pieces one by one. But halfway through he chickened out and spent the rest of his trip on his knees staring into the jigsaw fragments as if they were the entrails of Homeric birds, *telling him something.* Yesterday, when Steve went into his room to retrieve his bathrobe, he found the fragments glued onto oak tag: half a B.A. on the wall. Nothing else was any different: unmade bed, unread books, undressed George, sacked out in the bathrobe. Steve burned a wooden match and with the cooled char wrote R.I.P. on George's forehead. George did.

Susan was gone for hours. Sunday night. Steve sat crosslegged in his lifeboat and made up lists on 3-by-5 cards.

It was a joke that began when he was doing his honors

thesis at Harvard. On the backs of throwaway 3-by-5's he'd write

B—214:
Steve Kalman cites Marx—18th Brumaire—"Peasants shld be led into socialism by being asked to do housecleaning once a week."

He'd tape that to the bathroom mirror so the early morning peasants, recovering from dope and alcohol and speed, could hate him and get some adrenalin working. It was therapeutic.

Now the lists were different:

B—307:
Steve Kalman tells us in his definitive work on Engel's late period:

a) *learn karate*
b) *practice abdominal breathing while making love*
c) *read Marx's* Grundrisse
d) *read something through to the last page*
e) *"Be modest and prudent, guard against arrogance and rashness, and serve the . . . people heart and soul" (Mao)*
f) *specifically: fight racism, sexism, exploitation*
   (whew!)
g) *practice revolution*

When he felt it might be necessary to do something about an item on the list, he closed his eyes and meditated. Words sneaked in: what he might have said to Susan, what was the shortest route to Harvard Square, would he see his guru face to face the way Sam said he had, how many gallons would it take to do the kitchen. Aach, you should just get into the waiting, into this time without political meetings or leafleting at factory gates. Get into something.

In his mind's eye Steve saw Susan's face. All right, she wasn't Beatrice or Shri Krishna. But who was, nowadays?

*

She came in late from her support group; Steve was in a gloomy half sleep. She curled up behind him and touched her lips to the baby hairs on his back. He grunted and turned around: "And that's another thing—" He kissed her cheek, her nipple.

"What's another thing?"

"Your other nipple." Which he addressed himself to. "Listen. You come home after an exciting day at work while I've just swept the floors and wiped up the children's doodoo. Then you, you want to make love."

She held the cheeks of his ass and pressed him against her. They kissed. "Stephen, I don't have what you just said quite figured out, but I think you're making a sexist comment."

"Sexist? What sexist? I envy you your support group. You leave me nothing but the lifeboat and Chairman Mao."

"And a couple of years ago you'd have been up all night hammering out a 'position.' I think you're better off."

"We make love more, for sure."

"Let's make love, Steve."

And they did.

"Let's get out of Cambridge before it sinks. Cambridge is sinking."

Susan played with his curly black hair and beard, a Cambridge Dionysus. "You're silly. Cambridge is built on money. There are new banks all over the place."

"Then it's *us* who are sinking. We've got a lifeboat, let's go."

"Go where?"

"How about British Columbia? They need teachers. Or northern Ontario?"

"You'll get a lot of political thinking done up there."

"In exile? Look at Ho Chi Minh. Look at Lenin."

"Oh, baby. They were connected to a party."

"I love you. You're right. Let's go to Quebec and get away from politics."

"Away from politics? Quebec?"

"To Ontario."

"But, baby, you're away from 'politics' right here. That's what you're complaining about."

"But Cambridge is sinking."

At night in bed it was funny and they had each other. But daytime after they breakfasted and kissed good-bye and Susan would go off to teach her fourth-grade class and Steve would go off to the library to read Trotsky or Ian Fleming or he'd sub at a Cambridge junior high and sit dully in the faculty lounge waiting for his class to begin, then he'd think again, like the words of an irritating jingle that wouldn't stay quiet, about whether to go on for his doctorate in sociology so he could be unemployed as a Ph.D. instead of unemployed as an M.A.

*

Susan was off at work. Steve washed the dishes this morning. M.A. Ph.D. The dishes. If you called it karma yoga it was better than dishwashing. But he envied Susan her nine-year-olds, even if she were being paid to socialize them into a society with no meaningful work, a society which—*watch it:* do the dishes and stop the words.

He did the dishes—then spent the rest of the morning at Widener Library reading Mao's *On Contradictions.*

He was to meet George for lunch. On his way Jeff Segal passed him a leaflet without looking up.

The press loves to boast that the student movement is dead. It's alive and fighting back. And SDS is in the forefront of that fight . . .

My God—SDS. (Which meant, in fact, PL.) Well, Steve felt happy that somebody considered themselves a Movement, even a handful of people using the rhetoric of 1950's ad men.

Steve passed through Harvard Square—past the straight-looking Jesus freaks and the bald Krishna freaks dancing in their saffron or white sheets and their insulated rubber boots. In the corner news store, across from the kiosk (Steve remembered when they "took" the Square and people got up on the kiosk and the cops came. So the freaks charged off in all directions busting windows—called "liberating the Square"—while he, Steve, who'd helped organize the march and rally, walked quietly away)—in the corner news and magazine store there was George reading the sex books at the rear of the store.

"Hey, George!"

They got out into the street and stood blinking at the noon light like a couple of junkies oozing out of a basement. George took out from his army coat lining the copy of *Fusion* he'd ripped off. He thumbed through the record reviews and he headed down Boylston to Minute Man Radio. "You stay here, Steve. I know what you think about my ripping off."

Steve watched the young women of Cambridge pass. A lot of fine lunchtime arrogance that he delighted in; but, he considered, not a hell of a lot in their eyes to back it up. One blonde on the other side of Boylston, tall, with a strong walk and no-bullshit eyes: Steve fell in love with her right away and they started living together but she had kids and he didn't get it on with them and she had perverse tastes in bed and didn't understand politics so by the time she actually crossed the street and passed by they'd separated it was too bad but anyway there was Susan to think of and so on. But they smiled at each other. Then George came out with Bob Dylan—*Greatest Hits Volume II* and showed it to Steve when they'd sat down for lunch.

They ate in the Française under the painted pipes, ate their good quiche and drank French coffee. "George, I think this is a Hemingway memoir. I'm feeling nostalgia for this place while I'm still here. That's bad.

"I wonder where I'm going, George . . .

"I can't be Raskolnikov, George, as long as I can afford quiche for lunch. But it's the direction things are moving."

George ran his thick fingers through his wild red mane. "Not me. I decided. I don't want to be a casualty. I'm getting my MA in English and moving into a publishing house. I've got an uncle."

"Could you get your uncle to help you get your room cleaned up?"

"It's a pretty hip publishing house."

"I bet, George, that they make their profits off only the most freaky books."

"What's wrong with you, anyway?"

Steve bought George an expresso. "Here. Forgive me. This is so I can take our lunch off my taxes. I'm organizing you into our new revolutionary party."

"You couldn't organize your ass, lately."

Steve agreed. "I'm into getting my internal organs to communicate. I'm establishing dialogue at all levels."

After lunch Steve called Susan in the teachers' lounge at her school. "Hello, Baby? Cambridge is collapsing."

"Love, I can't do anything about that. Thirty-one kids is all I can handle."

"Pretend I'm a reporter from the *Times* and you're a terrific genius. 'Tell me, Miss French, how did you get to be such a terrific genius? I mean, here the city is falling down and nobody can stop snorting coke long enough to shore up a building, and here you are helping thirty-one human kids to survive. How, how, how, Miss French?' "

"Steve, you know better, you nut."

"Steve knows what he knows; me, I'm a reporter."

"Well," she cleared her throat, "I take vitamins, and I make love a lot with my friend Steve. And I ask his advice—"

"Ha! Fat chance!"

"—and I owe it to my sisters in the women's movement."

Steve didn't laugh. "It's true, it's true. Ah, anyway, love, I miss you."

Steve went up to the raised desk at the Booksmith on Brattle Street to ask the manager whether the one-volume reduction of Marx's *Grundrisse* was out in paper. The "manager"—long mustachios and shaggy hair like a riverboat gambler, fifty-dollar boots up on the desk where they could make a *statement*—aha, it turned out to be Phil. Hey, Phil.

Phil looked down from the counter, stopped picking his Mississippi teeth and grinned. "I've been meaning to stop by, Steve. You didn't know I had this gig, huh?"

"It's good to see you."

"Sure. I watch the motherfuckers on my closed-circuit swivel-eye TV setup, dig it, and I check out the Square when things are slow. It's okay. I'm learning. In a couple of months I'm going out to Brattleboro, open a bookstore. A hip, a very hip bookstore."

"In Vermont?"

"There's a whole lot of freaks in Vermont."

"You doing a movement bookstore?"

Phil began picking his teeth like waiting to look at his hole card. Grinned his riverboat grin. "My uncle's setting me up, Steve. I want to make bread, man. As much as I can make in two, three years, and then I'll sell and split for someplace."

"Where?" Steve played at *naif* to Phil's heavy hipoisie.

"Lots of time to work that one out."

Steve forgot to ask about Marx. But Marx was all right. He found a *Capital* and when the camera had swiveled away, he slipped it into his bookbag. Then a Debray. A Ché. Mao's *Quotations*. A Kropotkin. Into the lining of his air force parka. If Phil noticed, he didn't say. They grinned hip gambler grins at one another and Phil said, "Later, Steve."

*

Marx, Mao, Ché, Debray, and Kropotkin. A complete infield, including catcher.

Steve pitched his winnings out of his lining, into the lifeboat.

"*You*, Steve?"

"Everybody's got an uncle, George. Wow, I remember Phil when we took the administration building. He was up on a car that night doing a Mario Savio. And now—" Steve told George about the *very* hip bookstore in Brattleboro.

"Everybody's got an uncle, huh?" George grunted. "And you're pure, huh?" He assimilated it into his computer; it fit. He swallowed once, then his massive moon face framed by red solar fire, his face relaxed. He went back to his room.

Steve considered tacking up a 3-by-5 sign over the doorway: The Bestiary. Today he was a wall-eyed computer. Yesterday George was a griffin. Tomorrow he could expect a drunken red-haired cyclops.

What animal was Steve? Steve was *existentialops meshugenah*. Nearly extinct, thank God. Little survival value. Never looked down at the ground. Every bush a metaphor. Can't go for a picnic on a hillside without watching for a lion, wolf, and a leopard.

He shrugged. Ask Chairman Mao. He opened the *Red Book* at random:

We should rid our ranks of all impotent thinking. All views that overestimate the strength of the enemy and underestimate the strength of the people are wrong.

Good advice. But, plagued by impotent thinking, he climbed into the lifeboat and hugged his knees and sulked. He sat there till George, hammering up another picture on his wall, got to him. "George, will you cool it? Cool it, George. I'm miserable. The sky's falling down."

He tossed Mao aft in the boat, fitted real oars to the real oarlocks, and began to row in the imaginary water. It was smoother and easier than in real water—there was no struggle, and so, no forward motion. All things proceed by contraries. Blake or Heraclitus or Hegel or Marx. He rowed.

He rowed. Aha! It began to make sense. He was expressing precisely the "contraries" he felt in this year of the Nixon: him pushing, nothing pushing back but hot air from the radiators.

So. He closed his eyes. There was a forest on both sides. Tactical Police were utterly lost in the woods. Maybe it was a beer commercial. Inside his head Steve did up a joint and floated, eyes closed. The Tactical Police were stoned. Then he turned inside out and floated into a deep jungle world. There was a fat parrot with iridescent yellow and green, red and blue wing feathers. It was as big as a tiger.

George had a real parrot in his room, and it was the only thing George took care of. Including George. It wasn't very beautiful, certainly not iridescent or big as a tiger. It liked dope, ice cream, and Cream of Wheat. Like George. But now Steve floated while a very different bird floated overhead like a bubble or helium-filled crystal ball. He watched for the Good Witch of the West. Or for the Wizard of the East. But before any such visitation, he fell asleep.

Cambridge is a lie. Doesn't exist never existed. I am in my cups. The moon a cracked saucer. We are hardly acquainted.

In the graveyard of the Unitarian Church, sixteen-year-old runaways slept, dreaming of breasts with amphetamine nipples. They are all the time tired. Cats prowl the graveyard lean and angry. They suck blood and fly moonwards. The Unitarians underground are coughing uneasily. They are pressed down by the weight.

He woke up. He pretended it was a Caribbean cruise, this was the ship's boat, his jeans were a dinner jacket and tuxedo trousers. Susan was off to the captain's table getting champagne cocktails.

When she came back they walked through the Square arm in arm with champagne glasses and a bottle of Mumm's. It was spring; they kissed in front of a Bogart poster and poured more champagne for a toast. The Beatles were on again at the Brattle. There was nobody else in the theater. All the psychedelic flowers were fading, wilting dingy, like the murals on WPA post office walls. The submarine had faded to a rusty chartreuse. Steve remembered when it was bright yellow and Lucy looked just like an acid lady. You used to get stoned or drop acid and get into the colors.

The lifeboat was getting full. Harpo was asleep on a raccoon coat, and George and his girl, very stoned, were examining a wind-up see-through clock they'd ripped off at DR. Steve could hardly spread out his newspaper. It was a rush-hour subway except everybody had suitcases and guitars with them. "Is this the way to Charles Street?" The sign over the door said DORCHESTER.

They held on and on, the subway was behaving like a bad little boy; they were disappointed and wrote a strong note home but his government didn't reply. They floated through Cambridge trying to find the exit. They shouted FIRE! but it wasn't a crowded theater, and so they were stuck, everyone with their own suitcase and their own piece of the action.

Susan's key turned in the lock.

"Susan—hey, Susan! Let's go get dinner!"

*

The neighborhood food cooperative operated out of Ellen's apartment. Her twins crawled among the market boxes and noshed grapes.

"Stop noshing grapes!" Ellen warned. Susan put an Angela Davis defense petition on the table for coop members to sign. Chairman Mao sat cross-legged on a cushion slicing a California avocado with his pocket knife. He ate slice after slice of the creamy green fruit.

Coop members started arriving to pick up their orders. Twenty-three member households came in; only five ordered Angela Davis. Steve threw up his hands: "Dare to struggle, dare to win!" Chairman Mao shrugged sympathetically. He'd had trouble of his own with Cambridge intellectual types. Ellen hugged her twins and said, "But it's people that count, not politics." She put a Paul Klee on the stereo and recited W. B. Yeats.

Early Spring. Cambridge. Torpor, confusion, scattered energies. A return to sanity was advertised in *Life* and in the little magazines. Aha, you mean sanity's *in* again. Okay! The art show Steve and Susan took in after dinner so they could drink free wine and hold hands, it was all giant realistic figures and giant, colorful geometrics. He could imagine them in the lobby of the new, sane, John Hancock Building. They said EXPENSIVE, CAREFUL, INTELLIGENT, PURPOSEFUL, SERIOUS; but HIP. And look at the long hair on the doctors and PR men at the opening. Everyone was hip.

"They're into patchouli oil on their genitalia for sure!"

"Who're you kidding?" Susan laughed. "You don't want to see paintings, you came to kvetch. You're a silly man. I want a Baskin and Robbins ice-cream cone. And I'm willing to buy one for you, too."

"You're throwing your wealth up to me."

"Well"—Susan sighed and took his arm like a lady—"some

of us have firm positions in the world. Only Harvard Square trash does substitute teaching. This is a free country. Anyone with a little guts and brains and in-i-sha-tiff—"

"All right, I want an ice-cream cone." He stopped and right there on Mass Avenue kissed her, because she was so fine, because her tight jeans made him want to rub her thighs, because she kept him going through the foolishness.

They walked by the Charles River with their bridges burned behind them. There was nothing but to shrug. An invisible demonstration passed them from 1969 waving red and black flags and shouting old slogans. So they marched too. Steve lifted a revolutionary fist and shouted, "Take Harvard!" Susan said he sounded like a Princeton fan from the fifties.

"In the fifties I was a kid waiting for someone to push a button and end my having to go to school. I wouldn't blow up: just my school. The walls. Then in the sixties I expected us to tear down the walls."

"Well?"

"Now? Ah, Susan, where will we wind up?"

"In a clock factory?"

On the other side of the river the business students stood by the bank with almost long hair and fat empty pockets. They bought and sold dope and sincere greeting cards with pictures of couples walking almost naked by the edge of the sea. Since the bridges were burned, Steve could yell, "You think you smell any sweeter, baby?" The business majors at the bank ignored them. When they had their stock options, where would Susan and Steve be? In the bathtub making love? In their lifeboat on a stream in British Columbia trying to locate the Source?

They wanted to make love, so they went back to their lifeboat and opened a bottle of cheap champagne. "What should we toast?" she asked.

"The river that gets us out of here?"

Steve made love with Susan on a quilt in the bottom of the rubber boat, a raft made for saving drowned fliers.

*

Tuesday at lunch George and Steve spent a bottle of beer mourning the casualties.

"I decided again this morning," George said. "Not to be a casualty."

"Terrific."

"It's been a war of attrition. You know, 'I have seen the best minds of my generation . . .' "

"And some of the worst," Steve said.

"Sure. But like last night. Lynne came in to crash at two A.M. She didn't want to ball, just have a place. I think Paul kicked her out. This morning I woke up to the smell of dope, and she was getting sexed up and so we balled, but she didn't even know I was here. I can't get into that sickness anymore."

"Well," Steve said, "afterwards Lynne came into the kitchen, you were still in bed, Susan was off at work. We had coffee. I asked about her children. Her mother is still taking care of them. 'But I'm really together, Steve.' She's told me that about three times this past year. 'I couldn't stay in that hospital; nobody knew anything about where I was coming from. My *supposed* therapist had never done acid, but he's telling me about drugs. But anyway, they detoxified me. Cleaned me out.'

"I asked her how much she'd been doing. 'Wow, too much,' she said. 'I was exploring heavy things, I was deep into myself. But back-to-back acid trips . . . Too much. I think the hospital was good. But this psychiatrist with long hair, you know? . . . About my father.' Her voice started fading out. 'I had to split. I had to get back to my kids . . .' So she signed herself out.

"I reminisced about her kids—one day Susan and I took Lynne and the kids out to the Children's Zoo. So I was blabbing and fixing coffee, I turned around and Lynne was doing up a joint, and her clear blue eyes were really spaced out. She was fingering Nancy's old flute, recorder really, and she was talking to it: 'This side is blue, is Hegel, and the lower register is red, is Marx. The point is to listen down into the tone of God. Otherwise you're condemned to repeat the cycle.'

"I gave her a kiss on the cheek and went back to my life-boat to read. I understand you about casualties, George."

The casualties. And what about Lynne's two little girls? Today Nixon was on TV from Mars. He toasted a new "long march" of the American and Martian people. Two years ago we thought it was all set to autodestruct: General Murders and Lying Johnson and Noxious Trixter and Spirococcus Agony and the Chase Banana Bank. Now we're out looking for jobs. Peter, who put me down for getting a degree. Offered a job at Michigan if he'd finish his dissertation. He refused, lived on welfare and organized at factory gates. Now he's still on welfare, but there's hardly a movement to support him. Two years ago he was right. Now he's another kind of casualty.

The bridge is burning while we stand in the middle. Our long hair is burning, wild and beautiful. We are the work of art we never had time to make.

I don't want to be a casualty.

*

Feeling restless, uneasy, he sat cross-legged on a pillow in the orange boat. He tried paddling down a magic river of umbrella trees, giraffes with French horn necks, a translucent lady with hummingbirds flying out of her third eye. But the film kept breaking. To placate him or perhaps to make things more difficult, the projectionist flashed a scene out of his childhood: floating on a black rubber tube, a towel wrapped around the valve like the bathing suit that sheltered his own penis. He floated safe and self-sufficiently past the breaker rocks. Where nobody could touch him. Meanwhile his mother stood by the edge of the ocean waving a red kerchief she pulled out of the cleft between her heavy breasts. She called and called, she tried to interest the lifeguard in his case. Steve's lips and ears were sealed.

Steve opened his eyes. They burned a little from salt water although he was 24 years old, although this was a make-believe boat, a living room prop. He felt like a shmuck. Chairman Mao's face was red.

He didn't close his eyes again. "Hey, George? George!"

"I'm doing up a joint," George said from the other room. Then he came in and lit up. "Want a toke?"

"Listen, George—"

"I'm gonna get stoned and then get my room clean. Clean."

"George, first, come with me for a couple of hours. We'll wash our sins away in the tide."

They lifted the inflated rubber boat onto their heads like dislocated duck hunters. Through the French doors to the balcony, then by rope to the back yard. Steve lashed it to the top of George's '59 Cadillac. He wore a red blanket pinned at the collar, Indian style.

At the Harvard crew house they pulled the boat in the water and pushed off into the Charles. Metaphor of Indian so long ago no Prudential Center or Georgian architecture of Harvard. Nice to push off into the river wrapped in such a metaphor. But today there was oil and dirt on the surface of the Charles; perch, hypnotized or drugged, maintained freedom and consciousness by meditating on their own motion. Even the fish with hooks in their mouths were contemplating their Being and harking to a different drummer. That's all more metaphor, too, for who would go fishing in the Charles? Steve played a rinky-dink tune to the fish on Nancy's recorder, but they turned belly up and became free of their bodies and of the river. The smell was nasty.

George said he felt like Huck Finn. Steve thought that was possible. They floated under the Harvard footbridge and past the site of the future water purification plant to the River Street Bridge. Stench of traffic and *COCA-COLA* in two-story letters. The river curved. "I can see myself as Tom Sawyer," Steve said. "For me it wasn't quite real, getting Jim out of slavery. I always figured on Aunt Sally's investment firm to settle down into. But for you, George, it was a real plunge. You almost didn't come back out. You were almost a shaman who didn't return."

"What are you saying, you crazy fool?"

"We must steer the boat. Susan's school is by the left bank. She'll be getting out in fifteen minutes."

Kids in the playground on the other side of Memorial

Drive waved at the young man in the bright red blanket. Steve leaned over the chain link fence: "Peace to white and black brothers," he said, spreading his arms. "Tell Princess Afterglow we have come." George and a small boy tossed a ball back and forth over the fence.

"You're silly," a little boy told the Indian.

"Call Miss French. Ask Miss French to come down to the fence."

Miss French came down to the fence. Two little girls held her hands as they led her to the fence. She laughed and laughed and gestured "ten minutes" with her fingers.

George took up the recorder. It squeaked. "Steve. Those kids. That's where it's at."

"George, I don't believe you said that. Listen, George. I may dig being crazy or playing at being a child, but I can tell you that won't save me. Or being a freak. Or being an Indian. Metaphor won't save me. I got to save my own ass, so to speak. I mean, it's not any kind of revolution to float down the Charles in an orange boat."

"It was your idea. And who's talking about revolution? You're getting incredibly straight."

"And there—see—you can't make it on categories like straight. It's all over—the time you could think of *them* as bread and wine. So everything turns to shit in your mouth. Is bound to." He tugged at George's matted hair. "Except I don't feel like that this afternoon. I feel pretty manic and joyful."

Susan leaned against her bookbag in the stern and stretched back, her face parallel to the sky, and took it all in.

"Just smell this water. Don't let's fall in, friends," Susan said. "We'd be pickled in a minute."

They paddled upstream towards Harvard. Downstream, upstream. Circle Line sightseeing: on your right is a Stop and Cop, and the Robert Hall Big Man Shop. Fer you, George. Harvard crews raced each other towards the lifeboat; alongside was the coach's motor launch. The coach, in trench coat, scarf trailing crimson in the wind, stood droning into a bullhorn. For a second Married Students' Housing was upside down in the water; then a gust of wind shattered it into an impressionist canvas.

The shells raced by and the orange lifeboat rocked in their wake and in the wake of the launch. They shared an apple left over from Susan's lunch and didn't fight the rocking.

They rowed. They were rowing home. Home because

> The cat has to be fed.
> And the parrot.
> Because we are hungry and
> the place needs to be cleaned up bad.
> There are lots of books at home, and a telephone.
> Home doesn't smell as bad as this river.

No wild crowds on shore cheered this. From the footbridge no Radcliffe girls dropped white roses on their heads. Farther on, even more to the point, no marchers cheered them with raised fists, with red flags in the spring breeze, with a bull-horn dropped down off the Anderson Bridge so that Steve and Susan and George could address the crowd:

"Well, it's been a terrific five years. We've all learned how to make love and posters. We can really get into the here and now at times and we've learned to respect our fantasies. Yum yum. We're glad to be going home. We hope to see all the old faces tomorrow right after the revolution is over so we can clean up the paper we dropped."

After this didn't happen they paddled up Memorial Drive some more. The gulls were fishing. The shells raced past them going the other way and they rocked and bobbed, like a floater for fish. They sang,

> Fish on a line
> all strung out.
> If I cry the moon will go away.
> Are you with me?
> Plenty of conditions
> Sold by the millions.
> Nice to tell you
> can't hold water.

They drew pictures of fish in the water like invisible ink to be recovered later and read.

"We can't get anywhere this way," Steve said.

"Just float, man. The trouble with you is you never learned to float." George shrugged and reversed his oar, so the boat circled after itself like a dog after tail, like Paulo and Francesca. Infinite longing unsatisfied. But this was merely parody. George knew better than to long. The river stank but he had a cold. Steve and Susan were kissing on the bottom of the boat. Who knows how this fairy tale goes?

Why are the bridges all falling down? Why are the boats floating against bars of Ivory soap and turning over? It doesn't matter how the words go. They wound me up and didn't give me directions, Steve groaned, playing wind-up toy. But when he finished kissing his friend Susan, he took up paddle and coaxed George into rowing upstream past Harvard to the boathouse.

*

Steve—oh God, Steve, you've got to stop torchereeing yrself, Steve decided painfully. China wasn't built in a day. Steve closed his eyes and meditated, cross-legged in the wet lifeboat, on the career of Mao Tse-tung.

Susan and George carried in a brass tray with what was left of the champagne. But Steve was meditating.

"Join us, why don't you? We've got some heavy pazoola here on a fancy gold tray," George like a six-foot-three, red-haired genie wheedled. "Cut the meditating."

"Who's meditating? I'm telephoning Mao Tse-tung in Peking. *Hello, Peking?*"

"Well, tell us what he says."

Chairman Mao, Chairman Mao, Steve said inside his head. Tell us what we can do in this year of the Nixon.

Ah, yes, Mister Nixon . . .

It's been a long winter, Chairman Mao.

With no leaves on the trees, the wind shrieks; when leaves fill the branches, the wind rustles.

I think, Steve said, inside his head, I get what you mean.

The important thing, Chairman Mao said, is to get outside your head. Open your eyes. What do you see?

The rubberized canvas sides of my orange raft and a print of *Primavera* on my wall. My friends are offering me champagne on a gold tray. A brass tray to be exact.

Chairman Mao supposed a difficulty in translation. You, you behave like a blind man groping for fish. Open your eyes. Study conditions conscientiously. Proceed from objective reality and not from subjective wishes. Conclusions invariably come after investigation, and not before. Open your eyes.

"Open your eyes and your mouth," Susan said. "Here it comes." She tilted a glass of champagne to his lips.

"Well, nobody can say those are elitist grapes. Those are the people's grapes," Steve said, pursing his mouth.

"Connoisseur! Drink up!"

Picking up the pieces. Picking up the check. Somebody got to pay before we split and all them lights go out. Ah, well, but it's time to clean up and start almost from scratch.

Susan and Steve helped George clean up his room: Two green plastic trash bags full of wine bottles and dustballs, molding plates of spaghetti, old *Rolling Stones,* socks with cat spray, insulating felt strips chewed up by the parrot, Kleenex and Tampax and a cracked copy of Bob Dylan's *Greatest Hits Volume I* and a few cracked *ands* that broke open like milkweed pods and had to be vacuumed up in a search and destroy operation.

When George's room was swept and scrubbed, George decided to wash away the Charles River effluvium in the bathtub. So Steve and Susan sat cross-legged in the bottom of the lifeboat. Wiped out.

Then Steve pulled the plug. The boat hissed disapproval, deflated, expired. They were sitting in their own space, for better or worse.

JOHN WILLIAM CORRINGTON

Old Men Dream Dreams,
Young Men See Visions

(FROM SEWANEE REVIEW)

I TRIED TO REMEMBER if I had ever felt better. No, I had not ever felt better. And I could remember. I was only fifteen. And I was driving alone in my father's 1941 Ford to pick up Helena.

It was the first time I had ever had the car alone. That was a victory. My mother had fenced, thrust, and parried with my father, who said I was too young, too wild, too inexperienced to take a girl out in a car. Later, he said. How much later, my mother asked. Be reasonable, my father said. That's right, my mother answered. Be reasonable. The girl expects him. In the car. Do you want to shame him? He can be degraded, humiliated and dishonored as far as I'm concerned, my father told her. My mother gave him a distant wintry smile, one of her specialties. Like an advocate crossexamining an unacknowledged embezzler or black marketeer. Be reasonable, she said with smooth earth-scouring irony.

—All right, my father shouted, turning to me at last, admitting that I was party to the contest—indeed, the plaintiff vindicated.—Take it. Take the goddamned thing. Go out. Wreck it. Cost me my job. Kill yourself.

And then he tossed me the keys.

I parked in front of Helena's. She lived off Creswell Avenue in a nice part of town with solid houses and large pleasant lawns. We had met at one of those teen-age dances sponsored by parents who took great stock in supervised

61

activities. They were awful, except that you could meet girls. The day after, I had walked from Jesuit High over to the girls' school to catch her as classes finished in the afternoon. It was a long walk—no, it was a run, because she got out at the same time I did and they would expect her home within an hour. Her parents were very strict, she had told me at the dance.

So when she came upon me as she walked up Kings Highway, she smiled with delight, and wordlessly we walked past Fairfield, past Line Avenue and down the shallow hill that ran alongside Byrd High School, where the Protestants went, and where eventually I would go when the Jesuits determined that I was bound to end badly, indeed, already bore a bad name. We reached Creswell and slowed down. I took her hand. We stopped at the little bayou where the street dipped, where water stood several feet deep in the road after a heavy rain. We looked down at the brown water and she asked me what kind of fish might live in there. Before I could answer, she realized that we had walked a block past her house. She grinned and lowered her eyes as if admitting to an indiscretion. I shrugged and did not admit knowing all the time that we had passed that fatal street, ransoming ten precious minutes more by my pretense.

We met and walked so almost every day unless the weather was very bad and her mother drove to the school to pick her up. At last, one day, Helena asked me to come home with her to meet her mother. It was a beautifully furnished house, done in what I know now to have been good unobtrusive taste, though strongly feminine. Today I would put such a furnished house down as the work of a moderately talented interior decorator. But in 1949, I doubt that it was. People in Shreveport then had more substantial vices. They had not yet come to the contrefaction of sophistication.

As I waited for Helena to find her mother back in the unknown regions of the house, I stood caught up in a net of feelings that I had never experienced before. I saw Helena's round, bright, unremarkable face, her quick excited smile. I conjured her body, her slender legs and ankles. Sexuality was the least of it. That part was good and without complications because it was no more than an imagining, a vague aura that played around the person of every girl I met without settling into a realizable conception. Because then it seemed that an actual expression of unconcealed desire would surely smash itself and me against an invisible but real obstacle as unsettling as the sound barrier. No, it was something else that made me raise my arms and spread them as I smiled into a gold-framed mirror there in the foyer. I loved someone. It was a feeling composed and balanced between heights and depths that flared through me, leaving me exultant and ready for new things in the midst of a profound and indeterminate sadness. I looked at myself quizzically, arms akimbo, hair badly fingercombed. Was it the one or the other? Neither my own emotional history nor the mind that Jesuits had already forged in me had warned of ambivalence. It was disquieting and thrilling, somehow better than certainty. It was a victory taken from the flood of moments I lived but could not order. But even as I studied the physical shape of love in my face, I saw in the mirror, watching me from the parlor, a small face, serious, almost suffering, the face of a tiny Cassandra mute and miserable. For just an instant I thought insanely that it was Helena creeping up behind me on her knees. I was hot with embarrassment, chilled by something less personal, more sinister, as if a shard of some tomorrow had fallen enexplicably into the present. But the tiny disturbed copy of Helena's face vanished and I stood alone again fumbling a dog-eared Latin reader filled with the doings of Caesar.

Helena's mother was neat, attractive. The very picture of an efficient mother and housewife. Her eyes were dark, her face unlined in that metastatic poise of a woman who had passed forty by chronology but remains for months or a year as she must have been at thirty. She met me graciously, prepared Cokes for the three of us, and introduced me to Helena's small sister. I recognized the wraith in the foyer mirror. She did indeed look like Helena. Only without the smile, without the capacity to be excited and filled by a moment. I tousled her hair patronizingly, seeing in her eyes even as I did so a look that might have meant either *I know what you're really like*—or *help*.

It was a few days later that I asked Helena for a date. I had had a few dates before: humiliating affairs where my father drove me to the girl's house, took us to a movie, then came back and took us home afterward. But this would be different. This would be my first real date. And with someone I loved.

When I reached her house it was already dark. The air was chill. It was November, and the wind swept across my face as I opened the old car's door. Her porch light burned beyond the trees like an altar candle and I moved from the car toward it, key in my hand like power, into the circle of weak light close to Helena. When I rang, it was her mother who opened the door. Even entranced by the current of my triumphs and the size of coming pleasure, I noticed that her smile was forced. Had she had a tiring day? Or had she heard ill of me somewhere? That was possible. I had already the first stirrings of a bad name in certain Shreveport circles. But I forgot her expression as she introduced me to her husband, Helena's father.

He stood up heavily, a short red-faced man without charm or presence. He had reddish hair and that odd parti-colored complexion of certain redheaded farmers I knew who were most sensitive to the sun and yet obliged by their calling to work under it always. He looked at me as if I had come to clean the drains and was for some reason he could not fathom intruding into his parlor.

He shook hands with me perfunctorily and began at once to give me instructions as to where Helena and I might go, where we couldn't go. He brushed aside an attempt by his wife to make conversation and continued, making certain that I knew the time Helena was to be home. Eleven o'clock. He asked me to repeat the time back to him. I did so automatically, paying little attention because as he spoke I could make out the rank smell of whiskey on his breath, as if every word he uttered were being propelled up from his spreading shirtfront by the borrowed force of alcohol. As he went on talking, he looked not at me but past me toward the door, as if the effort of actually seeing me was more than he could bear. I stood silent, glancing at his wife. She was gnawing at the corner of her lip and looking down the hall toward the back of the house. At the edge of the dark hall I thought I could see, dim and distant, the face of Helena's little sister.

Then Helena came. She was dressed in a pale red woolen suit, high heels, a piece of gold jewelry like a bird of paradise on her shoulder. Her father turned from me, studied her, and said nothing. There was a flurry of last words and we were outside walking toward the car. As soon as the door closed, our hands met and clasped. We said nothing because both of us were back in the foyer of her house, the tension, her father and mother, vanished, annulled, decomposed by the look that had passed between us as we saw each other. We had sensed the whole garden of possibilities into which we were about to step. She came from her room assuming a schoolboy awaited her, only to find a slightly nervous young man in a sports jacket standing before her father armed with the key to an ancient car. I had been waiting for a girl but a young woman came to meet me. What joined us then, a current of our spirits, was all the stronger because neither of us had ever felt it flow forth to meet its counterpart before.

We reached the car. As I slid under the wheel, I turned to Helena. She was looking at me and her hand moved to meet mine again. We sat for a long moment until, embarrassed by the weight of our feeling, we drew apart and I started the car. Helena noticed that the inner door handle on her side was missing.

—That's to keep you in, I tried to joke, suddenly ashamed of my father's old car, seeing for the first time its shabbiness, the dusty dashboard, the stained head lining.

—I don't want to get out. Except with you, Helena said, her eyes large, the beginning of a smile on her lips.

For a while we drove. I headed in toward the city, driving up Highland Avenue past Causey's Music Shop, where I had learned the wherewithal of my bad name. I played trumpet every so often in a roadhouse across the Red River in Bossier Parish. It was called the Skyway Club and had bad name enough to splotch any number of fifteen-year-olds who could talk Earl Blessey, the bank leader, into letting them limp through a chorus of "Blue Prelude" or "Georgia on my Mind." Before the Skyway Club and I were done with each other, I would have lost and gained things there enough to be worth any number of bad names.

We drove into downtown and looked at the marquees of the Don and Strand theaters.

—What would you like to see, I asked Helena.

—I don't think I want to go to the movies, she said.

—What would you like to do?

—Could we . . . just go somewhere? And talk?

—Sure, I said. We could go to the Ming Tree over in Bossier . . . No, your father . . .

As I turned the car, I reached for her shoulder and drew her close to me. The lake was where people went when they had no reason to waste time with football games or movies. They went there to be alone, to construct within their cars apartments, palaces, to be solitary and share one another for a few hours.

Cross Lake was cold and motionless, a bright sheet under the autumn stars. Around us, trees rustled in the light breeze. But we were warm and I lit a cigarette and listened to Helena talk. She told me that she was sorry about her father. I said it was nothing. He was only thinking of her. He didn't know me. No, she said, he was thinking of himself. He drank at night. He sat drinking in the parlor, talking to himself, cursing his wife and children sometimes. Sometimes it was worse than that. She said she wanted me to know. Because if I were to think less of her . . .

—That's crazy, I said, turning her to face me. And we kissed.

It would not surprise me to find that moment, that kiss, the final indelible sensation last to fade from my mind as I lie dying. Not because I am sentimental. I have used and misused kisses and promises, truths and lies, honor and fraud and violence as the years moved on. That world where I knew Helena recedes from me more rapidly each day, each year, shifting red with the sting of its velocity, but never vanishing, its mass increasing in my soul toward infinity as, one who has managed the world as it is better than well, I am subtle enough to recover those fragments from the past which at the moment of their transaction were free from plan or prophecy or the well-deep cynicism of one who recognizes the piquancy of an apparently innocent moment precisely because he knows not only that it will not, cannot last, but because he has long before taken that fragility, that ephemeral certainty, into account in order to enjoy his instant all the more.

And so I remember that kiss. It was well-done. Our lips fused, moving together as if contained in them was the sum of our bodies. Without the conscious thought of sex we achieved a degree of sensuality unmatched in all the embraces I had still to seek or to endure.

—I love you, I told her.

—You can't mean it, she said.

We kissed again and then sat looking at the water, each of us touched beyond speech. We held ourselves close and sent our happiness, our exultation, out to move among the pines, over the water, toward the cold observant stars, keeping a time of their own. We sat that way for a long while.

In retrospect the appearances of banality are simple to determine. But the fact of it was not present between us that night. Banality presumes a certain self-consciousness, a kind of déjà vu, a realization explicit or implied that what one is doing has values other than those which seem. Or that certain values are missing. There must be a sly knowledge that the game in hand is not only not worth the candle, but hardly worth striking the match.

But Helena and I knew nothing then but each other and the shape of our victory. We were not repeating for the tenth or even the second time a ritual tarnished in its parts and lethally sure in its conclusion. We had for this moment conquered chance and youth, our fathers, the traps and distances laid for us. We were alone beside Cross Lake and no one on earth knew where we were. We belonged to ourselves, to each other. We did not know that neither of us, together or apart, would ever find this time and place, find each other like this again. It will always be exactly like this, we would have thought. Had we thought. It was not banal. The rest of our lives might be so, but not tonight.

Tonight we told each other of our troubles and our hopes. We said, each in a different way, that our fathers made us unhappy. That one day we would leave Shreveport, journey to London and Paris, to the farthest places we could imagine. Only now, after tonight, we would go together. We talked about much more, words cascading over each other as we exchanged all that we had been and done apart, all we planned and wished for together. Until, amidst a moment of silence, a pause for breath, Helena looked at her watch.

—Oh God, she gasped, her face stricken.

—What?

—It's . . .

—We're going to be late . . . ?

—It's . . . almost four o'clock. In the morning.

We stared at each other. I lit a match and looked at her watch. It was eight minutes to four. I closed my eyes. We were supposed to be home by eleven. Even my father would be aroused, knowing that I wasn't at the Skyway Club with Earl. I tried not to think about Helena's father but his squat body, his nearly angry face, rose in my mind again and again like a looped strip of film.

—O God, I do love you, Helena said.

We kissed again, touched, embraced. Her nylon-covered legs rose and touched my body. My hand found her breasts. None of this had we intended. The fruit of the tree in that garden we entered was the knowledge of time, of duration: time past, time lost. Even then, in those hysterical seconds, we were trying not so much to hasten passage from recognition to fulfillment as to claim what we might before it was too late, before we were separated and everything died.

But we stopped. We were not brave enough. We were too wise. We could not bring ourselves to wager what we had found against the sullen covenant of all our fathers. We kissed one last time hastily and I started the car, the beginning of an anguish inside me even as my heart beat insanely from her touch.

I cut the engine and coasted up in front of Helena's house. It seemed as if I had not seen it in centuries. Inside, many lights were on and I could see that the front door was a little ajar. Helena turned to me and touched my arm. I could see that there were tears on her cheeks, and the anguish grew.

—Go on, she said. Don't come up to the house with me. He'll be awful, really . . .

—No, I said without thought. I'm going to take you to the door.

I was not frightened, only apprehensive. I had been in too many hassles to spook before the event. There was always time to flush, sometimes only a second or two but always time. Anyhow, I had that fifty-yard walk to make, I knew. My bad name did not include cowardice, at least not of the overt and measurable kind. More important, there would be nothing left if I drove away, left the field and Helena upon it to her father. Our triumph would dwindle to an absurdity. I was not yet old enough to weigh those things against reality. What we had found in each other was real, I thought. And I was not a boy any longer. What you do not defend, you cannot keep: the oldest of all rules.

We walked toward the lights. Out of our world back into theirs. We did not walk hand in hand and later I would wonder how much of the future had been bent around that smallest of omissions. As we reached the door we could hear Helena's father. He was now very drunk and he was cursing and bullying her mother.

— . . . nice. Oh yes, Jesus son of God what do you reckon he's done . . . my baby. That little bastard. Telling her it's all right, taking off her . . . clothes . . .

I closed my eyes and blushed as if I were guilty of it all and more. Helena looked down at the concrete steps. Then she pushed open the door and stepped into the foyer to forestall any more of his raving.

—Hello, everybody, she said loudly, almost brightly, in that tone she used to greet me when we met after school each day.

Her father whirled about, his face red, thick, inarticulate with anger. Standing just behind Helena, I could not quite see the look that passed between them but it seemed to me that she nearly smiled, pale and upset as she was.

—Get to your room, her father spat out, swaying from side to side as he moved toward us. Toward me. No, don't say anything. I'll see to you later.

Helena's mother shook her head and signaled Helena to go, to leave it alone. But Helena wasn't ready.

—No, I want to say . . .

But her father pushed her out of the way roughly in order

to face me. Her mother stepped forward behind him and took her from the foyer. She was beginning to cry.

—What did you do, he rasped. Where did you take her? What kind of dirt . . .

He clenched his fists in front of my face. I thought coldly that he could smash me to pieces easily. But for some reason the realization meant nothing.

—We talked, I said. —I'm sorry we . . .

—Talked? You liar . . . you . . .

Helena's mother, her face anxious, truly frightened, came back into the foyer. She touched her husband's arm. He shook her off. Now he was swaying, blinking.

—Nothing happened, I said, considering the immensity of that lie.

—I think you'd better go now, Bill, Helena's mother said, motioning me toward the door with her anxious eyes.

I started to say something more, but I could think of nothing more to say. Then I backed toward the door, too old by far in the ways of Caddo and Bossier Parishes to show my back to a drunk who held a score against me, a blood score. The occasions of my bad name had made me cautious. Before I reached the door, there in the gloom of the dark hallway I saw, dressed in a long nightgown, the figure of Helena's little sister. Her face was pinched and no larger than an orange, it seemed. Her eyes were wide with excitement and certainty.

As I stepped outside, Helena's father, who had followed me with his inflamed eyes, began to weep. He twisted his fists into his eyes, his shoulders quaking. He turned to his wife, who looked after me one last time and then gave her attention to her husband, who leaned against her like a child swallowed in the skirts of its mother. Behind, the little girl stood alone, one hand pressed against that duplicate of Helena's face.

—My little girl, her father sobbed, as if he knew Helena to be dead. —My baby . . .

I turned then and breathed deeply, walking slowly toward the black mass of my father's sequestered Ford. I stopped at the car door and looked back at Helena's house under two cedar trees, dwarfed by a sweep of sky pricked with distant stars. I breathed again, taking in the chill early-morning air like one who stares down from some great height at the place where his lover sleeps or the field where his enemy lies broken. Then, full of some large uncertain joy, I sat down in the old car and jammed the ignition key home.

GUY DAVENPORT

Robot

(FROM THE HUDSON REVIEW)

DOWN THERE THE OCHER HORSE with black mane, black fet-
locks, black tail was prancing as if to a fanfare of Charpen-
tier, though it would have been the music of shinbone fife
and a drum that tickled her ears across the tall grass and
chestnut forests along the Vézère.

Coencas, tousled-haired, naked, and yawning, held Robot
in his arms, dodging with lifted chin his wet nose and gener-
ous tongue. The campfire under its spit of forked sticks, its
ashes ringed by rocks, looked abandoned in the woods light
at morning. The crickets had begun again, and a single night-
ingale trilled through their wild chirr on the slopes beyond
the trees.

The old priest was coming from Brive to look at the
horses, the reindeer, and the red oxen. He knows more about
them, Monsieur Laval had told them, than any man in Europe. More, *d'ailleurs,* than any man in the world.

Ravidat was awake, propped on his elbows in his sleeping
bag. In one of the pup tents Agnel and Estreguil lay curled
like cats. A leaf stuck to Estreguil's pink cheek. He had slept
in a sweater, socks, and hat. Agnel's knees were near his
chin.

Queroy and Marsal were asleep in the other tent under
Ravidat's canvas jacket.

Since Thursday they had lived with the tarpans of the Dordogne in their eyes.

72

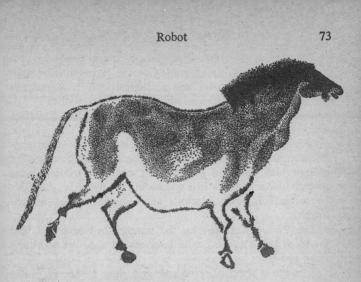

—Friday the thirteenth, Coencas said. *C'était par bonheur, la bonne chance.*

—We *felt* them on Thursday, Ravidat said, as when you know somebody's in the house without seeing or hearing them. They knew *we* were there.

—Scare me, Estreguil said, so I can scare Agnel.

Ravidat stretched kneeling, his open blue shirt that had bunched around his shoulders in sleep tumbling down his arched back like a crumpled piece of the September sky above them. He stood, naked but for his shirt, fell forward into ten brisk push-ups while Robot barked in his face, then rolled onto his back and pedaled his long legs spattered with leaf shadow in the sharp morning air.

—Ravidat, Marsal said gloomily from his tent, is having a fit.

—Show me, Estreguil said.

—*Et alors, mes troglodytes*, Coencas hailed the tents, help me get a fire going.

Estreguil crawled out in silly haste. Agnel rolled behind him. Robot studied them anxiously, looking for signs of a game.

Ravidat had pointed on Thursday toward the slope across the Vézère.

—He is over there! he called through cupped hands.

The others were catching up. Coencas had whittled a staff and was whacking thistle and goldenrod with it. Marsal put two fingers in his mouth and whistled like a locomotive.

Ravidat was watching the shaken sedge across the river where Robot nosed his way. He was seventeen, long of jaw, summer brown. His eyes were glossy black disks set in elm-leaf outlines of boyish lashes. His new canvas jacket smelled of pipe clay and gun powder. His corduroy trousers were speckled with beggar's lice and sticktights. Over his shoulder he carried his uncle Hector's old octagon-barreled breech-loader.

The Vézère was low, for the summer had been dry, and the reeds along its bank were thick with dragonflies and quivering gnats.

Through a stand of scrub oak and plum bushes as yellow as butter, the others filed toward him; Marsal with the other rabbit gun; Queroy with the sleeves of his sweater tied around his neck; Coencas in short blue pants, ribbed socks, a scab on one knee, brown cowlick over an eye; Estreguil sharp-nosed under a gray fedora; and little Agnel, who carried a frog.

The hum of an airplane had stopped them.

—Robot is over there on the slope, Ravidat said.

—A Messerschmitt, Coencas said. The Heinkels are much shriller.

—See my frog.

—When your hands are all warts where he's peed on you, Queroy said, we'll see your frog.

—The Stukas were so low we could hear them before we could see them, Coencas said. When a car stalled, or got hit, the people in the cars behind it would jump out and roll it in the ditch.

—They wouldn't roll *my* car in the ditch, Queroy said.

—They would, if you got kicked in the balls, like one man I saw. There were fights all the time. But when the Stukas came over the road, going down it with their machine guns *rat-a-tat, rat-a-tat*, everybody took to the fields, or woods if there were any. Afterwards, there were *burning* cars to get off the road.

Agnel watched Coencas's face with worried eyes.

—They are over there, Coencas said, pointing northwest.

Queroy spread his arms like a Stuka and ran in circles.

—Queroy is a Nazi, Estreguil said.

Estreguil was all dirty gold and inexplicably strange to look at. His hair was the brown of syrup, with eddies of rust spiraling in and out of the whorls of bright brass. His eyes were honey, his face apricot and the wild pale rose over the cheeks. He had been to Paris, however, and had seen real Germans on the streets, had heard them pound on their drums. Coencas had only seen the bombers. Agnel didn't know what he had seen.

—You might have to live forever in Montignac, Marsal said. The Germans may never let you go back home.

—I'm glad, Queroy said.

—*Merde alors,* Ravidat said. Then he shouted across the river:

—*Bouge pas, Robot!*

—He's going up onto the *hectares* of the Rochefoucauld, Marsal said.

—We can cross down at the meadow ford, Ravidat said, leading the way. Marsal and Coencas joined him, and the three little boys came in a cluster behind, Agnel's frog puffing its throat and swimming with a free hind leg. Estreguil's large gray fedora was a gift from Madame Marsal, Jacques's mother.

Robot had met them halfway up the slope, splashing his tail from side to side. His feet were still too big and he still fell when he wheeled. He squeaked when he barked and he squatted to pee, like his mother, which he did with a laugh, lolling tongue, and idiot eyes. He had never in his life seen a rabbit.

He thrashed his tail while Ravidat tickled him behind the ears.

—Find us a rabbit, old boy, Ravidat said. Find us a rabbit.

Robot let out his tongue in an ecstasy and rolled his tail.

—When the Nazi tanks turn, Coencas was explaining, they don't do it like an auto. It comes, *bram! bram! bram!* to a corner. If it's turning right, the right tread stops, *clunk!* and the left keeps the same speed, spinning it right around.

He swung his left leg out.

—And when it's facing the street it's turning into, the right tread starts again. Sparks fly out of the cobbles. Keen.

Queroy turned like a tank, spraying leaves.

—Are the rabbits just *anywhere* around here? Estreguil asked. Are they hiding?

They entered the oak forest at the top of the hill. The silence inside made them aware of the cricket whirr in the fields they had left, and the cheep of finches in the tall September grass. They could no longer hear the drone of the airplane. Caterpillars had tented over the oleanders.

The hills of the Dordogne are worn down to easy slopes, and outcroppings with limestone facings slice across the barrows of the hills.

—*C'est bien ajusté le slip Kangourou?* Coencas slapped Ravidat on the behind.

—*Va à ravir.* Ravidat laughed. *Et marche aussi comme un en pâte.*

—*Capiteux, non?*

Ravidat leaned his gun carefully against an alder, unbuckled his belt, unbuttoned his fly, lowered his trousers, and raised his shirt tail. He was wearing a pair of Coencas's underpants cut like swimming briefs, trim, succinct, and minimal.

—They're the new style from Paris, Ravidat explained. They are called *Kangourous.*

—Because you jump in them! Agnel squealed.

—Because your *queue* sticks out of the pouch when you want it, Estreguil said. *Idiot!*

—Has your peter got bigger still? Queroy asked. His was as yet a little boy's, his testicles no bigger than a fig.

Marsal, like Coencas, was old enough to have his aureole of amber hair, but Ravidat was already a man, full bushed in black.

—Let us see, Queroy said.

They looked at the rose heft of its glans with professional curiosity, the twin testicles plump and tight, Marsal and Queroy with envy, Coencas more complacently, though he felt his mouth going dry. Ravidat admired himself with animal pride.

Agnel considered these mysteries briefly and held out his frog to a tangle of gnats dancing in the air.

—Don't hurt him, Estreguil said. Will he eat the gnats?

Coencas slid his hand down into his short pants, stuck out his tongue in sweet impudence, and bounced on his toes.

—*Attendez!* Marshal said quickly, his voice hushed.

Robot was crashing through leaves. His tenor bark piped down the slope.

Ravidat stuffed his cock back into his shorts and the frog leapt from Estreguil's hands.

Ravidat held his gun, which he had grabbed, against his chest with his chin while he did up his trousers. Marsal was already away among the trees. Then they all galloped down the hill, elbows out for balance.

—Up and around! Marsal shouted.

—Show me the rabbit! Agnel cried from behind them.

Ravidat and Marsal were out front, stalking to the top of the slope, sighting along their guns. Coencas, his stick at the ready, was at their backs with Estreguil and Queroy.

—Say if you see my frog, Agnel said.

—Everybody stop! Ravidat cried. Keep quiet.

The woods were wonderfully silent.

—He went down the slope, Marsal said quietly, and then across, down there, and up again, didn't he?

—If he catches it, will he eat it? Estreguil asked.

—Shut up.

Robot was barking again. They turned together.

—Show me the rabbit, Agnel said, falling backwards.

They ran around him.

—How did the dumb dog get *behind* us? Ravidat asked.

They plunged down the hill, looking, jumping for a better look, kneeling for a better look. The familiar oakwood as they ran through it became unfamiliar and directionless, as though it had suddenly lost its ordinariness.

Agnel tripped and fell, spewing up a dust of leaves. Ravidat and Coencas bounded over fallen trees, their mouths open like heroes in a battle. Marsal was more methodical, sprinting with his gun at port arms.

—Everybody still! he shouted.

Only Agnel kept padding on behind them.

—I hear Robot, Marsal said, but damned if I know where.

The woods were all at once quiet. The distances were deepening dark.

Then they heard Robot. His bark was vague and muted, as if down a well. It was beneath them.

—Holy God, Ravidat said.

—Quiet!

Marsal went on all fours and cocked his ear. Robot was howling like a chained puppy. Then he began to whimper.

Robot! Ravidat called. Where *are* you? *Eh, mon bon bougre, où es-tu, hein?*

Marsal began to move on hands and toes.

—He's under the ground, Ravidat. In a fox den or rabbit burrow.

—He'll come out, Ravidat said. I'll bet he has a rabbit.

—Show me, Agnel said.

Marsal was walking around the hill, signaling for the others to follow. They could hear Robot's howls more distinctly as they clambered over an ancient boulder, a great black knee of stone outcropping. They came to the upended roots of a fallen cedar.

—He's down there! Marsal said.

The cedar in falling had torn a ragged shell hole in the hillside, and the weather had melted it down in upon itself. There was a burrow mouth at the back of the cavity, down which Ravidat, lying on his stomach, shouted:

—Robot!

An echo gave back *bô! bô! bô!*

—Get out of there! Ravidat coaxed. Come up, old boy! Come up!

Marsal gave a keen whistle.

—He's a hell of a long way down, Coencas said. You can tell.

Ravidat took off his canvas jacket, throwing it to Marsal.

—I'm going in after him.

—The hole's too small.

—Only the hole. You heard that echo. It's a cave.

—Sticks, Marsal ordered. Everybody find a good stick.

Agnel set to, arms over his head. Marsal drew his hunting knife and began to hack at the edges of the hole.

—It goes in level, he said. It must drop later on.

Estreguil came dragging a fallen limb as long as a horse. Ravidat brought a leafy length of white oak, stripping branches from it as he dragged it up to the hole.

—Let's get this up in there, he said, and walk it back and forth.

Ravidat and Coencas on one side, Marsal and Queroy on the other, like slaves at the oar of a trireme, they pushed and pulled, grinding the rim of the hole until Ravidat said that he thought he could crawl in.

—Go in backwards and feel with your feet, Marsal said. You can climb out then if you get stuck.

His legs in to the hips, he walked his elbows backwards, calling out, *Courage, Robot! Je viens!*

A half circle of faces watched him: Marsal's big gray eyes and tousled brown hair, Queroy's long Spanish face with its eyes black as hornets, Coencas's flat-cheeked lean face, all olive and charcoal, Estreguil's long-nosed, buck-toothed blond face with its wet violet eyes. Agnel's taffy curls and open mouth full of uneven milk teeth.

Level light from the setting sun shone on Ravidat's face.

—We ought to have a rope, Marsal said.

—It goes down here, Ravidat's muffled voice came out. There's a ledge.

He lowered his feet, loose rotten stone crumbling as he found footholds. His elbows on the ledge, he struck a heap of scattering objects with his feet. They must lie on something. He dropped.

—I'm on another ledge! His distant voice rose, as if from behind closed doors several rooms away. I'm standing in a muck of bones. It's a graveyard down here!

Earth poured on him in rivulets. An ancient dust, mortuary and feral, lifted from the bones he had disturbed. Coencas was wriggling in head first, loosening pebbles and sliding loam.

—Matches, he said, reaching down into the dark.

Then he said:

—I'm coming down!

Ravidat caught him, shoulders and arms, so that the one,

his feet still in daylight, hugged upside down the other standing in dark bones. They could hear Agnel saying:

—I'm next!

Coencas pivoted down, crashing onto the bones beside Ravidat.

—We're on a ledge, I think. Feel with your foot.

Coencas struck a match. White clay in striated marl beside them, utter blackness beyond and below, where Robot whined and yelped. Another match: the bones were large, bladed ribs in a heap, a long skull.

—Bourzat's ass!

—Queroy! Jacques! Ravidat shouted upwards. Last year, when old Bourzat's ass disappeared, you remember? Here it is!

—It was just about when that storm blew this old tree over. You're right, Marsal shouted down. You're right.

—Does it stink? Agnel hollered.

Another match showed that the ledge dropped at a fierce angle, but could be descended backwards, if there were footholds.

—Keep striking matches, Ravidat said. I'm going down. Robot had found a rhythm, three yelps and a wail, and kept to it.

—There's no more ledge. I'm going to drop.

A slipping noise, cloth against stone, and then Coencas heard the *whomp* of feet on clay far below him in the dark.

—*Robot,* he heard, *ici, ici, vieux bougre.*

—I hear Robot's tongue and tail, Coencas said upward. Everybody come on down. It's a long drop after this ledge.

Coencas lowered himself from the ledge of bones and fell lightly onto soft clay.

—We're here, Ravidat said from solid dark.

Marsal and Queroy were inside, handing down Agnel and Estreguil.

—Can we get back *out?* Marsal asked.

—*Qui sait?* Coencas said in the voice of Frankenstein's monster, and his words, full of grunts and squeals, rolled around them.

—Is the rabbit down here, too? Estreguil said, panting.

—Can we *breathe?*

—Here's the far wall.

A match showed it to be calcined and bulbous, a white bil-
low of stone. The floor was uneven, ribbed like river sand,
pot-holed, an enormous round-bottomed gully.

—I've never been so dark before, Agnel said.

—You're *scared!* Estreguil said.

—So are you.

—It keeps going back, Ravidat's hollow voice boomed in a
strange blur.

—I've got two more matches.

The hole through which they had entered was a dim wash
of light above them.

—Estreguil, Ravidat said behind them, take Robot. *Here!*
Keep steady with one hand. Hold on to Robot with the other.
Coencas is going to stand on my shoulders, and push you up
to the ledge. *D'accord?*

—Good old Robot! Estreguil said.

Ravidat braced himself against the wall. Coencas climbed
onto his shoulders, reached down for Estreguil and Robot,
pulled them up with a heave, and lifted them toward the
light.

—Stand on your toes, Ravidat, Coencas said. I think we're
just going to reach.

Estreguil pushed Robot onto the bone ledge. Then, skin-
ning both knees, he clambered up himself. Agnel went up
next, and had to come down again: he couldn't reach the
ledge from Coencas's shoulders.

—You go up, Queroy, Ravidat said, and pull Agnel up
when you get there.

Marsal went up next, showered them with dirt and pebbles, and hollered down:

—How are *you* going to get up?

—Get that long limb, Ravidat commanded. Poke it in, and
you four bastards hold onto it for all you're worth.

Coencas climbed out first, using the limb as a rope, and
Ravidat followed. The clarity of the long summer twilight
still held. Robot was in Agnel's arms.

—We have, Ravidat said in a level voice, discovered a
cave.

—Tell nobody, Marsal said. Estreguil! Agnel! You understand? *Nobody*. It's our cave.

—Find my frog, Agnel said.

—It's a damned *big* cave, Ravidat said. And Marsal and Queroy know what I'm thinking.

—What? asked Coencas. What is there to think about a cave?

At the ford Agnel fell into the Vézère. They dressed him in Queroy's sweater, and Ravidat carried him piggyback to the great spreading beech in Montignac.

—*Regardez les grands chasseurs!* the old men at their coffee sang out. Agnel had gone to sleep, Robot sat and let his tongue hang down, and Ravidat gave a confidential nod to the Catalan garage mechanic.

What he wanted, once they were leaning nonchalantly against the castle wall across the road from the beech and the elders, was grease. Old grease. And the use, for a day, of the old grease gun that had been retired since the new one arrived.

—Grease, my goose?

Precisely. The use to which it was to be put would be known in time. Meanwhile, could it be a matter among friends?

—*Seguramente*.

And he needed it first thing in the morning.

Queroy, Marsal, and Estreguil were to come out to the cave as soon as they were out of school. They could bring Agnel. Better to keep him in on it than have him pigeon.

—Meet me, Ravidat said to Coencas, at the flat rock on the river as soon as you're up. *Va bien?*

Bien. He heard the Heinkels in the night, and the cars of the refugees going through Montignac, headed south. He thought of the armies north and west, of white flares falling through the night sky, and of the long clanking rocking tanks that would most certainly come south. An old man under the great tree had said that the French battle flags had been taken to Marseille and had been paraded through the streets there. They were on their way, these flags, to the colonies in Africa.

By cockcrow he was up, making his own bowl of coffee, fetching the day's bread from the baker, as a surprise for his mother. He left a note for her saying that he would be back in the afternoon, and that he would be just south of town, in the Lascaux hills.

On the flat rock when he got there lay Ravidat's shoes and socks, trousers, canvas jacket, blue shirt, and Kangourou underpants. Ravidat himself was swimming up the river toward him. He stripped and dove in, surfacing with a whoop. Ravidat heaved himself out of the river and sat on the flat rock, streaming. The day was a clear gray, the air sweet and cool. He walked in his lean brown nakedness to a plum bush from which he lifted a haversack that Coencas had not seen. Inside, as he showed the wet, grinning Coencas, was a long rope, the grease gun, and a thermos of coffee.

—A sip now, he said, the rest for later.

They dried in the sun. The coffee was laced with a dash of cognac.

—What do you think we're going to see? Coencas asked.

—You'll see when you see.

They secured the rope outside the cave, and let themselves down the shelved clay. Ravidat lit a match and fired the grease gun: the kind of torch with which he had gigged frogs at night. The flame was greenish yellow and large as a handkerchief. Ravidat held it high over his head.

Neither spoke.

Everywhere they looked there were animals. The vaulted ceiling was painted, the crinkled walls, lime white and pale sulphur, were painted with horses and cows, with high-antlered elk and animals they did not know. Between the animals were red dots and geometric designs.

—Did you know they were here?

—Yes, Ravidat said. They had to be.

The torch showed in its leaping flare a parade of Shetland ponies bounding like lambs. Above them jumped a disheveled cow like the one in *Ma Mère l'Oie* over the moon. Handsome plump horses trotted one after the other, their tails arched like a cat's.

The cave branched into halls, corridors, tunnels.

They found long-necked reindeer, majestic bulls, lowing cows, great humped bison, mountain goats, plaited signs of quadrate lines, arrows, feathers, lozenges, circles, combs.

All the animals were in files and herds, flowing in long strides down some run of time through the silence of the mountain's hollow.

—They are *old,* Ravidat said.

—*Tout cela est grand,* Coencas said, *comme Victor Hugo.*

—They are prehistoric, like the painted caves of the Trois Frères and Combarelles. You have not been to them?

The cave was even larger than Ravidat had thought. It branched off three ways from where he had lit the torch, and two of these passages branched off in turn into narrow galleries where the floor was not clay but cleft rock. Their echoes rounded in remote darkness.

—It goes on and on.

They heard shouts outside: Marsal, Queroy, Estreguil, Agnel. They were out of school.

—Come look! Ravidat called up to them. It is Noah's Ark down here!

They told no one of the cave for three days. On the fourth day they told their history teacher, Monsieur Laval, who had once taken them to the caves at Combarelles and Les Eyzies. He came out to the cave, trotting the last steep ten meters. When they held the torch for him, he gripped his hands and tears rimmed his eyes.

—Of all times! Of all times!

He found a lamp by which the painters had worked, the mortar in which the colors were ground, the palette.

Coencas found another lamp, a shallow dish in which a wick soaked in deer fat had lit the perpetual night of the cave.

They began to find, sunk in the clay of the floor, flint blades, though most of them were broken. They found most of these shattered stone knives, thirty-five of them in all, just beneath the buffalo and the herd of horses.

—Maurice Thaon! Monsieur Laval said. We must get Maurice Thaon. He will know who must be told.

—Breuil, Thaon, who came the next day bringing a block of drawing paper, told them, is just over at Brive-la-Gaillarde with Bouysonnie, would you believe it?

Ravidat held the torch while he drew.

—I had a note from him last week. He will be frantic. He will dance a dance in his soutane. He will hug us all. The war has driven us all together here, and we have found the most beautiful cave of them all.

—Lascaux, he said, as if to the horses that seemed to quiver in the torchlight. Lascaux.

The postman went to Brive on the nineteenth with Monsieur Laval's note addressed to L'Abbé Henri Breuil, whom he had the distinguished honor of informing that in a hillside on the estate of the Comtesse de la Rochefoucauld a prehistoric cave with extensive paintings had been discovered by some local boys. Knowing the eminent prehistorian would like to inspect this very interesting site, he awaited word from him and begged him to accept his most elevated sentiments.

Thaon arrived later the same day with drawings.

—A car! the Abbé shouted. Do we have the petrol? For myself, I can walk.

They drove up the next day at the Great Tree of Montignac in the Abbé Bouysonnie's wheezing Citroën. Laval mounted their running board and directed them to the Lascaux hills.

Robot barked them to a halt.

—Here we are! Monsieur Laval said, shifting from foot to foot and waving his arms as if he were conducting a band.

The six boys, all with uncombed hair, stood in front of the automobile. L'Abbé Breuil herded them before him like so many geese.

—Brave boys, he cried, wonderful boys.

He stopped to look at their camp, shaking hands even with Estreguil and Agnel, who had never shaken hands with anybody before.

—I am decidedly prehistorical myself, is that what you're thinking, *mon gosse?*

Estreguil broke into a wide smile. He instantly liked the wide-backed old priest.

—Oh, I'm well beyond halfway to a hundred, and then some, he said to Agnel.

Then he turned to Ravidat, who stood with Robot in his arms.

—And that's the pooch to whom we're indebted, is it?

He patted the suspicious Robot, and mussed Ravidat's hair. They promptly forgot that this was the man who knew more about prehistoric caves than anybody else in Europe. He was simply an easy old priest with a wounded eye. His face was long, rectangular, big-eared, with strong lines dropping to comfortable pendules and creases under his jaws. A silken wattle hung under his chin. The gray bristles of his thick eyebrows rose and fell as if part of the mechanism of his meticulous articulateness.

—My eye? Prehistory got it. We've been climbing around Les Eyzies all week, Bouysonnie and I, and one of your indestructible bushes, through which, mind you, I was making my way in clear forgetfulness of my age, whacked me in the eye. I see lights in it, rather beautiful.

—But I'm forgetting my manners. This is Dr. Cheynier, who has come to help me, he said to the boys as if uncovering a surprise, and this is Monsieur l'Abbé Bouysonnie, who is an expert in primitive religions. And we're all anxious to enter the cave, if you are ready.

The first thing the Abbé's electric lamp found inside the cave was a rabbit.

It sat chilled with fear in the cone of light, its sides shivering. Marsal and Ravidat moved beside it just outside the beam, and the one chased it into the other's arms.

—We've not seen it the whole time we've been down here, Ravidat said.

—*He* was the first one in! Coencas said.

—Take him up, the Abbé said, and let him loose, and don't let the dog get him. He must be famished.

They heard Agnel shouting above.

—The rabbit! The bunny!

Light after light came on. A star trembled on the Abbé's horn-rimmed glasses. Silent, he looked. His weathered right hand was on Marsal's shoulder, as if he needed to touch the force that brought him here. A battery of lights shifted over their heads. Ravidat held the largest. Queroy aimed a long flashlight.

With his left hand the Abbé traced in the air the suave curves of a horse's back and belly.

—The colors! The tints! The gaiety of their movements! The wit of the drawing, the intelligence!

—They *are* old, are they not, Monsieur l'Abbé?

—Yes, *mon cher Laval,* no doubt at all of that.

He pointed higher, the lights climbing with his aim.

—They are as old as Altamira. Older, far older, than civilization.

A long cow faced her bull in the heart of the cave, the titan grandmother of Hathor and the cows of Africa upon whom the Nuer people still wait, burnishing their hair with her urine, imagining the female sun between her horns, replenishing the divine within human flesh with her holy blood.

With them run, as if pacing to the music of the first voice of the world, horses, elk, bears, and a spotted animal whose only portrait occurs here and whose bones have never been found. This first voice, the discourse of waters and rain, of wind in leaves and grass and upon mountain rocks, preceded the laugh of the jackal and the voices of the animals themselves, the rising wind of the cow's low, the water voice of the horse, the trumpet of the elk, bleat of the deer, growl of the bear.

In the Abbé's left eye trembled a jangle of red. He saw the prancing horse the color of crust through a snow of fireflies.

—Thaon brought me a drawing of this.

And of a line of reindeer:

—They were swimming a river. I have seen the motif before, carved on bone.

He worked the clay of the floor in his fingers.

—The bears were going when this cave was painted. Man could enter. The Aurignacian snow owl still drifted in at twilight, for the mice. One can imagine the sound of her wings in this stillness. The red rhinoceros was too blind to venture so much dark. The world belonged to the horse, the tarpan, the reindeer. Lion was terrible, but man could smoke him out of the caves, and lion, when the encounter came, was afraid of horse. The old elephants kept to themselves, eating trees.

They found the horse drawn upside down.

—Falling, do you suppose? Or weren't they oriented to the horizon, to the vertical? And these signs, these hieroglyphs! Are we ever going to read them, Bouysonnie?

They climbed out for lunch, cold chicken and mayonnaise and wine which Abbé Bouysonnie brought in two hampers, with Camembert and bread for dessert.

—It is a very great thing, is it not? Dr. Cheynier asked Abbé Breuil.

—So great that I sit here stunned. *Absolument bouleversé!* If there is a reason for my hanging on to such a disgraceful old age, it was to see this cave. A rabbit, a dog named—do I remember right?—Robot, these boys, a doctor's ration of petrol—he winked at Cheynier—and I suppose we must even give grudging thanks to the filthy *boches* for driving me from Paris. A veritable conspiracy of Providence!

Bouysonnie smiled.

—You've *always*, my dear Henri, been just around the corner from the discoveries, when, indeed, you weren't yourself the discoverer.

—I have, the Abbé said, I have.

He turned to the boys. Estreguil, who was sucking his fingers, was embarrassed.

—I have been around. Africa, oh yes, and China even. I was in China with a nephew of Voltaire who was quite close to his accomplished granduncle in spirit and brains. The church, in fact, thinks him too very much like his uncle, in a different sort of way. We went to China to look for the deep, the *very* deep, past of man. At Tcheou-kou-tien, a village some thirty-five kilometers below Peking, just under the lovely Fang Mountains—the Fang shan—*shan* is *mountain*—we found a very old skull, four hundred thousand, perhaps five hundred thousand years old. Five hundred thousand years old! *Cinq cent mille ans!*

He looked at each boy in turn, to make certain that they were following.

—Now, the cave bear, an enormous creature now extinct, was a kind of god, or totem. They broke his bones and sucked out the marrow after they had eaten his flesh and rendered his grease and dressed themselves in his hide. But they placed his skull reverently on ledges in open caves, looking outward, sometimes as many as fifty, all looking outward with their eye sockets; formidable I assure you, especially when they are found, as in the cave of the Drachenberg, covered with ten thousand years of dust.

—Fine dust, not quite half an inch thick. It looks as if the skulls were sculpted of dust.

—The snouts of these dread cave bears are all pointed out toward the sunrise, each in its hump of dust, its mask of dust, and each with its pair of empty bear eyes under a brow of dust. The lower jaws have all been removed, so that the long yellow teeth hang more bearlike in the dark while the sun, morning after morning for twenty thousand years, found the skulls on their ledges. It was like a shop with nothing to sell on its shelves but skulls of bears.

Estreguil and Agnel put their arms around each other.

—You have, some of you, the Abbé said to the boys, been to Combarelles and Font-de-Gaume, Monsieur Laval has told me. It was I who discovered them, oh years and years ago, when your parents were infants. So you see, you have been in my caves and now I have been in yours. *Nous sommes confrères!*

—You are not, you know, the first boys to have discovered a paleolithic cave, though it seems that you have found the most beautiful of them all.

—Three strapping fine brothers discovered Le Tuc d'Audoubert and Les Trois Frères. They were in their late teens when they found the Tuc, and soldiers home on leave from that other awful war when they found the cave that's named for them. Max, Louis, and Jacques de Bégouën they were. Their father is the Comte de Bégouën, Henri as he must always be to me, as I am Henri to him. He was retired after a lovely career of politics and owning a newspaper and such terrible things, to a house in the Ariège, near St. Giron, though he has never really retired. He is, if I can put it euphemistically, a man who has never lost his taste, bless him, for the good things of this life.

—His dear wife died early, leaving him three sons to bring up. We may note that they were brought up very well indeed, if just a touch wild, young wolves even in their Sunday best. And the Comte de Bégouën, never stinting his love of good food, a splendid cellar, and a gracious lady with which to share them, is now in his eightieth year, as hale as a prime bull.

—But I'm getting off my subject as if I were eighty myself. On the Bégouën property. Montesquieu-Avantès, the little river Volp runs right through a largish hill, in one side, out the other. What else must a boy do, I need not tell you, but build a raft of oil cans and wooden boxes, and paddle himself into that cave?

—That's what Max did, oh most decidedly. A farmer thereabouts, François Camel, had been as far up the Tuc d'Audoubert end of the mountain as where you can't go any farther unless you are a weasel, but that never stopped a boy, to my knowledge.

They *all* went, of course, Jacques and Louis too. They got to a kind of beach and, what do you know, they came across an inscription scratched there in the eighteenth century. They had to turn back, but not for long. They came back and hacked the weasel hole until they could get into it. They found that it was a *gours*, a chimney in the rock, and up it they scampered, forty feet.

—When we turned the rabbit loose that Robot chased into the cave, Estreguil said, he ran as if the Germans were after him!

—*Tais-toi!* Ravidat said. *D'où sors-tu?*

The Abbe sighed, and smiled.

—And what did they find there? Sculpture! The very first

prehistoric discoveries were of course sculpture, carved pebbles and bones, but this was modeled in clay, two bison, two bison moreover about to copulate. Close by they found the heel prints of children, such as Cartailhac would find later, also in the heart of a mountain, around the headless statue of a bear, with evidence that a real bear's head had been staked onto it. Both these sites seem to have been the occasion of a single ceremony. The animals were shaped by the light of a torch, who knows with what sacred dread, and children danced on their heels, and the cave was closed forever.

—The curious thing about this cave is that if you were to drill through the rock in the right direction you would come to the end of another cave, the Trois Frères, which the Bégouën boys found in nineteen sixteen. At the uttermost recess of *it* is that strange sorcerer, or god, a man dancing in a mask with a beard. He wears antlers, a horse's tail, bear's paws. His sex is human, but it is placed where a cat's is, under the tail. He is our oldest portrait of God.

—The caves are the first draft of the book of Genesis, when man was a minor animal, not suspecting that the divine fire in his heart was unique. He was thousands of years away from the domesticating of these animals. The dog was the first. He is man's oldest friend.

Abbé Breuil lit his pipe.

—Oh, Robot knew they were down there! He is one of them. I'm afraid I've already scandalized the archbishop—he winked at Agnel—with the heresy I can't get out of my head that animals most obviously have souls, but unfallen ones, as they did not participate in the sinful pride of our common parents. Ancient man must have been in some measure envious of the animal, suspecting its superiority.

—He was right, of course, he added.

A man in blue coveralls had come up behind them.

—Ramón! Ravidat called out.

It was Ramón's grease gun that had first illumined the cave. But he was signaling that he did not wish to be called to. He sat under a tree some meters away and lit his pipe. He winked at Ravidat and made himself comfortable.

—Abbé, are we going down again today?

—I think not, Thaon. I should rest my eye. It's full of lights again. Will the boys keep their guard?

—You couldn't drive them away, Monsieur Laval said. They're well set up in their camp. *Pour eux, c'est une aventure.*

—For us all. The Abbé smiled. We shall be at the Hôtel Commerce, he said to the boys, tweaking Agnel's ear and Estreguil's nose.

He shook hands with Ravidat, acknowledging his age and responsibility. His eyes indicated Ramón under the tree.

Let no one into the cave, he said.

—That's an old friend, Ravidat explained. He is the mechanic in Montignac.

—*Tiens. Jusqu'à demain.*

As the Citroën bounced down the hill, Monseiur Laval on the running board, the Abbé Breuil waving his handkerchief from a window, Ramón walked toward them, his hands in his pockets.

—Madame Marsal, he said, will be sending up hot soup.

He approached Ravidat with a look that was both intimate and inquisitive.

—Is it a big cave?

—It's a right good size, yes.

Ramón looked about him. He indicated with his eyes that he wanted a word apart. Ravidat followed him.

—Wait, Ramón said. *Marsal aussi.*

He put the flat of his hand out to the others. Then he stared at Coencas, who was looking at them from under his cowlick.

—You too, Ramón said. Come with us.

Queroy, Agnel, and Estreguil drew together, left out of a conspiracy.

—Why can't they come? Coencas asked.

Ramón's face showed that Coencas had jeopardized his own eligibility.

—What's it all about? Coencas was persistent.

Ramón saw his mistake. All or none, however dangerous that seemed. He stood in his indecision, pulling his nose.

—*Igual,* he said. Gather around.

He squatted, taking cigarette paper and a sack of tobacco from his pockets.

—This is a matter for *cojónes,* he said in a low voice. The priest will be through looking at the pictures in the cave in a few days. That's to be seen. I shall talk with him, too. And with the others. They're all French.

He sealed the cigarette with the tip of his tongue.

—The Germans are not here yet.

He looked at each of them in turn.

—They will be, in time. There are some of us who will be ready. Do you understand?

—I think I see, Ravidat said.

—We call ourselves the *Résistance.* We are all over France. Have you heard about us, Ravidat? No? Well, you have now. You and Marsal own guns. And you know your way about.

—You are a refugee, *hein?* he said to Coencas.

—From Charleville.

—And you and you, Ramón said to Estreguil and Agnel.

—They're old enough to understand, Ravidat said.

—I want you to swear, Ramón said. One hand on your balls, one on your heart. Swear!

—So help us God.

Ramón looked over his shoulder. It was only Robot jumping at a cricket. They sat quietly, listening to the trill of the nightingales and the wash of wind in the trees.

—The important thing at the moment, Ramón said, is a place to stash ammo. I can get straight off a consignment of Bren guns, if I can find a place to hide them. Is that cave big enough?

—You can hide anything in it, Ravidat said. It's as big as a castle down there.

—If you tell the preist, Coencas said, he won't let you. He'll be afraid you'll hurt the pictures.

—*Foutre les tableaux,* Ramón said. We won't tell him, then. We'll wait until he clears out.

—He's already said, Marsal put in, that he wants to keep the cave secret. That fits in. His secret and our secret will work out the same.

—Anybody who lets our secret out, Ramón said quietly, will have to answer to the *Résistance*. And we are many.

—When do we start? Coencas asked.

—I'll tell you when the time comes. The priest will be measuring the cave. Remember his figures. And tell me all his plans. When he's gone, we can begin to move.

He stood up.

—I'm going back down to the village.

He scooped Agnel up under the arms and held him above his head.

—You know about the Germans? he said. The war? If you tell anybody about this, we lose the war. If you don't, we win.

He set him down.

That goes for you too, he said to Estreguil, crooking his finger as if on a trigger.

—For all of us.

He set off, as casually as he came.

—*Ravidat*, he said, turning, *vous avez la verge la plus longue. Soyez le capitaine de ces voyous!*

—*Nous sommes soldats!* Queroy said.

—*Agents, au moins*, Ravidat said.

—*Des espions!*

The moon when it rose was red and perfectly round. Robot gave it a perfunctory trombone howl, joined by Agnel, answered by an owl.

Queroy hinted that Marsal was afraid to be in the *Résistance*, that his mother wouldn't let him if she knew, and got his lip split in a pinwheel of a fight by the fire. Ravidat parted them with slaps and made them shake hands.

Estreguil fell asleep in his clothes beside Robot, who slept facing the fire.

Coencas, standing in the red light, pulled off his shorts and studied his dick:

—Mine's the next longest, he said to Ravidat.

—Mine is, Marsal said, crawling back out of his bedroll.

—No, Ravidat said. Robot, I think, is next in rank.

Next morning they found the figure of the hunter in the shaft at the back of the cave, a mere stick of a man, bird-headed, ithyphallic, childish. Beside him is a carved bird on a staff. His spear has gored a bison whose bowels are spilling out. To the left of the hunter is a rhinoceros.

—These signs, Thaon! *What* do they mean? These quartered squares on legs, are they houses on piles, as in the Swiss lake wattle houses, houses perhaps for souls? Are those feather shapes arrows, spears?

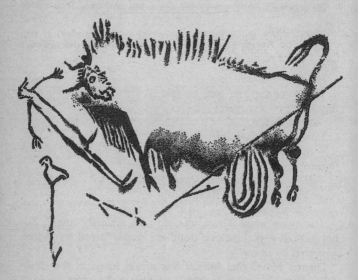

　—Your *houses*, l'Abbé Bouysonnie said, have four legs. Could not they too be horses? Written horses beside the drawn horses?

We've got onto a wall of cats. Mountain lions, probably. One old tom has his tail up, testicles well drawn, spraying his territorial boundaries.

—The artist, Abbé Breuil added, has observed the whiplash curve you get in a stream of water coming from a shaking source. We have all seen a cat wiggle his behind when he's peeing.

Another cat has an arrow in its side, like the Sumerian

lioness. These are engraved, not painted like the larger beasts.

Outside, over coffee, Abbé Breuil talked about the hunter, the disembowled bison, and the rhinoceros.

—The rhinoceros trotting off to the left is in heat, you can tell that from her arched tail, even if you've only seen a cow or a cat ready for the male. It was the realism of the *chat qui pisse* that led me to see that. The rhythmic dots drawn under her tail are her delicious odor, I should think. She is ready to breed.

—To the Aurignacian hunter she is ready to die. Except that it is not death he brings with his spear. It is mating in another sense. Nor does this picture mean that she is to die while in heat. It means that in the painter's vocabulary of symbols to die by the spear and to receive the male are cognate female verbs.

—Reality is a fabric of many transparent films. That is the only way we can perceive anything. We think it up. Reality touches our intuition to the quick. We perceive *with* that intuition. Perhaps we perceive the intuition only, while reality remains forever beyond our grasp.

—Man is the javelin bearer, the penis bearer. Woman conceives through a wound that bleeds every lunar cycle, except when she holds the gift of the child, magically healed. The hieroglyphs of these cave painters for wound and vulva are probably the same.

Monsieur Thaon frowned.

—The hunter with arms outspread before the wounded bison is embracing the idea of death, which to him is the continuity of life. The spilling entrails are an ideogram of the vagina. The bison is life under the guise of death. Who knows what metamorphosis death was to these archiac minds?

—The hunter wears a bird mask exactly like the bird on his shaman's baton. He is therefore not a picture of a man but of that intuitive film over reality we call myth. He has assumed the character that the bird totem also represents. Together they have brought the bison down.

The terrace of the Hôtel Commerce *cèpes paysannes*, Laval,

Thaon, Breuil, Bouysonnie, *truite meunière*. Ravidat is in a chair apart, his fingers laced together. Coencas, slapping his beret on his thigh, has just come in.

—I was at Altamira, bless you, in the year nineteen-o-two! the Abbé was saying. Eh! *It* was discovered by a dog, too. It was, it was! I have just now remembered the coincidence. It must have been Robot's Spanish grandfather.

—The cave, but not the paintings, which were discovered by a little girl. Her father, the owner of the property, had been going out to the cave for years, once his dog had found it, but he was looking for celts and flints. He had never once looked at the ceiling, if you can imagine. One day his little daughter came along with him, and walked in and looked up, first thing. *Papa,* she said, *los toros, los toros!*

—Carthailhac was convinced that those bulls were thousands and thousands of years old. I went down with him and began making drawings of them. I've been in the business ever since.

—One day at Altamira I was on my back drawing. They hadn't yet lowered the floor as they have now. I was working with crayons by candlelight, dabbed all over with dripping wax, drawing the great mural of bulls, when a very large-eyed young Spaniard came in on hands and knees. He had come from Barcelona, and his clothes were, I remember, of the Bohemian cut, as they said in those days.

The Abbé's eyes became mischievous and knowing.

—He said *bon jour* and I said *bon jour*, odd as it was, *vous savez*, to be of a civility deep in a Magdalenian cave. And *bon jour* was precisely all the French he had. He lay on his back, looking, looking. *Hermoso,* he kept saying, *hermoso*. He was not interested in the age of the drawings, but, *ma foi*, in their beauty. He asked, as best I understood his Spanish, if he might touch them, and I explained that pigments that had adhered to limestone for twenty thousand years weren't likely to rub off now. But he didn't touch them. He took one of my candles and followed the bold lines of the beasts as if *he* were drawing them. There was a terrible look on his face, wonder and admiration, and a kind of worship.

—I got his name straight once we were outside. Picasso. It meant nothing to me then, of course. Such eyes.

—*Picasso*. He did not forget Altamira. His eye has never forgotten anything. The bison at Altamira were to him *très moderne*. I have always thought of him as a Cromagnon painter out of time.

—The painted caves in Spain are in the north, in the Cantabrian mountains. They are all across, from San Román in the west to Santimamiñe in the east, and this last is outside Guernica where the dive bombers struck first in this awful war.

—And when Picasso painted his great symbolic picture of the bombing of Guernica, he made one of the bulls of Altamira dominate the design.

—But yes! said Abbé Bouysonnie. And I had never seen that at all.

—I like to think of that bull, whether at Altamira or in the angry and eloquent *Guernica*, as Being itself, in all its power and dumb presence.

And as if he suddenly found it more comfortable to change the subject, the Abbé Breuil turned to Monsieur Laval:

—What a beautiful old tree! he said of the Montignac beech that filled the *place* with its shade. They are cutting them down, you know, all over France, an obstruction to artillery sighting. A village without a tree is like a woman without hair. Some poet must write an elegy for the trees of the French villages, nay, for the trees of Europe. There was a vulnerable oak at Guernica, wasn't there? Some great pagan tree that burned when the dive bombers came. I keep coming back, it seems, to Picasso.

—But, Bouysonnie said, Picasso does not allude to the Basque oak in his mural, does he?

—No, no, Breuil said. It is not in the prehistoric genius to depict trees. This man Picasso *is* a painter from the Reindeer Age. The *Guernica* with its wounded horse, its hieratic bull, its placing of images over images, is a prehistoric painting. It honors and grieves and stands in awe. I have copied hundreds and hundreds of these beasts until they file through my dreams. God will take me to them when I die, to the saucy Shetland tarpans whose jet manes run the length of their backs, to the long red ox and woolly rhinoceros. But perhaps the *Guernica* I see is not the one everybody sees. The painting I see is as old as Lascaux.

The Drachenberg bears, their jaws full of shadow: *We are Ursus, companions of the Pole Star, god of the Finnmark, brothers of Artemis Diktynna, lords of the forest. We are Bruin, Arkturus, Baloo. We are eaters of the honey of the bees of Han, the golden bees of Mykinai and Tiryns, the red bees of the Merovingians. Man with his gods fire and flint drove us from the caves but put our souls on the walls along with blind bison, shrill horse, slow cow, royal salmon, wizard elk, cruel puma, idiot jackal.*

In the forecourt of the chthonic granary of souls at Lascaux two long cows shamble toward three long cows, dewlapped Indus horned cattle lowing and prancing on stiff forelegs. They are not domestic and pied but wild and brown, still in their eland grazing age. Nor are these aurochs yet Hathor nor the royal herds of Harappa. They are, bulls and cows together, female to the Magdalenian mind, creatures of the realm of woman. So were bison, ox, and mammoth. The male domain was horse, ibex, stag.

Breuil leaned on his geologist's pick and gazed.

The bison transfixed by the hunter's spear at the back of the cave is new to us. In a kind of visual pun the spear is drawn from the sexual parts downward and emerges along the bison's belly like a penis in a ventral foreskin. Men have read languages before now without a dictionary.

How could he decipher what men had forgotten twenty thousand years ago?

His eye hurt. He was old. This place was holy. To know, to know.

—*No, Breuil,* he said to himself aloud. *To see.*

Robot on his knees, the Abbé sat in the red rain of light that trembled through the shelved leaves of the great tree in the *place.* Ravidat sat at his feet in a seine of leaf shadow. Monsieur le Maire in his high collar and the tricolor across his breast rolled the wine in his glass. Agnel and Estreguil stood on each side of Maurice Thaon, whose hands rested on their shoulders.

—You cannot imagine Africa, the Abbé was saying. Djibouti in the Somaliland, on the gulf of Aden; Nizan, is it not, who calls Aden the worst place in the world? Djibouti, then, is the next worse place. Admiral Scott, you remember, when he first saw Antarctica, said, *Mon Dieu! What an awful place!* and I wish I could have said something as fine about Djibouti but I was speechless.

The Mayor looked from Thaon to a concierge in black stockings who was standing at a respectable distance from the men. He nodded with deep appreciation of the Abbé's words.

—You have lived all your life in France, *mes gosses, messieurs et dames.*

He, too, nodded politely to the concierge, who dared not acknowledge the honor except by folding her arms.

—The Somaliland is a baked waste. My American friend Monsieur Kelley once said that France smells of wine, urine, and garlic, but Africa smells of carrion, of *merde* ripened by flies as big as hornets, of rotten water silver with filth and green with contagion.

—Indeed, said the Mayor.

—Djibouti is ravaged dirt streets, shacks with blinding tin roofs, whole buildings of rust and packing cases wired together.

—*Il est poète*, the Major whispered to Thaon, *l'Abbé!*

—And all of this steaming rot is surrounded by white mountains, sparkling mountains of salt. Imagine that. I was there with Père Teilhard de Chardin, as in China, and with an extraordinary man, a Catalan with an almost French name, Henri de Monfreid, from the Roussillon, the half-brother of Madame Agnès Huc de Monfreid. Their father fell out of a tree some twenty years ago, strange way to die. He was Georges-Daniel de Monfreid, a painter and friend of Gauguin's, whose paintings he used to buy under the pretense of selling them, to encourage him.

Maurice Thaon was laughing.

—Since when is a priest not a gossip? the Abbé asked. I'm putting everybody to sleep.

Monsieur Thaon laughed the louder. The Mayor was confused but smiled nevertheless, rolled the wine in his glass, and leaned forward attentively.

—*Et Alors.* Where was I? The salt heaps of Djibouti. The stink of Africa. *Ah!* That extraordinary man Henri de Monfreid. He has been everywhere, everywhere that other people haven't been. He was the man who took Père Teilhard to Abyssinia, its awful deserts. Harar, where Rimbaud lived, Obok, Diredawa, Tajura. Prehistory is very rich around there. They found rock paintings, lovely graceful animals, hunters with bows, geometric designs all dots and angles.

Marsal came closer, sitting behind Ravidat.

—I went with them a bit later, like going to the moon. At Obok there is nothing alive. The old volcanoes are still in the week of creation, black and wrinkled. The silence lifts the hair on the back of your head.

—And then we got to Ganda-Biftu, where there are four hundred meters of paleolithic drawings across the face of a cliff. We climbed up, having built a scaffold for the purpose. I drew and drew and drew, as high up on the rock as the third story of a building. Sickle-horned African buffalo, lions, antelope. And lithe men, far more realistically drawn than in our European caves. And among the buffalo, quite clearly, were long black oxen. You see what that implies. Domestication.

The Abbé stared before him, sipping his wine.

—We found more pictures, found them at Diredawa, and then outside Harar. We went to the Porcupine Cave, as they have named it, that Teilhard had seen earlier. But I saw something he had passed over. It was a calcined protuberance, wonderfully suspicious, and with no trouble at all I found a bone beneath. A human jawbone, but not of man as we know him, but of the breed of men before us, the apelike man Neanderthal. He had never been found in Africa before, and it was not known that he was an artist. It was thought that he could only arrange stones painted red ocher, and set the mountain bears' skulls on ledges as in the cave at Drachenberg.

He drained his glass and set it on the table.

—But he could draw. *Mon Dieu,* he could draw.

The first boxes of ammunition were placed in the Shaft of the Hunter and the Bison late in October, when the moon was dark. Long cases of carbines packed in grease, grenades, flares, .45s rose in neat stacks to the black shins of the prancing horses.

At Drachenberg the bears' skulls sat on their ledges, hooded in dust older than Ur or Dilmun. Their muzzles all pointed to the rising sun, which fell upon them dimly in the depth of their cave in the cliff, lighting all but the sockets of their eyes.

Historical Note

The cave at Lascaux, on the estate of the Rochefoucaulds near Montignac in the Dordogne, was painted between 20,-000 and 15,000 B.C. by men about whom we know nothing except that they hunted with arrowheads shaped like laurel leaves and were draftsmen as accomplished as Hokusai and Carpaccio. The passage by which they entered the cave has never been discovered, but it is evident that they worked in darkness by torchlight. The animals they depicted all belonged to species now extinct. The outlines of the figures were engraved or brushed, and the pigment sprayed on.

Sealed for two hundred centuries, the cave was discovered on September 12, 1940, first by a rabbit, and immediately afterward by a dog named Robot, who was chasing it. Robot belonged to a boy from Montignac named Ravidat. Jacques Marsal, who was with Ravidat and Robot, is now a guide at Lascaux, though he only shows slides rather than leading visitors through the cave, which has been closed for over a decade and is expected to be closed indefinitely. The warmth of human breath had caused bacterial cultures to grow on the paintings.

M. André Leroi-Gourhan, whose work on the European prehistoric caves is the most brilliant and searching since that of the greatest of prehistorians, Abbé Henri Breuil (1877-1961), says in his monumental *Treasures of Prehistoric Art* that Lascaux "was discovered in 1940, quite accidentally, by two local boys, Ravidat and Marsal." Mlle Annette Laming (now Mme Laming-Emperaire) attributes the discovery to four boys. "Two of the boys," she says in her *Lascaux: Paintings and Engravings*, "Ravidat and Marsal, are natives of the Commune (Montignac in Périgord) and subsequently became guides to the cave—indeed they still fill this office. The third, Agnel, was on holiday in Montignac, and the fourth, Coencas, was a refugee there."

Mr. Glyn Daniel recognizes five discoverers, and is the sole historian of archeology to have recorded Robot's name. "On the morning of September 12, 1940," he says in his *Lascaux and Carnac*, "when the Battle of Britain was being fought out and France itself was divided into an occupied and unoccupied zone by a line that ran from Bordeaux north-east to Burgundy, five young men from Montignac went out rabbit-shooting. They were Ravidat, Marsal, Queroy, Coencas, and Estreguil. Ravidat, Marsal, and Queroy were local boys; the other two were refugees from occupied France. Ravidat, aged seventeen at the time, was the oldest of the five and the leader of the party. They had with them two guns and a dog—a famous dog to whom archeologists should erect a statue—the little dog Robot."

That Lascaux was used as a secret ammunition cache by the Résistance is recorded in André Malraux's *Anti-Memoirs*. The presence of Picasso at Altamira with the Abbé Breuil is affirmed by Alan Houghton Broderick's *Father of Prehistory: The Abbé Henri Breuil, His Life and Times*. The resemblance between the *Guernica* and the Sanctuary of the Bulls at Altamira is a perception which I assume occurred to Père Breuil. Other perceptions of the great prehistorian are actually ideas later worked out by M. Leroi-Gourhan, and some of them, such as the theory that the red dots at the rumps of the tarpans are graphs of sexual odor, are imaginary.

My story is an *assemblage* of facts insofar as they can be known. All the characters are real, including the Spanish mechanic, and the time scheme is as I have used it. The discovery of Lascaux was a pattern of coincidences which no professional storyteller would ask any reader to believe. It is slightly preposterous that the greatest living authority on prehistoric art was only a few miles away at the time of the discovery, though it is not surprising that schoolboys should be learned in the subject of painted prehistoric caves, as the region roundabout is rich in them, and their history teacher was an ardent amateur prehistorian.

M. Jacques Marsal told Daniel M. Madden in 1969 that he "and three other boys" discovered Lascaux [*New York Times,* January 4, 1970, "France Saves Lascaux Grotto, But Public Is Still Barred"]. The number of codiscoverers fell to two when M. Marsal talked with André Malraux earlier. Ravidat became a contractor, but holds with Marsal the honor of being an official guardian of the cave. The fortunes of Coencas, Estreguil, and Agnel I have failed to ascertain. Queroy was killed in the Résistance.

WILLIAM EASTLAKE

The Death of Sun

(FROM COSMOPOLITAN)

THE BIRD SUN was named Sun by the Indians because each day their final eagle circled this part of the reservation like the clock of sun. Sun, a grave and golden eagle-stream of light, sailed without movement as though propelled by some eternity, to orbit, to circumnavigate this moon of earth, to alight upon his aerie from which he had risen, and so Sun would sit with the same God dignity and decorous finality with which he had emerged—then once more without seeming volition ride the crest of an updraft above Indian Country on six-foot wings to settle again on his throne aerie in awful splendor, admonitory, serene—regal and doomed. I have risen.

"Man Feodor Dostoevski said," the white teacher Mary-Forge said, "without a sure idea of himself and the purpose of his life cannot live and would sooner destroy himself than remain on earth."

"Who was Dostoevski?" the Navajo Indian Jesus Saves said.

"An Indian."

"What kind?"

"With that comment he could have been a Navajo," Mary-Forge said.

"No way," Jesus Saves said.

"Why, no way could Dostoevski be an Indian?"

"I didn't say Dostoevski couldn't be an Indian; I said he couldn't be a Navajo."

"Why is a Navajo different?"

"We are, that's all," Jesus Saves said. "In the words of Sören Kierkegaard—"

"Who was Sören Kierkegaard?"

"Another Russian," Jesus Saves said.

"Kierkegaard was a Dane."

"No, that was Hamlet," Jesus Saves said. "Remember?"

"You're peeved, Jesus Saves."

"No, I'm bugged," Jesus Saves said, "by people who start sentences with 'man.' "

"Dostoevski was accounting for the high suicide rate among Navajos. Since the white man invaded Navajo country the Navajo sees no hope or purpose to life."

"Then why didn't Dostoevski say that?"

"Because he never heard of the Navajo."

"Then I never heard of Dostoevski," Bull Who Looks Up said. "Two can play at this game."

"That's right," Jesus Saves said, sure of himself now and with purpose.

"What is the purpose of your life, Jesus Saves?"

"To get out of this school," Jesus Saves said.

Jesus Saves was named after a signboard erected by the Albuquerque First National Savings & Loan.

All of Mary-Forge's students were Navajos. When Mary-Forge was not ranching she was running this free school that taught the Indians about themselves and their country—Indian country.

"What has Dostoevski got to do with Indian country?"

"I'm getting to that," Mary-Forge said.

"Will you hurry up?"

"No," Mary-Forge said.

"Is that any way for a teacher to speak to a poor Indian?"

"Sigmund Freud," the Medicine Man said, "said—more in anguish I believe that in criticism—'What does the Indian want? My God, what does the Indian want?' "

"He said that about women."

"If he had lived longer, he would have said it about Indians."

"True."

"Why?"

"Because it sounds good, it sounds profound, it tends to make you take off and beat the hell out of the Indians."

"After we have finished off the women."

"The women were finished off a long time ago," the Medicine Man said.

"But like the Indians they can make a comeback."

"Who knows," the Medicine Man said, "we both may be a dying race."

"Who knows?"

"We both may have reached the point of no return, who knows?"

"If we don't want to find out, what the hell are we doing in school?"

"Who knows?"

"I know," Mary-Forge said, "I know all about the eagle."

"Tell us, Mary-Forge, all about the eagle."

"The eagle is being killed off."

"We know that; what do we do?"

"We get out of this school and find the people who are killing the eagle."

"Then?"

"Who knows?" Mary-Forge said.

Mary-Forge was a young woman—she was the youngest white woman the Navajos had ever seen. She was not a young girl, there are millions of young girls in America. In America young white girls suddenly become defeated women. A young white woman sure of herself and with a purpose in life such as Mary-Forge was unknown to the American Indian.

Mary-Forge had large, wide-apart, almond-shaped eyes, high full cheekbones, cocky let-us-all-give-thanks tipsy breasts, and good brains. The white American man is frightened by her brain. The Indian found it nice. They loved it. They tried to help Mary-Forge. Mary-Forge tried to help the Indians. They were both cripples. Both surrounded by the white reservation.

High on her right cheekbone Mary-Forge had a jagged two-inch scar caused by a stomping she got from high-heeled

cowboy boots belonging to a sheep rancher from the Twin
Slash Heart Ranch on the floor of the High Point Bar in Gallup.

Mary-Forge did not abruptly think of eagles in the little
red schoolhouse filled with Indians. A helicopter had just
flown over. The helicopter came to kill eagles. The only time
the Indians ever saw or felt a helicopter on the red reservation was when the white ranchers came to kill eagles. Eagles
killed sheep, they said, and several cases have been known,
they said, where white babies have been plucked from play-
pens and dropped in the ocean, they said.

You could hear plainly the *whack-whack-whack* of the
huge rotor blades of the copter in the red schoolhouse. The
yellow and blue copter being flown by a flat-faced doctor-
serious white rancher named Ira Osmun, who believed in
conservation through predator control. Eagles were fine
birds, but the sheep must be protected. Babies, too.

"Mr. Osmun," Wilson Drago, the shotgun-bearing sado-
child-appearing copilot asked, "have the eagles got any white
babies lately?"

"No."

"Then?"

"Because we are exercising predator control."

"When was the last white baby snatched by eagles and
dropped into the ocean?"

"Not eagles, Drago, eagle; it only takes one. As long as
there is one eagle there is always the possibility of your losing
your child."

"I haven't any child."

"If you did."

"But I haven't."

"Someone does."

"No one in the area does."

"If they did, there would be the possibility of their losing
them."

"No one can say nay to that," Wilson Drago said. "When
was the last time a child was snatched?"

"It must have been a long time ago."

"Before living memory?"

"Yes, even then, Drago, I believe the stories to be apocryphal."

"What's that mean?"

"Lies."

"Then why are we shooting the eagles?"

"Because city people don't care about sheep. City people care about babies. You tell the people in Albuquerque that their babies have an outside chance, any chance that their baby will be snatched up and the possibility that it will be dropped in the ocean, ker-plunk, and they will let you kill eagles."

"How far is the ocean?"

"People don't care how far the ocean is; they care about their babies."

"True."

"It's that simple."

"When was the last lamb that was snatched up?"

"Yesterday."

"That's serious."

"You better believe it, Drago."

"Why are we hovering over this red hogan?"

"Because before we kill an eagle we got to make sure what Mary-Forge is up to."

"What was she up to last time you heard?"

"Shooting down helicopters."

"All by herself?"

"It only takes one shot."

"You know, I bet that's right."

"You better believe it, Drago."

"Is this where she lives?"

"No—this is the little red schoolhouse she uses to get the Indians to attack the whites."

"What happened to your other copilots?"

"They got scared and quit."

"The last one?"

"Scared and quit."

"Just because of one woman?"

"Yes. You're not scared of a woman, are you, Drago?"

"No, I mean yes."

"Which is it, yes or no?"

"Yes," Wilson Drago said.

Below in the red hogan that was shaped like a beehive with a hole on top for the smoke to come out, the Indians and Mary-Forge were getting ready to die on the spot.

"I'm not getting ready to die on the spot," Bull Who Looks Up said.

"You want to save the eagles, don't you?" Mary-Forge said.

"Let me think about that," Jesus Saves said.

"Pass me the gun," Mary-Forge said.

Now, from above in the copter the hogan below looked like a gun turret, a small fort defending the perimeter of Indian Country.

"Mary-Forge is an interesting problem," Ira Osmun said—shouted—above the *whack-whack-whack* of the rotors.

"Every woman is."

"But every woman doesn't end up living with the Indians, with the eagles."

"What causes that?"

"We believe the Indians and the eagles become their surrogate children."

"That they become a substitute for life."

"Oh? Why do you hate me?"

"What?"

"Why do you use such big words?"

"I'm sorry, Drago. Do you see any eagles?"

"No, but I see a gun."

"Where?"

"Coming out of the top of the hogan."

"Let Mary-Forge fire first."

"Why?"

"To establish a point of law. Then it's not between her eagles and my sheep."

"It becomes your ass or hers."

"Yes."

"But it could be my life."

"I've considered that, Drago."

"Thank you. Thank you very much," Wilson Drago said.

Sun, the golden eagle that was very carefully watching the
two white animals that lived in the giant bird that went
whack-whack-whack, was ready.

Today would be the day of death for Sun. His mate had
been killed two days before. Without her the eaglets in the
woven of yucca high basket nest would die. Today would be
the day of death for Sun because, without a sure idea of himself, without purpose in life, an eagle would sooner destroy
himself than remain on earth. The last day of Sun.

"Because," Mary-Forge said, and taking the weapon and
jerking in a shell, "because I know, even though the Indians
and us and the eagle, even though we have no chance ever,
we can go through the motions of courage, compassion, and
concern. Because we are Sun and men, too. Hello, Sun."

"Stop talking and aim carefully."

"Did I say something?"

"You made a speech."

"I'm sorry," Mary-Forge said.

"Aim carefully."

Mary-Forge was standing on the wide shoulders of an Indian named When Someone Dies He Is Remembered. All the
other Indians who belonged in the little red schoolhouse
stood around and below her in the dim and alive dust
watching Mary-Forge revolve like a gun turret with her
lever-operated Marlin .30-30 pointing out of the smoke hatch
high up on the slow-turning and hard shoulders of When
Someone Dies He Is Remembered.

"Why don't you shoot?" More Turquoise said. He almost
whispered it, as though the great noise of the copter did not
exist.

"The thing keeps bobbling," Mary-Forge shouted down to
the Indians.

Looking through the gunsights she had to go up and down
up and down to try and get a shot. She did not want to hit
the cowboys. It would be good enough to hit the engine or the
rotor blades. Why not hit the cowboys? Because there are always more cowboys. There are not many eagles left on the
planet earth, there are several million cowboys. There are
more cowboys than there are Indians. That's for sure. But

what is important now is that if we give one eagle for one cowboy soon all the eagles will have disappeared from the earth and cowboys will be standing in your bed. No, the helicopter is scarce. They will not give one helicopter for one eagle. A helicopter costs too much money. How much? A quarter-million dollars, I bet. Hit them where their heart is. Hit them right in their helicopter.

But it danced. Now Mary-Forge noticed that although it was dancing it was going up and down with a rhythm. The thing to do is to wait until it hits bottom and then follow it up. She did and fired off a shot.

"Good girl," the Medicine Man said.

"That was close," Ira Osmun said to his shotgun, Wilson Drago. "Now that we know where Mary-Forge is we can chase the eagle."

Ira Osmun allowed the chopper to spurt up and away to tilt off at a weird angle so that it clawed its way sideways like a crab that flew, a piece of junk, of tin and chrome and gaudy paint, alien and obscene in the perfect pure blue New Mexican sky, an intruder in the path of sun. Now the chopper clawed its way to the aerie of Sun.

The eagle had watched it all happen. Sun had watched it happen many times now. Two days ago when they killed his mate was the last time. Sun looked down at his golden eagle chicks. The eaglets were absolute white, they would remain white and vulnerable for several months until the new feathers. But there was no more time. Sun watched the huge man junk bird clawing its way down the long valley that led to Mount Taylor. His home, his home and above all the homes of the Indians.

Like the Indians, the ancestors of Sun had one time roamed a virgin continent abloom with the glory of life, alive with fresh flashing streams, a smogless sky, all the world a sweet poem of life where all was beginning. Nothing ever ended. Now it was all ending. The eagle, Sun, did not prepare to defend himself. He would not defend himself. There was nothing now to defend. The last hour of Sun.

"Catch me," Mary-Forge shouted from the top of the hogan, and jumped. When she was caught by More Turquoise, she continued to shout, as the noise of the chopper was still there. "They've taken off for Mount Taylor to kill Sun. We've got to get on our horses and get our ass over there."

"Why?"

"To save Sun," Mary-Forge shouted. "Sun is the last eagle left in the county."

"But this is not a movie," the Medicine Man said. "We don't have to get on horses and gallop across the prairie. We can get in my pickup and drive there—quietly."

"On the road it will take two hours," Mary-Forge said. "And we'll need horses when we get there to follow the chopper."

"What would Dostoevski say about this?" the Medicine Man said.

"To hell with Dostoevski," Mary-Forge said.

Outside they slammed the saddles on the amazed Indian ponies, then threw themselves on and fled down the canyon, a stream of dust and light, a commingling of vivid flash and twirl so when they disappeared into the cottonwoods you held your breath until the phantoms, the abrupt magic of motion, appeared again on the Cabrillo draw.

"Come on now, baby," Mary-Forge whispered to her horse Poco Mas. "What I said about Dostoevski I didn't mean. Poor Dostoevski. I meant seconds count. We didn't have time for a philosophical discussion. Come on now, baby, move good. Be good to me, baby, move good. Move good, baby. Move good. You can take that fence, baby. Take him! Good boy, baby. Good boy, Poco. Good boy. I'm sure the Medicine Man understands that when there are so few left, so few left Poco that there is not time for niceties. You'd think an Indian would understand that, wouldn't you? Still the Medicine Man is a strange Indian. A Freudian Medicine Man. But Bull Who Looks Up understands, look at him go. He's pulling ahead of us are you going to let him get away with that Poco?" Poco did not let the horse of Bull Who Looks Up stay ahead but passed him quickly, with Mary-Forge swinging her gun high and Bull Who Looks Up gesturing with his gun at the tin bird that crabbed across the sky.

"You see, Drago," Ira Osmun shouted to Wilson Drago, "we are the villains of the piece."

"What?"

"The bad guys."

"It's pretty hard to think of yourself as the bad guy, Mr. Osmun."

"Well, we are."

"Who are the good guys?"

"Mary-Forge."

"Screw me."

"No, she wouldn't do that because you're a bad guy. Because you kill eagles. People who never saw an eagle, never will see an eagle, never want to see an eagle, want eagles all over the place. Except the poor. The poor want sheep to eat. Did you ever hear of a poor person complaining about the lack of eagles? They have got an outfit of rich gentlemen called the Sierra Club. They egg on Indian-lovers like Mary-Forge to kill ranchers."

"Why?"

"They have nothing else to do."

"You think Mary-Forge actually has sex with the Indians?"

"Why else would she be on the reservation?"

"I never thought about that."

"Think about it."

"I guess you're right."

"Drago, what do you think about?"

"I don't think about eagles."

"What do you think about?"

"Ordinarily?"

"Yes."

"Like when I'm drinking?"

"Yes."

"Religion."

"Good, Drago, I like to hear you say that. Good. What religion?"

"They are all good. I guess Billy Graham is the best."

"Yes, if you're stupid."

"What?"

"Nothing, Drago. Keep your eye peeled for the eagle."

"You said I was stupid."

"I may have said the Sierra Club was stupid."

"Did you?"

"No, how could you be stupid and be that rich?"

"Why are they queer for eagles then?"

"They are for anything that is getting scarce. Indians, eagles, anything. Mary-Forge is against natural evolution, too."

"What's natural evolution mean?"

"When something is finished it's finished, forget it. We got a new evolution, the machine, this copter, a new bird."

"That makes sense."

"Remember we don't want to kill eagles."

"We have to."

"That's right."

The eagle that had to be killed, Sun, perched like an eagle on his aerie throne. A king, a keeper of one hundred square miles of Indian Country, an arbiter, a jury and judge, a shadow clock that had measured time for two thousand years in slow shadow circle and so now the earth, the Indians, the place, would be without reckoning, certainly without the serene majesty of Sun, without, and this is what is our epitaph and harbinger, without the gold of silence the long lonely shadow beneath silent wing replaced now by the *whack-whack-whack* of tin, proceeding with crablike crippled crawl—the sweet song of man in awkward crazy metallic and cockeyed pounce, approached Sun.

Sun looked down on the eagles in the nest. The thing to do would be to glide away from the whack-bird away from the nest. To fight it out somewhere else. If he could tangle himself in the wings of the whack-bird, that would be the end of whack-bird. The end of Sun. Sun jumped off his aerie without movement, not abrupt or even peremptory but as though the reel of film had cut, and then proceeded to a different scene. The bird Sun, the eagle, the great golden glider moving across the wilds of purple mesa in air-fed steady no-beat, in hushed deadly amaze, seemed in funeral stateliness, mounting upward on invisible winds toward the other sun.

"If he climbs, we will climb with him, Drago. He is bound to run out of updrafts."

Wilson Drago slid open the door on his side and shifted the Harrington & Richardson pump gun into the ready position.

"How high will this thing climb, sir?"

"Ten thousand feet."

"The bird can climb higher than that."

"Yet he has to come down, Drago."

"How much fuel we got?"

"Fifty gallons."

"What are we consuming?"

"A gallon a minute."

"Shall I try a shot?"

"Yes."

Sun was spiraling upward in tight circles on a good rising current of air when the pellets of lead hit him. They hit like a gentle rain that gave him a quick lift. Sun was out of range. Both the copter and Sun were spiraling upward. The copter was gaining.

"Shall I try another shot?"

"Yes."

This time the lead pellets slammed into Sun like a hard rain and shoved him upward and crazy tilted him as a great ship will yaw in a sudden gust. Sun was still out of range.

Now the upward current of air ceased, collapsed under Sun abruptly and the copter closed the distance until Ira Osmun and Wilson Drago were alongside and looking into small yellow eyes as the great sailing ship of Sun coasted downward into deep sky.

"Shall I try a shot?"

"Yes."

Wilson Drago raised the Harrington & Richardson shotgun and pumped in a shell with a solid slam. He could almost touch Sun with the muzzle. The swift vessel of Sun sailed on as though expecting to take the broadside from the 12-guage gun that would send him to the bottom—to the floor of earth.

"Now, Drago."

But the gliding ship of bird had already disappeared—folded its huge wing of sail and shot downward, down down down downward until just before earth it unleashed its enormous sail of wing and glided over the surface of earth—Indian Country. Down came the copter in quick chase.

There stood the Indians all in a row.

"Don't fire, men," Mary-Forge shouted, "until Sun has passed."

As Sun sailed toward the Indians the shadow of Sun came first, shading each Indian separately. Now came the swifting Sun and each mounted Indian raised his gun in salute. Again separately and in the order which Sun arrived and passed, now the Indians leveled their guns to kill the whack-bird.

"Oh, this is great, Drago," Ira Osmun shouted, "the Indians want to fight."

"What's great about that?"

"It's natural to fight Indians."

"It is?"

"Yes."

"Well, I'll be."

"My grandfather would be proud of us now."

"Did he fight Indians?"

"He sure did. It's only a small part of the time the whites have been that they haven't fought Indians."

"Fighting has been hard on the Indians."

"That may well be, Drago, but it's natural."

"Why?"

"Because people naturally have a fear of strangers. It's called xenophobia. When you don't go along with nature you get into trouble. You suppress your natural instincts and that is dangerous. That's what's wrong with this country."

"It is? I wondered about that."

"There's nothing wrong with shooting Indians."

"I wondered about that."

"It's natural."

"No, Mr. Osmun there is something wrong."

"What's that?"

"Look. The Indians are shooting back."

Ira Osmun twisted the copter up and away. "Get out the rifle. We'll take care of the Indians."

"What about the eagle?"

"We've first got to take care of the Indians who are shooting at us and that girl who is shooting at us."

"Is she crazy?"

"Why else would she have intercourse with the Indians?"

"You mean screwing them?"

"Yes."

"She could have all sorts of reasons. We don't even know that she is screwing them. Maybe we are screwing the Indians."

"Drago, we discussed this before and decided that Mary-Forge was."

"What if she is?"

"Drago, you can't make up your mind about anything. You're being neurotic. When you don't understand why you do something you're being neurotic."

"I am?"

"Yes, get out the rifle."

"I still think it's her business if she is queer for Indians and eagles."

"But not if she shoots at us when she's doing it; that's neurotic."

"You're right there, Mr. Osmun."

"Get the rifle."

"O.K."

"You know, Drago, people, particularly people who love the Indians, are suppressing a need to kill them. It's called a love-hate relationship."

"It is? You can stop talking now, Mr. Osmun. I said I'd get the rifle."

Below the helicopter that circled in the brilliant, eye-hurting, New Mexican day, Mary-Forge told the Indians that the copter would be back, that the ranchers would not fight the eagle while being fired on by Indians. "The ranchers will not make the same mistake Custer did."

"What was that?"

"Fight on two fronts. Custer attacked the Sioux before he finished off Sitting Bull. We are the Sioux."

"We are? That's nice," the Navajo Bull Who Looks Up said. "When do we get out of this class?"

"We never do," Jesus Saves said.

"Get your ass behind the rocks!" the teacher Mary-Forge shouted. "Here they come!"

The copter flew over and sprayed the rocks with M-16 automatic rifle fire.

"That should teach the teach that we outgun them, Drago," Ira Osmun said. "Now we can get the eagle!"

The golden eagle called Sun spiraled upward again, its wings steady, wild, sure, in the glorious and rapt quietude of the blue, blue, blue New Mexico morning, a golden eagle against the blue, a kind of heliograph, and a flashing jewel in the perfect and New Mexico sea of sky. The gold eagle, recapitulent, lost then found as it twirled steady and upward in the shattered light, followed by the tin bird.

Sun knew that he must gain height. All the power of maneuver lay in getting above the tin bird. He knew, too, and from experience that the tin bird could only go a certain height. He knew, too, and from experience that the air current he rode up could collapse at once and without warning. He knew, too, and from the experience of several battles now with the bird of tin that the enemy was quick and could spit things out that could pain then kill. All this he knew from experience. But the tin bird was learning, too.

The tin bird jerked upward after the golden eagle. The golden eagle, Sun, wandered upward as though searching and lost. A last and final tryst in the list of Indian Country because now always until now, until now no one killed everything that moved. You always had a chance. Now there was no chance. Soon there would be no Sun.

"Remember, Drago, I've got to stay away from him or above him—he can take us with him. The last time when we got his mate he almost took us with him; I just barely got away when he attacked the rotors—when the rotor goes we go, Drago—we fall like a rock, smash like a glass. They will pick you up with a dustpan."

"Who?"

"Those Indians down there."

"Mr. Osmun, I don't want to play this game."

"You want to save the sheep, don't you?"

"No."

"Why not?"

"I don't have any sheep to save."

"You don't have any sheep, you don't have any children. But you have pride."

"I don't know."

"Then fire when I tell you to and you'll get some."

"I don't know."

"Do you want eagles to take over the country?"

"I don't know."

"Eagles and Indians at one time controlled this whole country, Drago; you couldn't put out a baby or a lamb in my grandfather's time without an Indian or an eagle would grab it. Now we got progress. Civilization. That means a man is free to go about his business."

"It does?"

"Yes, now that we got them on those ropes we can't let them go, Drago."

"We can't?"

"No, that would be letting civilized people down. It would be letting my grandfather down. What would I say to him?"

"Are you going to see your grandfather?"

"No, he's dead. We'll be dead, too, Drago, if you don't shoot. That eagle will put us down there so those Indians will pick us up with a dustpan. You don't want that, do you?"

"I don't know."

"You better find out right smart or I'll throw you out of this whack-bird myself."

"Would you?"

"Someone's got to live, Drago. The eagle doesn't want to live."

"Why do you say that?"

"He knew we were after him. He knew we would get him; he could have left the country. He could have flown north to Canada. He would be protected there."

"Maybe he thinks this is his country."

"No, this is a civilized country. Will you shoot the eagle?"

"No."

"I like the eagle and the Indians as well as the next man, Drago, but we have to take sides. It's either my sheep or them. Whose side are you on, Drago?"

"I guess I'm on theirs."

The helicopter was much lighter now without Drago in it. The copter handled much better and was able to gain on the eagle.

Ira Osmun continued to talk to Wilson Drago as though he were still there. Wilson Drago was one of Ira Osmun's sheepherders and should have taken a more active interest in sheep.

"The way I see it, Drago, if you wouldn't defend me, the eagle would have brought us both down. It was only a small push I gave you, almost a touch as you were leaning out. By lightening the plane you made a small contribution to civilization.

"We all do what we can, Drago, and you have contributed your bit. If there is anything I can't stand, it's an enemy among my sheep."

The copter continued to follow the eagle up but now more lightsome and quick with more alacrity and interest in the chase.

The Indians on the ground were amazed to see the white man come down. Another dropout. "Poor old Wilson Drago. We knew him well. Another man who couldn't take progress—civilization. Many times has Drago shot at us while we were stealing his sheep. We thought anyone might be a dropout but not Wilson Drago. It shows you how tough it's getting on the white reservation. They're killing each other. Soon there will be nothing left but Indians."

"Good morning, Indian."

"Good morning, Indian."

"Isn't it a beautiful day. Do you notice there is nothing left but us Indians?"

"And one eagle."

The Indians were making all these strange observations over what remained of the body of the world's leading sheepherder, Wilson Drago.

"He created quite a splash."

"And I never thought he would make it."

"The last time I saw him drunk in Gallup I thought he was coming apart, but this is a surprise."

"I knew he had it in him, but I never expected it to come out all at once."

"I can't find his scalp. What do you suppose he did with it? Did he hide it?"

"The other white man got it."

"I bet he did."

"They don't care about Indians anymore."

"No, when they drop in on you they don't bring their scalp."

"Please, please," Mary-Forge said, "the man is dead."

"Man? Man? I don't see any man, just a lot of blood and shit."

"Well, there is a man, or was a man."

"Well, there's nothing now," Bull Who Looks Up said, "not even a goddamn scalp."

"Well, Drago's in the white man's heaven," More Turquoise said. "On streets of gold tending his flock."

"And shooting eagles."

"Drago's going higher and higher to white man's heaven, much higher than his what-do-you-call-it—"

"Helicopter."

"—can go," Jesus Saves said.

"I don't like all this sacrilege," Mary-Forge said. "Remember I am a Christian."

"What?"

"I was brought up in the Christian tradition."

"Now you're hedging," When Someone Dies He Is Remembered said.

Ah, these Indians, Mary-Forge thought, how did I get involved? And she said aloud, "Once upon a time I was young and innocent."

"Print that!" Bull Who Looks Up said.

"We better get higher up the mountain," Mary-Forge shouted at the Indians, "so when Osmun closes on the eagle we can get a better shot."

"O.K., Teacher."

"There's only one white guy left," she said.

"I find that encouraging if true," More Turquoise said.

"Load your rifles and pull your horses after you," Mary-Forge said.

"My Country 'Tis of Thee," Ira Osmun hummed as he swirled the copter in pursuit of the eagle. You didn't die in vain, Drago. That is, you were not vain, you were a very modest chap. We can climb much higher without you, Drago. I am going to get the last eagle this time, Drago. I think he's reached the top of his climb.

Sun watched the tin whack-bird come up. The tin bird came up *whack-whack-whack*, its wings never flapping just turning in a big circle. What did it eat? How did it mate? Where did it come from? From across the huge water on a strong wind. The evil wind. Sun circled seeing that he must get higher, the tin bird was coming up quicker today. Sun could see the people he always saw below. The people who lived in his country, filing up the mountain. They seemed to be wanting to get closer to him now.

Ira Osmun felt then saw all the Indians in the world firing at him from below. How are you going to knock down an eagle when all the Indians in the world are firing at you from Mount Taylor? It was Mary-Forge who put them up to it, for sure. An Indian would not have the nerve to shoot at a white man. You don't have to drop down and kill all the Indians. They—the people in the East—who have no sheep would call that a massacre. Indians are very popular at the moment. If you simply knock off Mary-Forge, that would do the trick. Women are not very popular at the moment. Why? Because they have a conspiracy against men. You didn't know that? It's true, Drago. The woman used to be happy to be on the bottom. Now she wants to be on the top.

No?

Did you say something, Drago?

I thought I heard someone say something. I must have been hit. My mind must be wandering. What was I saying? It's part of the conspiracy. What's that mean? Something. I must have been hit. What was I doing? Oh yes, I was going to get Mary-Forge—the girl who is queer for Indians and eagles. The eagle can wait.

And Ira Osmun put the copter in full throttle, then cradled the M-16 automatic rifle in his left arm with muzzle pointing out the door. With his right hand he placed the copter in a swift power glide down.

Sun saw the obscene tin bird go into its dive down. Now would be a chance to get it while the tin bird was busy hunting its prey on the ground. Sun took one more final look over the aerie nest to check the birds. The eaglets were doing fine. Drawing the enemy away from the nest had been successful. The eaglets craned their necks at the familiar shape before Sun folded his great span of wings and shot down on top of the tin bird.

Mary-Forge mounted on Poco Mas saw the tin bird coming, the M-16 quicking out nicks of flame. She could not get the Indians to take cover. The Indians had placed their horses behind the protection of the boulders and were all standing out in the open and were blasting away at the zooming-in copter. Mary-Forge was still shouting at the Indians, but they would not take cover. They have seen too many goddamn movies, Mary-Forge thought, they have read too many books. They are stupid, stupid, stupid, dumb, dumb, dumb Indians. How stupid and how dumb can you get? They want to save the eagle. Standing exposed naked to the machine gun. The stupid Indians. Mary-Forge raised her rifle at the zooming-in copter in a follow-me gesture, then took off in a straight line, the horse pounding, and the flame-nicking copter followed, so did Sun. So now there were three.

The tin bird was alive in flame all at once, something had hit the fuel tank and all of everything exploded in fire, the rotors of the tin bird were still turning and fanning the flame so that it was not only a streaking meteor across Indian Country but at once a boil of fire that shot downward from the terrific draft laying a torch of flame across the desert so that the mesquite and sagebrush became a steady line of flame ending where the tin whack-bird hit into the rocks and went silent in a grand tower of flame.

"It was Sun that did it," More Turquoise said.

The death of Sun.

All of the Indians and Mary-Forge were standing around

the dying fire of the big whack-bird in the smoke that shrouded the death of Sun.

"When an eagle," the Medicine Man said, "—when a true bird has no hope—"

"Yes?"

"When the eagle is no more," the Medicine Man said.

"Yes?"

"Then we are no more."

"Yes," every person shrouded in smoke said.

Look up there. It was within three months when Someone Dies He Is Remembered remembered that an eagle named Star by the Medicine Man sailed in one beginning night to reclaim the country of Sun. Now Star's wide shadow passed over the dead tin whackbird then he, the great eagle Star, settled on his throne aerie in awful and mimic splendor, and again admonitory, serene—regal and doomed?

ALVIN GREENBERG

The Real Meaning of the Faust Legend

(FROM THE NEW AMERICAN REVIEW)

WHO IS THERE who isn't peddling himself to the devil in some way? There are those who do it according to the tradition: for knowledge and power. There are those who do it for fame and money. There are those who do it to maintain the status quo and those who do it for the sake of revolution. There are those who do it to keep their children fed, to quiet their own consciences, to make the sun rise tomorrow morning, or to torment their heirs. There are those who do it for what most of us might agree are sufficiently good reasons, and others whose reasons, well, leave something to be desired. Why do I do it? I do it for a .368 batting average.

Fame, you might say. Not hardly. I don't hit that for the Reds or the White Sox. Not even for Indianapolis or Louisville. I hit it for Muncie of the Three-I League. I never wanted the fame, believe me; I only wanted to hit .368. And not even that on a regular basis. I wanted it as a lifetime average. The nice thing about that is that it leaves a lot to chance: I might hit .318 one season, but I might also hit .427—as, in fact, I did three years ago. The logical question, of course, is how fame can fail to come to one who hits consistently up there where I do, but the answer is equally logical. I hit it for Muncie. In other words, I have had my chances higher up— have them most every spring, as a matter of fact. Muncie is a farm club, after all. So there I am down in Tampa or Sarasota every March, and people who know what I did at Muncie last year are watching me each time I take batting practice, and all those out-of-shape big-league pitchers who are sweating off their bellies doing laps around the outfield are just waiting for the first intersquad game. And with good reasons, too, because they know how good I'm going to make them look. I play on "B" teams in the Grapefruit League and end up hitting .187, so naturally when we break camp for the exhibition swing heading north, you know where I'm going.

Every year, of course, my season gets interrupted at Muncie when somebody at Denver breaks a leg or goes into a two-month-long slump and the big brass decide to call up the leading hitter in the minors to fill the gap, but for the most part my stays in the lofty altitudes of Triple-A ball are mercifully short. I'm in a slump the day I suit up. I may have hit safely in the last thirty-two games for Muncie, with two or more hits in twenty of them, as is frequently the case, but suddenly I'm 0 for 18 before I trickle one between first and second that rolls dead before the right-fielder gets to it. Once I even got peddled to the Yankees in a stretch drive, but you don't want to hear about that one. Muncie is where I always end up.

And why not? There are people who think I must be on the verge of suicide, being able to hit the way I do at Muncie and then not making it at all anywhere further up the ladder, and my previous manager, who never hit more than .250 himself, was one of those who had the notion that all I needed to make it in the majors was confidence. But he was dead wrong. I *knew* I could hit .368, I had perfect confidence in my ability to do so; after all, I did it—or something close to it—every year, and how many ballplayers can say that, even in the minors? So Billy cost the parent club a good bit in psychologist and hypnotist bills with his silly theory, and then one summer cost himself a sizable measure of pain over his investment in double-up bets when I had a fat hitting streak in the beginning of August. I had gone 5 for 8 in a Sunday doubleheader, including a pair of bases-loaded doubles in the second game, and had hit safely the last three times at bat, and on the bus home from Peoria Billy got on my back again about the confidence thing.

"No, Billy," I told him, "you're dead wrong. I've got so

much confidence I'm willing to bet you I hit .385 for the season. I'll pay you a hundred dollars for each point I hit below that and you pay me a hundred for each point above." He looked at me then and fell silent and took off his cap and scratched his head. He was obviously tempted—maybe only to see if I really had the confidence to shake hands on a bet like that—but the fact was that I was already hitting .379 and was on a pretty hot streak, so he thought better of it and shook his head no. And that was a good thing for him because I ended the season at .397. But I didn't want to let him off that easy.

"All right then, Billy," I said, because I wanted to show him just how wrong he was about his confidence theory. "How about a five-dollar bet that I get a hit first time up next game?"

Well, that was all right with him, especially since the next game, though at home, was against Des Moines, which was currently leading the league by a good twelve games and had a couple of hot young pitchers who were sure to be called up by the end of the month. That may have made a difference to Billy, but not to me. After Johnson and Feathers went down on called strikes in the first, I patted Billy on the shoulder and went up there and lined the first pitch over the third baseman's head and down into the corner for a stand-up double.

Sitting on the bench during the next inning, I asked Billy if he wanted to double up his bet on my next at-bat, giving him a chance to come out five ahead. He was paying more attention to the kid on the mound than to me, but he mumbled, "OK, why not?"

I didn't get a turn at the plate again till the last of the fourth with one out, because that kid hadn't allowed one out of the infield since my first-inning double, and maybe Billy wasn't even thinking about our bet by then because we were losing 4-0 and he had to get a scouting report in on the kid by noon the next day. This time I waited out a couple of pitches, till I was sure Billy was watching, and then lined one up the middle. Took off my cap and waved at Billy from first base and he just stood on the dugout steps and shook his head at me and that was where we both stayed while the next two guys fouled out to the catcher.

When I came up again in the last of the sixth, with two out and none on, we were seven runs behind, and besides me nobody had gotten to base except the catcher, Wiltz, who had walked the inning before. Billy was juggling relief pitchers and looking very sad, so I had to shake him a bit to get his attention. He looked irritated when he turned around; as far as he was concerned it wasn't anything but a hot, lost, miserable afternoon, and there wasn't much anyone could do about it at this point. What's more, it was dragging on endlessly, for in spite of the way we were being set down, Des Moines had kept up enough action on the bases and in our bullpen so that the game was almost two hours old already. I just stayed calm though.

"Double up again, Billy?" I asked him.

"What's that?" he said, like he didn't even know what the name of the game was.

"It was five on my first at-bat," I reminded him, "and ten on my second. Want to go for twenty this time?"

"Shit," he said, squinting up at me, "that's five straight since Sunday, you can't keep that up against a kid like this, he's major-league stuff."

"We're on then?"

"Right," he said as I headed for the on-deck circle, "we're on."

I was first-ball hitting again and went with the pitch, which was a nice outside slider that I lined to right just beyond the first baseman's reach. And stayed on first base again while Kryzinski struck out for the third straight time.

By the time I came up to lead off the last of the ninth, Johnson had got us a run, and our only hit beside my three, with an inside-the-park homer that the Des Moines outfielders, worn out from chugging around the bases all afternoon, just didn't seem to have the energy to run down. Billy, who had just finished calling me a smart-assed old man but had agreed all the same to one more bet, for forty dollars this time, was standing by the water cooler shaking his head. And the kid on the mound, who could understand the stupidity that had led to the home run but couldn't understand how

I had hit him three straight times, was grinding the ball in his glove and staring at me. I was thirty-five bucks ahead and would be out only five even if I lost this time, and besides I wasn't arrogant enough to really think I could go on getting consecutive base hits forever, so I decided I would at least have a little fun. He was throwing hard but sharp and obviously wanted to get me this time, as I'm sure he had a right to. He wanted to be a major-leaguer, that was what he was peddling himself to his devil for. His first two were curve-ball strikes, and I just let them go by with no intention of swinging. I was ready on the next, but it was low and away. Then he came in with the fast ball, and 1 and 2, nine to one, forty dollars and all, I just let my bat hang out there in front of it and dropped a lovely little bunt down the third-base line and skipped on down to first while the pitcher, catcher, third baseman, and poor Billy most of all just stood there and watched it roll dead on the grass as if they'd never seen such an obscene thing in the middle of a ballfield before.

Now I wasn't at all worried about that kid pitcher, even if he did blow sky-high after my bunt and walk the next two men on eight straight pitches. He was going to be a major-league star and that was all there was to it. Fame, money, and women, and nothing short of a broken back in an automobile accident or an all-out war was likely to stop him. I even doubted if war could. He'd probably turn up 4-F in the spring and pitch three hundred innings that same season. So naturally with the bases loaded and no one out in the last of the ninth, he struck out Henry on a 3 and 2 count and got Goldburg to bounce into a double play. That kid was no different than anybody else, just a particularly obvious case.

I was more worried about Billy, who was already muttering, even as we walked off the field, about getting it back tomorrow afternoon. He was also an obvious case, in a way. I think he never really wanted to be a hitter, even though he broke in on a long-ball reputation, but mostly just wanted to be in baseball, somehow or other. So when he found out what it was like, standing up there at the plate four, five times a game, he bargained himself into a managership. Now he didn't know that was going to mean seven years at Muncie, but you deal for managership and you get a managership; nothing guarantees it's going to be in Detroit or San Francisco. If he'd peddled himself for Detroit he could surely have had that, but maybe he'd have ended up there as a used-car salesman, who knows. Also he didn't know that every time he put a decent team together he'd be raided in the middle of the summer by the parent club and end up finishing the season with the same ragtag bunch that had come in 24½ games behind the year before. He didn't know he'd have to live with things like his big dumb catcher slipping on the dugout steps and stomping down on the toe of tomorrow's starting pitcher in the middle of today's dismal loss. Yes, and there was that poor kid, who hadn't yet made up his mind whether or not this was what he wanted to peddle himself for, sitting in the locker room watching his big toe swell up bigger and bigger. It was time for him to decide. And poor Billy surely didn't know he'd end up the day $75 in the hole, with $80 riding on the first inning of the next day's game, to a thirty-five-year-old left-fielder who was an eleven-year veteran of a minor-league team he not only couldn't hit his way off of, even with the leading average in the Three-I League for eight of those years—to say nothing of the longest stay on record at Muncie—but didn't even seem to care about.

"Al," he said, when we were having a beer at McDougal's after the game, "when are you going to grow up and do something with your life?"

"Billy," I told him, "I am doing something with my life. I'm hitting .386 after today's game." He looked up at me and emptied the pitcher that was on the table between us into his own mug. He hadn't paid up yet, but I supposed that as long as I was ahead, even if only on the books, I was going to have to buy the beers, so I carried the pitcher over to the bar for a refill. When I came back he was waiting with an empty glass.

"Look," he said, while I filled it for him, and then poured myself one as well, "why don't you be a good boy and go hit .386 for the Pirates, or the Yokahama Giants, if that's what'll make you happy?"

"Billy," I told him, "I am happy." But he went right on as if he hadn't even heard me.

"Maybe you'll have to settle for .322, or even an occasional season at .298, but you could do it. Al, I know you could. All you need's a little confidence."

"Billy," I reminded him, "I've got plenty of confidence. Didn't I already show you that today?"

"You smart-assed college kids are all alike," he muttered, finishing the pitcher off again. "You'll get a little lucky and right off you think you know it all." He pushed the empty pitcher across at me, so I went and got it filled again.

"Billy," I reminded him when I came back, "I'm not one of your smart-assed college kids that comes and goes here. I may have gone to college, but that was a long time ago, when I didn't know what I wanted yet, and you don't see me tripping on my degrees while I'm running the bases, do you? I'm no kid, either, Billy, I'm as old as you, or maybe a little bit older. And I didn't get lucky, as you damn well know, unless you want to say I've been lucky for the past eleven years. No, Billy, what I had was confidence that I could go up and get a hit each one of those times today, and I've got confidence I can do it first time up tomorrow, too, if you're still on, and for as long after that as you want to keep it up." I got up to leave, before I got stuck buying another pitcher.

"On," he said. Feathers and Goldburg were standing at the table by then, and when they heard that the bet was still on for tomorrow, they wanted a piece of the action too. But this was strictly between Billy and me, so when I left the two of them were sitting on either side of Billy trying to arrange a bet between just themselves. Billy, between them, had his chin in his hands and was staring at the empty beer pitcher.

I had three hits in the first four innings the next day, including a single, a double, a triple, and five RBI's before Billy pulled me out with the excuse that we were already eight runs ahead and put old Falucci in for me. Falucci had always wanted to have the strongest arm in baseball, and he probably did. He could throw strikes across the plate from anywhere in the outfield. But he couldn't hit well enough to stick on any team, and so he had spent a couple of decades bouncing around from one minor-league club to the next and never getting in enough playing time to fulfill his dream of throwing out all those runners at the plate. Meanwhile, it had become a real obsession with him: everything hit to him he fired to the plate, whether it was a bases-empty single or a fly ball with a man on first. You had to have a sharp catcher, which we didn't, to remember to be ready for a Falucci peg every time somebody banged one to left. But meanwhile, we were ahead 13-5 when I went out, I was glad to see the lefty with the swollen toe was determined to hang in there long enough to pick up the win, and I now had ten straight hits and $635 of Billy's money, though I had yet to see any of his real cash.

Thursday, when I came in from left field after the top of the first, I saw that someone had propped a chalkboard up on the bench in the dugout and was keeping a record of the progress of our running bet. It read "11—$640" and then further over on the same line it said "$1275," which was the total of what Billy would owe me if I got a hit the first time up. I did. Johnson walked leading off, Feathers drilled one to right on the hit-and-run, and I bounced one off the left-field wall, scoring both of them.

When I came up again in the third, we were ahead 3-0 on Wiltz's second-inning triple and a wild pitch, and the chalkboard read "12—$1280—$2555." I looked over at Billy from the on-deck circle and he looked grim but he shook his head up and down. They didn't give me much to hit at this time but I was determined not to take a walk, even though that wouldn't have lost the bet for me but only postponed it till my next at-bat. I got the first two pitches in the dirt and the next one behind my back. The 3 and 0 pitch was a curve spinning low and away but I went for it all the same, got underneath it just like I wanted, and lofted it high down the right-field line. It stayed up there, in the still air under dark clouds that were building up all around us, and dropped over the fence just inches inside the foul pole.

By the last of the fifth Des Moines had gone ahead 6-4, the chalkboard read "13—$2560—$5115," and when I stepped up to the plate with two out and McKay, who had singled for the pitcher, on first, the thunderstorm that had been threatening suddenly broke and sent us all scampering for the dugouts. We sat for forty-five minutes and watched the heavy downpour before the umpires called it off, and Billy who had been deep in silent thought all the while, carefully pointed out to me that since the game had now been cancelled and wouldn't appear in the record books, my two hits were wiped out, and so were his losses for the day. I couldn't argue with him and didn't want to.

Friday it rained all day so Des Moines went home, and Saturday, when Fort Wayne came to town, the field was still too soggy to play on, so Saturday's game was rescheduled as part of a Sunday doubleheader. But when Billy fell suddenly quiet after standing there in the locker room Saturday afternoon telling us that, I could see just what was going through his head. Even wiping out my two hits in Thursday's rained-out game, I had ten straight and he was $635 behind. A doubleheader, if I played both games—and he didn't have another left-fielder except Falucci, whom he couldn't really justify using in my place unless we were way ahead—could mean as many as ten more times at bat for me for the day. He had already had a taste Thursday of what just a couple more hits could cost him, and even if I had to hit a couple more in place of those two that had been wiped out, he was clearly beginning to have his doubts. If I went to the plate four times in the first game, he'd be betting $5120 against that fourth hit. The times and the bet would be up to $327,680! Which was a good bit more than he could afford. He just stood there and looked at me where I sat on the bench in front of my locker. Everybody else was picking up to leave. I just sat and stared at the floor, not wanting to look him in the eye. I didn't know whether to pick up and go myself and let him sweat it out or to take pity on him and offer to call it off, and I was afraid I'd offend him either way, which never was my aim. All I ever wanted to do was hit .368. Not even .370. I thought that zero at the end made it sound a little too astronomical, a little arrogant. Just a nice ragged .368. It didn't make any difference to me where I hit it. None at all. The fact that there were rarely more than five hundred fans in the stands or that I wasn't getting $100,000 a season or that I didn't have my picture on trading cards, my signature on bats, and Marilyn Monroe on my arm didn't bother me in the least. It wasn't fame or fortune I peddled myself for. It was, as I said, a .368 average.

When I looked up Billy was gone and so was everyone else. The locker room was empty, and damp and chilly from two days of rain, and I felt pretty much the same way myself. I went home and tried to watch the nationally televised game, Senators at Boston, but both teams seemed to be trying to set a major-league record for pop-ups, and I couldn't stand that sort of boredom for long. Watching some-one else play was never my idea of baseball anyway. I strolled down to McDougal's, but when I looked in the win-dow and saw Billy sitting at a table with half a dozen of my teammates around him, I felt too embarrassed to go in and join them. Instead I went back home and with some trouble got my old Ford started—I never used it much during the sea-son because you can't hop around all day and night if you want to hit .368, that's part of the price—and went and had dinner by myself at the Country Kitchen and then came back in to the Drive-In and sat and ate popcorn and watched a horror movie triple-feature until one-thirty A.M.

Sunday was bright and clear again and not too hot. We even had a decent crowd, for a change. And Billy had a sur-prise for me. Fort Wayne scored twice in the top of the first, mostly on walks and a couple of errors. When I came in from left field Billy was standing on the dugout steps holding my bat out to me.

"Don't sit down," he said "you're leading off."

"Billy?" I said. What was he trying to do, pushing it like that? Why, leading off I might even get a couple more at-bats in, as he had to know. The chalkboard was still there in the dugout, but it was lying under the bench and there was noth-ing written on it, as if whoever had thought it up in the first place had realized it was a bad joke and was now trying to ignore it. A little calculating on the way to the plate told me that a pair of extra chances, beyond the ten I'd already fig-ured on for the afternoon, would get our bet up over a mil-lion dollars. I didn't know whether to laugh or cry.

But one way or another, I didn't wait. Their first-game pitcher was an aging major-leaguer sent down to work out some mid-season shoulder miseries, but from what I could see of his warm-up pitches he hadn't worked out much of anything yet. I stepped up, tugged at my cap, tried to smile over at Billy but I couldn't spot him right off in the dugout shadows, and cocked my bat. The first pitch was right down the pipe and had nothing on it. I took my swing and sent it bouncing on nice even hops right out to the shortstop. Then, just to make sure, in case that damn-fool high school kid let it go through his legs without touching it, I fell down on my way to first base.

Billy didn't have a great deal to say to me for the rest of the season after that. He let me stay in the number-one slot, which was all the same to me, and I finished the year, like I said, at .397. When we had our final little get-together at McDougal's after the last game and just before everybody took off, most of them to play winter ball in Mexico or the Caribbean, Billy to go back to his wife and kids in New Jersey, he seemed a little sad and distant, and not much interested in all the beer that was flowing. We hadn't been there more than an hour before he stood up and announced he had to get on his way. He said good-bye and thanked everybody and then went around the tables, shaking hands with each of us. I was last. When he came to me, I got up and walked to the door with him. At the door I shook his hand and then reached in my pocket and took out a five-dollar bill, which was what I still owed him from all those bets, and tried to give it to him, but he wouldn't take it.

"Use it to buy the boys some more beer with," he said, and then he turned and left. I did, and then I left too.

Next season we had a new manager, a red-headed wild man, and I heard that Billy was managing Amarillo in the Texas League. Red, who had been a fine catcher till arthritis had started creeping into all his broken finger bones and knuckles, had the idea that a manager's job was to manage as much as possible, so he juggled the outfield around every couple of days or so and had me batting everywhere in the lineup but ninth. I never knew from one day to the next what field I'd be playing or where I'd be hitting. Curiously enough, we weren't doing any worse than under Billy. But it was all very unsettling for me, and the result was that around mid-season I found myself in the midst of the worst year I could remember. I was hitting .306, watching a lot of fat ones go by, and settling for a hit a game, mostly singles at that. Red wasn't very happy with either my attitude or my style of play and was platooning me with a fat farm boy who had a penchant for hitting tremendous homers with the bases empty and then striking out four times in a row with men on. But what did all that have to do with what I really wanted to do? Nothing, I realized, and then took off.

It was a Fourth of July doubleheader, and when I went 4 for 5 in the first game Red let me stay in for the second. I picked up three more hits in that one and kept on going. I had the hottest three weeks anybody ever saw. By the end of July, even with that chubby strike-out king getting his chances now and then, I was over .350 and going strong, even though Red still couldn't decide whether to have me bat first, third, or fifth. We were in Peoria and had just won the last of a three-game sweep with a 9-0 shutout in which I'd walked twice and then banged out three straight doubles to the exact same spot in left center. When I came out of the shower, I found Red waiting for me next to my locker. He sat on the bench and smoked a cigar without saying a word while I dressed, then he asked me to come with him. He had driven his own car up so that he could cut over to Chicago on our off-day to visit his family, so we sat in the car in the parking lot outside the ballfield until he finished his cigar and threw it out the window. Then he turned to me and started telling me what a fine job I was doing for the club, and what a great hitter I was.

"I know," I told him. "I've been hitting like that for a good many years now."

"Al," he said then, "I talked to the general manager this morning." I knew just what was coming next: "He said they could use a boost in their batting order up there."

"Red," I told him, "forget it. I've been there before. I hit here." He had a sudden pleading look in his eyes. They must have offered him a fat bonus if he could send someone up who would have a hot bat for the next few weeks. Even an old man like me.

"Look, Al," he said, "you can do it, I know you can. I've

watched you hit. All you need is a little confidence." That did it.

"Red," I asked him, "what am I hitting?" He told me without even having to look it up: .357, including today's game.

"Red," I said, "that's not what I mean. I want to know what's my lifetime average." That took him back a bit, but since he was a hot one for managing and a demon for statistics, he was carrying all the club's record books with him. He reached over and got the big cumulative team book out of the back seat, along with the current season's book and a pencil and pad of paper. Then he lit up another cigar and sat and figured and chewed on it and relit it a couple of times and finally turned back in my direction.

"Well," he said, "I've checked it and double-checked it and it keeps coming out the same. Like I said, you're a fine hitter, Al."

"Red," I asked him, "Just tell me what it is."

"Well," he said, holding the paper up close to his face, "it figures out exactly at .36802."

"Red," I said, "I quit."

It was just that easy, for me at least. Red spluttered and argued, and I was a little taken aback myself when we got back to Muncie and I went over to watch a Wednesday afternoon game with Cedar Rapids and Red wouldn't let me in the players' entrance but made me go around through the main gate and buy a ticket. I was about the only paying customer in the stands. He started to make some noise about my contract too, until he found out that it had been a good three years since I'd had anything more formal than a letter announcing my salary for the season. In spite of how angry he was, he still wanted to keep me on. I guess he thought I was at least some sort of stabilizing force on the team, good for the rookies going up and the veterans coming down. Fact was, I'd been around so long that some of the rookies I'd once seen going up were now the veterans on their way back down. The team, for that matter, didn't seem to do much different with or without me, and the farmer was already beginning to learn something about easing off on that wild swing of his.

What now? you may ask. Well I don't know. In a way I've jumped back a dozen years or so to where I was standing with a B.A. in one hand, an M.A. in the other, five years of semi-pro ball in my bones, and a little voice in my head saying, What do you want? What do you want? I didn't know, then I knew, then I got it, now I don't know again. I only know that I didn't just quit while I was ahead, unless you consider .00002 ahead. I know I got exactly what I peddled myself for. Who doesn't, as long as he's willing to go all the way with it? And I know I didn't get much else besides. Who does? I don't know what else I know.

JULIE HAYDEN

In the Words of

(FROM THE NEW YORKER)

TWO PEOPLE ARE IN A FIELD in the Catskills. He is painting a watercolor. She is lying on a scratchy picnic-stained blanket, facedown, reading field guides, listening to the chipping sparrows burr in the scrub oaks that stud the old pasture, a too loud towhee, some kind of woodpecker booming beyond a stone wall that once kept the cows out of the woods.

She goes over to see what kind. Near the wall is a patch of spring beauty, rose-veined, and white and lavender hepaticas. The field was filled with the hot smell of strawberry flowers when they were here last May. They meant to come back for the strawberries when they ripened. According to Euell Gibbons, you can eat the roots of the spring beauty, boiled.

One, two, three red-tailed hawks spin over the valley, riding the thermals, back and forth like prowl-car inspectors. She tracks them with the binoculars he gave her for her birthday, which is the same as his.

He swishes a broad-tipped paintbrush around in one of two coffee cans full of brook water, makes a wash, considers, and removes a fine-pointed brush from the box she gave him to hold the tubes of paint—alizarin crimson, burnt umber, forest green, Payne's gray.

The sky over the valley is an unpainterly cerulean.

Finally the painting is finished and they climb over another stone wall out to the dirt road. The road's other side is wide open to the hills, cleared land dropping away below them for miles. There are apple trees, buzzing with sparrows, above a white farmhouse, the closest landmark, and below that the increasingly flat perspective of stone-delineated fields, green-on-green polygons that recede in size and color like the paintings of Josef Albers. The fields fall to the valley crease, and on the other side the forest rises to join the sky.

The road is parallel to the valley; they begin to walk it without any discussion. Yellow-bellied sapsucker. Phoebes building a nest under a shelf of rock. A mushy spot in the road where water ran down from the mountainside (this is the watershed area); green shoots poking up in it. A brown thrasher asking everything twice, like a boring five-year-old. They walk close together, silent as painted people.

Words, after a while. She asks a question: "What is your day like?"

"Oh," he says, "I get up when I always did, go to bed at the usual time. It's important to make rules for yourself, and stick to them . . . The trucks wake me," he adds, "and it takes me a long time to fall asleep again. I try to think about what to paint."

"Why don't you take something?"

"I'm through with props."

The road looks as though it must lead to a farmhouse. But it doesn't; they followed it once before, two birthdays ago. It leads deep into the woods and up a mountain. The trees as they walk get taller and older, blocking the valley view. An unkempt tangle of lilac which somebody planted, an unfamiliar fruit tree suggest some former habitation. (In the watery ditch last May bloomed forget-me-nots gone native out of some long-ago garden.)

"What do you have for breakfast?"

"Toast, coffee, juice."

"No more croissants?"

"Dr. Fellman told me I should lose ten pounds."

He looks thinner, almost ascetic; he has lost weight. Mostly around the face, a closening of skin to the bone structure, heightening the hawklike tenseness of his expression. There is a smudge of chemical green on one check.

"How do you spend the morning?"

"I'm taking a class at the New School. Just so I can have a place to paint with the right equipment, the right light. I paint there all morning." He considers a moment. "It takes a lot out of you, painting."

"Who do you eat lunch with?"

"Nobody. People in the class. Well, when I go uptown, fellows from the office if it isn't too late for them. Tuesdays, I have to lurk around the Bureaucracy."

"What do you do in the afternoon?"

"Usually I go home. Some afternoons I do another painting. Or answer letters and pay off the creditors. I try to take in the galleries; you can always learn from other people's successes and failures. Right now I'm hunting for a studio where I can paint all the time, and give classes."

"And give up the apartment?"

With surprise: "Oh, no. I'd never do that."

At this place in the road they saw, last time, a silly woodchuck trying to make a burrow in the hard dirt.

"Where have all the woodchucks gone?"

"I don't know." With better eyes than hers, he used to point out woodchucks spaced territorially along the Thomas E. Dewey Thruway, when they drove up to spend weekends at the Inn of the Four Seasons, or, in the words of the French, L'Auberge des Quatre Saisons. The seasons are deerslayers, skiers, fishermen, and swimmers.

"What do you do in the evening?"

"I would have been teaching that class at Brooklyn College. But only seven people signed up for it. You needed eight."

"Perhaps the word will have spread by next semester."

"Perhaps. It's hard," he admits, "to block in the time. The martinis get earlier and earlier. Five o'clock, then four-thirty, then four."

Except for one occasion, they haven't seen each other in six months. It was his idea for them to revisit this scene.

"Do you invite people to dinner?"

"Daphne has high blood pressure and I haven't located another cook."

"Don't you get invited out?"

"Extra men are always being asked to dinner, thank you. Who wants to be *that*? Last night I ate at Barney and June's."

"How is Barney?"

"Barney's doctor told him his heart is six years older than the rest of him."

"How do you stand weekends? Saturday nights and Sunday afternoons?"

A slim sapling like a rod of copper, speckled white, some kind of fruit tree. Nothing here is in leaf or flower, not even the shadbush.

"I try to arrange things for weekends."

There are no more signs of a homestead, the road is well into the forest, wide enough for a jeep but redder and muddier and rutted, no longer going anywhere in particular, except up. They keep pausing, as birds shuttle back and forth across the road and she pursues them with the field glasses.

"Read any good books lately?"

"No."

"What about the theater?"

"I took in *Oh! Calcutta!* It was rotten."

"Haven't you kept up the subscriptions—Shakespeare, American Place?"

A shake of the head.

"Flicker, flicker," says a yellow-shafted one deep in the trees. It gets snowier the higher you go. Between the roots of the trees, gritty patches linger like white toes. And other things—a shotgun shell casing, a gold Ballantine beer can.

"Look—sportsmen," she says.

"People don't care what they throw away."

She sighs. "How long do you think it will be before the others discover this place?"

"They're probably on their way right now, Twig. It's going to be A-frames and Dairy Queens and beer cans and pay toilets right to the top of the mountain. People won't stop spreading. The trees are going to have to go."

From the throat of the woods the drumming of a large woodpecker, like the sound of an ax.

"But we need the forest. This is the watershed."

"They're going to flood this valley for a new reservoir. People won't stop breeding and spreading. In five years' time you won't recognize this place."

"What's the point of Earth Day, then? Zero Population

Growth, recycling, antiexhaust laws—" She stops when she sees he's not paying attention.

"Too late."

The valley is doomed. Water will lie upon the fields, the oriole-harboring orchards, the untidy, worthless back-country farms. This is the age of expenditure and success, expenditure and failure.

Climbing, a bit out of breath, into an earlier season: more snow and, on the north face of the rocks, frozen water like stopped fountains. They have never followed the road to the end.

"How far can we go?"

"We ought to begin to head back now. I've thought of some things to do to my painting."

"Let's get the car."

"Last time, if you will remember, we nearly got stuck to the hubcaps."

An enormous black bird explodes beside them, crosses the road stridently, and is absorbed by the trees before she has a chance to focus the binoculars.

"A pileated woodpecker!" She runs to the edge of the forest, searches for it. He looks at the sky, then at his uncle's heirloom watch.

"It was only a bluejay, Twig."

"Much larger than a jay. They're rare now, and I've never seen one. I need it for my life list."

But already he is walking away.

He is lighter, but his step is heavier, and his shoulder blades protrude in the chamois-cloth shirt that she ordered for him from L. L. Bean for Christmas. Like wings, but not the wings of a hawk.

Ask me a question, pessimistic sojourner. I'll tell you no lies.

"Don't you want to hear about me?"

Silence.

"Perhaps I talk too much; you don't talk enough. If only I could get inside your head for two seconds."

"In answer to what you said *first:* I'm aware that I'm not

as communicative as some. So what? I'm so tired of always trying to please people."

"Wouldn't it be easier to look for a new job?"

"Listen, I'm trying to learn to enjoy my freedom ... Freedom, I keep telling everybody, is for the birds."

"You are too hard on yourself always. Someone ought to tell you to be happy, for a change."

"I don't need anybody *else* to tell me anything. Look. I appreciate your intentions. Maybe you've gained a whole lot of insight. But I have to work things out my way. I just haven't got the future sketched in yet. Wait a few months."

"What about the cost of living?"

"The last time I paid my taxes I realized that I earned about the same amount as I get from the brokers. Well, I figured, I'm supposedly being paid a living wage, enough to support a family. So, since the only one I'm supporting is myself, I don't really need a salary, do I? In the words of Euclid, Q.E.D."

"What if we'd been married?"

"I don't want to talk about it."

"Did you ever really want to?"

"I *said*, I don't want to discuss it."

In silence the two of them descend, watching out for the wet spots, past the detritus of the hunters; the lilac bush that tells of a family that wrested a homestead out of the wilderness, cleared a field, fenced it in from the woods with the rocks from it, planted a garden and lilac, quit farming or died; the phoebes' nest of clay and debris. The forest reaches over the walls, sends out advance parties—alders in the marshy low places, scrub oaks in the dry.

The trees march down the hillside. But the people are flocking out of the cities. Having drunk up the snow, the troglodytes erupt into the valley and begin climbing the hill, irresistible in number, thrusting on and devouring everything along the way.

If only the trees could fight back: a leafy, shadowy army. There would be trees enough to take on every man, woman, and child. Hand to hand, branch to branch, who would win? Wood is harder than flesh. But flesh has hands, and metal, and the secret of fire.

Fully illuminated, the valley is completely still, except for the wind, and the birds; in the middle distance a few clouds are shaping up. A scarlet station wagon is parked alongside the pasture wall.

"Why didn't you buy a car with a convertible top?" The wind blew her hair into spaniel ears when, in the old car, they swooped over the top of the hill for the first time and discovered all this land, vacant of people for miles and miles, except for the dirt-poor farms tucked into side roads like this one, with forest, fields, and, at the bottom, the meander of the valley stream.

Halfway down is a tiny cemetery on a little plateau, fenced in tidily like a rock garden, lonely as a moor. The state bird strolled bluely among the tombstones, mama and papa and four juveniles—a new species for her life list.

Pause. "Haven't you heard, Twig? The Great American Convertible as a species is extinct. Detroit doesn't make them anymore. The tops were always getting slashed."

"Let's drive down," she urges.

But he has returned to his easel; finds a need for another dark in the upper left, mixes burnt umber with forest green, wets the paper, strokes in color, which runs and feathers, dabs at it with a sponge, stands back. He has painted that tree over by the stone wall, lightning-struck, against a background of winter woods. On paper, it looks as if it were calling for help.

"It's good and strong. But I thought you had transcended your dead-tree period."

"I'm mostly abstract now, of course. You like it, Twig?"

"If you were a bird, what would you be?"
"An ostrich."
"What kind of landscape?"
"Flatness. The tundra. The veldt."
"Flower?"
"A lichen."
"That's not a flower."
"They survive."
"What weapon?"
"Anger."

He taught her to play that game when they drove for long distances at night and couldn't look at birds or landscapes. She said, "You," but the answer was "My father."

Only a month ago he had called. "Just checking in." Then he sighed deeply and said, "You might as well be among the first to know. They're letting people go down at the Lie Factory. Ten of us got the ax this morning."

"Who's us?"

"If you see a fellow selling apples at the corner of Madison and Forty-ninth, that'll be me. I'll save you a juicy one." A few minutes later, her phone rang again.

In an apartment, his, but she could tell you the number of floorboards in the living room, which seemed smaller: no rug. "The painters got more on my things than they did on the walls. I had to send it out for cleaning."

"You've moved the Mexican statue. I liked it under the skylight."

"The vandals smashed it."

He clutched her like a drowning person. "I'm going to miss the old place, I truly am. It's like losing your family. I've always had an office to go to. I even liked grinding out the fibs. Where am I going to? What am I going to *do* all day?"

"You'll find another job."

"The old man used to hide behind the papers at breakfast so we couldn't see the look on his face—there was such emptiness in his eyes. I felt ashamed when I left for school, knowing he probably wished he could come along." He held on and on. "My mother was watching him once and she whispered, 'The poor little thing.' I didn't know who I wanted to choke, him or her."

Later he repeated several times, "I'm so frightened. I'm so afraid it's too late."

She told him it was not too late. She said anybody would be frightened. Quite a number of her friends were out of work. To be sure, they were living in hard times. Yet, with his abilities, his experience, she was sure he'd hit upon something. It was nothing to be ashamed of.

"Why did you come here? I'm so ashamed."

Then he remembered his plan. "I thought it all out while I was waiting for you to come." He'd go to the chief and ask if they couldn't keep him on as a consultant at, say, half of his present salary, and perhaps he could free-lance on the side. So that when business picked up— "I feel as though I'm too old to go looking for another job. I need my job. I need my family."

His heart thudding. She couldn't look at his face.

He whispered, "You shouldn't have come here. It is too terrible."

That was only a month ago. And now he has no family—a man who so desperately loathed weekends he'd go to the office on Saturdays, before he took up with painting and her, not necessarily in that order. His old hat is jammed down over his forehead; his voice drops at the end of every sentence, angry, abrupt, and hollow. Every day is a weekend now.

Something like a bad cold inundates her eyes, her throat. Sorrow? Pity? No, she refuses to savage him with her pity. He is not a poor little thing. *They* are not poor little things.

Last week she opened a book and a picture floated onto the bed, a photograph of him, grinning at the camera and slightly out of focus. His hair was black; a piece of it fell over one eye. He looked as if he were about to ask a question.

Once he said, "I want to die," and she believed he would die without her. Whom does he talk to now about his paintings and the household gods, rage, futility, loneliness, anxiety, and despair? After a martini or two he sometimes would pat her knee: "Twig. You're not so bad. There's a lot going on behind that smiling face. You've wisdom enough for both of us, if we just knew how to tap it." Eyes across the valley, where the water-bearing cumuli are streaming, receding like years, like five years.

Five years ago she was drowning and called out to him. And he saved her; he pulled her in, gave her artificial respiration, dried her off, permitted her to continue. How did she know he couldn't swim either? Cravenly she attacked his resources, insisting that he flourish, take an interest; she encouraged him to paint, which he is doing full time now, morning, noon, and night, though the martinis get earlier and earlier and he wakes at three in the morning.

Oh dear, she filled his days but she could not add to them. Ultimately he was exhausted. He betrayed her: He got old—

Inclining always, anyway, toward death, away from life, stubbornly chopping at the foundations. At a distance she must follow him, strolling toward death in his L. L. Bean shirt and his old hat. Like a tortoise she had, a dry-land creature with a yen for streams and rivers; put him down near the bank and he struck out at once for the water. It whirled him away upside down in his shell, like a rudderless boat. No matter how you turned him around, he swerved back, ineluctably heading for the torrent. She held him back for a while but she couldn't turn him around, he was so eager to get away, perhaps more eager than ever.

In the watershed region two people stand overlooking a lit valley, watching the clouds that move up from the ocean like buckets, dropping water that runs through leaves and tree roots down the slopes into trout streams with Indian names, streams that feed into the reservoir, to flow through the aqueduct pipes for a hundred miles to rise in the dirty, thirsty city where they live. In the rich and airy landscape she gropes for a way out of sorrow, can find none.

"Oh, why did we live together so long? What was the point?"

Looking down at the valley soon to be drowned, he replies finally, remotely, without tenderness, "Don't ask me, Twig."

In the words of W. H. Auden, "Thousands have lived without love, not one without water."

GEORGE V. HIGGINS

The Habits of the Animals: The Progress of the Seasons

(FROM THE NORTH AMERICAN REVIEW)

RIGHT after I got back from Korea—I had a certain amount of money—I took every nickel I had and bought a piece of land up in New Hampshire, south of Center Ossipee. That was in 1954. The chrome on most cars was about a whisper thick and there was some kind of clear lacquer on it that had a tendency to peel and whiten when you washed it. But you could buy woodlots in New Hampshire for about twenty-five dollars an acre; I bought fifty-three acres, more or less, on a pond, and it cost me sixteen hundred dollars. It was all you could do to buy a halfway decent Chevrolet for sixteen hundred dollars then, and I got an apple orchard all gone to seed, some fine oak trees and pines, and several meadows full of tall grass and sloping very gradually down to the pond. There were beavers in the pond, and in the evenings it was still.

My wife was fit to be tied. It was not that she wanted, really, the Chevrolet. What she wanted was a house in, say, Framingham or Braintree or maybe Swampscott, Massachusetts. Definitely not any apartment in Quincy, which was what she had had during the war, and what we had had before the war. To do her justice, it wasn't much of an apartment. It was about the kind of an apartment that a police officer could expect to be able to afford those days, which is about the same as saying it was the kind of apartment a police officer could expect to afford these days: not much of an apartment.

I tried to convince her that the kind of house we could afford to replace the apartment wouldn't be much of a house either, but that didn't work. If I had gone out and gotten the house she wanted, she wouldn't have liked it, once she lived in it for a while. But it wasn't the house itself—the house we could have swung with the down payment I used for the land, instead—that I was fighting: it was the idea of a house. That was a lot harder, because it included cozy evenings by the fireside and prize-winning roses and gin and tonics on the porch in the summer evenings with the fireflies going on and off. It was not just a lot harder. It was a losing proposition.

I lost as graciously as I could. That was not very graciously. I was kind of annoyed that she seemed to be glad to have me back chiefly because she thought it meant I would now do what she wanted me to do, and that was to buy some rattletrap house that'd fall down if she snapped the shades. But I did my best to avoid talking about that, and I took a lot of grief. I figured that when the flak was over, I would still have the land in New Hampshire, and I wanted that land badly enough to put up with the abuse.

It took me a very long time to understand that there was more involved than the abuse. I tended to assume that when the noise died down, the matter was over. I neglected the lingering resentment. For ten or twelve years that neglect was all right: the resentment was still there, and it cropped up in most arguments (there will be a few when you spend the better part of your life away from a crummy apartment, at the barracks or on patrol), but I didn't understand that the fury I caught from time to time was really the continuing reaction to the New Hampshire land. I honestly thought that was over. So, where I would have gotten mad if I had understood that she was still flogging me for buying the land, ten or twelve years after I thought the matter was settled, I did my best to shrug off the complaints because she stated them as something else. Such as: Why the hell don't you get out of police work and into something that pays enough so I don't have to work all the time?

I didn't get out of police work for two reasons. First, because I couldn't; I was too old. When I got back from Korea—it was my second hitch—I was thirty-two years old. I had six years in, which left fourteen for a pension, and I was just too old to start in all over again, going to school and selling storm windows nights. Second, because I didn't want to. I liked police work. I still do. I was perfectly satisfied to spend my time working on murder cases to make a living, and doing the living that I made on the land I bought on the pond.

There wasn't much to the property but the natural advantages I have already described. The man who sold it to me was an old swamp Yankee that farmed it on and off when he felt like it, and didn't when he didn't. Mean-tempered old son of a bitch, I gather; if he ever had a wife he didn't have her when I got there, he didn't mention ever having one, and there wasn't any evidence of a woman ever having been around the house. The day I arrived to look the property over he was wearing one of those dark gray shirts and a pair of pants that'd gone out at the knees several times, and he nodded toward the house and said: "I lived here since I was a boy, forty years or so, and I'm sick of it. Going up to Maine. Not going to haggle. Sixteen hundred dollars, cash. Take it or leave it." To go with the house—three rooms: kitchen and sitting room down, one large bedroom up, cramped bathroom that'd obviously been converted from a pantry—there was a small barn getting ready to fall down and a fruit cellar dug out of the side of a slope, with a leaky roof There was a stone wall that marked off the easterly boundary of the land, and the remains of a wooden fence leading away from the barn toward the orchard that never quite made it, made of tarpaper and the door all choked in with brush. but fell away into the tall grass before it reached the trees. I took it all.

Buying it was like joining a church, because it committed me to spending every weekend I could get, at least in the summers, working on the place. I started with the house. I jacked up the foundation and ripped out the plumbing. I replaced every pipe in that house with copper, and then I repaired the walls and painted them light colors, white and yellow. Most of the windows needed new sash cords and I had to reglaze every light of glass in the house. I stripped the floors downstairs, sanded and varnished them, and upstairs I covered the naked beams with wallboard and painted it light blue. I did all the wiring I could—most of it—and spent two weekends working paid details on the highways to get enough extra cash to pay an electrician to do the rest. I took out the rusty black stove in the sitting room and put in a Franklin stove that I got from Sears; when the doors were open, it was just as good as a fireplace and it threw a lot of heat. There was a massive iron stove in the kitchen that burned wood for heat and range oil for cooking. I left that where it was, but I gave it the first polishing it'd had in at least twenty years. I put in a used refrigerator and I ripped out the old slate sink—it leaked—and put in a porcelain one. Then I built up a cabinet around it, and I did the same thing in the bathroom and put in a shower, too. It took me almost six years to do all those things, and when I finished I decided I wasn't content with the heat. So I went back and put in radiators and a gas burner in the cellar—I had to make a concrete platform for it on the dirt floor—and I built a small shelter to conceal the propane tanks outside the kitchen window. I put a bird feeder on the corner of that shelter and on Thanksgiving morning in 1960 I got up early and went downstairs and watched several sparrows doing their best to frustrate a bluejay after the suet and grain. There was a heavy frost on the meadow that sloped down to the pond and there was ice at least ten feet from shore that reflected the sunlight in the frozen weeds. My wife slept late. She generally did on such days. She said holidays depressed her because we had no children and holidays were meant for children, so she slept away as much of the day as she could.

With the house repaired, painted white on the clapboards with dark green trim and the roof reshingled, I became better acquainted with the land itself. I set out to prune the apple trees and clear away the brush that was stunting them, having it in mind to bring in a crop every year. The idea appealed to me. The few dwarf Macks that I rescued from the local deer tasted good. But I consulted some people who actually knew what they were doing and they told me that spraying and cultivating an apple orchard probably wasn't the way I wanted to spend the rest of my life, and they said it would take about all of that. So I lowered my sights a little. I just cleared out the orchard, removed the brambles, and burned over the deep grass. Even that small attention seemed to make a considerable difference: the trees seemed to straighten themselves up, and the apples the next year were noticeably larger. The real improvement, though, was the way the orchard began to attract animals. Particularly in the early spring, and from the middle of September on to about the first snow, deer came in groups of two or three to browse in the morning and again in the late afternoon and evening. There was a knoll about fifty yards away, and by sitting below the crest, to avoid frightening them with my silhouette, I got a good two or three hours' entertainment every week or two, watching the deer. I posted the property.

I left the stone wall alone. It had been constructed well—from which I concluded it was probably at least a hundred years old, because the previous owner never would have done anything that well. Anything that has lasted a century deserves to be let alone. But I brought in new poles and rails for the fence and I painted the barn the appropriate red and used it to store my tools. I chopped up the wood from the old fence and burned it, along with the usable pieces of wood I had saved when I tore out the fruit cellar, in the Franklin stove.

In the spring of 1964—I believe it was May—I discovered a family of squirrels in the barn loft, apparently getting along nicely with the barn swallows, and a noticeable increase in the number of pheasant around the property. There had always been a lot of rabbit tracks around the place in the snow, but now I began to see them often. In April I had disturbed a fox hunting in the field south of the house, and during the summer I saw the vixen herding her cubs along the edge of the pond. There were groundhog holes in the field, of course, but I found tracks around the barn that I matched in a book with raccoon prints. From time to time I heard an owl.

These things gave me pleasure, and did not offend my wife. Perhaps she was so completely annoyed at spending all of our leisure time at the place that it took a complete catastrophe to upset her. At least that was what I concluded later, after the skunks.

I found the skunks the next year, keeping house in the darkest corner of the old fruit cellar. Fortunately I saw them going home, and was able to watch from a safe distance to see where they went. I had no interest in exciting them. At the time there were two, fully grown. I suspected that there might be offspring around, but I did not investigate.

My wife's ability to contain her enthusiasm for my wildlife observations had long before gotten me into the habit of saying nothing about what I had seen. In that instance, having some premonition of her likely reaction, I said nothing. On the Fourth of July she saw a small grass snake crawling away from the propane tanks, and nearly lapsed into hysterics, and I reflected on the wisdom of my silence about the skunks.

I saw the skunks again, from time to time, but I never saw them with any young. Occasionally I would see one skunk, and more often the pair, but I never saw anything to indicate that more than two of them were holed up in the fruit cellar. Always I saw them at the northerly end of the place, out of sight of the house, and in a careless sort of way I rather hoped that they would confine themselves to those precincts. For three years they obeyed my silent wishes.

On Easter morning of 1968, my wife, doing dishes at the sink, looked beyond the bird feeder and saw the skunks peacefully mincing across the front of the barn, heading back to where they lived, I suppose. She was very concerned, and directed me to shoot them at once. I refused. I can summarize what happened next a lot more comfortably than I can report everything that was said. She permitted herself the hysterics she had narrowly avoided when she saw the snake, and to me, at least at the time, seemed perfectly incoherent. The substance of what she said was that I preferred the skunks to her, because I would not kill them as she wished. I told her about Wicklow.

In 1948 I made corporal in the State Police and was assigned to Holderness barracks. There was a rule that you were not supposed to drink in the barracks, any barracks, and there was a long-standing custom of drinking in all of the barracks. Particularly at Holderness, which was away the hell out in the woods ten miles from God, but centrally located, as far as geography was concerned, on Route 81. In the Holderness barracks in 1948 there was also a big stupid trooper from Worcester named Wicklow.

Along with everyone else, except Sergeant Fitzmaurice, who had stomach trouble, Wicklow drank in the barracks. Pehaps the rule against it was declared to prevent the kind of things that happened when Wicklow drank: he wasn't a bad fellow, really, but he couldn't drink and he did. He did not become belligerent, or anything like that. It was simply that he was stupid when he was sober, and alcohol did not help him to be smarter.

The procedure of forbidden drinking at the Holderness barracks was as follows: prohibited beverages were consumed from their original containers in the two unoccupied bathrooms at the rear of the second floor. When the container was empty, the consumer raised the bedroom window and, using an underhand delivery with a lot of snap in the wrist, flipped the dead soldier out over the cruisers in the parking lot below and into the gully beyond them. The gully was full of underbrush, and in the course of time it also acquired a lot of empty pints and beer bottles. Two years ago, I understand, they burned over the gully in the process of enlarging the parking lot, and when the fire went out they found they had to go and get a dump truck to cart the empties away. Headquarters was furious, and for several weeks afterward, I am told, nobody drank in any of the barracks.

Wicklow and the rest of us deserved, although we did not, of course, receive it, a substantial measure of that anger. There were prodigious drinkers in the Holderness barracks in 1948, and we kept the gully rustling just about every night.

The local animals kept it rustling after we had gone to bed. There were rats and mice and rabbits and squirrels— and foxes and owls and hawks that came to hunt them—and skunks. Rats and mice and squirrels and skunks congregate at convenient trash piles. Partly they came looking for the sandwich wrappers and so forth. Partly they came because there is nothing a scavenger likes better than the nice starchy dregs of an empty beer bottle.

One night in July, Wicklow came back from patrol and pulled the cruiser into the parking lot just in time to see a skunk on the early shift heading for the gully. Wicklow was not completely stupid: he knew enough to stay in that cruiser until the skunk got well out of range. Then he came into the barracks with his bag of beer and he was all upset. He was outraged. "There's a skunk out there," he said, as though there'd never been a skunk anywhere before. "Right out there under the goddamned *windows*."

No one paid much attention to him. He went upstairs and joined up with some other gentlemen, also having a cold glass on a warm night. He sat there drinking his beer and going on about the skunk and getting thicker and thicker about the whole thing. When he finished the last bottle, he raised the screen, and when he did that he saw a skunk coming up out of the gully, going home. A little unsteady on his feet, too, weaving out of that dark gully, full of beer, halfway dazzled by the light in the parking lot.

"There's the bastard now," Wicklow said. "I'm going to shoot him."

Wicklow was a pretty good shot, drunk or sober, but no one was interested enough in his announcement to think about the possibility that he might hit the skunk. He got out his service pistol and he shot that skunk, a nice clean shot that took its head off. And that headless skunk went ass over teakettle and started spinning around just like a pinwheel, except that what was coming out of his back end wasn't sparks. Wicklow hit the skunk fat, and the skunk hit the cruisers— one had the windows open, not that it mattered—and the back door of the barracks and the nice, porous brick walls and the curtains in the mess (someone had left the windows up after dinner). It was six weeks and more before the place was fit to live in, and the smell got into the uniforms and the bedding. We woke up with it and we carried it with us on patrol and speeders grinned at us when they handed over their licenses and registrations, and our wives claimed we brought it home with us.

I reminded my wife of the summer of 1948 when she said

I preferred the skunks to her. She was not persuaded. She said that if I didn't start doing something to make the place livable, beginning with shooting the skunks, she was never coming back to the property. The skunks proceeded delicately into the grass in the sunlight on the anniversary of the Resurrection of Our Lord and Savior Jesus Christ and I stood there staring at that woman I had married twenty-two years before. Considering Korea and the other hours I spent away from her on other obligations, I figure we had spent the better part of those twenty-two years away from each other, learning things separately that were so different that we ended up never further apart than when we were together. Last November we were up there for the first snowfall, and in the early morning I saw three deer feeding on the tender branches of the apple trees. I made no effort to report this to her. I did not shoot skunks, and she each week comes more than close enough to keeping her promise, though she is there in the still evenings when we do not speak.

WARD JUST

Burns

(FROM THE ATLANTIC MONTHLY)

ANONYMOUS THEN, Burns joined the State Department in May of 1959, the week John Foster Dulles died. He carried with him a letter of introduction from his history tutor at Columbia, but was never able to use it because the dying Secretary was refused visitors. Burns tucked the letter away, sad because he admired the old man's Bourbon audacity (nothing learned, nothing forgotten) and wanted to meet him; he disapproved of the *weltanschauung* but liked the *geist*. He'd arrived in Washington with two suitcases and a half dozen cartons of books, all of it stuffed into the rear seat of a red Volkswagen. An officer of the Foreign Service of the United States of America. Diplomatic immunity. A black passport. He and a friend from Columbia rented a small furnished house in Foggy Bottom, within easy walking distance of the Department, and the summer passed pleasantly, without incident.

Burns was eager, trained in economics, and an accomplished linguist as well: excellent German, French, and Italian, passable Russian. Intelligent, watchful Burns had a thoughtful nature, and his career proceeded logically and without sensation. The first year, he was assigned to the European section as a cable clerk. Burns found the State Department agreeable, he liked its stillness and atmosphere of deliberation, quiet days broken only by the old hasty moments when the entire section would turn to drafting instructions for an ambassador or a memorandum for the Secretary.

The Department was a forest of hat racks, scholarly in its way; Burns was reminded of low-keyed university seminars. That first year, he spent much of his time with the head of the German desk, listening to droll stories of Berlin in the 1930s; the head of the German desk had known Dorothy Thompson and Christopher Isherwood, and was a nimble raconteur.

The second year he was posted to Turkey, stamping passports, and the next three years spent in Bonn, in the office of the economic counselor. These were rewarding and exciting years; Burns felt he was doing useful work and was wise enough to take frequent holidays throughout Europe. He saw all of Germany and the Low Countries and most of Switzerland and Rome with friends. In somnolent Bad Godesberg he lived in a small suite in the Yankee ghetto, the large bleak block of flats near the embassy that the American government had built as a communal residence. No living off the land! The staff hated its isolation. Burns did not mind; he could walk to the Rhine, and he had a girlfriend who lived on the Nibelungenstrasse. The ghetto was amusing in its way, Mother America caring for her children, the government surrounding you even as you slept; but the building was truly inelegant. The part of the job that he hated was the necessary contact with traveling American businessmen, many of whom thought that the State Department was a division of the U.S. Chamber of Commerce. Burns cultivated objectivity: he was no good at all out front.

His record was excellent and studded with commendations. He was discreet, reliable, and hardworking. By the time he left Bonn, Burns knew most of the important older German labor leaders and all of the unimportant younger ones. Burns was building for the future, for the day ten years hence when he'd return. He got on well with the younger Germans, finding to his surprise that he shared their taste for the livid and the grotesque: gargantuan meals, carnival sideshows, Grosz and Brecht, and the underground university theater. Burns often filled in for the cultural attaché at benefits and openings, and at embassy receptions for visiting American artists and writers. Through his contacts in the German labor movement and his skillful analysis of the direction of the German economy, he was brought into frequent contact with the Deputy Chief of Mission, a diplomat of long and varied experience. The DCM encouraged his career and coached him in the ways of the Department. Burns particularly remembered one bit of advice, given late one night over schnapps:

"The Department values loyalty, intelligence, and calm—in that order. The Foreign Service is something apart from the run-of-the-mill American bureaucracy. Remember that. We are not action people, we are analysts. Leave the action to the pickle factory and the pentagon, they are the ones with the resources (and the ones who'll evade the blame). Stay close to the bureaucracy," Burns was told. "It is an elite, and the better for it. Not as elite, mind you, as it was. But elite nonetheless. Study diplomatic technique. Read history. Always be cautious, always be firm . . ."

"Firmly cautious or cautiously firm?" Burns inquired with a flicker of a smile.

"Very," said the DCM.

Burns was surprised and disappointed in the fall of 1965 when he was ordered back to Washington and informed he was being loaned to CIA. He was told only that the agency had a major project underway, which required the participation of many of their economists. It left them shorthanded, and meanwhile the State Department had been directed by Congress to cut its own budget. The loan would not be for long, perhaps no more than one year. Burns should think of it as a net plus, if not a clear advantage; he could have been transferred to AID. He'd been requested by name, and the transfer had the blessing of the Department.

The first day at Langley he was shown his office, and it was not in the German section, as he'd been told.

"Here you are," the chief of section said. "Everything you'll need. Paper, pencils, slide rule, computer room down the hall. Filing cabinets there. Toilet down the hall and to your right. Staff meeting every day at nine, and sometimes again at six."

"I thought it'd be the German . . ."

"This is not the German."

"Yes, but I was told the arrangement."

"That is on another floor. That is on the third floor, quite different and apart from this. That is another section, something distinctly separate from what we do here."

"I know, but . . ."

"You can ask them about it. You'll get an answer. Perhaps there was a snafu. There sometimes is. Are. Snafus."

"Son of a bitch," Burns said.

"You were in Bonn?"

"Three years."

"Well, they probably thought that a change of scene . . ."

"But I am an FSO."

"You'll come to like it here," the chief of section said.

The first year at Langley was disagreeable in all but one respect. Burns watched the bureaucratic gavotte as it was danced by experts, and learned lessons he never forgot. They were lessons in bureaucratic technique, and the uses of firmness and caution. At first, Burns told himself that these were lessons he wished he did not know, but he found out that once known they were impossible to ignore or forget; in the beginning, he thought it was like learning something damaging or unpleasant about a friend. The friendship changes, usually for the worse—and yes yes, he knew it was naïve and unrealistic but it was the way he felt nevertheless. He found himself admiring the small ways a man moved ahead, the ways in which a man identified the winners and then placed his bets. There was no question of political or ideological conflict—the agency was too sophisticated for that; it was mainly a matter of technology and the skill with which a bureaucrat managed to force his ideas, and thereby gain a purchase on the future. CIA Burns was able to learn with a clear and objective mind, because he was a man on loan; in time he would be returned to the State Department, where he belonged.

Burns had no ax to grind, but the Department dawdled amid procedural inertia and the budgetary restraints imposed by Congress. Burns remained at Langley although he yearned for the security and familiarity of the Foreign Service, the satisfaction of fashioning American foreign policy; he felt

himself an artist among artisans, made few close friends, and
denounced (privately) the rules and regulations, which
seemed to him frivolous when they were not corrupting. The
spooks ran as a pack, and considered him an outsider. But
the job had its moments. Paper. He tried to explain it, his life
inside the bureaucracy. Burns translated French documents
relating to the economy of a small African nation, a small,
pivotal African nation, in the vernacular of the Board of National Estimates. Every day the documents arrived in pouch,
and Burns would translate them and summarize the contents.
Some of them were official, some not; some of them were
agents' reports. The précis went to the chief of section, who
would include it in the running commentary on the economy
and politics of the country.

"Think of yourself as Charles Dickens," the chief of section told Burns. "Writing a novel, a new installment every
month. Odd turnings of plot. But a bold metaphor. Except
that this novel goes on forever and forever, of course."

"A sort of *Pickwick Papers* in triplicate," Burns said.

"You've got it exactly," the chief replied.

The government of the small, pivotal African nation was
fledgling and incompetent, and one week, the reports said,
owned by the Russians, the next by the Chinese. Conscien-
tious Burns received State Department cables as well (there
were channels, and these he eagerly awaited, particularly the
commentary of the chief political officer, a sardonic and
witty diplomat who doubted everything, including agents' reports: "Buy the government? You can't even rent it for an
afternoon." For the first two years the work was interesting,
and even valid in a perverse way. The Prime Minister had
committed "significant errors" in the management of his
country's finances, and it was beguiling—often amusing—to
try to put the pieces of fact together to make a conprehensi-
ble whole. Burns threw himself into it, juggling trade figures,
cash flow, tax revenues, production, employment, resource
management, inflation, and all the other classical indices of
economic fortune. One afternoon he created an entirely ficti-
tious Gross National Product, which he dropped in his out
box on a lark. It turned up later in the National Estimate,
and that worried Burns. At the time, the country was on the

verge of collapse, indeed the statistics indicated the country had collapsed. According to the numbers, the bottom line as Burns called it, the country was bankrupt and not functioning—except that it continued as before, the vitality and innocence of the people defying all known economic laws, or anyway those laws that were promulgated by American economists. Burns conceived the novel idea that his statistics had nothing whatever to do with the situation. Novel to Burns, not novel to his section chief.

"You're learning," the chief said.

"Remember the GNP figure?" Burns was in the mood for a confession.

"Four hundred eighty-two point something-something million? Sure."

"It was all cock," Burns said. "Doesn't exist."

"Strange," the chief mused. "It seemed to fit in so well."

"Some of the figures were real. But I made most of them up. The GNP is meaningless."

"Yes," the chief said sadly.

"I'll play around with it again, if you'd like me to. Perhaps a new figure . . ."

"Please do."

"I suppose I shouldn't have said anything."

"It doesn't matter," the chief said. "So long as I know."

"Well, I'm sorry if it's embarrassing in any way."

The chief looked at him, surprised. "Why should I be embarrassed?"

Burns was nearing the end of two years in National Estimates, and most of his friends were overseas, some of them in Southeast Asia where the wars were being fought, and their infrequent letters home made him long for the symmetry and rhythm of the State Department, anything real. He became a nostalgic, recalling the details of his flat in the ghetto and the look of the Rhine at dawn, during his salad days in Bonn. He remembered the long talks with the DCM, and his satisfaction at filing skillful reports. Now he'd been passed by. One man he had known briefly in the embassy at Bonn had actually been a member of the Working Party negotiating the test ban treaty with the Soviet Union. His former roommate was ADC to the Ambassador in Saigon, and that man was Burns' own age and grade. Other friends were in Europe or the Middle East, living well in Amsterdam or Beirut. Meanwhile, Burns reflected bitterly, he pushed paper at CIA and watched experts maneuver the bureaucracy. His polite requests for return to the State Department elicited polite replies, mere acknowledgments, no more.

In the evenings in Washington, home alone with his drinks and his dog, Burns would undertake National Estimates of his own life. A personal GNP, entirely factual and aboveboard. Big, bearish, awkward Burns, b. 1937 N.Y.C., father an M.D., mother a psychologist, "professional people." Medical talk at the breakfast table, mind-numbing Saturday afternoons at Yankee Stadium: good father, obedient son. But his childhood and adolescence were mostly blank, seventeen blank years until he entered Columbia University, became fascinated with economics and history, graduated with honors, and joined the Foreign Service. This became the central objective of his life, membership in the Diplomatic Corps, and an understanding of the interplay ("the confusion") of politics and economics. The stress was on manipulation and management—of national interests, of alliances, of various political and economic crises, all of it huddled together under Reason and the Rule of Law. It was no place for an eccentric. Burns admired professional diplomats—men who were cool, collected, in control, rising to a geopolitical *crisis* (he liked the word—his doctor father first defined it for him as the point in the course of a disease when the patient either recovers or dies). He saw himself as one of a dozen men in a small room, an anteroom in a foreign chancellery (Belgrade? Helsinki?) conducting secret negotiations, ADC to a giant, Bohlen or Kennan, taking on the Russians and, by sheer force of logic and remorseless dialectic, arguing them back, turning their own deceptions against them. Forcing an agreement, and then a laconic cable to the Department: *Negotiations concluded* . . .

But that was a joke now. What he had to show for eight years in the Diplomatic Service were a few commendations, and some flimsies of cables he'd sent. He had a Q Security Clearance; now he could read intercepts from anywhere,

from Havana or Hanoi or Pyong-yang. And he had a filing
cabinet full of economic analysis of a wretched country
which had, if the analysis were correct, collapsed. He had all
those things plus a flat stomach, owing in part to his noon-
time squash games with an overweight colonel who was, similarly, on loan to CIA. He did not know the colonel's job,
and did not want to know.

To an empty room, at midnight on a Monday night: "Celebrated Diplomat. Superspy Burns, the hired gun. The cloak-
and-dagger man from National Estimates. A fast man with a
document, that Burns. Hard. Resourceful. Adroit."

Burns was a man of routine, at home as at his office. There
were no crises in his section of the agency, so he arrived
home in Foggy Bottom punctually at seven each evening.
He'd feed the dog, and select a recording with great care; a
different recording each night. He prepared a shaker of cocktails, and at nine would put a steak on the grill and frozen
potatoes in the oven. He stood at the counter in the kitchen,
drinking his drink and slowly breaking lettuce into a salad
bowl. As the steak cooked, he selected his wine. The wine selected, Burns moved to his bookcase for the evening's read.
Something British, he thought, and ran his thumb along the
spines of his books. Disraeli. Cromwell. Melbourne. Yes,
Melbourne—William Lamb, alone and distracted at the end
of his life, the affections of Victoria detached from him and
fastened on another. Melbourne, the quintessence of controlled inaction. He prowled among the books, glass in hand,
then paused. He had not read his latest issue of *Revue de
Défense Nationale,* the authoritative guide to the thinking of
the French general staff. It was there now, arrived in the
morning mail, on the coffee table. unopened, waiting. He
glanced through the table of contents. Arms control. The Indian subcontinent. Ah. General J. Nemo would bear careful
evaluation: "Étude sur la guerre de Vendée (II)."

Burns smelled the steak and the potatoes and returned to
the kitchen. He uncorked the wine, and set it gently on the
table. He'd set his place that morning, the knife, fork, and
spoon on one side of the plate, the wooden salt and pepper
shakers to his left, the white napkin folded just so, a fresh

candle in the silver holder. Then Burns sat down with the
steak and the potatoes, the salad and the wine, and began to
read "Étude sur le guerre de Vendée (II)." Inside his mind,
General J. Nemo competed with the memory of a candlelit
dinner in Munich four years ago. The dinner was followed by
visits to half a dozen nightclubs, ending at dawn. Burns finished in thirty minutes, then slowly washed and wiped the
dishes and the silverware. He spoke to the dog and returned
to the living room, where the backgammon board was waiting.

He carefully prepared his pipe with the tobacco purchased
that evening, and bent over the board, playing both sides, but
mentally betting on white. He smoked three pipes, then lay
back on the couch, thinking.

"Nemo appears to have got hold of something interesting
in the new *Revue*. Pertinent to our own situation, it seems to
me."

"I haven't seen ... that number."

"I recommend Nemo and Mourin."

"Ah, Mourin. The historian."

"Some new insights into the Sovs on the subcontinent."

"How much time do you spend on that stuff?"

"Well, not much; I read it, is about all."

"Blast, I wish I could find the time."

"Important stuff."

"Burns, you're bullshitting me."

Every Friday night Burns and five others forgathered at
one house or another to play poker or backgammon. Except
for Burns on loan, all of them were State Department people. By civil servant standards, the stakes were high: at backgammon, a dollar a point; at poker, a ten-dollar limit. Burns,
bearish over the backgammon board, was the big winner. He
played a loose conservative game—with occasional light and
daring moments, when he felt the dice were right or when he
found himself in untenable positions. He lived on the backgammon board, absorbing himself in the moves, studying
probabilities, odds this way and that. Straitlaced men tended
to be erratic at games, and Burns watched for the break, the

wrong move when the dice were cold or the odds close, but not close enough. More interesting than chess, because the dice were 30 percent of it—all other things being equal, which they never were. The edge was in the double; he paid attention to the utility of the double. The psychological double or the administrative double or the deceptive double.

It was rather like diplomacy in that way, and as interesting, because Burns had learned the fanciful nature of world affairs. A carapace of madness, concealing the tortoise beneath; the revisionists saw it the other way around, but the revisionists were wrong. He inspected the men around the tables, all of them young like himself and ambitious in diplomacy; they had outflanked him, their careers were secure. The dice rattled, the counters flashed: doubled here, redoubled there. Acceptance. Refusal. Failure of entry. He played backgammon now as a substitute for diplomacy. Dulles was dead, had died the year he came to Washington. The letter of introduction hadn't been worth a damn.

2

They knew *what* had happened, that was clear enough. They also knew, within limits, *how* it happened. They were less certain about the *who* and the *why*. But the government of the pivotal African nation had fallen, and the capital was now in the hands of insurgents. These were insurgents from the army and from the economics ministry, something of a queer alliance: the army officers were presumed to be reactionaries and the economists Communists. At ten in the morning they met in urgent session, representatives from the Agency, the Pentagon, the State Department, and the White House. They met downtown in the Executive Office Building, entering underground. Burns was in on it, as the Agency man closest to the economics ministry. They had tried to hash it out beforehand.

"Names, Burns, do you have names? You can bet your booties that the Pentagon will have names. Christ, they'll have a file on every colonel in that ragtag army. Half of them probably attended Leavenworth."

"I'll ransack the files."

"You do that, Burns. Do that right away."

But in Burns' section they had not concentrated on names. They had assembled numbers, numbers of bewildering variety and degree. They knew the names of the economic minister and his deputy, and the chief adviser to the Prime Minister. But these were not men who would participate in a revolt. These were men who were in the pay of others, or were said to be. So Burns went to the files, and spent a feverish hour rummaging through them. The warning—the opportunity!— rang in his ears.

"Burns, we want control of this operation. If there *is* an operation. We've got men on the ground, we've got very good op-con. American interests are involved, and don't forget that. This is what the Deputy Director wants, and that is what we will have. But you've got to find the names. And give identity to the names . . ."

The meeting began slowly. Burns noted with satisfaction that there were two dozen men in the room, four or five from each agency. It meant there would have to be a second meeting. The Pentagon man, an Army general, spoke first, and it was an astonishing stroke of luck because he was inarticulate and ill at ease with the Gallicized African names. The Deputy Director scored a point straightaway.

"Our intelligence indicates that the leader is a major," the Pentagon man said. "Name's Hubert . . . Fooshing?"

"Ah yes," the DD said. "Ooo-bear. Foo-saw."

"You know him?" the Pentagon man inquired politely.

"Burns knows him," the DD said. "But we'll get to that later."

Rattled, the Army general continued with his briefing. It was a disorganized briefing, but the names had been there. There were about two dozen names in all, mostly mispronounced. All the facts were there—ominous, compelling—but it required an effort of will to organize them. Burns saw the DD smile and make notes on the back of an envelope.

The representative of the State Department followed, and Burns sat back in his chair and listened. It was a *tour d'horizon*, the politics and economics of the country briefly, brilliantly, sketched. The geography and demographics of the country, its relations with its neighbors, its natural resources, its investments. There was a side excursion into cultural anthropology, a long reach back into prehistory for the national metaphors. Burns was dazzled; the State Department man had them in the palm of his hand. Finally, almost casually, he brought them up to the present moment, and the question of the American interest. This was done lucidly and skillfully, a history of diplomatic relations between the world's most powerful nation and one of the world's weakest. The diplomat stood at the head of the table, his hands in his pockets, speaking without notes. A low, musical voice: "The truth of the matter is this, gentlemen. The United States has no interest in this country. Sad, but true. Lamentable if the country falls to the Communists—Russians, Chinese, Cuban, whomever . . ." Burns noted the correct "whomever," and nodded in appreciation. "But in any serious analysis, not important. Too much risk against no gain. Gentlemen, let us leave them be. And remember the Armenian proverb: *A thousand men cannot undress a naked man.*"

He'd taken it all, ears and tail, hooves and bull.

The DD said nothing for a moment; Burns watched his jaw work. In the general conversation that followed the State Department presentation, he heard the DD mutter, "Oh fuck," but no one else heard. Now he was in a jam: not only had he to outmatch the diplomat's logic, but his elegance of speech as well. Burns watched the DD rise, and pause for dramatic effect.

"I hope none of us falls into the trap of disregarding the fate of a sovereign nation simply because it is small," the DD said. "Or black. Or without resources. Or generally friendless in a hostile world. Or in the fist of revolution"—not bad, Burns thought—"its national identity not yet fully forged from the tangled threads of its own tribal history, and the odious legacy of colonial exploitation. A nation without a center of gravity. A nation which looks to the United States of America for leadership . . ."

"Last month they burned down the embassy," the State Department man murmured, just loud enough to be heard.

". . . *They* didn't, the *Communists* did. And that's the difference. Easy for us here in the capital of the United States

to shrug off this *minor*"—the word was spoken harshly—
"country's agony, these infaust events . . ." *Infaust,* Burns
thought: the DD was pulling every lever he possessed. There
weren't a dozen people in Washington who knew what the
word meant—except the diplomat, who nodded, slight smile.

Burns was anxious, the DD made a good case. He was pulling the levers available to him. The diplomat had not been
specific, he'd given them a brilliant *tour d'horizon,* nothing
more. Presently the DD lapsed into fact, so much American
investment, the strategic value of the Nbororo river, the
threat to peaceful neighbors.

"I think we ought to very carefully consider putting a team
in on the ground. Civilians, no more than forty or fifty. But
before we come to that, I would like Burns to say a word,
about the sort of men who run the economy of . . . this 'naked' country."

Well played, Burns thought. He rose, a tightness in his
throat. The DD had them now; they could not ignore the
facts. Facts were the DD's strong suit, and now he was calling on Burns to back him up. The DD looked at him, encouraging a strong response. Burns stared across the table at
the diplomat, hand loosely clasped on the table. The diplomat's expression was benign; he'd made his case. That was
the trouble with the State Department. They didn't *fight;* they
were gentlemen. They didn't read each other's mail. Well,
they deserved what they got, Burns thought. If they did not
control events, events would control them. Laissez-faire had its
limits. For Castlereagh, Chamberlain. Burns cleared his throat.

"There is no question they will expropriate American prop-
erties," Burns said. Then he named the economists, two who
had received instruction at Lumumba University, Moscow; a
third from Havana; two or three others who'd cruised
through the L.S.E. "One of these"—he mentioned a name
and an age—"has unusually strong ties with the . . . black
movement . . . in the United States. So there is a domestic
political spin to all this . . ."

The agency, at that meeting and at later meetings, carried
the day. Forty men were dispatched up the Nbororo river in
rafts. They landed, and reported the town quiet. There was
no shooting, nor any signs of upheaval. The communications

worked splendidly. In time, most of them returned. There was a different government, but no expropriations.

They were good about it. They wanted him to stay, to "pack it in" for keeps at the State Department and become permanently attached to the Agency. They liked him. Burns did intelligent, careful work. Sometimes, when the problem truly interested him, he was brilliant. They indicated to him, but delicately, that his habits were somewhat bizarre—but fully within the . . .

"Ah, parameters."

"Of what?"

"Behavior, acceptable."

"Oh, yes."

"Look, Burns. If you will do no more than trouble yourself to get an M.A., preferably in your field, economics, the future here is very bright, very very bright. Limitless, really."

"Forget economics, how about this, something stronger? an M.A. in the diplomatic history of Europe."

"Not as good, but acceptable."

"The . . . eastern religions?"

The personnel man smiled. There were already more ersatz Buddhists than the Agency could comfortably tolerate. SEA Section smelled like an incense factory, gnomic sayings sprouted like tulips. No, definitely not "the eastern religions."

"Too bad," Burns said.

"Look, if you're tired of Africa, we can . . ."

"I am tired of Africa, Africa is tired of me," Burns said.

"All right, we understand that. Like pinning Jell-O to the wall, no?"

Burns smiled.

"So let us turn elsewhere."

"The field," Burns said, and the personnel man shook his head. No, not possible. Burns was an inside man, an analyst from the inside; anyone could see that. Outside men were something else altogether. Burns wasn't one of those, probably wouldn't ever be.

The personnel man was encouraging. He tempted Burns. "Look. One immediate jump in grade. That's a couple of thou a year more for you. What will it be? Seventeen, seventeen-five. You have another income. You can move to George-town. Or Chevy Chase, and really go with the high rollers."

Burns was expressionless, though surprised. But of course they would know about the gambling.

". . . A couple of thou more a year."

Burns smiled bleakly; he had no need of money.

"And a change of venue." The personnel man mentioned two countries, one in Asia and the other in Latin America. The Latin American country was an interesting proposition, no doubt about it. Its economy had even less to recommend it than the African. But other aspects were more favorable. It was clearly a nation in crisis.

"Not exactly the Soviet Union, is it?"

The personnel man smiled and shrugged.

"Or Germany."

"You know the ropes here now. You know us, we know you. We all get along together. We don't have to finish sentences, do we? Saves us a lot of bother both ways, no?"

"I suppose it does."

"There's another compensation. If you take the LatAm job, you can go down there for six weeks, see the place yourself. Eyeball it firsthand. We'll set you up. We're very liberal about that sort of thing, as you know. On your way down you can stop off at Puerto Rico, Freeport . . ."

"For the casinos?"

The personnel man smiled.

"Who do you think I am, Nick the Greek?"

". . . Break up the return trip in Jamaica, Tobago."

"Six weeks, you say."

"More or less."

Burns mused: "It takes time to really get into these countries. They're complicated. The people, the statistics. It takes time to know what makes them tick . . ."

"This place is no Girard-Perregaux, Burns."

"And when I get back?"

The personnel man explained the job again, and its title. The location of the office, and the men immediately above and below him. His superior would be a man sixty-one years old, near retirement. Burns would be in line. From there would come a shot at the Secretariat itself, the Board. If everything broke right, Burns would be on the front line, on the inside, at forty-five, forty-six years old.

"I've always thought about the field."

The personnel man said nothing, and looked at the clock on the wall.

"Give me a week to decide?"

"Of course."

"I want to check in with some friends at State. Get another opinion. It's a radical move."

"State's agreeable," the personnel man said quickly.

"Oh?"

"Quite agreeable."

Burns shook his head. His old friend the DCM in Bonn was correct. Once he'd left the Department, there was no returning. He'd left their files, become a memory attached to another agency. Others now competed for attention. It always happened in government; once you broke your career chain it was curtains, and you ceased to exist. You were elsewhere, no longer in their control. Burns supposed that the State Department suspected that he'd picked up bad habits at Langley; they assumed no one ever *quit* the place, as indeed no one ever did. The procedures were different, and these would become habits that would divide his loyalties. That was the other thing they thought about, the loyalty of the man to his agency. That was critical, particularly if you were truly of the bureaucracy and on your way up, not an inner and outer, but a career professional man. If your loyalty were divided, there was no end of potential disagreement and therefore of conflict and strife. You were not a man whom they could count on in a crisis.

"I'll tell you in a week," Burns said.

"I don't understand this one thing," the personnel man said. "What exactly is your reluctance? You've a clear shot here."

"I always wanted to be a diplomat."

"Well, there's a lot of action here. More than the other place. You're doing essentially the same thing, analysis. It's just going into a different pipeline. And of course . . ."

"You know, the Congress of Vienna."

". . . you're anonymous."

"That's the only thing that appeals to me," Burns said.

JAMES S. KENARY

Going Home

(FROM THE MASSACHUSETTS REVIEW)

HE CAME IN FEELING GOOD. It's funny, he thought, that I should be feeling this way, but what the hell, I'll be going home now, and my wound isn't so bad that it will be with me forever. The medics rushed Will from the chopper, stopping momentarily to check his leg, then moved inside and set him on a rack in a small, makeshift emergency room. He moved his head stiffly to one side and was suddenly frightened by the sight of a massive, fat man peppered with red marks ringed in blue and with thick, white patches on his eyes. It was hard for him to look at the man, so he turned away, but he could still hear the hard, sputtering gasps of his breathing, and he felt very sorry and sick.

The nurses came by and cut away his clothing and his boots that dripped blood in a trail along the floor, and then a young, pale doctor put a needle into the bend in his arm and attached a bottle of clear fluid to a metal pole above his stretcher. Without his clothes he felt cold, but he did not mention it because he was finally safe, and he did not want to lose that. A nurse stopped by him and punched a needle into his upper arm and he smiled into her face. She smiled too, and rushed away as quickly as she had come. He apologized for not having worn underwear, but she had gone and did not hear him.

The room was crowded with wounded men after the attack, and Will liked the excitement and the security. He wished that one of the nurses would spend some time with him, touch him, but none of them could stop. His blood was rushing through him madly and he felt fully alive like after an attack when all of them would come together and talk about it wildly.

A medic, starched and uneasy, approached him clutching a clipboard.

"Can you talk?" he asked timidly.

"Sure," Will said, glad to have a release. "What do you need?"

"I've got to get some information as long as you're able to talk."

"Okay."

"What's your name?"

"Garrett, William S."

"Service number?"

"Two-two-three-eight-seven-nine-eight."

"Would you like anyone to be notified of this?"

"No," Will said sharply. "Underline that, will you?"

"Don't worry. No one will be notified."

"That's the main thing, okay? Make sure of it, will you?"

"Sure. Really. Don't worry about it." The medic looked at Will for the first time, expression grave, as if trying to understand the intensity of the demand.

A nurse went by, then stopped and looked back at Will. He felt good having her eyes on him, but it did not excite him in a sexual way. It was the same feeling he had had when the small village girls had clung to him as he passed through their streets, then watched him move away.

"I'm sorry about not having worn underwear, Nurse," he called, raising himself with his elbows. "I don't wear any in the bush. None of us do. Anyway, I didn't plan on this."

"That's all right. I've seen it before. Just don't make it a habit."

Will laughed with the nurse and was suddenly ecstatic with the affection in her voice, the security of the room, and the knowledge that soon he would be going home. He would settle for the clean comfort of the hospital for a few days, but not for longer, because still there would be the distance, the inmeasurable space between the war and the dream, and until that had been closed, nothing could soothe his fear.

Another man was carried in and set down next to Will. He recognized him as someone from his own unit who had gotten it from the same round, and whom he had tried to help before realizing that his own leg was hit and immovable. He had not known him well, but now he felt that they were very close and wanted desperately to console him.

"Hey, Bart? How are you feeling?"

Bart groaned, almost wailed. Will was frightened by the transformation that had taken place in him since the wound. The sobbing and the writhing and the setting had changed him into another man, an apparition, and his face seemed relined and misshapen. He was incomplete, formless, as if something more than skin and blood and bone had been torn from his body, and Will thought sadly that he would never know him as he had been before this day.

"Are you okay, Bart?" Will leaned toward him. "Do you want me to call someone?"

"Did it go through?" Bart asked, teeth clenched and caked with dried dirt and pieces of brush. "Can you see if it went through?"

"You mean through your leg? I'll look." Will hung over the edge of his stretcher. He could not see well through the thick, clotted blood, but he knew that it had gone through and that only a few pieces of the leg were left. He looked away and worked himself squarely back onto his stretcher. A hard clod burned in his throat. He turned his head toward Bart again who was lying with his eyes shut, his parched lips moving, searching for saliva.

"It's okay, Bart. It didn't go through. You're going to be all right. Really."

The nurses were around Bart now and they seemed worried as they prepared him for surgery. He cried, sensing the urgency, but a medic jabbed a needle into his arm, and after a short, spasmodic fit of trembling, his body relaxed and his head dropped limply to the side. Will felt better that Bart was unconscious, but he could hear that the fat man was dying and he wanted to be taken away from the death.

He had seen a man die once before—an enemy—and had remembered it clearly since then, especially in the night when he had tried to sleep it away. They had found him on a trail, pushed like heaped clothing to the side, and his breathing had been like the fat man's, enormous explosions of sputtering life, and his legs and his chest had moved convulsively. They had all stopped and watched him die, and some had even laughed toughly through it, jabbing and kicking at the dying man. Will was remembering that now as he listened to the sporadic bursts of half-life next to him, and he did not want to see it again, or to be near it. He called a medic.

"He's dying, medic," he whispered.

The medic nodded. "Yeah, I know."

"Can't you move him?"

"No room now. We'll have to wait," he said moving away. "It won't be long."

The medic was gone and Will knew that he would have to see it and hear it and remember it again. His leg began to throb and burn, and the coolness of the room became damp. He could hear the fat man going, and the nurses were suddenly next to him with a doctor, and there were muffled voices combined with gasps, and then it was very quiet, except for the rustling of a sheet and the wooden sounds of the stretcher.

Will was uncomfortable next to the dead man. It seemed that a wet coldness came from that side, a gnawing, persistent reminder of the death, of its finality, and Will shivered, his naked body defenseless against the severe chill. For a long time, he waited on his stretcher listening to the *hack-hacking* of the choppers outside and to the moaning and the crying and the frightened laughter in the room. He looked at the ceiling, not wanting to see any more of the wounded men, or the nurses who were too busy for him. He tried to forget the pain in his leg and wished that he could sleep or dream of going home. But his mind and his body were tense, inflexible, and would not allow it. He still relished the cleanness and security of the hospital, but he had lost the ecstasy he had felt in the beginning when its detachment and its safety had been new, and when the nurse had stopped to joke and laugh with him.

Finally two medics rolled him onto a movable stretcher and pushed him down a hallway full of thick heat into a small, steaming room.

"X ray," the medic announced. "Give this to the doctor when he gets to you." He handed Will a manila envelope.

Will started to ask a question, but the medic had gone. He had wanted to know why he was being treated this way, why the nurses hadn't grouped around him, talked to him, touched him, why he was being made to hold his own records. I'm wounded, he thought. I shouldn't have to do this. How about a little consideration, or do I have to be dying to get that? Maybe if I had my leg shot off like Bart. That might do it. That might at least earn me a pat on the head. Oh, cut this out. Forget it. I'm going home. That's all that matters. I've got a good wound. If the nurses don't have time for me, the hell with it. I'll be out of here in a few days anyway.

The doctor came and asked to see Will's records. Will was glad to have some attention.

"So you got it in the leg, huh? How's it feel?" the doctor asked.

"Not too bad. It burns a little."

"Well, we'll take a look at it and see how deep the piece is, okay?" The doctor turned. "Medic, wheel this man into x ray."

The medic pushed Will into the dark room. "You're going to have to get up on the table so I can get a picture. Can you move by yourself or are you going to need some help?" His voice was cold.

"I can do it." You arrogant bastard, Will thought. I wouldn't let you help me if both my legs were shot off. Will pulled himself slowly, painfully, onto the table, dragging his bad leg across the stretcher. The burning intensified with movement and he closed his teeth and his eyes, battling the pain and the indignation. They're making me pay for it, he thought, watching the stiff leg slide sluggishly along the table. Going home is never easy when the wound is a good one.

After the x rays had been taken and given to Will in the manila envelope, he was wheeled to the pre-op room, a noiseless tomb that seemed to have a pain of its own. A nurse greeted him, took the envelope, and looked firmly into his eyes. He could feel a loosening process take place, a gentle, flowing heat that moved along the senses, relaxing them, obscuring the injustice, and he smiled thankfully in return.

"Aren't you cold?" she asked. "You must be freezing with this air-conditioning the way it is. I'll get you a blanket." She left briskly, and Will sat up slightly to watch her. She wasn't pretty, but she had a special beauty that came from the moment and from his need for her. She looked strange in the green clothes and jungle boots, but they didn't matter. None of that mattered now as it had once before.

She returned with a blanket and covered Will. "The doctor will be here soon," she said. "We've all been pretty busy."

"I know," Will said. "This was the worst it's ever been. They must have hit us with everything they had."

"I hope it ends soon." She sighed, lowering her eyes.

"Why are you here?"

"I guess it's because of my brother. He was killed here." She looked at Will; her face showed a composed sadness. "At first I came here because of him, but now it's for something else. It wasn't right when it was only for him." She smiled easily, as if from some exclusive knowledge or recollection.

Will was watching her so closely that he was not aware of the silence. He was studying the smile and the eyes and the thin, fine lines that trailed delicately beneath them. The mouth still held the smile, as one holds onto hope, and the eyes were bright and clear.

"I hope it ends soon too," he said finally, disrupting the silence. "I don't want any more of it."

"It will." She touched his head lightly.

He was sorry when she left, but his body was loose and relaxed now, and he had forgotten the bad treatment. He closed his eyes and waited for the doctor. More men were being carried in on stretchers and he listened to the movement. Some were crying and swearing strongly, others were quiet, pensive, like himself.

The doctor came and looked briefly at Will's wound without speaking. Here we go with the cold treatment again, Will thought, but his bitterness had ebbed because of the nurse, and he looked into the light on the ceiling that hung swaying with the air of the room. He wanted it to end. Take the piece, sew the wound, and send me home. That's all. Do it fast and well, and then I'll leave you. I'll just forget some of the bad treatment because I know what a strain it must be taking care of all these guys. I realize how hard it must be to watch them crying and dying and going home. I understand. So I'll forget it. Just fix me up, and I'll be gone, because I've got a going home wound.

"Are you sleeping?" Will heard the nurse's voice, as if from a vast, peaceful distance. He opened his eyes.

"I'm going to wash your wound now so that the doctor can look for the fragment." She smiled and Will was warmed again. He lifted his head to watch her work, but not to see the wound.

"How does it look?" he asked.

"Good. It's a clean wound, but it may be deep."

"I'll be glad to have it out," he said looking beyond her to a stretcher being wheeled from the operating room. He could not see the face of the man on it, but he knew that it was Bart. He watched the medics for a sign, an indication of Bart's condition, but their expressions were tired and vacant, and revealed nothing. The condition of all men is the same to them, Will thought. Blood and skin, life or death. That is why I cannot read their faces. But I know that it is bad. I can feel that myself without having to watch them, and I am sorry that I never knew him until the wound, because now it is too late.

"Do you know anything about him?" Will motioned toward the stretcher with his eyes.

"Who?" The nurse looked up.

"That one. The one they're wheeling out."

"He lost his leg." She faced Will. "Do you know him?"

"He was in my unit. I tried to help him today, but I couldn't move."

"There was nothing left of it. They would have saved it if they could, but it was almost all gone." Her eyes closed for an instant before she looked down.

"I know. I saw it. I told him it was all right. But he knew that I was lying. Maybe I should have told him the truth."

"No." Her head came up sharply. "You were right. He'll know the truth soon enough, and if he remembers, he'll forgive you."

Will felt her working on his leg, and despite the pain, he wanted her to go on. The rubbing of the cloth against the wound drove heat into his thigh, and stabbing, steellike pains into his knee and ankle and foot, but the hand that did not work, except to hold his leg steady and to comfort him, seemed to stop the worst of it, the agony, from moving further than the wound itself. It could have forced its way into his system and made him suffer, but she controlled it with her hand and her touch, and the pain was good because it let him feel her more. His eyes without his mind watched the light above him. If only he could carry this with him—this good, comfortable feeling from the nurse—and use it to get him by the details, it could be very easy. Stay with me, he begged silently. Make it easy for me, and I'll take you away from the war. But that's not what you want, is it? You told me about it before and I could sense then that you loved it here, that, for you, this is more important than going home. You have come here to calm and soothe, and to watch the grateful faces of men like myself, and if that is what you want and need, then I am all for it, if only somehow I could keep it exclusively until I am home. But that would be selfish, and I could not ask you to stay by me alone. And so, I will have to leave without you, but I will always remember your love for this place as compared to my contempt, and because you have shown it to me so clearly, I will understand.

She finished with the cleaning and went to find the doctor. The leg was cool where the wet cloths had been pressed, but without her hands rubbing and moving there, the pain began to run beyond the wound, surging hotly, then icily, then hotly and icily again and again in flashing repetitions that made the heat and the cold the same, indistinguishable. He shut his eyes and felt anger tears forming and a damp hardness in his throat that would make them come unless he could stop the thrust now before it took him over. Think of it, he thought. It's almost here. What you've been waiting for. Going home. The doctor will come to tell you soon. He'll say it when he sees the wound. "Well, it looks like you're going home with this one," he'll say. And you won't smile too wide, because you don't want to lose it now. So you'll just nod and sigh and close your eyes and say, "Yeah, I guess so," but inside you'll be repeating the words, celebrating them, and you'll know that it has finally come—the beginning of the going home process—and you will suddenly be sure of keeping your life, and be beautifully on your way. On your way home.

Will continued to imagine how the process would be, and how he would pass through each separate stage of the trip home. When he could think of it no longer, because of the anxiety that was beginning to sicken him in the stomach, he sat up and scanned the room. He liked it now only because it seemed invulnerable, separate from the war and the world, surrounded by cold space. But he hated it for its lifelessness and its well-scoured dullness, and he wondered if men who might have lived died because of it. He was angry that those who worked here had never noticed the passive quality of the walls, had never thought to paint them, to make them more alive, more hopeful. The room had the same stillness as the places he had been just before or after battle, and it did not help a man to recover, or to want to recover. It's because none of them here know how it is in the bush, he thought, that they make it like this. If they knew, they would change it, and more men would live or recover because of it. But maybe they don't want it that way. And as much as he hated to think of that, he felt that it might be true, that possibly there was a reason for the deathly color of this room, and suddenly he believed it and was frightened.

The nurse was next to him and his fear. "Are you afraid?" She bent close to him.

"I don't know." He fell back on his stretcher. "I've just been thinking and it hasn't done me much good."

"Do you want something? Something to make you sleep?"

"No." He breathed more easily. "Not that. What I really need is to be on my way home. That's all that can help me, except your being here, which is a damn good substitute."

"I guess that's what all of us need."

He did not like the answer because of its righteousness, and he looked away, eyes closed.

"The doctor should have been here," she said, as if aware that she had been too curt. "But he's terribly busy, and there's been some bad wounds."

"I'll wait."

"Are you sure you're all right?"

"I'm fine," he said, then turned to watch her go.

He was asleep when the doctor came and did not feel the needle that was pumping in his leg to numb it. He wanted to be more awake, but he could not return easily, and he felt that he was losing some of the goodness and the excitement of the process. His eyes fluttered between sleep and consciousness; he could not hold or control them. He perceived only in stages and felt nothing. There was a great distance from him to the doctor, who was at the wound, and an even greater distance from there to the end of his leg that he could see vaguely, as if it were a part of the wall, or another body. He wanted it closer to himself. He wanted the total experience, from the beginning to the end, because now it was for him, finally and surely for him. For too long it had been withheld and he had begun to think that he might never have it, but now with the wound and the removal from the war, he knew that a change was taking place.

The doctor was working with difficulty, and Will was jarred by the pulling and the digging in his leg. There was no feeling, only rough movement. He lay still and wooden, more confident, more in control than he could remember since the day that he had been taken and prepared for war. He was certain that he was on his way now, and he was anxiously happy. He wondered how long the doctor would work and how big the piece would be. He wondered too about the words he would be told with, how they would sound, how he would react. It was coming closer. All of it was a service to him now, a preparation. I'll let it happen, he thought. I'll just lie here, and then when the words come I'll play it out right, and from there, they can wheel me through the rest of it. It will be slow, and I'll worry through it, but it will be nothing like the bush and the searching and the hurting. Now, if only it would start, I would feel better, and I could prepare myself for all of it, because even though it is what I want and need and love, it will not be easy.

And when the doctor stopped working and seemed finished, Will tensed with the excitement of the impending announcement. The doctor looked tired. His eyes were set deep and framed roughly with wild, scowling lines like trenches. Will hated and respected him immediately.

"How do you feel?" he asked Will with a voice that seemed to come from somewhere other than his mouth.

"Not too bad."

"I'm sorry we didn't get to you sooner, but we've had so many worse ones that we had to take them according to their condition."

"That's okay. Did you get the piece?"

"No, I couldn't find it." The doctor frowned. "It must be deep, and it's probably not worth going in after. Sometimes it does more harm than good, digging through all that muscle."

"You mean I'm always going to have it in my leg?"

"Maybe not. A lot of times shrapnel will work its way right through the skin. One day it might just pop out," he said smiling. "Your piece may stay there, though, because it's very deep. Scar tissue will form around it, and it will probably be there for the rest of your life." The doctor seemed pleased to be giving the details.

"What about infection?" Will asked. "Could it get infected?"

"It could, but it's not likely. When the shrapnel entered your leg it was so hot it was sterile. Actually you're very lucky. It looks good, and you shouldn't be bothered by it after it heals."

The doctor went to the end of the stretcher and picked up the chart that had been left there. He wrote in it hurriedly, occasionally lifting his eyes to study the wound while Will lay silently watching his abrupt, professional movements, hating them terrifically, but depending on them to keep his hope alive. When the doctor had finished writing he called a nurse and handed her the folder. He glanced once again at Will's wound, then walked away quickly. Suddenly, as if remembering a small obligation, he spun and returned to Will.

"Okay!" He slapped Will heavily on the good leg. "You can go back to your unit now. Stop by in about four days and we'll sew you up. We have to leave the wound open for awhile in case of infection."

Will tensed and smiled incredulously at the doctor who was ready to leave, to discard his case without sending him home.

If he had not planned so carefully the details of his trip home, if he had not created the stages so precisely, he could have turned and strained for a moment, allowing the truth to settle. But he had projected beyond his limit, had built a certainty from a hope and a need.

"You want me to go back to my unit?" Will asked.

"Can you get someone to pick you up?" The doctor did not feel the plea.

"I don't know. I guess so," Will stammered. "They were pretty well scattered when I left, but there should be someone around. Can I call from here?"

"Sure. Right over there."

"Do you think the piece will ever have to come out?"

"I don't think so. It shouldn't bother you much. There might be some nerve damage, but it will only be minor."

How can I say it, Will thought. How can I tell him what I want? Please doctor, send me home. I'll pay for it. I'll send money to you for the rest of my life. Just let me out of here, I've seen enough, I'll never make it. They'll get me again. There was a time when I thought I couldn't be hit. But I've lost that now, and I'm terrified. I'm fucking terrified. What stops me from telling you, begging you? I shouldn't care what you think. I can't go out there again, that's all. There's nothing left to prove. I'm a target now, a wounded, limping fear-target, and everything is pointed at me. They'll get me for sure. I can't escape them. Come on! Say it! Tell him how you feel. Tell him you can't go back out there. Tell him you won't.

The doctor broke the pause. "Is there anything else I can do?"

Will was roused from the warring in his mind. "No. No, thank you. I'll be all right, I guess. I'll be back in four days."

"Good. I'll see you then." The doctor rushed away, leaving Will shaken and weak, a great, scalding wetness in his eyes. He tried to rise and sit, but the trembling in his body stopped him, and he fell back, working to control the outrage. His eyes were closed to restrain the rush of tears that he could feel coming, his arms were up across his face to hide the breakdown. He waited for the torrent to burst and over-whelm him, but mysteriously it lost its intensity, and he could feel its stinging dissipation, its dryness, and suddenly he was alone with the realization that he was not going home.

He lay motionless, arms still across his eyes, until he could think of it no longer. The room was almost empty now, and he sat up slowly, squint-eyed, forcing movement, hating it, wincing from the pain. He stretched his legs out fully in front of him, testing them for strength. Why couldn't I tell him? Why couldn't I explain to him how I feel? He might have let me go. It might have been easy. If I had asked him, I would have known. But I was afraid. Of what he'd think? Of my own cowardice? Haven't I learned anything here? None of that matters anymore. Staying alive is all that is important. But I used to do the same thing in the bush. We'd come back in to the rear area and get together at night, and I'd say I'm never going back out there again. And then, the next day when the order came down and all of them started putting their gear together and grumbling about the war, I'd do it too, and I'd go right back out there and get into it again. Won't I ever learn? It's like a curse, and the worst thing about it is that someday it might just kill me.

Will lifted his good leg over the edge of the stretcher and let it hang down loosely. He watched it swing, freely, easily, and thought of the other leg, stiff and hot, and of how difficult it would be to move. When he was ready, he stretched the good leg to the floor and put his weight on it, at the same time sliding the other one cautiously to the edge of the stretcher. The burning started with the pulling, and when he had finally dragged it over and down, the pain was more severe than if he had set it into a deep fire. He dropped his head.

The nurse saw his pain and came to him.

"Can I help?" She bent to see his face.

"I think I'm going to need some crutches and something to wear."

"You mean the doctor didn't give you anything?"

Will shook his head in his hand, then looked up, eyes fierce. "No, he didn't give me anything. Not a goddamn thing."

"Well, I'll get you some, okay? I'll be right back."

Will dropped his head again, sorry that he had shown his

contempt. The nurse returned immediately with the crutches, and he took them indifferently.

"The medic is getting you some pants," she said. "We're all out of shirts."

"It doesn't matter."

"I hope you'll be all right."

Will did not respond. He knew that he could not have her anymore. The medic brought the pants.

"Can I help?" the nurse asked.

"You can hold the crutches."

He bent at the waist and strained, fitting the bad leg into the pants. The other leg went in more easily, but the burning was greater from the shift of weight. When he stood up, his face was fever red, and he turned away from the nurse as he buttoned his pants, calming himself.

"Will you be back to see the doctor?" she asked.

"In four days." Will struggled forward.

"Maybe I'll see you then." She moved next to him.

"Maybe."

At the door she left him, and he did not watch her or look back into the barren room. He leaned heavily on his crutches, squeezing the handgrips until the heels of his palms were chafed, but he did not reach for the door. Instead, he thought of what he had lost, of what the war would be like now that he had come so close to being removed from it. Without this, he thought, I could have made it, but now that I have seen it and touched it and it has fooled me, I am not right for going back. Oh Christ, I hate to think of leaving here. I cannot control my fear. It has me completely, and I'm only moving because I have not yet died. But I will die. I'm sure of it. They'll destroy my chance to live again, to return home. Oh God, what can I do?

Will opened the door brashly and was struck with a rush of light and heat that held all of it again—the discomfort, the lethargy, the uselessness—and it sucked in at him, as air would rush into a vacuum. For a moment, he floundered in the brilliance of the sunlit hallway, attempting to adjust to the sudden change.

When he could see clearly, he stopped and looked down the narrow hallway. Standing against the wall opposite him were two of them—the lieutenant and the Top. They had come to take him back. Will froze, afraid to face them, afraid to submit himself once more to their authority. He saw their pallid faces, despising them, possessed entirely now by the horror of the return. They hated him. He knew that. They had come only as a formality. Their offer of concern, their willingness to help, was nothing more than a means of priming him for recovery, of keeping as many men as possible between them and the war.

They didn't even wait for my call, Will thought. They're frantic. And so, now I've lost my chance to return to the unit at my own pace. I could have made my way back slowly, but now that they are here to pick me up, it is too late. I cannot fool myself any longer. They will take me—the ones who make it worse than the actual war, the ones that made the war for all of us—and now it will never be the same. Oh God, I hate to think of going back, of fighting it again, of losing it. The leg will heal and they will watch it and know when I am ready, and although I'll try to hide it, I will not evade their plan. They'll send me out again and I'll remember all of it as it was—the going home process. The whole of it. And I will think only of how close it seemed to take me to the proper distance from the war land, how close I seemed to home.

Will did not speak to them. He did not have to, now. He had something more than they had, something because of them, and he accused them with his silence. They went outside to bring the truck around, and Will moved slowly down the long hallway toward the intense brightness at the end. He could see it in the open door and remember the feel of it and how it had burned his eyes. He knew that he would be in it soon, just as he had been in it before the wound, and now, convinced at last that the possibility of escape was finally gone, and that he would never have it again, the crying began, first with a series of spasms, then with weaknesses in his legs, and then with an explosion of tears that dropped him to the floor in a heap like the man he had seen on the trail that day and had not been able to cry for.

WALLACE E. KNIGHT

The Way We Went

(FROM THE ATLANTIC MONTHLY)

WE WERE AT AN ARTFULLY CHOSEN SPOT about forty yards from the bridge and near the graveled driveway of a store, our suitcases side by side so that sign on Fooey's—GOING TO—and on mine—CHARLESTON?—composed what we thought was a clever plea. From there we could see south-bound cars coming for a full half mile. We knew we would have plenty of time to get up and stand attentively behind our suitcases, cupping cigarettes discreetly, so that any driver, having slowed down to take the sharp turn at the end of the bridge, would see us at our best, smiling and thumbing.

Fate, driving a pickup, had left us at Adrian, and so Fooey and I had looked the situation over and walked across the bridge and established our station where the grass was deep and pleasant. We sat and smoked. The sun was high. Four or five cars passed.

Before us the two stingy lanes of Route 4 curved marvel-ously around a hill to descend to French Creek and the bridge. We watched the point of the road's appearance hope-fully.

And here came a car like a panther, alternately black and twinkling as its glass caught the sun, coming so fast its roar down the hill didn't reach us for a second. It started to brake and throw dust halfway down, touching the berm and swaying; momentarily it was hidden behind trees and a build-ing, and then it was on the bridge, screeching, and Fooey and I jumped up slack-jawed and stuck our thumbs out.

191

The car had to slow down. It almost stopped, whipping sideways and spraying dust and gravel, and then it was by us and I glimpsed two faces, thrust up near the windshield.

I thought I saw sparks. The car skidded and crouched and stopped, and then shifted and started coming back, and a man hung out of the door yelling.

At such times there are things to be done. I grabbed my suitcase and jumped back, and Fooey reached for his and fell over it, onto the pavement, kicking by the time he hit until he was standing up again with grit in his palms and bag retrieved. I caught the back of his jacket and jerked, and his heels came down on my toes. We swayed together, occupying nearly the same space.

Over the gunning of the engine came voices. They were shouting "Get in! Get in!" and so we got in fast, interlocked, and sprawled across the pinstriped back seat. The car started forward, and I twisted up and slammed the door.

Nobody said anything for a moment, and then the driver, pulling the car into high, raised his chin and tilted back toward us. "You fellows going to Charleston?"

"Yes, sir," said Fooey.

"Well, you're lucky because that's where we're going," said the driver. The speedometer needle climbed steadily to 80.

He was a plump man, thirty-five or forty, with a creased roll of fat across the back of his neck that a baseball cap leaned on, its bill pointing toward the sun visor. Brown hair stuck out all around it. I glimpsed, as he turned—he bounced around a lot, fixing his fingers on the steering wheel and shifting his weight—a long nose, lean for his round face. One ear was higher than the other.

"I'm Bruce Hammond," he said, straightening the car out of a gentle turn and accelerating to 95, which until that day was as fast as I'd ever seen a car go. He threw the words over his shoulder. "This is Merv York. How about you boys switching places and you"—indicating me—"pull your box over in front of your feet and leave the other one in the middle."

I slid over and squared my suitcase across my ankles, as instructed, and Fooey climbed across me and then sat back, looking ill.

"What's your name, son?" the driver said, apparently to both of us, jerking his head again in our direction.

"Harold Fletcher," said Fooey. "I go to school in Buckhannon, and we were looking for a ride to Charleston to go home. For the weekend." He said this very fast, as if he were driving 95.

I told them my name and said we appreciated getting picked up and then I asked the question. "What are you driving so fast for?"

The driver laughed, and the other man—York—laughed too, cautiously, and then York said they liked to get where they were going so they could relax when they got there. He was a lean man, younger than Hammond, with dark, darting, humorless eyes.

"You're going to get a long weekend," he added. "You'll get lots of time to spend in Charleston."

"Hell, Merv, go ahead and tell them," said Hammond. "You tell them, and I'll get us going."

Already we had crossed over into Lewis County, flying up the valley of the right fork of the Buckhannon River. In a brand-new high-bodied Hudson sedan. Quick. With pinched-in sides, vestigial running boards, thunder.

So Merv told us. "We got this bet. We bet this car can get us from the front of the courthouse in Buckhannon to the front of the court house in Charleston in two hours flat. Got a hundred dollars each on it, and we took off at one o'clock sharp."

Two hours. I think it's 136 miles. And these guys were going through country where the creeks planned the roads, with towns and railroad tracks and one-way bridges and farmers everywhere driving wagons.

Fooey was pale, I noticed, and I think I was, too.

"Why did you pick us up?" I asked.

"You're ballast," said York, grinning.

And that's the way we went to Charleston once in the spring of 1947, through lovely country that few people know, relatively speaking, as the world is so large. We went out of Upshur County and across the southern neck of Lewis, past Ireland, which is a cluster of cottages in green, and into the watershed of the Little Kanawha, into Braxton County, to

Falls Mills and Bulltown, out of the Kittanning coal country and into the Pittsburgh seams, across the Roanoke syncline and the Orlando anticline, through Wine Gap to Heaters and Flat Woods, and then down Granny Creek to Sutton Junction.

And there, as you may know but probably have never had the chance to know, runs the Elk, shallow and sometimes clear, snaking and straggling all the way to Charleston, past some other remarkable places.

"Fooey," I whispered, leaning toward him as we swept into another turn. I wanted to ask him how we could get out. I nudged his leg. He never heard me, or at least he didn't look at me. "Fooey," I whispered, "for God's sake, listen here." He didn't.

Fooey, who later got killed in a motorcycle wreck, was skinny, dark-haired, had acne scars, and customarily was quietly pleasant. We roomed in the same house in Buckhannon, and there we had found we were both from near Charleston, not near enough to know the same people but familiar with the neighborhoods and football teams and so forth. We had thumbed back together two earlier Fridays during the winter, and we'd meet at the Greyhound station Sunday afternoons and ride the bus to Buckhannon on the slower, surer road through Spencer and Weston.

He got his nickname from a movie—I've forgotten its name—in which there was a ship's doctor named Louie who was a drunk. Harold Fletcher wanted to be a doctor, and he liked beer, so we started calling him Louie. He spoonerized well, and so became Fooey Letcher, but eventually the Letcher had been dropped.

This process can be harsh. A sophomore girl whose name was Dorothy Snider—Dottie—was turned into Snotty Dider, and I think it affected her personality. Fooey didn't seem to mind being spoonerized, though.

We had been taking some bad turns, and York swiveled and stared back at us.

"Boys," he said, "you're going to have to help a little. Lean away from the curves. Lean uphill. This car's tall, and we got to keep her square." Hammond nodded without saying anything, and so did Fooey and I. We were back to 80 now, and

Hammond had been straightening bends by easing over to the left when the road rolled left, touching the right berm when we turned right. He continued to bounce around and adjust his grip, and he'd mutter and even occasionally chuckle. He was pleased with the pace, I think.

I saw the Bulltown marker flash by, and saw the river and low field to the right. I had stopped here once while riding with an old couple from North Carolina, and we had read the brief statement of its history. Everyone should read markers.

Bulltown is notable only for a mistake.

There had been a man named Stroud who lived deep in the Glades of the Gauley. Once, in 1772, he came to Bulltown for salt, and got to know the Indians who lived there, a small band of displaced Delawares who were friendly and mild. When he went back south across the mountains to his home he found the bodies of his wife and children, scalped, and the trail of his livestock led back toward Bulltown.

So Stroud had taken off north again and as he trotted through the forest he quit grieving and started hating. He gathered friends from Hacker's Creek and the Buckongehanon country and led them back to Bulltown. There, in a few moments, they killed everybody. John Cutright, who lived to be 105, past the Mexican War, said they scalped the Delawares and threw the bodies into the Little Kanawha. It's quite shallow, so the mess must have been around for some time.

A few days later the men learned that Stroud's family had been murdered by Shawnees, who had purposely left signs pointing toward Bulltown. Tricked, damn it, Stroud sank out of history. A Mrs. Cutright was the cook for our rooming house, an admirable woman who baked excellent pigs in a blanket, and she said John was her great-grandfather. Bulltown was named for Captain Bull, a chief. A rush of wind and we were past it.

Nobody was talking, but the car was filled with noise. Both vane windows were open a quarter inch, and wind whistled across them, low and powerful and at the same time with a persistent warble modulated by every sway. Bumps brought loud clicks as well as jolts; the shock absorbers weren't what they should have been. And there was a rattle up front that I took, after analysis, to be a loose horn button. The seats made noises, and the frame creaked, and I felt that my body was making noises too. And from outside came the almost constant cry of the tires.

I looked out of the window directly to the side and could see almost nothing, as trees and weeds and grass blended into a yellow-green smear occasionally interrupted by a mud smear or a house smear. Little else was identifiable. A bridge was a noise, rather than something seen.

I have never enjoyed the rides at amusement parks or fairs; I get sick. A park manager told me once, with professionalism leaning on every word, that there were riding families and nonriding families, and if this is true, I'm from a nonriding family. The Hudson was becoming a car on a roller coaster, swooping and fluttering and falling, and queasiness crept in beside my fear. So I started looking ahead, over the driver's shoulder.

We came to a railroad track, a quick dip to the right, skidded, straightened out, and flew ahead, the road smooth and fast, and were in Flat Woods, a town that hadn't pulled itself together but stood in its own wide fields, with just a school and a few stores and neat homes.

Flat Woods, according to collectors of things, is the geographical center of West Virginia. I'm not sure how such things are decided. If you draw a line from the southernmost point in the state to its northern tip, and then from the farthest east to farthest west, the intersection is somewhere near Linden in Roane County, thirty miles east of Flat Woods. I never heard of anybody at Linden getting excited about this, but at Flat Woods there definitely is pride in centerness. If West Virginia didn't have such an irregular border, perhaps it would be easier to find the middle.

Flat Woods is where the Braxton County Monster visited in, I think, 1953 or 1954; actually, it was near Flat Woods. He was a great green giant ten feet tall with a red face and a helmet that seemed to have horns, and he landed on a forested hill and got out of his luminous spaceship to look around. The odor was harsh and penetrating and persistent, and this was vividly recalled by the woman and four boys who met him. They ran off, and presumably so did the monster. Others smelled the stink, though, and saw burned places.

If you think it is a small thing to be so visited, you're wrong. This monster stopped no place else on earth, but stood above Flat Woods and looked down toward Cedar Creek, and what visions he gained came from here and no place else. "It's a damp place," he could have said, "dewy and rather dark, but I made out many white oaks and shagbark hickories and meadows lined with thorns and sumac, and a fair amount of cedar. There was greenbrier pulling at my boots. The earth is beautiful."

Of course, this had not yet happened when Fooey and I and Bruce Hammond and York raced through there in 1947. But it was going to happen.

McNutt's next on Route 4, and then Karl's Siding on the B&O. It's on Granny Creek.

Hammond glanced back again. "You all watch this one," he said as we arced down an easy hill. "Right up here we're going to bust or win. This is where the trooper parks."

It was a flat statement, cold and reckless. We were coming to Sutton Junction, where the highway joins the Elk at an angle leading off east to Sutton itself, a placid, messy town. But here we had to turn acutely west. Prudent people drove up beside the restaurant and filling station at the junction, stopped, looked both ways, and eased off in low. We weren't going to do that, I knew.

I saw the restaurant and a clutter of gasoline pumps and cars in front of it. It seemed in the air flying at us. Hammond pumped the brake, jerking us, jerking down from 90 to 60 and sliding us forward in our seats. Then he cut off the road—right off the road and into a backyard tangle of garbage cans and junk behind the station, making a dust cloud that must have billowed for minutes, and sending a big dog up and over a barbed-wire fence like a deer. We dipped and the Hudson's body banged down on its springs and my head hit the roof hard. Down again and up again, with the car turning sideways under me. And then we were going west, with the calm Elk to our left, picking up speed and going faster and faster.

"I didn't see him," said York.

"I didn't either," Hammond answered.

So presumably the state trooper was someplace else.

"I didn't see him either," said Fooey.

The next place is Gassaway—another place to look out for, with two traffic lights, a bad bridge, two sharp turns a block apart, and a clutter of slow people.

Henry Gassaway Davis is the man it was named for, a gloriously rich man who made his money from coal and timber and railroads, and who entertained Presidents, looked out for things in the Senate (1871-1883), and went to international conferences in behalf of the interests of the United States. When he was young he lived for a while in a boxcar, and later he built the Coal & Coke Railroad, 175 miles long, that opened this part of the world so that its wealth could pour out. When the Coal & Coke came here, Gassaway was born. When Henry Gassaway Davis was an old man, he gave every school in West Virginia a state flag. On the whole he lived a good life, as he gave people things to do. He took long rifles out of their hands and gave them green and red lanterns to swing, and you must remember that this had never been done here before. He destroyed a wilderness, which once was considered commendable.

He preferred to ride horseback.

Over the bridge, into town, through a green light, through a red light, quick right past the depot, quick left to keep from landing on the tracks—his tracks—and we were out in the country again.

"That was Gassaway," York told us. "It's easy from here on in."

That is not necessarily true. It has never been true, as the hills are old and ragged. Sometimes, I've been told, even the creeks here have gotten lost. A man at Frametown once told me, as if he believed it—and he frowned and left when I laughed—that he had found a place where a creek got confused and tried to run up a hill. It had gone up and run into a hole under an overhang, and then had turned around and come back. Water ran both ways, he said; leaves floated upstream and down. It sounded to me as if he found a spring. But think of William Strange if you think that's odd, be-

cause Bruce Hammond now was getting us to Strange Creek.
I saw the store beside the riverbank a little ahead, and the
old steel bridge to the left, and the rush of the car smeared it
away. I looked back at it momentarily.

William Strange had come here in 1795 to hunt and to
map the ground. He was with a party that came up the Elk,
and actually they shouldn't have had any trouble. In 1795
there were forty or more people living in Charleston, which
had been chartered the year before; Kentucky already had
become a state; and the last man to die at the hands of Indians in this region, hapless Shadrack Harmon, was four years
buried.

But Strange got lost. He couldn't find his friends, and they
couldn't find him. He got hungry, but he couldn't get anything to eat. Maybe he lost his powder. And so he did a very
unusual thing. He carved a poem into a tree. It said, haunt-
ingly, with rhythm and grace:

> *Strange is my name*
> *And I'm on strange ground,*
> *And strange it is*
> *I can't be found.*

Probably it was a beech, with even gray bark and a trunk
large enough for such a message.

Several years later his rifle was found leaning there, and
his bones were nearby.

I'm not skeptical, as it's better to believe that improbable
things frequently occur than it is to demand the common-
place, but I do find William Strange's death inconsistent with
the nature of the region, so rich in game and fish and Queen
Anne's lace to eat. Perhaps he just sat out there and thought,
"I've written four lines too good to leave ..." Or perhaps
sometimes the streams do run back and forth.

Strange Creek is where the big bend in the Elk comes. On
to Villa Nova, which has a post office named Duck, by the
county line, by Ira and Groves to Ivydale, long and narrow,
past Standing rock, following closely the turns in the river to
Clay Junction. The magisterial district to the north had been
Otter; to the south, Buffalo. Now we were in Henry District,

man having come to conquer forests, and the fiercest barriers were behind.

Clay, seat of Clay County, is off Route 4 a mile or so; the road turns west from the river and runs up Lower Two Run toward Maysel and Laurel Creek. Lower Two is logically named; it is south of Upper Two. And so we went away from the valley of the Elk for a while, across the Handley syncline and the Hansford anticline and toward the Grassland syncline, along which the old oil field north of Bomont is located.

The character of the land changed as if Hammond were sweeping it away and substituting new sights by turning the Hudson's wheels. We went up and up, flashing past cottages set in nooks and stores held together with Nehi and Clabber Girl and SSS Tonic signs.

I tried to talk to York once, when he looked back.

"You guys live in Buckhannon?" I said tentatively.

"He does," said York, pointing to Hammond. "I live up at Lorentz."

"Do you all come this way a lot?" I asked.

"Not this way. We get to Sutton sometimes, but not down here. I haven't been here since I got drafted. It's too far."

"I can tell you some things about this road," Fooey broke in. "There's a God-awful turn up here a few miles, going down the hill to Procious. It just keeps turning. I'll tell you when we're coming to it."

Hammond had been sagging back a little, but now he bounced up again.

"Kid," he said, "you just hold your corner of the car down and I'll watch this corner. When we get to a turn I can't make I'll let you know."

I knew the turn Fooey meant. When we got there the tires started to scream, and they screamed, evenly and long, until we were through it. It wasn't bad. And we were back beside Elk River again.

In the next two miles we left Clay County and went into Kanawha County by King Shoals Run. Then we looped back into Clay County for a long bend, perhaps a thousand yards, and took off west once more. Behind us was farmland and riverland and tangled hills. Ahead was Clendenin, mainly on the other side of the river but still big enough to put cars in our path, and Falling Rock, Blue Creek, Elkview, Big Chimney—places where children and dogs played, trucks backed out, and buses and tank wagons and timber haulers crept.

"We're going to be coming to a lot of traffic," I said. "Have you figured on that?"

"Well, I figure on not stopping," Hammond answered after a pause. "Nothing's on the road here from noon until the school buses start out. And by the time they start, we'll be in Charleston."

I leaned up and got a quick look at York's wrist watch. It was 2:30 almost exactly.

When I looked ahead again there was a wall in front of us and Hammond was trying not to hit it. It was a dusty brown wall with red lights all over it and it was across half the road and towering over our windshield. I must have yelled, but I heard only the brakes and saw, like dust devils, two cars whip by us going east.

"Slow son of a bitch," York shouted. Hammond said something and then cut right, onto the narrow berm, and passed the truck on the right side. He whipped back into the roadway and Clendenin Bridge was before us. We sidestepped it. I looked back and saw the brown truck ponderously jackknifing just short of the abutment.

Fooey, who hadn't said anything since before Procious hill, started to speak now, very emphatically.

"You let me out of this goddamn car or I'll wreck it," he said. He threw himself against me. "We'll tip over on the next turn. Stop, or I'll throw your keys out!"

Behind his acne Fooey was white. He started to push me into the corner of the car, and then he began to bounce heavily, wildly.

"Boy," said York, swinging around lightly, "you're almost dead."

He looked straight at Fooey, but I felt the power of his gaze from my place deep in the corner.

"You're going to kill us all and lose my hundred dollars, and even if you live I'll kill you."

It was not a very logical thought, but it was effective. Fooey, as I did, had a vision of sundering steel and shattered glass, the car flipping over and over, and York rising from the wreckage and choking him and then all of us sinking into flame and going to hell together. Fooey shut up and slid over, and slowly, after more glowering, York turned around. We passed the refinery at Falling Rock and the high school and the funeral home at Elkview and the base of the chimney at Big Chimney, the chminey itself having been torn down long before.

Twenty till three. There was traffic: a bread truck, three cars, an RC delivery truck, and a stubby flatbed. We passed them all in one heroic rush, and then got caught behind an old Packard as other cars plugged the left lane. There was nothing to do except cut to 40 and fidget, which Hammond did. "Goddamn."

He started blowing the horn. He blew the car ahead of us off the road. Kids stared out of every window.

And so we went up the last hill and down, through Elk Forest, down and across railroad tracks with a bitter, skidding bounce, turned past a greenhouse, and roared on the straight stretch by the river—still the Elk, of course—toward the Charleston city limits. It was our last roar, and the needle reached 90. At ten till three.

I wasn't really scared anymore. I don't think Fooey was, either. We had begun anticipating an end to the ride, win or lose, and although I hadn't thought about getting out and saying thank you and watching the black Hudson drive off, I felt now this could happen.

Had I felt this at Flat Woods or Gassaway? I don't know. I don't think so. Gassaway was past, and consequently had become unreal. Strange Creek was not real, either—something imagined. And Villa Nova, where people sat waiting for the train on a bench at the end of the station, was so far away I'm not certain it ever existed. I've been there and watched the bustle, and they seemed like actual people, those who walked over and talked to the conductor, people from the other side of the Elk, but I know if you went there today they would not be there. Duck Post Office; a ridiculous name.

It was all a part of time's passage. Some passed there

slowly, turning over rocks and looking under them for mussels. Some, such as we, passed fast.

To become a part of a place, one must cut marks into it. Henry Gassaway Davis did, and so did William Strange. So, for that matter, did the Braxton County Monster, scarring the stone exposed by wind on Cedar Creek, burning a message: "Came from far off. Left something to talk about. I was more here than Grover Cleveland, and, as Grover Cleveland lived, so too did I."

Dodge to the right, over tracks and a rise past homes crowded on narrow lots; this was Bigley Avenue, Charleston. And we got behind a bus.

There wasn't any room to pass, none at all. A row of parked cars was beside us, the bus in front, and cars passing swiftly to our left. Hammond nosed out and dipped back, three times, four times. The bus let people off and took others on, stopping in the street as there was no place to pull over.

"We've got time," York yelped. "Seven minutes." He turned around and looked at me. "Now, where's the courthouse?"

"You don't know where it is?" I gasped. "You've come all this way and you don't know where to stop?"

"Bruce, this kid's arguing with me," York yelled just as Hammond jerked the wheel, gunned out, and stopped the other lane so that every car for a block rocked and began honking. The bus stopped too, and its horn was high-pitched and excited as we dipped in front of it. York flipped up on his knees in the front seat, facing me, with his arms dangling as if he wanted to grab me.

"I am not," I shouted. "I just didn't think you wouldn't know."

Hammond started shouting now, an awful noise in the car with the windows up. "How far is it and how do we get there?"

I had to think and couldn't. I'm not good at giving directions anytime. Fooey giggled and didn't try to save me, but I realized later it was a scared giggle.

"Well, there are several ways—" I started.

"Lord God!" screeched York. "Point!"

I pointed straight ahead, down Bigley, felt like crying, and then collected myself. "Straight ahead to the next railroad tracks, and then turn left, over to Pennsylvania Avenue, and then right on down to Virginia Street. It's maybe a mile or so."

York deflated. He sank back to his seat and pointed for Hammond, who was shaking his head slowly from side to side. He seemed unaware that cars were all around us, moving slowly, and that we were dodging them with sometimes only inches to spare. As if in slow motion, but terribly fast, Hammond drove up to their bumpers, blew, gunned, braked.

They had expected a tall building with an enormous clock, a stone building at the very center of a round city, and consequently they hadn't asked if this were so. Buckhannon's courthouse doesn't have to be inquired about, nor does Clay's or Sutton's. Why should Charleston's?

Fooey's finger tips gouged my leg, and when I realized what it was I remembered he had been poking at me for a long time—for seconds. I looked irritably toward him. He mouthed words I couldn't hear, and then I heard.

"Take them over the Spring Street bridge," he said. "It's quicker."

Spring Street led to a part of town I didn't know much about, a tangle of warehouses and wholesale places and can-covered lots; and the bridge itself was narrow and old. I didn't want to go that way. It would be too easy to get mixed up and lost.

Why did Fooey do this, confusing me when I had enough trouble already? York turned around to Fooey, bright eyes narrow, and shouted:

"What did you say about a bridge?"

"Fooey, you gutless bastard," I shrieked, "they're not going to let you off at any bridge. We're going to win this thing if you'll shut up!"

York sneered and spun away, and Fooey and I looked at each other. Neither of us said anything. I tried to create an expression that indicated I'm sorry but I'll explain later, but I couldn't. Fooey's expression was shocked and awful.

Ten seconds and we crossed Spring Street, and I looked left, trying to take in the view photographically. I saw Spring

Street bridge and it was empty. Not a car or a person on it. And Fooey saw it too.

Hammond sped on and I leaned forward and pointed the way across his shoulder. He cursed the cars. Space seemed to pluck at us. Hammond fought it, but nothing helped.

More cars crept into our way, more and more and more, and then there were the traffic lights at Washington Street and Fayette, and the one at Virginia Street. Every one was red. Finally we turned onto Virginia and went up its wide old arching bridge with our tires chipping on and off the gleaming unused trolley tracks. We were past the center and going down when York sighed and threw back his head.

"Quit it, Bruce," he said. "We lost. We lost two minutes ago."

Almost imperceptibly our pace slackened. Hammond eased, but very gently. "Are you sure?" he said.

"Yes. Just over two minutes."

We rolled, glided, coasted, stopped. Another red light. Virginia Street was busy, but not too busy; an ordinary afternoon.

"Now," said Hammond. "Where's the courthouse?"

"Just up there on the right. It's the stone building with the tower," Fooey told them. "It's too bad you lost," he added.

I scooted back and turned toward Fooey, full face. We looked at each other, and then he said, only to me, but loud and evenly, "Of course you could have won if you weren't so goddamn dumb."

Oh God, Fooey. He stared at me and I turned away and Hammond pulled over to the curb at Summers Street, stopping the car so that it rocked. He jerked down the bill of his ball cap and the two of them, Hammond and York, both turned around.

"Now, you just tell me, kid, where I was so dumb," Hammond said, low and angrily.

"Well," Fooey told him, like a lecturer, "first, you wasted a minute picking us up. You could have sandbagged the back of this car. And second, you could have driven at night and missed all the traffic. Your bet was for two hours—any two hours."

Hammond looked at York and I kept watching Fooey, but

now he wouldn't look at me. And then Hammond sighed.

"I guess you're right. Damnation, you're right. But I don't like to be called dumb right after I lose a hundred dollars."

York laughed. It was the only time he had laughed since we got in the car. It was a high-pitched snorting. "That's the best time, Bruce," he said. "That's the right time."

I opened the car door and pulled my suitcase up on my knees. I was embarrassed, and, too, I was feeling the absence of sound. I seemed in a hollow. So I asked a question just before I got out, partly to fill in and partly to know.

"Tell me," I said, "who knows you lost? You only came in three or four minutes late."

"There's a guy in the assessor's office," York answered. "We were supposed to get up there and tell him. He has half the bet against us."

"I saw him," Hammond added. "He was on the steps. He saw us, too."

Well, we got out and they drove off. And Fooey and I were back in town at ten after three.

We stood on the sidewalk and I said, "Fooey, I hope you know why I cut you off like I did. I didn't want to go on Spring Street. I was afraid we'd get lost."

Fooey looked at me with great seriousness. It was an open, overwhelming look. "It's all right," he said. "I knew you were afraid."

I've forgotten what I did the rest of the afternoon, although I expect I went over and bummed a ride home with Dad at five o'clock, when he got off work. But my memory stops with Fooey going up Summers Street beside the discolored bulk of the Kanawha Hotel and me standing and watching him out of sight.

Sometimes I still think, though, what might have happened if we had crossed at Spring Street. Probably we would have made it, and Merv York and Bruce Hammond would each have had a hundred dollars, which was a lot more then than it is now.

But I console myself by thinking of the infinite number of other ways we could have come. An infinite number, as the Kanawha County Courthouse, thought of in those terms, was at the very center of everything.

KONSTANTINOS LARDAS

The Broken Wings

(FROM THE SOUTH DAKOTA REVIEW)

HEAVEN WAS GREAT WITH SNOW. The starry flakes on the highest mountains of Icaria. Then, irresistibly prevailing over all, they crowned the island and its surrounding sea with their dawning and with their swirling mist.

The boy was caught within the warmth and safety of his ancestral home. Gazing through the kitchen window, he saw the snow falling on the boulders; melting, changing the dark brown color of the rocks to a glistening and to a dripping red.

He looked upon the whitest sky. He knew that soon the storm would end, that all the flakes would melt, that they would rise in ordered majesty into the firmament again. Tasso knew that he would see the swollen clouds once more made heavy by these sparkling flakes.

The kitchen, all the rooms which held him warm, imprisoned, were washed in lime; even the outside walls were white. His home was the brightest and greatest snowflake in the universe. And here, crouched from the cold this morning, he waited with his black-robed, widow-shrouded *yiayia* for the funeral procession of Anastasia.

Seeing the snow, he had not, like a child, run to the garden to frolic in the season's freshest gift. He had remembered last year's first falling snow. He had recalled his fear. He had remembered Anastasia walking towards him in the night when he was lost, when he was cold and lost.

Now, she was dead. She who had taught him love. And the snow was a spreading mantle, not of joy, but of despair.

From the window, he saw the wetness of the snow, felt its cold breath; knew he was bound to snow as he was bound to her.

Tasso's grandmother sat on the bench in front of the fire staring at the flames. She wore her homespun black, closed at the neck and wrists, long, sweeping the floor. She wrapped the black shawl tight across her shoulders.

Tasso did not move from the window. For hours he sat there. Watching him, dividing her concern between the blazing fire and Tasso, his *yiayia* thought that he would soon grow dumb or sick with his quiet mourning, with his dry-eyed grief.

The holy light, suspended by a copper chain above the window, burned and flickered in the oil-filled cup and made a sputtering sound, the only noise in the room. Tasso's mind was stopped and his senses were numbed by the sweet odor of the basil plants lined along the windowsill. He raised his hand and rubbed the mist from the window. He placed his forefinger against the glass until a snowflake melted; and then, moving it over, he touched another snowflake through the cold, wet glass.

Yiayia sighed. She rose from the bench; placed a fresh pine log on the fire. "God"—she crossed herself—"why did it have to happen to Anastasia and the boy?"

As Tasso thought of Stasia, his eyes showed wet and shiny like the windowpanes. He remembered how he had first seen her in the town, how she had been with him in the snow, in the night.

Last winter, he had gone, late one afternoon, down to the village, Therma, to surprise his *yiayia* with the mineral water which would cure her of her stones and of her pains.

It had been a cool day, and he had worn his sweater. Yet, the excitement of going to the larger town warmed him and made him think of those festive Saturdays in America, when his mother had saved enough coins and given them to him, so that he too could go to the movies with his friends.

He wandered through the twisting streets of Therma. And though there were no movies here, life reeled before him through the open doors and windows of the town. The many-childrened families, bursting with life, seemed always to be calling him, to be inviting him to enter their homes.

Once, as he had passed by Kleis' home, he had seen her mother sitting on the wooden steps of the deserted street; her one breast bared to her suckling son. The sight, the hungry noises of the squirming baby, had resounded in his ears and it had seemed to him, that moment, that he had been trapped in a deep canyon from which he could never escape.

He loved these narrow streets; the sights, the loud sounds of happy people, the smells of garlic rising to his nostrils from the roasting lambs, the heady odors of fermenting wines.

Most, he liked looking through the windows of the coffee houses where old men whiled away their time. They sat on thin black chairs, which always seemed to Tasso to be too fragile for the men. Always, he waited for the chairs to break and splinter in a thousand bits. They leaned on marble tables, playing at cards and backgammon, drinking their coffee and eating their powdery *loukooms*.

That afternoon, he too had bought a white *loukoom*. As he walked along the cobbled streets, with his first bite into the soft smoothness of the cube, he saw Kleis walking toward him. He greeted her with a nod, but as she smiled at him, he felt the need to greet her with some words, and as he spoke and smiled "hello," his breath was caught in the first exciting moment of love, and the white powder, sucked into his windpipe, choked him and made him reel in urgent, uncontrollable coughing.

Kleis ran to him, smiling still, and yet, concerned. And when the twisting coughing quieted in Tasso, she spoke to him.

"Tasso, you are just in time. Anastasia is at the steps. This is the last performance of her puppets. Let's see them together."

Tasso walked beside her to the bay. With each kicking of his toes, he thought not of the stones that he propelled before him, not of the dust that swirled about his feet, but thought of her; her smile, her lips, her laughing eyes, her black and shining hair. He thought of the Kleis that he could not turn to see, but who he knew was walking at his side.

When they came to the bay, he saw that the stone landing pier and the steps that led up to it were swarming with children, and that at its widest and highest point, a curtained booth was raised above their heads. Kleis took his hand and ran with him towards the steps; led him twisting through the labyrinth of squatting children, to where they knelt together at the foot of the booth.

Magically, the curtains parted; as if they had been waiting for Tasso and for Kleis. A puppet king appeared. King Minos stalked the battlements of his Cretan palace; spoke to a lowly man whom he addressed as Daedalus. "No, Daedalus. Here you will stay. Never to Athens again. You and your son shall be my guests forever."

Tasso and Kleis and all the children of the island watched as the wooden puppets moved across the stage. They spoke the words, they played the fabled legend of Icaria's beginnings.

Boldly, King Minos threatened. But when he left the stage, Daedalus began his secret preparations for escape. The puppets came to life for all the children. The boys and girls looked for the eagles' feathers on the stage and called to Daedalus when he had missed the one that lay there in the corner. "There. There. There's one for you. And one for Icarus."

Slowly the tale unfolded. The children cowered on the stones when Minotaur, the flame-snorting, ferocious bull-god breathed his fire near Daedalus.

Tasso, dreading the bull, waited for the young Icarus to come and to subdue him. But Minos shouted to the god and the huge beast obeyed and leaped from the stage, down through a secret trap door, to cringe in the dark dungeon that Daedalus had built beneath the palace.

Tasso, startled by the sudden surging of the bull, felt at the same time a sharp rap on his shoulders. He turned; was face to face with Yanni, the tall, thin leader of the children, the one who loved Kleis only. His face was sharp and deadly as the face of Minos. His eyes said, "Tasso, she is mine. Leave her to me."

Tasso turned to see the play. Saw the imprisoned Daedalus fashioning wings for himself and for his son. Saw the white wings that would soon help them flee from their island prison, the wings that would soon send them soaring through the skies.

Tasso waited for the appearance of the son. Felt still the deep burning of the hand that had hurt his shoulder and that had now moved down against his hip to erect an impregnable bastion, holding him apart from Kleis. He waited for Icarus to come. And finally, when he came, the most perfectly fashioned of all the puppets, he and all the children clapped and shouted welcome to the youth.

Icarus did not speak. Lightly he walked across the stage, touched his old father on the shoulder, and helped him don the wings that he had made. They seemed heavy; and Daedalus was weighted, bent by them. But Icarus was like a gloriously plumaged bird. He seemed to fly even before his feet rose from the Cretan earth.

Then began the long flight. And, as Icarus was lifted from the ground, Tasso, watching the strings that carried him aloft, saw the supple arms, the quick fingers that manipulated the soaring youth. Tasso watched Icarus; watched as the hands and fingers bore him high and higher, higher. Then, as Icarus approached the burning sun, high in the heavens, Tasso saw the youth, saw the hot sun, saw too, the face of Anastasia above the screening skies, saw that her gentle, blond and quiet face contorted to a scream, a scream of "Father, Father, I am falling!" Her anguished lips were crying out the words of Icarus, but Tasso saw and heard and knew them only as the words of Anastasia.

None of the other puppeteers possessed her anguish. The girl that spoke for Daedalus, his sorrow for the falling son, spoke only words. Her face did not betray the sorrow of the words.

Only Anastasia seemed to be crying out the hopeless cries. Only her face revealed the anguish in the falling puppet. And as he fell, Icarus was crushed upon the wooden floor, upon the waves that dashed against the rocks of the new-found Icaria. And Anastasia's face, and Anastasia's voice, were crushed.

The curtains closed. Tasso, too, was broken. He jumped from his kneeling posture and ran from the landing pier, past all the children, down the stone steps, forgetting Kleis, forgetting Yanni, forgetting all but Icarus and Anastasia.

Wandering through the streets now, he only heard the voice that called out, "Father, Father, I am falling!"

And with these cries of pain he remembered also *yiayia*'s pains and thought that he must buy the waters that would calm her cries.

Tasso saw dark clouds above his head. The southern winds propelled them, dashed them against the rocky sides of high Mount Pramnos. They broke against the mountain and billowed forth like frothy, giant waves, spewing their misty foam over the towns and villages sequestered in the hills.

Tasso was near the landing pier again. Across from it, close to the shore, he saw the white pavilion. Bold letters on its steps proclaimed UNDYING WATERS.

He climbed the steps, opened the door and entered the pavilion. He saw the hot waters bubbling from a deep cut in the earth, spilling over smooth slabs of stones, flowing into a cistern. The excess waters from the filled cistern were funneled to a pipe which bore its way beneath the sand and emptied in the sea.

Tasso bought the hot "Undying Waters" which would help his *yiayia*. In a huge earthen jug he carried them and watched the steam spill over its smooth lips.

As Tasso climbed the path that led him out from Therma, the jug grew heavier and heavier, until he thought that he would never be able to bring it home to *yiayia*.

Then the snow began to fall; the huge flakes that blotted out the path, the flakes that fell across his eyes and blinded him, the flakes that blew dark clouds across Icaria bringing the night with them.

Tasso, carrying the jug, stopped many times to rest. The water was cold. No longer steamed. He stopped to catch his breath. Fear dashed across the skies. Darkness descended over him.

He felt that something else, something besides the night, something besides the snow, was closing in on him; and he hurried, hurried.

"Tasso! Tasso!" someone called.

Tasso turned; saw Yanni standing on a gutted boulder at his rear. "Tasso! Remember me! Remember me!" And Yanni reached down, picked up a stone, aimed it, hurled it with all his might. And the jug that Tasso carried on his shoulder was shattered; and the water burst, as a great dam bursts, and it cascaded down his shoulders, engulfing him in flood.

Bent double, laughing, Yanni leaped from the rock. Looked Tasso in the face. Yelled, "Remember not to bother me again!" Was gone. Was lost.

Wet, wedged between the boulders that jutted to protect him from the falling snow, Tasso tried to stop his voice from crying out, but he could not, and the tears and the anguish burst from him and cried out louder than the winds.

But through his tears, beyond the snowflakes, coming from the spot where Yanni had stood to throw the rock that broke his jug, Tasso saw a blazing light floating towards him. The snow seemed to be dashing headlong towards the moving light and as it drew close to him, he saw that Anastasia bore the lamp.

"Tasso, you will die out here. Come, let me take you home. Your *yiayia* will be mad with fear."

"Anastasia, I'm lost," he told her.

"I know, Tasso. You are like Icarus. But hush now. You are not broken yet, as he. You shall not be."

She took him close to her and led him to his home. And with his *yiayia*, she helped to dry him and to boil the herbs that would prevent the cold from entering deeply in his body.

Then, as he lay in bed, Anastasia sat beside him and held his head until he fell asleep.

The next morning, Tasso woke hoping to find her still next to him, but when he looked at the chair in which she sat, he saw only a puppet. He reached for it. It was the broken boy. The shattered Icarus. The broken wings hung limply at his side.

For Tasso, this was the greatest gift. He would mend the wings. He would revive the boy and give him back to Anastasia.

After that night in the snow, Tasso had often gone to Anastasia's home. Always she gave him spoonfuls of rose-petal sweets. Always they sat together in her garden eating the white *loukooms*.

She had refused to take back the puppet that Tasso had carefully repaired.

"He is for you to keep, Tasso. I have no use for him now. That was the last performance of my puppets. My husband has asked me to give them up. We shall soon have our own. Our own son. Our Icarus."

As the summer months dragged slowly into autumn, and as their love expanded, Anastasia had begun to call him Tassaki and even, sometimes, Icarus. And though Tasso had liked these names, though he had liked to hear her soft voice call him in this way, he hoped that no one else would ever hear her.

Coming from her lips, the names of Tassaki and of Icarus were like the names, the cries of some mysterious birds, flying, goalless, forever in the sky.

Often, she called him, "Icarus, my winged boy. Like Icarus you came to me. But you will leave again. You will return to that strange land where gold is in the streets, where many kings, where many gods abound."

Tasso remembered, also, last week, when he had touched her body, when he had tried to play with Niko and with Yanni. He had forced himself to leave the silence of his garden, and to wander up to them, so that he too could take a turn at catching the red ball that they were tossing to each other.

Yanni and Niko had smiled and winked knowingly. This he had seen, but could not now escape. They greeted him with smiles and with the sounds of "Yes, Tasso, yes. Come play with us."

And they made him stand between them, and for a long time, had tormented him by forcing him to leap into the air in efforts to catch the ball which they always threw in high, spirally curves to one another.

Vainly he tried to catch the ball. But his leaping, his every bounding into the air, was one sustained and never-ending leap. How long? How long? How many times? How many countless times had he jumped towards that ball?

And in their happy mood, Yanni and Niko had yelled,

"Oh, *Amerikane*, you'll never catch the ball. Perhaps the sun. If you jump long enough and high enough. But not this ball."

And as his agony and his humiliation grew, the sweat gushed forth from every pore of his body, drenching him, soaking his shirt and his white pants.

He could not stop; and as they continued with the tossing of the ball, they yelled, "Look, he has wet himself. Oh, what an *Amerikano*."

Tasso jumped again to catch the flying ball, but as he leaped he saw that out of nowhere, Stasia had appeared and she stood next to him; holding the red ball. She handed it to him. And as she placed the ball in his cupped hands, her mouth, her face showed suddenly a greater pain than he had seen when she had screamed the puppet words of Icarus, the words of "Father, Father, I am falling!" Not words. Only wild noises issued from her lips. The unintelligible noises of great pain.

Yet she did not fall. She stood. She clutched her stomach. She wildly dug her fingers into her groin.

This was the deepest pain; and Tasso, filled with remorse, took the red ball, strained to expend his fullest power in hurling it at Yanni.

Again, they laughed. Only louder, louder; for the ball, meant to destroy them utterly, flew wide of its target, rolled and was lost amidst the tangled heather.

And the two friends, joined in the shadow of a pine tree, arms circling one another, far from Tasso and from Anastasia, cupped their hands to their mouths, yelled out to her, "You have a swelling ball under your dress. No. Not a ball. A big balloon.

"BallOOON. BallOOOON. BallOOOOON. BallOOOOO-ON," trailed their voices as they ran from Tasso and from Anastasia. "A baby-filled ballOOOOOOON. Where were you playing, Anastasia? With whom? With whom?"

Tasso sank to the ground. Ashamed to look at Stasia. Ashamed of himself. Ashamed because of what he had heard from the mouths of the two boys.

Stasia, recovered now from the pain that had forbidden her to fall, knelt next to him and took him in her arms. "Come, Tasso, let's go home. I have some sugared rose petals boiling in the pot. Rose-petal sweets and cold, cold water. That's what we need. Fly to me, Tasso. Gather your wings and learn to fly.

"You must be tired now, after all that playing with your friends."

Tasso looked at her. "My friends. What did they mean, Stasia, about your belly?"

"Here, Tasso"—she smiled, pressing her hands about her thighs, showing the outline clearly of her swollen belly—"is a new life. Here is the son that we have dreamed about for five years now. He will grow strong and handsome as my husband. He will grow true and keep his watchful eyes upon his father when they are out there in the deep waters, fishing, fishing, fishing.

"He will grow up to be his father's joy, his one companion in the caïque that will ever sound the depths, that will ever circle this island. Oh, he will be a fisherman, a mender of huge nets. Too, my own joy, my sorrow and my fear."

"Stasia, let me see. Let me touch your son."

Stasia smiled at him and drew him close to her. Unbuttoning her dress, she took his hand and placed it firmly on her belly.

He saw the taut and swollen skin protruding round her belly. Lightly he touched her, and, touching her, immediately he knew that he would never haltingly approach a growing child, that he would never touch another one again; never, anything like this.

This touching was to be remembered for all time. Reverently. And he knew that even when he was grown, when he was a man, when he would have his own first, even his own last child, this he would never do again. Even with his own wife. With his own child.

This he would never touch again. Never, the delicate, paper-thin feeling of taut skin covering, protecting a new child.

This was like touching snow. This was like being next to God. And something made him fear this touching. He recoiled from it. For he knew that its beauty, its perfection would somehow be despoiled, profaned, by this, his human touch.

"Stasia, you should not have stretched so hard for that ball."

"It was for you, Tasso. I was careful. I would do it again."

Touching the windowpane, Tasso felt her swollen body on his finger tips. He felt the new life swelling and throbbing in her body, the new life which would soon cut him from her love.

Tasso turned his eyes away from the window and the snow. He saw the sprawled puppet on the shelf beside the icon of the Virgin. He grabbed it. He dashed it to the floor. Again, the wings of Icarus were broken.

He looked out to the snow again. He watched the snowflakes as they transformed the earth, the rocks, the trees into a magic land of white. This was a setting for a new myth. For a new puppet show. But no. Never again. For she was dead.

There, on the path on top of the hill leading to the church, he saw the procession. The priest, dressed in black, walked ahead of the people. His tall, black miter jutted above the gold crosses held high up by the altar boys and chanters. The procession wound on through the now-fast-falling snow. Tasso saw the coffin. Lidless.

"There! There!" he cried running out into the snow. "They're taking her away."

"Wait, Tasso," his *yiayia* called to him as she hobbled towards him, towards Anastasia.

Tasso saw no one. Only to Stasia did he turn his eyes. Saw her with snowflakes dancing in her hair.

Then, slowly, he looked about, and saw that next to her, her husband, like a hoplite, followed straight and true. She was the queen, fallen in battle, now borne by warriors in a makeshift coffin back to her palace, to a waiting tomb. Lightly her husband bore the lid that would soon shroud her in eternal night. Lightly he bore it at his side, a warrior's black shield to guard her from her enemy, from death.

Seeing her face, now shining, smiling radiant in death, Tasso knew that he would never be offended, that he would never be afraid again of life. Stasia was now become the moving light on which converged the myriad flakes of snow, leading him from her own radiance, the nimbose, aureated queen; out from the world that they had known together for a little time, out, out into the greater world beyond.

Now he saw *yiayia* walking in sorrow next to him. Darker than he had ever known her. Black as the sea. She babbled to herself, half-heard by Tasso in an echoed cry, "God. God. Why this? What joy the baby would have brought us all. Why death for Anastasia, for her unborn son? Why this black death for Tasso?

"Why? Why? Oh, God, why this black death for him?"

But Tasso, transported now by love, looked straight ahead, saw Stasia as the snow, striking the light that she had held before her when she was walking through a raging storm, once, towards the sea. He felt again the comfort of that blazing lamp, the warmth of Stasia's smile. And in that smile, he understood the meaning of her name, the name of Stasia, Anastasia, the meaning of the Resurrection.

Now, stopping at the turning of the road, he saw her borne beyond him, carried along the twisting way. And Tasso, silent and still, faced, smilingly, alone, the snow that kissed his eyes, his lips, his hand; the sea that broke against the rocks, the waves that sounded mightily for him.

JAMES ALAN McPHERSON

The Silver Bullet

(FROM PLAYBOY)

WHEN WILLIS DAVIS tried to join up with the Henry Street guys, they told him that first he had to knock over Slick's Bar & Grill to show them what kind of stuff he had. Actually, they needed the money for the stocking of new equipment to be used in a pending reprisal against the Conchos over on the West Side. News of a Concho spring offensive was in the wind. But they did not tell Willis this. They told him they had heard he had no stuff. Willis protested, saying that he was ready to prove himself in any way but this one. He said that everyone knew Slick was in the rackets and that was why his bar had never been hit. As a matter of fact, he did not know this for certain, but did not really want to do the job. Also, no one could remember having seen Slick around the neighborhood for the past three years.

"Slick ain't in no rackets!" Dewey Bivins had screamed at Willis. "You just tryin' to get outta it on a *humble!* Slick died of t.b. over in Jersey two years ago. And don't come tellin' me you don't know that." Dewey was recognized as the warlord of the group, and there were many stories circulating, some dating several years back, about the number of dedicated Concho assassins who were out to get him. Some said that at least two of the Concho membership had taken a blood oath and waited at night in the darker areas of Henry Street for Dewey to pass. Others maintained that the Concho leadership, fearing disproportionate retaliations, had given orders that Dewey, of all the Henry Street guys, should go un-

219

molested. Dewey himself argued that at least four guys were looking for him, day and night, and liked it known that he walked the streets unarmed, all the time. In fact, each time he was seen walking, his reputation grew. People feared him, respected his dash, his temper, the way he cocked his purple beret to the side. The little fellows in the neighborhood imitated his swagger. He was a dangerous enemy, but a powerful associate. So Willis decided to give it a try.

But first he went around to see Curtis Carter, hoping to get him to go along. Carter wanted no part of it. "I know for a fact that Slick ain't dead," he pointed out. "You'd be a fool to mess with his establishment."

"Aah, *bull*shit!" Willis replied. "When was the last time you seen Slick? There's another guy runnin' the joint now." But his voice was not as convincing as he wanted it to be. And Carter was not moved, not even when Willis suggested that this job could lead to a closer association for both of them with the Henry Street guys.

Carter was not impressed. "If Slick takes after you," he said, "how can them guys help you run any faster than you'll have to run by yourself?" Willis did not like to think about that possibility, so he called Carter a ball-less son of a bitch and announced that he would do it alone.

But now that he was forced to do it alone, Willis began to really wonder about Slick's connections with the rackets. He remembered hearing stories about Slick in the old days. These stories frightened him. And even with Slick gone for good, the bar might still be covered. He wanted to ask around about it, but was afraid of calling attention to himself. Instead, he made several brief trips into the place to check out the lay of the land. The bar opened sometime between 11 and 12 o'clock, when Alphaeus Jones, the bartender, came in; but it did no real business, aside from the winos, until well after three. He figured that two o'clock would be the best time. By then the more excitable winos would have come and gone and the small trickle of people who went in for the advertised home-cooked lunch would have died away. Alphaeus Jones took his own lunch around one-thirty or two, sitting on the stool at the end of the counter, just in case any customer entered. And the cook, Bertha Roy, whom Willis recognized as a neighbor of his aunt's in the projects over on Gilman, left the place around that same time to carry bag lunches to the ladies at Martha's Beauty Salon down the block. This kept her out of the place for at least half an hour. He did not want Bertha to see him, so he decided the best time would be the minute she left with the lunches.

Again he went to Curtis Carter, begging for help. Curtis worked in an auto-parts warehouse about four blocks away from Slick's. Willis told him that the job would be much softer if they could pull it off together and then make a run back to the warehouse to hide out until after dark. But Curtis still did not want any part of the operation. He made a long speech in which he stressed the importance of independent actions, offering several of his own observations on the dependability of the Henry Street guys; and then disclosed, by way of example, that he already had a nice steady income produced by ripping off, from the stock room, new accessories and mended parts, which he sold to a garage over on the West Side. "There ain't no fair percentage in group actions," he concluded, the righteousness of a self-made man oiling his words. Willis called him a milk-fed jive and said that he was after bigger stuff. Curtis checked his temper and wished him luck.

The following afternoon, Willis waited across the street, leaning against the window of a barbershop and smoking a cigarette, until he saw Bertha Roy come out the door with the lunch bags. When he was sure that she was not going to turn around and go back, he threw the cigarette into the gutter and crossed over, trying to work up a casual amble. But his knees were much too close together. He pushed through the door, sweeping with his eyes the few tables against the wall on his left. The place was empty. Alphaeus Jones, a balding, honey-colored man with a shiny forehead, looked up from his lunch. A blob of mustard from the fish sandwich he was eating clung to the corner of his mouth. "What you want?" he asked, chewing.

Willis moved closer to the end of the bar and licked his lips. "What you got?" he asked.

Jones raised his left arm and motioned to where the sunlight glittered through the green and brown and white bottles on the shelves behind him. With his other hand, he raised the fish sandwich and took another bite. Willis licked his lips again. Then he shook his head, trying hard to work the amble up into his voice. "Naw, man," he said, his voice even but still a bit too high, "I mean what you got in the register?" And he made a fist with his right hand inside the pocket of his jacket.

Jones eyed him, sucking his teeth. Then he said, "A silver bullet." And, looking up into the space above Willis' head, his right hand lifted the sandwich again. But just before it reached his mouth, he looked Willis directly in the face and asked, impatience hurrying his voice on, "You want it, Rosco?"

"It ain't for *me*," Willis said very fast.

"Ain't for nobody else. You the first fool to come in here for years. You want it now, or later?"

Willis thought it over. Then, ever so slowly, he took his right hand out of his jacket pocket and laid both hands, fingers spread, on the bar.

Jones sucked his teeth again. "You done decided?" he asked.

"A beer," Willis said.

When he reported to the Henry Street boys what had happened, Dewey said: "You a silver-bullet lie!" The other guys crowded round him. They were in the storage basement at 1322 Henry. There was no door. "Chimney" Sutton, high on stuff, stood by the stairs leading up to the first floor, smashing his fist into his open palm. Besides needing the money for the coming offensive, they did not like to have an initiate seem so humble in his failures. "First you come with that mess about Slick," Dewey said. "Now you say old Jones bluffed you outta there on a bullshit tip." He paced the floor, making swift turns on his heels and jabbing an accusing brown finger at Willis, who slumped in a green metal chair with his head bowed. Sutton kept slamming his fist. The others—Harvey Gomez and Clyde Kelley—watched Willis with stone faces. "I know what your problems is," Dewey continued. "You just wanna get in the club without payin' no dues. You didn't never go in there in the first place."

"That ain't true," Willis protested, his hands spread out over his face. "I'll pay. You guys know how bad I wanna get in. But there wasn't no sense in takin' a chance like that. A guy would have to be crazy to call a bluff like that," he said, peering through his fingers at Dewey. "I tell you, his hands was under the counter."

"Aah, get off my case!" Dewey shouted. He jerked his head toward the stairs where Chimney Sutton was standing, still pounding his fist. Willis slid off the chair and eased across the room. Sutton was about to grab him when he saw Dewey wave his hand down in a gesture of disgust. Sutton moved a few inches away from the bottom step. Willis got out of the basement.

He hurried away from Henry Street, thinking it through. He still wanted to get into the organization. He felt that a man should belong to something representative. He was not against people going to work or joining churches or unions if these things represented them. But he wanted something more. And the Henry Street guys were not really bad, he thought. The papers just made them out to be that way. Several of them were family men. Dewey himself had been a family man at one time. That showed that they respected the family as an organization. But this by itself was not enough. There was not enough respect in it. And after a while you realized that something more was needed. Willis was not sure of what that thing was, but he knew that he had to try for it.

In the late afternoon, he went back around to the warehouse to see Curtis Carter. It was near closing time, but Curtis was still sorting greasy valves and mufflers into separate piles on the floor. His blue overalls were dirty and rust-stained. When Curtis saw him come in, he motioned him over to the john in the rear of the shop, where McElrath, the manager, could not hear them. "You do it?" Curtis asked, his voice hollow with suppressed excitement.

"No."

Curtis grinned. He seemed relieved. His mouth was smeared with black grease from his hands. "Couldn't get up the balls by yourself, huh?"

Willis told him about the silver bullet.

Curtis laughed aloud and said, "That's some more jive. Jones wouldn't never shoot nobody in there. In the afternoon they wouldn't have no more than fifty dollars in the register, anyhow. You think he wanna get in the news for somethin' like that?"

Now Willis felt bad. He knew that, from all angles, Curtis was right. He could see that Curtis knew it, too. He began to feel cheated, tricked, a laughingstock. "What can I do now?" he asked. "The guys are gonna be hard on me 'cause I didn't deliver."

"I told you so in the first place," Curtis said. "Now you go'n get it, no matter whichaway you turn. Don't think that old Jones go'n keep his mouth shut about what happen today."

"What can I do?" Willis asked, his lowered voice begging support.

"Get yourself some protection," Curtis said. "Maybe try a new approach."

"Like what?"

Curtis, still with the air of an objective adviser, told him about some guys with a new approach. They were over on the West Side. He offered no names but gave Willis the address of an office that, he suggested, might be friendly to Willis' situation.

On Wednesday morning, Willis took the bus over to the office. Once he had located it, he began to suspect that he might have been given the wrong address. This office had the suggestion of real business about it, with large red lettering on the window that read: W. SMITH ENTERPRISES. When Willis entered, he saw two new hardwood desks and tall gray file cabinets on either side of the small room. On the floor was a thin, bright red, wall-to-wall carpet; and behind one of the desks sat a man who wore a full beard, with a matching red shirt and wide tie. The man was watching him and looking very mad at something. Willis approached the desk, holding out his hand as he introduced himself. The man ignored the hand and continued to look very mad. The new hand-carved name-plate on the desk said that his name was R. V.

Felton. He was the only person in the office, so Willis had to wait until Felton was through surveying him. Finally, still not seeming to focus on the physical presence before him, the man named Felton asked: "What you want?"

Willis said what he had been told to say: "I got a problem in community relations."

R. V. Felton looked even madder. His cheeks puffed out. His nose widened as he sat erect in the brown leather chair. Then, as if some switch had been clicked on, he began to speak. "Well, brother," he said, "that's our concern here. This office is committed to problems vis-à-vis the community. That's our only concern: an interest in the mobility of the community." His voice, as he talked, seemed tightly controlled and soft, but his hands suddenly came alive, almost of their own, it seemed to Willis, and began to make grandiose patterns in the air. The index finger of his right hand pumped up and down, now striking the flat palm of his left hand, now jabbing out at Willis. The hands made spirals, sharp, quick-cutting motions, limber pirouettes, even while the fingers maintained independent movements. "There are profound problems that relate to community structure that have to be challenged through the appropriate agency," he continued. "We have friends downtown and friends in the community who see the dynamics of our organization, vis-à-vis the community, as the only legitimate and viable group to operate in this sphere. They support us," he said, his eyes wandering, his hands working furiously now, "we support the community dynamic, and together we all know what's going down. That's our dynamic. Dig it?" And he fixed a superior eye on Willis' face.

"Yeah," Willis said.

Now R. V. Felton relaxed in the chair and lifted a pencil from the new brown holder at the edge of his desk. "Now, brother," he said, "suppose you articulate the specifics of your problem."

At one-thirty that same afternoon, Willis, with R. V. Felton behind him, walked into Slick's Bar & Grill. Bertha Roy was back in the kitchen, preparing the bag lunches; at the end table in the far left corner of the room, a single customer was getting drunk. Jones was pulling his own lunch out of the kitchen window with his back to the door. When he turned and saw that it was Willis standing by the bar, he smiled and asked, "A born fool, hey?"

R. V., looking especially mean, came up to the bar and stood beside Willis. Jones sighed, laid the plate on the bar and dropped both hands out of sight. "How much this place earn in a week?" R.V. demanded. He had puffed out his cheeks and chest, so that he now looked like a bearded Buddha.

"We eat steady," Jones told him, still smiling.

Bertha Roy looked out at them from the kitchen, her sweating face screwed up in puzzlement.

R.V. sighed, intimating ruffled patience. "A fat mouth make a soft ass, brother," he said to Jones.

"What you boys want?" Bertha called from the kitchen. Her voice sounded like a bark.

"Tend your pots, Momma," R.V. called to her. Then he said to Jones: "How much?"

"You better get on out," Jones told him.

Willis, standing beside R.V., tried to look as mad. But his cheeks could not hold as much air, and without a beard, he did not look as imposing.

"Now, listen here, brother," R.V. said to Jones. "As of this minute, I declare this joint nationalized. Every dollar come in here, the community get back twenty-five cents, less three cents for tax. Every plate of food pass over that counter, the community get ten percent of the profit, less two cents tax. Paying-up time is Friday mornings, before noon. You can play ball or close down now."

"Can I ask who go'n do the collecting for the community?" Jones asked, his voice humble.

R.V. snapped his fingers twice. Willis moved in closer to the bar. "This here's our certified community collector vis-à-vis this bar," R.V. announced. "Treat him nice. And when he come in here on Friday mornings, you *smile*."

"Why wait for Friday?" Jones asked. "I'll smile right now." And he raised his hands from under the bar. He was holding a 12-gauge shotgun. "See how wide my jaws are?" he asked.

"I'm smiling so much my ass is tight. Now, what about yours?" And he lifted the gun and backed off for range.

"Let's go, man," Willis said to R.V. He was already moving toward the door.

But R.V. did not move. He held up one long finger and began to wave it at Jones. "A bad move, brother," he said.

"Why don't you boys go on home!" Bertha Roy called from behind Jones. "You oughtta be *shame* of yourselfs!"

"Bertha, you don't have to tell them nothin'," Jones said over his shoulder. "They'll be goin' home soon enough."

Willis was already at the door. He did not mind being the first one out, but then, he did not want to leave without R.V. "Let's go, man," he called from the door.

"Tomorrow's Thursday," R.V. said to Jones, ignoring Willis. "We'll be in to inspect the books. And remember, if you get any ideas about disrupting the progress of our dynamic here, there'll be some action, vis-à-vis *you*." Then he turned sharply and walked toward Willis at the door.

The drunk over in the corner lifted his head from the table and peered after them.

"You boys need a good whippin'," Bertha Roy called.

Jones just watched them go, smiling to himself.

That night, Willis went into Stanley's pool hall and told Dewey Bivins what had happened. He explained that since R. V. Felton and his organization had taken over, there would be a guaranteed cut of 12 percent for him, Willis, every Friday. And since he had decided to join up with the Henry Street guys, rather than with R.V., this would mean a weekly income of from twenty to thirty dollars for the gang. He said that he envisioned new uniforms for the guys, better equipment and a growing slush fund for more speedy bail bonding. But Dewey did not seem to share his enthusiasm. He laid his cue on the table, frowned and asked, "Who is these guys, anyhow? They don't live round here. This here's *our* territory."

Willis tried to explain, as concretely as possible, the purposes of the organization. And though he made a brave effort to repeat, word for word, the speech that R.V. had given him, he could tell that without the hand movements, it sounded uninspiring. In fact, Dewey said as much even before

Willis had finished. "That's bullshit!" he said, his face going tight. "They ain't go'n pull that kind of shit round here. Any naturalizin' that's done, *we'll* doin' it!"

"Nationalization," said Willis.

"And we'll be doin' it, not them phonies."

"But then I'll be in trouble," Willis explained. "These guys have already taken over the job. If I let you take it from them, they'll be after *me*."

"That's your problem," Dewey said, his eyes showing a singlemindedness. "You wanna be with them or us? Remember, we live round here. If you join up with them, the West Side ain't go'n be far enough away for you to move." He allowed a potent pause to intervene, then asked, "Know what I mean?"

Willis knew.

The following morning, he waited outside the barbershop across the street from Slick's. He smoked, walked up and down the block several times, then got into a throw-to-the-wall game with the boy who worked in the shop. He lost seventeen cents, and then quit. The boy went back into the shop, shaking the coins in his pocket. Willis waited some more. He had planned to go in with the group that arrived first; but as the wait became longer and longer, he began to consider going in alone and apologizing to Jones for the whole thing. He decided against this, however, when he saw Bertha Roy leaving to deliver the lunch bags. The place seemed unsafe with her gone.

Finally, a little after two, R. V. Felton and another fellow drove up in a dark blue Ford. R.V., behind the wheel, was wearing green sun shades. He double parked and kept the motor running while his man got out and went into Slick's. Willis crossed over and leaned against the car. R.V. was looking especially mean. He looked at his reflection in the rearview mirror, and then looked at it in the side mirror. Willis waited patiently. Finally, R.V. said, "We talked it over. Six percent for you."

"You said twelve!" Willis protested.

"Six," R.V. said. "This here's a small dynamic. Besides, I had to cut Aubrey in on your share. You'll get twelve, maybe more, when you line up some more of these blights on the community."

"I don't wanna get involve no more," Willis said.

"I figured that. That's why it's six."

Willis was about to make further protests when Aubrey came back to the car. He opened the door on the curb side, leaned in and said, "R.V., you better come on in, man. That dude done pull that heat again."

"Aah, fuck!" R.V. said. But he got out of the car, pushing Willis aside, and followed Aubrey into the bar. Willis entered behind them.

Jones was standing behind the bar, holding the shotgun.

"You want some trouble, brother?" R.V. asked.

"There ain't go'n be no trouble," Jones said.

"Then let's have them books."

"We don't keep no books," Jones said.

"A strange dynamic," R.V. said, pulling on his beard. "Most strange."

Jones cradled the gun butt against the bend of his right arm. "And here's somethin' stranger," he said. "If I was to blast your ass to kingdom come, there wouldn't be no cops come through that door for at least six hours. And when they come, they might take me down, but in the end, I'd get me a medal."

Now R.V.'s lips curled into a confident grin. He shook his head several times. "Let me run something down for you, brother," he said. "First of all, we are a nonprofit community-based grassroots organization, totally responsive to the needs of the community. Second"—and here he again brought his fingers into play—"we think the community would be very interested in the articulation of the *total* proceeds of this joint vis-à-vis the *average* income level for this area. Third, you don't want to mess with us. We got the support of college students."

"Do tell," Jones said. "Well, I ain't never been to college myself, but I can count to ten. And if you punks ain't down the block when I finish, that street out there is gonna be full of hamburger meat." He braced his shoulder and lifted the gun. "And one last thing."

"You better say it quick, then," R.V. told him.

"I'm already way past five."

Willis, backing off during the exchange, had the door almost open when it suddenly rammed into his back. Before he could turn around, Dewey Bivins and Chimney Sutton pushed him aside and stepped into the room. As Sutton pushed the door shut again and leaned his back against it, Willis glimpsed Bertha Roy, her face a frightened blur, moving quickly past the window and away down the block. He turned around. Dewey, a tight fist pressed into either hip, stood surveying the room. Both he and Sutton were in full uniform, with purple berets and coffee-colored imitation-leather jackets. Dewey swung his gaze round to Willis, his eyes flashing back fire. Alphaeus Jones, still in the same spot behind the bar, held the gun a bit higher.

"Who are you dudes?" R.V. asked Willis.

Willis, trying to avoid Dewey's eyes, said nothing.

"Who the hell are *you?*" Dewey asked.

"Nine," Jones said.

Willis was still trying for the door. But Sutton moved up behind him, forcing Willis to edge almost to the center of the room.

Dewey walked closer to R.V. "Where's the money?" he demanded.

R.V. began to stroke his beard again. He looked more puzzled than mad. "Brother," he said, "there's some weird vibrations in here. What we need now is some unity. Think of the ramifications that would evolve from our working together. This here's a large community. The funds from this one joint is pure chicken shit compared to the total proceeds we could plow back into community organizations by combining our individual efforts into one dynamic and profound creative approach."

"Yeah?" asked Dewey, his head cocked to the side.

R.V. nodded, looking less puzzled. "Our organization, for example, is a legitimate relevant grassroots community group," he said, making hyphens with his downturned fingers. "We have been able to study the ramifications of these here bloodsucking community facilities. We have the dynamic. You have the manpower. Together we can begin a nationalization process—"

"You a naturalizin' lie!" Dewey screamed. "*We* the only group operate round here. You better take that bullshit over to the *Conchos*."

"Let's git 'em," Chimney hissed, moving forward and pounding on his fist.

Jones grinned and raised the gun.

The room tensed. Chimney and Dewey stood close together, almost back to back. Similarly, Aubrey inched closer to R.V. and both stood facing Chimney and Dewey, their backs to Jones. Eyes narrowed in assessment, hands began to move toward pockets, fingers twitched. Dewey turned to Willis, standing near the door. "Which side *you* on?" he asked through his teeth. Without answering, Willis began to move toward the center of the room.

"Hey, Alphee!" someone said.

They all looked. A man was coming through the door. "Hey, Alphee," he said again, seemingly unaware of the fury he had temporarily aborted, "a cop out there writin' a ticket on that car that's double-parked. The owner in here?" He walked past the group and over to the bar, his face betraying no curiosity.

"Could be," Jones told him, now lowering the gun. "But you know how these big-time businessmen can fix tickets."

The man smiled, then, in the same loud voice, asked "What you doin' with that gun, Alphee?"

"Fixing to swat some flies," Jones answered.

Now the man turned and looked at the five in the middle of the room. "Them?" he asked, nodding his head as he surveyed the faces.

Jones smiled. "That's right."

The man smiled, too. He was dressed in a deep green suit and starched white shirt open at the collar. "Which one's the big businessman, Alphee?" he asked, the suggestion of amusement tugging at the corners of his mouth.

"You got me," Jones said.

"Is it you?" the man asked R.V. "You the only one in here don't look like a bum."

"Lemme take 'em, R.V.," Aubrey said.

But R.V. didn't answer. He was obviously in deep thought. Dewey and Chimney began to look troubled. Willis' mind was racing. He looked out the window. The cop was standing with his left foot on the bumper of the car, writing. He began to wish that Bertha Roy would come back or that the cop would finish quickly and then go away.

"Now, a *real* businessman," the man was saying to no one in particular, "he would own him at least six cops, a city councilman, one and a half judges and a personal letter from the mayor. He wouldn't have to worry about one little old cop writin' a ticket." He paused and the smile left his face. "You own anything like that?" he asked R.V.

"Let's go, man," R.V. said to Aubrey in a low voice.

The man walked over and slapped R.V. across the face. "You own anything like that?" he asked again, his voice suddenly dropping the hint of amusement.

R.V. stiffened and drew back his fists. The man slapped him again. "What you wanna do that for?" R.V. whimpered.

"Floor the mother!" Dewey said. "He come in here tryin' to take over."

The man turned to Jones. "Who's that?" he asked.

"Some of them punks that hang out on Henry Street."

"Get out," the man said to Dewey.

"For what?" Dewey asked. "We on *your* side."

"No, you ain't," the man said. "Now, get out before I change my mind."

Dewey and Chimney headed for the door. Willis followed them.

"Not you," the man called after Willis. "You with these other businessmen, ain't you?"

Dewey turned at the door. "Yeah," he said, malice in his voice, "he ain't wearin' our uniform."

"I told you to get out," the man called.

"You go'n let him talk that way?" Chimney asked Dewey.

"Shut up!" Dewey hissed at him, an unfamiliar fear in his eyes.

Willis watched them go out the door. He felt trapped. Now there was only Bertha to hope for. Through the window, he could see that the cop had already left the car. Turning to the room, he saw R.V. and Aubrey standing unnaturally straight, like mechanical toys. R.V.'s lips were pushed out, but now the mean look had been replaced and R.V. was sulking like a little boy. The man stood at the bar, seemingly engaged in some private conversation with Jones. But after a few seconds, he turned to R.V. again. "Alphee, here, says I should just let you fellows go. He got a good heart and don't want to see you boys in any more trouble." Then he hit R.V. again, this time a quick, hard blow with his fist. R.V. screamed as the knuckles thudded into his face. "Waste him, Aubrey!" he moaned, his face turning deep brown.

But Aubrey did not move. He was looking past the man. Willis looked, too, and saw Jones holding the shotgun again and smiling. "Ten," Jones said.

R.V.'s head fell. He backed off, roughly pushing Aubrey aside. "You go'n be sorry you done that," he muttered, fighting to contain his rage. "We got—"

"Give the boys a beer before they go, Alphee," the man said.

"Let 'em pay," Jones said, following R.V. with the gun.

The man smiled. "Just a regular businessman, huh?"

"We don't want nothin' from here," Aubrey said. R.V. was standing behind him, nursing his face. He didn't say anything.

"Then take that dummy out of here," Jones ordered.

R.V. and Aubrey slowly moved toward the door. Again, Willis followed.

"Not him," Jones said. "He been in here three times already. I want to make sure he don't come back."

Willis stopped. The two others went on out, R.V. pausing only long enough at the door to say, "You ain't seen the last of our dynamic," and to shake his fist vengefully.

"Punks," Jones said.

Now Willis stood alone, frightened and frozen, eager to be going, too. He faced the man. "I didn't know," he said, his voice little more than a tremble.

"Know what?" the man asked in a softer tone.

"That this place was covered by the rackets."

The man laughed. He closed his eyes and kept the laugh suppressed in his throat. He laughed this way for almost a minute. "You hustlers kill me," he said at last. "All that big talk and you still think a black man can't have no balls without being in the rackets."

"I didn't know," Willis said again.

"Aah, *go on* and get out!" Jones said.

"Let him have a beer, Alphee," the man said, still containing his laughter.

"No," Jones said. "Go and get out. You give me a pain."

"They just young," the man told Jones.

"The hell with that," Jones said.

Willis moved toward the door. Any moment he expected them to call him back. But all he could hear as he moved was the jerking laughter coming up from deep inside the man as he made low comments to Jones. When he was going out the door, he heard Jones say, "Sure, I was young. But I ain't never been no *fool*."

Willis ran down the block. As he passed Martha's Beauty Salon, Bertha Roy saw him and raced to the door. "You!" she called after him. Willis turned. Bertha's face was stern and her eyes flashed. "Your momma oughtta give you a good whippin'," she said.

Willis pretended he had not heard and ran faster down the block.

BERNARD MALAMUD

God's Wrath

(FROM THE ATLANTIC MONTHLY)

GLASSER, A RETIRED SEXTON, a man with a faded beard and rheumy blue eyes, lived with his youngest daughter on the top floor of a three-story, red-painted house on Second Avenue near Sixth Street. He hated going up and he hated going down; he felt tired, irritable. The oak doors of the old synagogue in the neighborhood had been nailed shut, its windows boarded up; and the white-bearded rabbi had gone off to his son in Detroit. The sexton, sixty-five, received social security and a small pension from the synagogue he had served faithfully for thirty-four years. Lucille, the only child of his recently deceased second wife, a heavy-breasted girl of twenty-six who called herself Luci on the phone, was an assistant bookkeeper in a linoleum factory during the day. She was by nature a plain and lonely girl. The telephone in the house rarely rang.

After his shul had closed its doors, the sexton rode twice a day on the subway to a synagogue on Canal Street. On the anniversary of his first wife's death he said kaddish for both wives and barely resisted saying it for his youngest daughter. He was at times irritated by her fate. Why is my luck with my daughters so bad?

Still in all, though twice a widower, Glasser got along, thanks to God. He asked for little and was the kind of man who functioned well alone. Nor did he see much of either of his daughters from his first marriage, Helen, forty, and Fay, thirty-seven. Helen's husband, a drinker, supported her badly, so Glasser contributed a few dollars now and then; Fay had a goiter and five children. He visited both his married daughters every five or six weeks.

Lucille he had more affection for, and sometimes she seemed to have affection for him. Sometimes not; it was his second wife's doing: she had been a dissatisfied woman. The girl did little for herself, had few friends—once in a while a salesman asked her out—and it was quite possible, even likely, she would in the end be left unmarried. No young man with either short or long hair had asked her to live with him. The sexton would have disliked such an arrangement, but had resolved, if ever the time came, not to oppose it. If God, in His mercy, winks an eye, He doesn't care who sees with two. What God, in His mystery, won't allow in the present, He may permit in the future, possibly marriage for Lucille. Glasser remembered friends from the old country, some were Orthodox Jews, who had lived for years with their wives before marrying them. It was a way of life. Sometimes this thought worried him. If you opened the door of the house a crack too much, the wind might take over the bedroom. The devil might hide in a cold wind. Glasser shivered. Still, better a cold bedroom than one without a bed. Better a daughter ultimately married than an empty vessel all her life. The sexton had seen some people come to happier fates than had been expected for them.

At night after Lucille returned from work, she prepared supper, and Glasser cleaned up the kitchen alone so she could study, or go to her classes. He also thoroughly cleaned the house every Friday; he washed the windows and mopped the floors. Being twice a widower he was not bothered by having to do domestic chores. What had deeply disappointed the retired sexton in his youngest daughter had been her lack of ambition. She had wanted to become a secretary after finishing high school and was, five years later, an assistant bookkeeper. About a year ago, he had said to her, "You won't get better wages if you don't have a college background." "None of my friends go to college anymore," she said. "So how many friends do you have?" "I'm talking about some people I know who started and stopped," Lucille said; but Glasser finally persuaded her to register at Hunter College at night, where she took two courses a term. Although she had done that reluctantly, now, once in a while, she talked of teaching.

"Someday I'll be dead," the sexton remarked, "and you'll feel better off with a profession."

Both of them knew he was reminding her she might be an old maid. She seemed not to worry, but he heard her, through the door, later, crying in her room.

Once, on a hot summer's day, they went together on the subway to Manhattan Beach for a dip in the ocean. Glasser wore his summer caftan and a black felt hat of twenty years; he had on white cotton socks, worn bulbous black shoes, and a white shirt open at the collar. Part of his beard was faintly brown and his complexion was flushed. On the train Lucille wore tight bell-bottom white ducks and a lacy, short blue blouse whose sleeves could be seen through; she wore clogs and had braided her dark hair to about six inches of pony tail, which she tied off with a green ribbon. Her father blushed at an inch of bare midriff and the tightness of her pants, but said nothing. One of her troubles, he thought, was that however she dressed, she had little to say, and he hoped the college courses would help her. Lucille had gold-flecked grayish eyes, and in a bathing suit showed a plumpish but not bad figure. A yeshiva bocher, dresesd much like her father, stared at her from across the aisle of the subway train, and though Glasser felt she was interested in him, her face self-consciously stiffened. He felt for her affection and contempt.

In September Lucille delayed, then would not register for night college. The sexton argued kindly and furiously, but she could not be moved. After he had shouted for an hour she locked herself in the bathroom and would not come out when he swore he had to urinate. The next day she returned late from work, and he had to cook an egg for himself for supper. That ended the argument; she did not return to her classes. As though to make up for that, the phone in her room began to ring more often, and she called herself Luci when she picked up the receiver. Luci bought herself dresses, leotards, two leather skirts, new sandals and shoes, and wore them in combinations and bright colors he had never seen on her before. He did not protest because he thought she was determined to get married. And though no one ever appeared at the door to call for her, she seemed to be going out more often. So let her go, Glasser thought. He watched television and was usually asleep when she got home from a date. "So how was your evening?" he asked in the morning. "That's my own business," said Luci. When he dreamed of her he was usually upbraiding her for her short dresses; when she bent over you could see her behind. And for the disgusting costume she called hot pants. And the eye liner and violet eye shadow she now used regularly.

One day when the sexton was davening in the shul on Canal Street, Luci moved out of the house on Second Avenue. She had left a brown-ink note on lined paper on the kitchen table saying she wanted to live her own life but would phone him once in a while. He telephoned the linoleum office the next day, and a man there said she had quit her job. Though deeply shaken at her leaving the house in this fashion, the sexton felt, with God's help, it might come to some good. If she were living with someone, all he asked was that it be an honest Jew.

On Third Avenue, one night on his way home from Helen's house, he passed a prostitute in the street. She was a heavily made up woman of thirty or so and did not attempt to solicit him. She glanced at the old man and walked on, but at the sight of her he became instantly nauseated. Glasser felt a weight of sickness on his heart and was moved to cry out to God, but could not. For five minutes, resting his swaying weight on his cane, he was unable to walk. The prostitute had taken a look at his ashen face and had hastened away. If not for a young man who had held him firmly against a telephone pole until he flagged down a police car that drove the sexton home, he would have collapsed in the street.

In the house he pounded clasped hands against the wall of Luci's room, bare except for her bed and a chair. He wept, wailing.

The sexton telephoned his eldest daughter and cried out his terrible fear.

"How can you be so positive about that?"

"I know in my heart. I wish I didn't know, but I know it."

"So in that case she's true to her nature," Helen said. "She can't be otherwise than she is; I never trusted her."

Glasser hung up on her and called Fay.

"All I can say," said Fay, "is I saw it coming, but what can you say about such things?"

"What should I do?"

"Ask for God's help, what else can you do?"

The sexton hurried to the synagogue and prayed for God's intervention. When he returned to his flat he felt unrelieved, humiliated, miserable. He beat his chest with both fists. He blamed himself for not having been stricter with her. He felt he had affronted God; he was enraged with Luci for being the kind she was and sought ways to punish her. Really, he wanted to beg her to return home, to be a good woman, to ease the pain in his heart.

The next day he woke in the dark and determined to find her. But where do you look for a daughter who has become a whore? He waited a few days for her to call, but when she did not, on Helen's advice, he dialed information and asked if there was a new telphone number in the name of Luci Glasser.

"Not for Luci Glasser but for Luci Glass," said the operator.

"Give me this number."

The operator, at his impassioned insistence, gave him an address as well as a telephone number, a place on midtown Ninth Avenue. Though it was still September, the sexton put on his winter coat and took his rubber-tipped heavy cane. He rode, whispering to himself, on the subway to West Fiftieth Street, and walked to Ninth Avenue, to a large new orange apartment house.

All day, though it rained intermittently, he waited across the street from the apartment house until his daughter appeared, late at night; then he followed her. She walked quickly, lightly, as though without a worry, down the avenue. As he hurried after her she hailed a taxi. Glasser shouted after it, but no one looked back.

In the morning he telephoned her, and she did not answer, as though she knew who was calling. That evening Glasser went once more to the orange apartment house and waited across the street. The sexton had considered going in and asking the doorman for her apartment number, but was ashamed to. At eleven that night Luci came out. From the way she was dressed and made up, he knew at once he had not been mistaken.

She turned down Forty-eighth Street and walked to Eighth Avenue. Luci sauntered calmly along the avenue. The sidewalks were crowded with silent men and showily dressed young women. Traffic was heavy and there were lights everywhere, yet the long street looked dark and evil. Some of the stores, in the in spotlit windows, showed pictures of men and women in sexual embrace. The sexton groaned to himself. Luci wore a purple silk sweater with red sequins, almost no skirt, and tight black net stockings. She paused for a while on a street corner, apart from a group of girls further up the block. She would talk to some of the men passing by, and one or two would stop to speak with her, then she waited again. One man spoke quietly to her for a while as she listened intently. Then she went into a drugstore to make a telephone call, and when she came out, her father, half-dead, was waiting for her at the door. She walked past him.

Incensed, he called her name, and she turned in frightened surprise. Under the makeup, false eyebrows, gaudy mouth, her face had turned white, eyes anguished.

"Papa, go home!" she cried in fright.

"How can a Jewish girl do such a terrible thing to her father?"

"Papa, go home!"

"What did I do to you that you did this to me?"

"It was nothing to do with you. I do it because I like the life. It's not as bad as people think."

"If it's not bad it's worse; it's filthy."

"Not if you don't think it is. I'm not lonely like I used to be. I meet all kinds of people—some Jewish."

"A black year on their heads."

"You live your life, let me live mine."

"God will curse you, He will rot your flesh."

"You're not God," Luci cried in sudden rage.

"Cocksucker!" the sexton shouted, waving his cane.

A policeman approached. Luci ran off. The sexton, to the man's questions, was inarticulate.

When he sought her again Luci had disappeared. He went into the orange apartment house, and the doorman said Miss Glass had moved out, he could not say where. Though Glasser returned several times the doorman always said the same thing. When he telephoned her number he got a tape recording of an operator saying the phone had been disconnected. The sexton walked the streets looking for her, though Fay and Helen begged him not to. He said he had to. They asked why. He wept, enraged. He sought her among the streetwalkers on Eighth and Ninth avenues and on Broadway. Sometimes he went into small cockroachy hotels and gave her name, but nobody knew her. A month passed. Late one October night he saw her on First Avenue near Twenty-third Street. Luci was standing in midblock near the curb, and though it was cold she was not wearing a coat. She had on a heavy white sweater and a mirrored leather mini skirt. A round one-and-a-half-inch mirror in a metal holder was sewn onto the back of her skirt above her plump thighs, and it bounced on her buttocks when she walked. There was another round mirror in front, at her crotch, and a line of small heart-shaped mirrors around the hem of her skirt.

Glasser crossed the steet and waited through her fright of recognition.

"Lucille," he begged her, "come home with your father. We won't tell anybody. Your room is there."

She laughed angrily and walked off. She had gained weight, grown heavy. When he followed her she called him dirty names. He hobbled across the street and waited in an unlit doorway.

Luci walked along the block, and whenever a man approached she spoke to him. Sometimes the man stopped to speak to her. Then they would go to a run-down, dark, squat hotel on a side street nearby, and a half hour later she returned to First Avenue, standing between Twenty-third and second, or higher up the avenue near Twenty-fourth.

The sexton followed her and waited on the other side of

the street by a bare-branched tree. She knew he was there He waits. He counts the number of her performances. H⌐ punishes by his presence. He calls down God's wrath on the prostitute and her father.

JOYCE CAROL OATES

Silkie

(FROM THE MALAHAT REVIEW)

WELL, HERE WE ARE standing side by side on the bridge, and who's going to speak first? Getting here was one thing; it's easy to stay quiet when you're walking and pretending you have somewhere to go. But when you get there the clumsiness sets in.

It is late summer. Evening. If there were something to say about the river—the "river"—down below I'd say it, or Nathan would say it. But it just moves on beneath us the way it has for years and years, nothing new, the same old river we've been seeing since we played in this part as kids or took the long way home from school to get horse chestnuts from the front yards of the Park Drive houses. Those were houses we never even thought of as houses people might live in, people like us—big brick houses with doors painted a bright happy yellow and windows framed with that yellow, and old big colonials with shutters painted dark blue or dark green, and lawns that rose up from the street so that you couldn't see in the front windows if you tried.

Maybe Nathan is thinking about this, or maybe he is thinking about my trouble. I am conscious of everything about him. For a few years his family rented on our street, a little soiled-white frame house like Mama's, and we played in the same gang; then his father ran off and what was left of the family moved to the outskirts of town to live with his mother's sister. But our town has just one high school, of course—that big old brick monstrosity across from the build-

ing that has both the police station and the library in it—so
Nathan and I stayed friends all along. He always "liked" me,
even when he was a kid and could be teased about it. He was
always waiting for me to get tired of the boy I was going
with so I could go out with him a few times, then he'd be
waiting again while I got tired of the next one or he got tired
of me. Some of them were nowhere near as nice-looking as
Nathan, either. He is nice-looking, yes. If you look at him
the right way, without him knowing, there is something about
his dark hair and the serious straightness of his eyebrows that
catches at your heart.

"What's the matter?" he says, seeing me watching him.

I raise my shoulders to indicate I don't know, and try to
laugh. My laughter is a little thin but Nathan smiles to make
it easier for me.

"You're silly," he says.

This is how he shows affection. In school I was one of the
flighty, silly girls, just the way Bernice Chamberlain and Alice
Dwyer were hardworking, serious girls. You got in one of
those categories in ninth grade and never got out, even if you
wanted to. Being one of the "silly" girls was nice; it meant I
could go out all the time and make dates with two boys for
the same time and pretend to be sorry, and everyone thought
it was cute. All my girl friends were the same way and we
spent afternoons after school being driven up and down the
highway by boys lucky enough to have cars, or by men
young enough to take us out and not get into trouble for it,
or we wandered through the five-and-ten looking at things
and winding up by the magazine rack where we could read
through *True Romance* and *True Confessions*. The sales girls
were our older sisters or cousins and never hollered at us.

"I was just thinking that you didn't used to look so handsome," I say to him. "You used to be skinny. Your skin
wasn't nice."

Nathan laughs. Because I am taking this particular line—
imitating myself—it is easier for him. He takes out a pack of
cigarettes and selects one. The guys in our town always took
smoking seriously. It was the one serious thing they did,
along with drinking and joining the navy.

"Well, you look the same. Better," he says.

He lights the cigarette with his Ronson lighter, his Christmas present to himself a few years back. He was always proud of that lighter. When the cigarette is lit he lets his eyes move onto mine, shyly, and I can see that he means what he says—he is in love with me, what can he do?

"Yeah, well, I could do something with my hair. I could cut it."

This is just talk but he says, "Don't you ever cut it, Silkie," as serious as if we'd come out tonight just to discuss my hair. "Don't you cut it, never. I'll get mad."

Because he speaks like that of the future, slipping it in, we both have to look away. There is nothing to stare at but the river and we lean against the railing together. In late August the river is down, of course, and the banks are strewn with napkins and beer cans and other junk. It surprises me, all this mess. When we were little kids the river was always exciting and we didn't compare it to a real river—the Shedd River, for instance, about ten miles away. It was our own river and that was that. But now Nathan and I are stranded here, grown up, like two people drawn down to the shore to get some mysterious gift from the sea, but it just turns out to be a dried-up creek in a park that is running down. And some of the big old places on Park Drive need paint and one of them is even boarded up. There are some things that catch at my mind and want to make me think about them, like cockleburs you can't shake off, but I can never get those things into focus. I can never understand all there is.

"Give me a cigarette too," I say to Nathan. He takes out the pack at once even though he hates to see me smoke. He was always a polite boy, even years ago, and where it comes from nobody could say—his brothers are all pretty wild and his mother drinks and of course his father ran off and left them. But here's Nathan, a surprise. A gift. "Thank you, honey," I say. He smiles at this, fast to hide his surprise; that word pleases him. He lights the cigarette for me and it takes a few seconds, giving us time to think about what to say next. What is safe? But how can we stay safe and still get said what is unsaid between us?

I rest my hand on top of his, like a woman in a movie, framed by sweet overdone colors and backed with music coming out of the air itself. It does not mean anything. But Nathan's gaze drops and he purses his lips the way he does when he is not quite ready to acknowledge something. He works in a gas station all day long and from two to eight on Sundays, so he has to have two parts to himself—the one that takes everything in clearly and the one that stays drawn back and hidden, not open to receive the loud hellos and how-are-yous people are so free with when they drive in. It's his face that makes people friendly and open. There are some boys' faces that look as if they'd been shaped by razors, all sharp lines and sharp, icy eyes. Not Nathan. Mama always liked him, the best of all the boys who came around to the house. She'd say, "Why don't Nathan come around anymore?" and I'd have to make up some excuse. "He's a real nice boy. He never kept you out too late," she would say. Poor Mama—cleaning the house up and down, washing the walls, scrubbing the floors and stairs, out on the front porch in cold weather and leaning around to wash the windows no matter if she risked her neck—all because of my crabby old grandmother. Poor Mama is sitting at home right now watching television and trying to make herself see the figures on the screen and not other people—for instance me—and trying to remember where she went wrong. Where did she make her mistake with me? Why did it happen? I love Mama because she didn't scream at me the way other mothers would, and then what could you do? Nothing else but run away from home. But Mama did not get angry. If she'd gotten angry I could have talked back, but she was just sorry, just sad as if it was her the same as me, and I wasn't alone in it. That was the second biggest shock of my life: finding out how much Mama loved me, after all.

"Well, how's old Marsh?" Nathan says. Mr. Marsh owns the drugstore I work in. "Still kicking around?"

"Still kicking."

"He must be eighty-five, or something."

"I guess so."

"How's your job going?"

I shrug my shoulders again in a way I must have picked up from someone. It isn't a habit I like. So to make it softer I brush my hair back from my face and let it fall down behind my shoulders. It's long, long hair, not as blond as I'd like it, but enough to make men stare around even if they're driving by fast. I was going to get it cut the last three summers but each time Mama got the newspapers down on the kitchen floor and got ready I changed my mind; I felt like crying. Old as I am I'm still silly. I could lie on my bed and cry for hours, even before I had something to cry about. Now that I do have something worthwhile to cry over I find there's no point in it—better to sit dry-eyed and do a little thinking. Last night after I talked on the phone to Nathan I couldn't sleep for all the thinking I did, which was probably more thinking than I ever did before in my life. And, like Mama said, making a hard-mouthed little joke, if I had done some thinking a few weeks back I wouldn't need to be wearing myself out with it now.

"Oh, Mama!" I said, and in spite of everything I laughed. There are times when a laugh forces its way out of you no matter what the situation. When Pa died it was all so strange, the house was upset and Mama's sisters were running in and out, my Aunt Bea looked so foolish with her reddened eyes and frizzy hair that I almost—almost—laughed. But lucky for me I didn't because it would be one more thing I'd never hear the end of.

Right now I'm afraid I might laugh too, because I am so silly. Silly or exhausted—or beaten down—or terrified. I don't know which. If only I could go back to the way I was a few years ago, before I quit school, and we'd all drive out to the Moonlight Rotunda on Saturday nights where they'd serve the boys and let us dance, then I'd be safe. I did so much laughing then, so much giggling. I had a pretty laugh. The boys would make jokes and we'd sit giggling helplessly, our long hair falling into our faces, our eyes shut tight and our heads tilted back a little so that the pink light from the neon tubing came to us blurred and mixed up with the music from the jukebox and the smell of our own perfume. It seems to me that the hundreds of times I did things like that were just one single time, locked safe somewhere with me, still that age and safe from growing up, and I could maybe get back to it if I knew how. Like an old photograph, maybe, everyone in it locked together in one instant and kept young and safe. But here I am standing with Nathan and we aren't even touching, as if we were already married and had been married for ages . . .

"Well," Nathan says slowly. He is awkward and shy, beginning. If we could spend this time the way we spent so many hours, in each other's arms, he would forget his shyness like all boys. And if I could get that close to him so that I could almost forget who he was, the way I did with all of them except Johnny, everything would flatten out and there would be no clumsy talk to get through. There would be no need to talk. Johnny had never talked much and that was one of the ways he kept himself from me, no matter how many times we were together. He never gave himself to me by saying the words Nathan is getting ready to say. "Well, what do you want to do? It's up to you," he says.

I let the cigarette fall down into the water, to let him know that I am not afraid. "You said to me, if I wanted to see you or anything, if I needed help—you would always be there." Saying this is awful; I can't look at him. But I force myself to look around, a gentle sideways glance that fastens itself right on his eyes.

"Well, yes, ma'am," Nathan says, trying to smile. He has dark, dark eyes and a patient face, and how I want to hurt him! How I want to punish him for not being the right person! But he knows nothing of this. "Say, Silkie," he says, off on another subject, "you remember when Davey died? You remember that?"

He slides his arm around my shoulders. "Of course I remember."

"And all the kids went to the funeral and I kept watching you . . . You had a white hat on. You had white gloves."

"Oh, Nathan—"

"I don't know why I thought of it. It's funny, Davey seemed so old but now we're older than he was. He never got this old."

We were silent for a while. Finally I say, "You have to get up at six tomorrow?"

"Yeah."

"My job, God . . . Mr. Marsh is getting real bad. He says everything three times and gets mad over nothing."

"He hadn't better get mad at you."

This is all so nervous, so brittle. His arm around my shoulders isn't just anyone's arm but is so much Nathan's that I want to push him away. I want to escape. But I say, slowly, "I guess I need you, after all. You can figure out what I mean."

"I already know that," he says. He sounds slow, tired, as if he had planned all these words and practiced them too much. Or maybe he is noticing how warm and desperate I am and is thinking, "This is Silkie? *This* is Silkie—" for the first time in his life. Not just an idea of a girl or someone waving at him from a car going past, and not just a face that was lucky enough to be born pretty, but the real person standing here in black flat shoes wore over at the heel and a skirt that already feels too tight even if it is my imagination, both of us maybe thinking ahead to the same thing; a room in somebody else's house, Nathan up at six to drive out to the gas station, me left alone with straightening up and maybe sick because of the baby, or, later on, feeding the baby and changing it and fixing myself up nice enough to take a walk downtown or out to see Toni or Laney or even Mama. I can even see the General Electric clock on the wall that somebody is sure to give us, a nice bright red like a sun gone screaming crazy, nailed up on the wall over the kitchen table, and I can see the rumpled bed and the dishes in the sink from the night before, and that's that. I know that I will die in that room, that I will live out my life and die there or in a room just like it somewhere else or in a rented house with three or four rooms like it, and we'll go to the show when it changes and out drinking with our friends, who'll be getting married too, and we'll have more kids, and he'll spend his life showing how he loves them all the same, the first one just as much as the ones that are really his.

"Well, he didn't want to stay around here," I tell Nathan. He is touching my hair and pretending a need to smooth it down. "He said he'd go crazy in this dump, but he never said anything about taking me along and I didn't bother telling him there was any special reason for him to do it. I didn't know him that well."

"Okay."

"He's got all kinds of ideas about traveling around. And him going on thirty, and already one wife behind him—he said she was a nice little girl but didn't go on to say what he found wrong with her. How do you like that?" And I make myself laugh to show how ugly it is. "So I thought what the hell, let him go. There's nothing going to keep him in one place anyway."

"Yes," Nathan says.

"You want me to tell you about it, don't you?"

"I don't know."

"But if you're—if we—"

"You don't need to make it hard for me," he says. I can hear him swallow, as if he's afraid. Why is he so shy, why is he so weak? Does love make people like that? Because he never loved me Johnny was strong and it was his strength I had to love, I couldn't help it, even the way he left and never even bothered to lie about writing to me . . .

"Don't you want to know what happened?" I ask him.

We look at each other. It is getting dark. He is a year older than I am and we have known each other all our lives, but the way we stand not touching, with our faces tightened and pale, you'd think we were two strangers who happened to meet on this bridge for the first time in our lives.

His face tells me No, but he says, "All right."

"I don't want no secrets between us. Mama said I had no need to tell but I'm not Mama, I'm myself."

"Yes."

"I made some mistakes," I tell him. My heart is pounding so hard I am afraid he will hear it and pity me. "I got hurt pretty bad for them, and I wouldn't do all of it again. I—"

"Why don't you forget it?" Nathan says.

"But later on you would think about him and get mad at me—"

"I won't get mad at you, Silkie."

"You don't know. Look at your father."

"Oh, the hell with him."

"Some men are like that."

"So what?"

A few kids are coming by on bicycles. I don't want to look at them so I lean on the railing. There is no reflection down below, just dark. The kids yell at each other and their bikes thump up on the wood floor of the bridge and then they're gone.

"Well, I was with Riley Summers when I met him. You know Riley, he's Baxter's cousin? We were at this place in Hampton that's by a lake, and you can dance out by the lake. It was real nice. I had on my pink dress. Tony and her boy friend were with us, then when Johnny came we went off by ourselves, we shook Riley—he's a real nice guy but— Johnny was there alone and came right over to me, we danced a few times and decided to leave for somewhere else. I never did that before with a guy, like that."

"Okay. I know it."

"I couldn't do anything about it," I tell him. I would like to scream this at him to make him understand, but he can't understand because he can't know what that night was like or what Johnny was like. "I didn't want to go but I did anyway and—and Riley was mad like you heard—and I couldn't ever stop it, all the different times I was with him. He was—"

"For Christ's sake!" Nathan says.

"But don't you want to know? Are you afraid?" My voice is higher than I would like it to be but I can't control it. It keeps getting thin and shrill as if it wants to fly at Nathan and punish him for something that isn't his fault and he couldn't ever help. "Don't you want to know?"

He is staring at me in a way I have never seen before.

"You're a coward, you don't want to hear about him!" I scream into his face. "You're afraid of him! You don't want it hard for you, coming in where another man was, you want to pretty it up and forget about it—you don't want to think how I was with him all those different times. He took me all the way to the beach once—he was—"

"What the hell do you want from me?" Nathan shouts.

"I want—I want—I don't know what I want—" I turn away from him, crying now, and the ugly little park and the first row of houses just beyond it are all broken up in the dusk, smeared and ruined. I feel as if I could snatch up Nathan and me and squeeze us into a tiny ball, crumple us up and throw us away and not ever give a damn.

Nathan turns me around. I can see his hand moving fast

and then my head jerks back. Where his hand struck my face is burning. Nathan stares down at me and I have to see so much in his eyes, in his face, that is sick with watching and listening to me all these years. Maybe he's going to spit in my face or hit it again, I've never seen him like this, or maybe he's going to strangle me and push me over the railing—

"Are you coming with me or not?" he says angrily.

He doesn't mean just back to my house. We both know what he means. He starts off the bridge and I watch him go and think, all wild inside where the slap is just getting to me, that I could let him walk away and go home by himself and then what would happen? What would happen to me? But when he hears me coming he waits for me to catch up. He doesn't look around at me; his shoulders are a little slumped.

When I finally get home it's late and there's one light on in the parlor, waiting for me. But Mama wakes up and calls out from the back bedroom, "Joan? Joan?"

"Yes, Mama, it's me."

I snap off the light on the table as if I'd like to snap off her voice forever, and that name "Joan" along with it. The fringe from the stupid old lampshade tickles my hand.

"Is it—is it all settled?" she says.

"Yes."

"Is it? Is it all settled?" I can almost hear her breathing, waiting for me to answer. "I prayed to God that—"

"It's all settled, Mama," I say, to cut her short. "We don't need to worry anymore, either one of us." I stand there with my eyes shut tight even though it's dark and hope to God I won't hear the springs in her bed, meaning she's on her way out here and to me.

SYLVIA PLATH

Mothers

(FROM MC CALL'S)

ESTHER WAS STILL UPSTAIRS when Rose called in at the back door. "Yoohoo, Esther, you ready?"

Rose lived with her retired husband, Cecil, in the topmost of the two cottages in the lane leading up to Esther's house—a large, thatched manor farm with its own cobbled court. The cobbles extended under the stout, nail-studded oak door into the dark hall between the kitchen and scullery.

The oak door was the back door; everybody but the random stranger used it. The front door, yellow-painted and flanked by two pungent bushes of box, faced across an acre of stinging nettles to where the church indicated a gray heaven above its scallop of surrounding headstones. The front gate opened just under the corner of the graveyard.

Esther tugged her red turban down around her ears, then adjusted the folds of her cashmere coat loosely so that she might, to the casual eye, seem simply tall, stately and fat, rather than eight months pregnant. Rose had not rung the bell before calling in. Esther imagined Rose, curious, avid Rose, eyeing the bare floorboards of the front hall and the untidy strewing of the baby's toys from front room to kitchen. Esther couldn't get used to people opening the door and calling in without ringing first. The postman did it, and the baker, and the grocer's boy, and now Rose, who was a Londoner and should have known better.

Once when Esther was arguing loudly and freely with Tom over breakfast, the back door had popped open and a hand-

253

ful of letters and magazines clapped onto the hall cobbles. The postman's cry of "Morning!" faded. Esther felt spied on. For some time after that, she bolted the back door from the inside, but the sound of tradesmen trying the door and finding it bolted in broad day, and then ringing the bell and waiting until she came and noisily undid the bolt, embarrassed her even more than their former calling in. So she left the bolt open again and took care not to argue so much, or at least not so loudly.

When Esther came down, Rose was waiting just outside the door, smartly dressed in a satiny lavender hat and checked tweed coat. At her side stood a blond, bony-faced woman with bright blue eye-lids and no eyebrows. This was Mrs. Nolan, the wife of the pub keeper at the White Hart. Mrs. Nolan, Rose said, never came to the Mothers' Union meetings because she had no one to go with, so Rose was bringing her to this month's meeting, together with Esther.

"Do you mind waiting just another minute, Rose, while I tell Tom I'm off?" Esther could feel Rose's shrewd eyes checking over her hat, her gloves, her patent-leather heels as she turned and picked her gingerly way up the cobbles to the back garden. Tom was planting berry plants in the newly spaded square behind the empty stables. The baby sat in the path on a pile of red earth, ladling dirt into her lap with a battered spoon.

Esther felt her little grievances about Tom's not shaving and his letting the baby play in the dirt fade at the sight of the two of them, quiet and in perfect accord. "Tom!" She rested her white glove, without thinking, on the earth-crusted wooden gate. "I'm off now. If I'm late getting back, will you boil the baby an egg?"

Tom straightened and shouted some word of encouragement that foundered between them in the dense November air, and the baby turned in the direction of Esther's voice, her mouth black, as if she had been eating dirt. But Esther slipped away, before the baby could heave up and toddle after her, to where Rose and Mrs. Nolan were waiting at the bottom of the court.

Esther let them through the seven-foot-high, stockadelike gate and latched it behind them. Then Rose crooked out her two elbows, and Mrs. Nolan took one, and Esther took the other, and the three women teetered in their best shoes down the stony lane past Rose's cottage and the cottage of the old blind man and his spinster sister at the bottom, and into the road.

"We're meeting in the church today." Rose tongued a peppermint drop into her cheek and passed the twist of tinfoil round. Both Esther and Mrs. Nolan refused politely. "We don't always meet in church, though. Only when there's new members joining up."

Mrs. Nolan rolled her pale eyes skyward, whether in general consternation or simply at the prospect of church, Esther couldn't tell. "Are you new in town, too?" she asked Mrs. Nolan across Rose's front, leaning forward a little.

Mrs. Nolan gave a short, joyless laugh, "I've been here *six years.*"

"Why, you must know everybody by now!"

"Hardly a *soul,*" Mrs. Nolan intoned, causing misgivings, like a flock of chilly-toed birds, to clutter at Esther's heart. If Mrs. Nolan, an Englishwoman by her looks and accent, and a pub keeper's wife as well, felt herself a stranger in Devon after six years, what hope had Esther, an American, of infiltrating that rooted society ever at all?

The three women proceeded, arm in arm, along the road under the high, holly-hedged boundary of Esther's acre, past her front gate and under the wall of the churchyard. Flat, lichen-bitten tombstones tilted at the level of their heads. The road, worn deep into the earth long before pavements were thought of, curved like some ancient riverbed under its slant banks.

Along past the butcher's window, with its midweek display of pork hocks and cartons of drippings, and up the alley by the constabulary and the public conveniences, Esther could see other women converging, singly and in groups, toward the churchyard gate. Burdened by their cumbersome woolens and drab hats, they seemed, without exception, gnarled and old.

The interior of the church seemed curiously light. Then Esther realized she had never been inside before, except at night for evensong. Rose led Esther and Mrs. Nolan to an empty pew halfway up the aisle. She pushed Mrs. Nolan in first, then stepped in herself, drawing Esther after her. Rose was the only one of the three who knelt. Esther bowed her head and shut her eyes, but her mind remained blank; she just felt hypocritical. She opened her eyes and looked about.

Mrs. Nolan was the one woman in the congregation without a hat. Esther caught her eye, and Mrs. Nolan raised her eyebrows or, rather, the skin of her forehead where the brows had been. Then she leaned forward. "I never," she confided, "come here much."

Esther shook her head and mouthed "Neither do I." That was not quite true. A month after her arrival in town, Esther had started attending evensong regularly. The month's gap had been an uneasy one. Twice on Sundays, morning and evening, the town bell ringers sent their carillons pounding out over the surrounding countryside. There was no escape from the probing notes. They bit into the air and shook it with a doggy zeal. The bells had made Esther feel left out, as if from some fine local feast.

A few days after they had moved into the house, Tom called her downstairs for a visitor. The rector was sitting in the front parlor among the boxes of unpacked books. A small, gray man, with protruding ears, an Irish accent and a professionally benign, all-tolerating smile, he spoke of his years in Kenya, of his children in Australia and of his English wife.

Any minute, now, Esther thought, he's going to ask if we go to church. But the rector did not mention church. He dandled the baby on one knee and left shortly, his compact, black figure dwindling down the path to the gate.

A month later, still perturbed by the evangelical bells, Esther, half in spite of herself, dashed off a note to the rector. She would like to attend evensong. Would he mind explaining the ritual to her?

She waited nervously one day, two days, each afternoon readying tea and cake, which she and Tom ate only when the tea hour was safely past. Then, on the third afternoon, she was basting a nightdress of yellow flannel for the baby when she happened to glance out the window toward the front

gate. A stout, black shape paced slowly up through the stinging nettles.

Esther welcomed the rector with some misgiving. She told
him right away that she had been brought up a Unitarian.
But the rector smilingly replied that as a Christian, of whatever persuasion, she would be welcome in his church. Esther
swallowed an impulse to blurt out that she was an atheist and
end it there. Opening the Book of Common Prayer the rector
had brought for her to use, she felt a sickly, deceitful glaze
overtake her features; she followed him through the order of
service. The apparition of the Holy Ghost and the words "resurrection of the body" gave her an itchy sense of her duplic-
ity. Yet when she confessed that she really could not believe
in the resurrection of the body (she did not quite dare to say
"nor of the spirit"), the rector seemed unperturbed. He
merely asked if she believed in the efficacy of prayer.

"Oh, yes, yes, I do!" Esther heard herself exclaim, amazed
at the tears that so opportunely jumped to her eyes, and
meaning only: How I would like to. Later, she wondered if
the tears weren't caused by her vision of the vast, irrevocable
gap between her faithless state and the beatitude of belief.
She hadn't the heart to tell the rector she had been through
all this pious trying ten years before, in comparative-religion
classes at college, and only ended up sorry she was not a Jew.

The rector suggested that his wife meet her at the next
evensong service and sit with her, so she should not feel
strange. Then he seemed to think better of it. She might prefer, after all, to come with her neighbors, Rose and Cecil.
They were "churchgoers." It was only as the rector picked up
his two prayerbooks and his black hat that Esther remembered the plate of sugared cakes and the waiting tea tray in
the kitchen. But then it was too late. Something more than
forgetfulness, she thought, watching the rector's measured retreat through the green nettles, had kept back those cakes.

The church filled rapidly now. The rector's wife, long-faced,
angular, kind, tiptoed back from her front pew to pass out
copies of the Mothers' Union Service Book. Esther felt the
baby throb and kick, and placidly thought: I am a mother; I
belong here.

The primeval cold of the church floor was just beginning its deadly entry into her foot soles when, rustling and hushing, the women rose in a body and the rector, with his slow, holy gait, came down the aisle.

The organ drew breath; they started on the opening hymn. The organist must have been a novice. Every few bars a discord prolonged itself, and the voices of the women skidded up and down after the elusive melody with a scatty, catlike desperation. There were kneelings, responses, more hymns.

The rector stepped forward and repeated at length an anecdote that had formed the substance of his last evensong sermon. Then he brought out an awkward, even embarrassing metaphor Esther had heard him use at a baptism ceremony a week earlier, about physical and spiritual abortions. Surely the rector was indulging himself. Rose slipped another peppermint between her lips, and Mrs. Nolan wore the glazed, far look of an unhappy seeress.

At last three women, two quite young and attractive, one very old, went forward and knelt at the altar to be received into the Mothers' Union. The rector forgot the name of the eldest (Esther could feel him forgetting it) and had to wait until his wife had the presence to glide forward and whisper it in his ear. The ceremony proceeded.

Four o'clock had struck before the rector allowed the women to depart. Esther quit the church in the company of Mrs. Nolan, Rose having caught up with two of her other friends, Brenda, the wife of the greengrocer, and stylish Mrs. Hotchkiss, who lived on Widdop Hill and bred Alsatians.

"You staying for tea?" Mrs. Nolan asked, as the current of women ferried them across the street and down the alley toward the yellow brick constabulary.

"That's what I came for," Esther said. "I think we deserve it."

"When's your next baby?"

Esther laughed. "Any minute."

The women were diverting themselves from the alley into a courtyard at the left. Esther and Mrs. Nolan followed them into a dark, barnlike room which reminded Esther depressingly of church campouts and group sings. Her eyes searched the dusk for a tea urn or some other sign of conviviality, but fell on nothing but a shuttered upright piano. The rest of the women did not stop; they filed ahead up an ill-lit flight of steps.

Beyond a pair of swinging doors, a brightly lit room opened out, revealing two very long tables, set parallel to each other and swaddled with clean white linen. Down the center of the tables, plates with cake and pastries alternated with bowls of brass-colored chrysanthemums. There was a startling number of cakes, all painstakingly decorated, some with cherries and nuts and some with sugar lace. Already the rector had taken a stand at the head of one table, and his wife at the head of the other, and the townswomen were crowding into the closely spaced chairs below. The women in Rose's group fitted themselves in at the far end of the rector's table. Mrs. Nolan was jockeyed unwillingly into a position facing the rector at the very foot, Esther at her right and an empty chair that had been overlooked at her left.

The women sat, settled.

Mrs. Nolan turned to Esther. "What do you do here?" It was the question of a desperate woman.

"Oh, I have the baby." Then Esther was ashamed of her evasion. "I type some of my husband's work."

Rose leaned over to them. "Her husband writes for the radio."

"I paint," said Mrs. Nolan.

"What in?" Esther wondered, a little startled.

"Oils, mainly. But I'm no good."

"Ever tried watercolor?"

"Oh, yes, but you have to be good. You have to get it right the first time."

"What do you paint then? Portraits?"

Mrs. Nolan wrinkled her nose and took out a pack of cigarettes. "Do you suppose we can smoke? No, I'm no good at portraits. But sometimes I paint Ricky."

The tiny, extinguished-looking woman making the rounds with tea arrived at Rose.

"We can smoke, can't we?" Mrs. Nolan asked Rose.

"Oh, I don't think so. I wanted to the worst way when I first came, but nobody else did."

Mrs. Nolan looked up at the woman with the tea. "Can we smoke?"

"Ooh, I shouldn't think so," the woman said. "Not in the church rooms."

"Is it a fire law?" Esther wanted to know. "Or something religious?" But nobody could say. Mrs. Nolan began to tell Esther about her little boy of seven, named Benedict. Ricky was, it turned out, a hamster.

Suddenly the swinging doors flew open to admit a flushed young woman with a steaming tray. "The sausages, the sausages!" pleased voices cried from various parts of the room.

Esther felt very hungry, almost faint. Even the ribbons of clear, hot grease oozing from her sausage in its pastry wrapper didn't stop her—she took a large bite, and so did Mrs. Nolan. At that moment everybody bowed their heads. The rector said grace.

Cheeks bulging, Esther and Mrs. Nolan peered at each other, making eyes and stifling their giggles, like schoolgirls with a secret. Then, grace over, everybody began sending plates up and down and helping themselves with energy. Mrs. Nolan told Esther about Little Benedict's father, Big Benedict (her second husband), who had been a rubber planter in Malaya until he had the misfortune to fall sick and be sent home.

"Have some dough bread." Rose passed a plate of moist, fruity slices, and Mrs. Hotchkiss followed this up with a three-layer chocolate cake.

Esther took a helping of everything. "Who made all the cakes?"

"The rector's wife," Rose said. "She bakes a lot."

"The rector"—Mrs Hotchkiss inclined her partridge-wing hat—"helps with the beating."

Mrs. Nolan, deprived of cigarettes, drummed her fingers on the tabletop. "I think I'll be going soon."

"I'll go with you." Esther spoke through a doughy mouthful. "I've to be back for the baby."

But the woman was there again, with refills of tea, and the two tables seemed more and more to resemble a large family gathering from which it would be rude to rise without offering thanks, or at least seeking permission.

Somehow the rector's wife had slipped from the head of her table and was bending maternally over them, one hand on Mrs. Nolan's shoulder, one on Esther's. "This dough bread is delicious," said Esther, thinking to compliment her. "Did you make it?"

"Oh, no, Mr. Ockenden makes that." Mr. Ockenden was the town baker. "There's a loaf over, though. If you like, you could buy it afterward."

Taken aback by this sudden financial pounce, Esther almost immediately recollected how church people of all orders were forever after pennies, offertories and donations of one sort and another. "I'd love a loaf," she said, a bit too brightly.

After the rector's wife returned to her chair, there was a muttering and nudging among the middle-aged women at the table's foot. Finally, on a spatter of local applause, one woman rose and made a little speech calling for a vote of thanks to the rector's wife for the fine tea. There was a humorous footnote about thanking the rector, too, for his help—evidently notorious—in stirring the batter for the cakes. More applause; much laughter, after which the rector's wife made a return speech welcoming Esther and Mrs. Nolan by name. Carried away, she revealed her hopes of their becoming members of the Mothers' Union.

In the general flurry of clapping and smiles and curious stares and a renewal of plate-passing, the rector himself left his place and came to sit in the empty chair next to Mrs. Nolan. Nodding at Esther, as if they had already had a great deal to say to each other, he began speaking in a low voice to Mrs. Nolan. Esther listened in unashamedly as she ate through her plate of buttered dough bread and assorted cakes.

The rector made some odd, jocular reference to never finding Mrs. Nolan in—at which her clear, blonde's skin turned a bright shade of pink—and then said, "I'm sorry, but the reason I've not called is because I thought you were a divorcée. I usually make it a point not to bother them."

"Oh, it doesn't matter. It doesn't matter now, does it," muttered the blushing Mrs. Nolan, tugging furiously at the collar of her open coat. The rector finished with some little welcoming homily that escaped Esther, so confused and outraged was she by Mrs. Nolan's predicament.

"I shouldn't have come," Mrs. Nolan whispered to Esther. "Divorced women aren't supposed to come."

"That's ridiculous," Esther said. "I'm going. Let's go now."

Rose glanced up as her two charges started to button their coats. "I'll go with you. Cecil will want his tea."

Esther glanced toward the rector's wife at the far end of the room, surrounded now by a group of chattering women. The extra loaf of dough bread was nowhere in sight, and she felt no desire to pursue it. She could ask Mr. Ockenden for a loaf on Saturday, when he came round. Besides, she vaguely suspected the rector's wife might have charged her a bit extra for it—to profit the church, the way they did at rummage sales.

Mrs. Nolan said good-bye to Rose and Esther at the town hall and started off down the hill to her husband's pub. The river road faded, at its first dip, in a bank of wet blue fog; she was lost to view in a few minutes.

Rose and Esther walked home together.

"I didn't know they didn't allow divorcées," Esther said.

"Oh, no, they don't like 'em." Rose fumbled in her pocket and produced a packet of candies. "Have one? Mrs. Hotchkiss said that even if Mrs. Nolan wanted to join the Mothers' Union, she couldn't. Do you want a dog?"

"A what?"

"A dog. Mrs. Hotchkiss has this Alsatian left over from the last lot. She's sold all the black ones, everybody loves those, and now there's just this gray one."

"Tom *hates* dogs." Esther surprised herself by her own passion. "Especially Alsatians."

Rose seemed pleased. "I told her I didn't think you'd want it. Dreadful things, dogs."

The gravestones, greenly luminous in the thick dusk, looked as if their ancient lichens might possess some magical power of phosphorescence. The two women passed under the churchyard, with its flat, black yew, and as the chill of evening wore through their coats and the afterglow of tea, Rose crooked out one arm, and Esther, without hesitation, took it.

ERIK SANDBERG-DIMENT

Come Away, Oh Human Child

(FROM THE KANSAS QUARTERLY)

IT WAS ONE OF THOSE UNFORGIVING DAYS when the world seemed full of cripples. He'd signed off the tanker *Tanner Compton* in Wilmington before sunrise, making his way on thumbed rides up to Philadelphia, and from there to the suburbs by three o'clock. Everywhere he stood, waiting for a lift, with his ageless duffel, there seemed to be cripples. A blind man moving quietly in the shadows. A legless man, ragged and dirty, pushing his way along on a coaster-supported platform. Even, on Chestnut Street, a brown-spotted dog limping in a manner identical to his master's. Overcome by a feeling of helplessness in their presence, he would grit his teeth, or curl his toes, until pain shifted the focus of attention back to himself.

He'd been at sea seven months—the last two from Tokyo, with only an eight-hour stop in Puerto La Cruz, Venezuela, to take on oil. There was no shore leave. He'd almost forgotten about cities, and people. After the clean, vast ocean, they were only things to be avoided, that occasionally caused him to shiver with pity for their condition.

But in any case he had not signed off to go to the big city. He was from the country. Even now, after fifteen years out, he longed for a field when at sea almost as much as for the waves when ashore. With seasonal regularity he was driven to land, always without knowing why. One time he returned to sea satisfied after reaching his father's grave and shouting that he "never gave a damn for you and never would!" Another time the release came after giving a lump of sugar to a horse. Just that, nothing else. She belonged to a junkman in Newark, New Jersey, and took the lump gently. Then, crushing it noisily between her teeth, the mare nudged him with a slobber for more. Suddenly it was all over. He signed on the first ship with an open berth. He never had known what would do it until it happened.

This time was no exception; he had to go ashore. The reason was still to come. When it did, an inexplicable emotion, not awareness, would leave him free again.

A few miles from Swarthmore he came to the first field large enough to hold the developments back from sight. He found it by instinct, beyond several streams of contoured streets. Walking slightly stooped as always, he passed variegated houses paced off on either side, their low, rambling silhouettes set on lawns spotted with green and studded with miniature trees, but still muddy from the bulldozer. He headed towards a tall stand of bare ash, not noticing a red bicycle lying where the sidewalk ended abruptly. A strip of well-trampled dirt led across the edge of what had once been pastureland. A little further along the path, an unattached storm sewer indicated the course of future progress. Then at last untended brush and trees were left behind on the hill as he descended into a hollow—if not a sleepy hollow, at least one not fully prodded into the present.

North, by the sun, lay a shifting meadow beginning to green, topped with fluttering lemon-colored butterflies. South, the hollow dipped into trees. No doubt there was a creek in that direction. As he crossed the corner of open land, burrs of last year's plants, dried brown by time, snagged his corduroy slacks and wool jacket, demanding to be carried on. In the shade of evergreens he listened with amazement when he thought he heard a whippoorwill. It was dark beneath the pines, but not dark as night. He strained to hear it again, but there came to his ears instead the raptured murmur of a flowing stream. He ran wildly through the undergrowth and flaying branches of brush.

The brook was small, but clean. Dropping the duffel blindly on a clump of lilies of the valley, he threw himself onto the mossy mounds at the water's edge. His outstretched left hand broke the flow of icy water and tingled. He felt joy. The sensation of cold had always been a sign of life, of awareness, just as being hot was. A comfortable temperature was negation, because one wasn't really aware of it.

He lay there till the clear water turned black with the early darkness of the forest. As a child, he used to pass the stream on Olsten's farm on his way home from school, often wishing he could slither off the bank into the stream like a lizard. Swimming. A fish among fish heading upstream, fighting the current. He was slipping back, behind the others. Back downstream . . . He screamed, sitting up and pulling his chilled hand into his lap, as if it were maimed. The silence of the forest, mimicked in the bells of the stream, surrounded him.

"Hello."

Although startled, in the split second before turning his head, he recognized the voice as friendly. So his movements were languid. She was young: ten, twelve, fourteen? He had no way of guessing. In the dusk she seemed smaller, more delicate, than she probably was. An aluminum pail in her hand caught the last rays of sunlight and held them. Her hair was long, sweeping around her oval face, her—

"My name's Jan. What's yours?"

No. He didn't want to talk to anyone. He had all he wanted. Letting his right hand run along the cool ground, he located a pebble by the water's edge. He picked it up.

"I— Didn't your mother tell you not to talk to strangers?"

She jumped back in response to his harsh tone. "Well, yes. But you looked so—"

"Beat it."

"But—"

"No buts." The pebble was beginning to gather the warmth of his hand. It grew smoother.

Jan bent down on the other side of a large, gray boulder just upstream of the lilies of the valley. She scooped up water from a quiet pool. "So long."

When she was out of sight he threw the pebble softly in the direction of her departure. It landed in the distance with barely a rustle.

The moon rose. Tired, and unrelieved of whatever burden

drove him forward, he longed for sleep. Removing the blanket from his duffel, and filling the space with his boots, he prepared for the motionless night of land. The duffel rested beneath his head, the carrying loop under his shoulder. If it was too high for a pillow, it was at least safe that way. The blanket was warm. He was hungry, but that did not matter much; it was more of a craving than real hunger. Staring at the moon through the winter-nuded branches, he knew, with the certainty of a child a week before his birthday, he would suddenly, soon, for a moment feel wonderful.

When he woke later than usual the next morning, she was sitting on the moss-covered boulder looking down. About to shout, he held back, choosing instead to ignore her. He got ready for the day, repacking his duffel, slipping into his boots, and splashing cold water into his face. He had about two hundred left from when he signed off, but no idea of how long it had to last. Vaguely he was considering hitching to the coast. That would take time. Still, a good breakfast ... Besides, he hadn't eaten dinner yesterday. She'd probably know a place. "Say, kid ..."

"I'm no kid."

"Go to hell!"

"I told you my name's Jan. Why can't we be friends?"

"Because I don't like friends, that's why."

"Oh ..." She hooked her little fingers together. Pulling and twisting them, Jan did not look at him as she spoke. "Want to come to my house for breakfast?"

"Just what do you think your mother would say if you brought a stranger home for breakfast?"

"Not her house, silly. I said my house. Over there." She pointed up the hill about two hundred yards to the right of where he had descended.

"Come on." She jumped off the boulder, her short blue dress lifting to expose thighs still slender with youth. She headed up a path he had not noticed before. Following, he stumbled twice on old, gnarled roots protruding invisibly through ground leaves.

In a gully where the hill folded in upon itself, they came to the house. He was a couple of yards away before he noticed the woven branches, boards, and vines that, carefully held together by twine, enclosed an area the size of a car, with not much more head room. He smiled. He couldn't laugh, it reminded him too much of the tree house he had built by the oak grove on the far corner of Olsten's place. Twenty years of his life vanished, almost as quickly as they had in reality.

"Well, don't just stand there. Come on in."

Inside, he was surprised to see how carefully it was constructed. The plastic-lined roof seemed waterproof, the walls much denser than he had realized, impenetrable except to the eye looking out.

"You can sit over there." She pointed to one of two stumps bordering a third topped by a broad plank.

Obediently he dropped his duffel in a corner as he sat down. For the first time since entering, he was able to stretch out. "Well, what's to eat, kid?"

"Don't call me kid! Anyhow, first you gotta tell me your name."

"Oh ... right. It's Hugh. Hugh Mullin."

"Hello, Hugh."

"Hello." It was pleasant. But an undefined anxiety began to rise within him, calling him to leave.

"You like bacon and eggs?"

It wasn't until his stomach rumbled in reply that he noticed there was a regular wood-burning stove in the house. Just a small one—still ... "Say, that could start a fire, you know!"

"No, it's insulated. See?" She pointed to the asbestos sheeting that surrounded the cast iron wherever it made contact with the woven walls.

Hugh wondered if he'd have been smart enough at her age to do that.

"We got it up at the old hermit's cabin they tore down last year, when he died. Kathy and I did ..."

"Kathy who?" Hugh tensed, immediately suspicious of more people. He had no desire to see people. That's not what he had come ashore for.

"Kathy Gibson," Jan answered, beginning to cook. "She moved to New York after Christmas vacation. Don't see her anymore. But she's written me twice. Real letters. You want to see?"

Hugh's perspective jarred. In the diminutive room, with its

miniature stove, Jan had looked adult. The whole time he felt as if he'd been taken in by some kind woman. "She's only a child," he told himself, trying to place everything in proper scale.

"Later, maybe."

"You like them over or sunny?"

"Sunny's fine."

Jan brought over an aluminum plate with two perfect eggs and three strips of bacon, fire-toasted bread, eating utensils, salt and pepper, even a paper napkin. She sat down on the opposite stump.

'Say, aren't you going to eat?"

"No, I ate at home."

That was it, he suddenly realized, home, parents, school. "Say, why aren't you at school?"

"Silly, it's Saturday! I live here all weekend when it's warm enough. Except at night."

"What do your folks say?"

"Oh they don't care. So long as my grades are good. I never really see them anyhow. Dad's always out of town for some meeting, and Mom's very important in the League of Women Voters and things. She comes home very late."

"Doesn't anyone take care of you?"

"Sure, Aunt Edna. She lives with us. But all she ever does is sleep, or talk about how smart her cats are. So I almost live here. Kathy used to spend all her time here too. But nobody else. It's our Secret Place. We've only lived here two years and she was the only friend I ever had."

Satisfied, Hugh began eating. Breaking off pieces of toast, he dipped up the yolk. Then he ate the rest of the eggs and the bacon in quick succession.

"That sets the stomach, it does! Now a cup of coffee . . ."

"Oh"—her face puckered—"I forgot. I don't drink coffee, not even instant."

"That's all right. It was delicious." He took out his cigarettes, catching himself before offering her one. He smoked peacefully, gazing around the house, as she departed to go down to the stream to do the dishes.

He ate well that day and the next, even had coffee Jan brought along with other things smuggled from her home.

They explored the hollow, while she talked of school, and Hugh of typhoons in the China Sea, and taking on cargo in the East, where the smells of the crowd and incense were stronger than that of oil, and of wild bananas and oranges in the jungle waiting to be picked. Jan told him how bare the trees were in Pennsylvania; no one could live off them.

"You're wrong there. It's just a matter of knowing. Take that, for instance." He pointed to some clover just beginning to sprout.

"That's just clover."

"But a special kind, look." They bent down together. He showed her where it was beginning to branch off. "You see, it looks almost like a tiny bush. In a month or two it'll be five or six inches tall. It's really very good." He plucked a few stems, "Here, try some."

"It's sour." She chewed hesitantly.

"Sure, that's why they call it sour clover. You can eat regular clover too if you get really hungry."

Monday morning he sat by the creek alone. It was warm and sunny, with unseen birds to be heard. The buds on nearby bushes were opening so rapidly he could observe their progress hour to hour, while Jan was in school. At sea the changes were constant but unpredictable, without time. Ashore, the thing that held him most was the cycle of growth. Which was no doubt why spring and fall were the times he came. Leaves unfolding, their valiant, colorful death in the fall, these anchors in time, he felt, were the reason he periodically ran away to land, as it were.

Jan returned from school by way of her parents' house, bringing with her some cold chicken, half a loaf of bread and a can of peaches for the four-o'clock snack they called dinner. They ate in silence, the company of each other sufficient. They sat at opposite ends of the table, not moving their feet, which touched accidentally.

As she gathered the empty plates Jan asked, "What do you do when you're ashore? Before you came here, I mean."

"I wander around most of the time. Nothing special, you know. Just wander a lot, until I've had enough. Then I go back to sea."

"That's all you do?"

"I read a lot too, I guess. Whenever I'm in a city I go to the library. They have free men's rooms. While I'm there I read the paper. Usually the microfilm 'cause I can doze in the reader."

"The reader?"

"Yeah, they have this machine, like a small metal tent. There's a projector on the top. You stick your head in, where it's dark, and you can read whatever you put in. I read the papers from the thirties last time I was ashore. Doesn't make much difference what year you read. They only change the names, the news is about the same."

"Oh, now you're being silly again."

"Am I?"

"Yes, you are."

"Well then I'll stop."

"I'm going down to the stream to clean the dishes. Wanna come?"

"No, I'll wait inside, okay?"

"Okay."

The first day she had asked if he wanted to play house, the prefix *play* was completely unreal to him ... Yet he couldn't dissociate from it. At that moment Hugh had known that most of his life had been only an unreal playing at existence. But what alternative was there in this case? And so he had said yes. Perhaps because he didn't want to hurt her, more likely because it was as good as anything. Hugh said yes even though he realized his perspective was blurred by their differences. The house, however, brought things into focus. He found himself spending most of his time with Jan indoors.

When she was at school he wandered the woods freely. Picking flowers, bringing in dead wood for the stove, or otherwise striving to provide for their home. But full satisfaction was lacking. Hugh thought about setting a squirrel trap. He'd been good at it while in high school.

The few years he attended, that is. He had left when he was sixteen. He hadn't even hated his folks then, he just wanted to get away from their constant silence. An unintended silence, not consciously produced, but the result of their having nothing really to say to each other except, as the years continued, how they would meet retirement. Retirement and old age were things he did not even pretend to understand, and which they in any case did not expect to share with him. So even as with the years they became more conversant, the silence, measured by the chimes of the grandfather's clock in the living room, continued for Hugh. He could hear its mellow tones as he lay upstairs on his bed, with the door shut tight. Every fifteen minutes, with precision, he had a friend; for a few seconds the emptiness was filled.

Tuesday she didn't come by four as usual. It was almost quarter to five before, pacing in their house, he saw Jan through the window. She was struggling through the brush with a guitar case. Hugh sat down and whittled on a little statuette he'd been working on since they first met. It was slowly taking on a semblance of Jan. His back was to the door.

"Hugh."

"You're late. Where've you been?"

"Music lesson."

"You never told me about no music lesson."

"I always have them on Tuesdays."

While she made a peanut butter sandwich, Hugh picked up the guitar and began strumming. "Did you ever see a robin weep/ When leaves begin to die/ That means he lost the will to live/ I'm so lonesome I could cry . . ."

"Robins can't cry," Jan said emphatically, as she placed a sandwich and a half in front of him. She began eating the other half as she sat down.

"Sure they can. You've just never seen one."

"Mr. Hagart wouldn't like that. He'd say you're only telling stories."

"Who's Mr. Hagart?"

"He's our science teacher. He's really sharp."

Hugh began eating, bringing the sandwich to his mouth with an almost sullen thrust.

"Last week he had us grafting plants. You know we're going to have an apple tree with three different kinds of apples on it? And maybe even pears, if the graft takes."

"Pears on an apple tree? How come you believe in that nonsense, but can't believe in robins crying?"

"I've seen pictures. Lots of pictures. Even with plums on a peach tree."

"Fake."

"No they weren't either. They were real. Just as real as you are."

"Just as real as me, huh?"

"That's right."

"I wonder . . . I wonder how real I really am. How real all this is." His arms swept the far corners of their house, almost touching the walls and ceiling.

Jan stared at his motions with a frown, as if he had asked her to solve a riddle. A riddle she couldn't even understand. "You know, sometimes you talk funny."

"Maybe that's because I'm grown up." He stopped. Somehow that wasn't what he meant to say. Hugh looked down at the empty plate and dabbed up some crumbs with a moistened thumb. "What about your folks, don't they talk funny sometimes?"

"I guess." She took the guitar from him gently, tucking it back into its case. Jan reached over to her books. "I brought you this." She handed him a small volume. "You said you liked to read."

"Rob White. *The Lion's Paw*. Where the hell'd you get that? I'm surprised it's still around. I read it a hundred times when I was a kid. That and *The Invisible Island*." He leafed through the book slowly. "You like it?"

"Oh yes, very much."

"Guess it's the living without parents that appeals. But I thought that was for little boys, not girls. Would you like to live without your parents?"

"I'd like to be an orphan best, just like Penny." She pointed to the book. "That way I could have the parents I wanted."

"What kind of parents would you like?"

"Sorta like you, I guess." Somehow she felt that was wrong. A blush rose to her cheeks. "I gotta run. Promised I'd be home by five-thirty. Takes me fifteen minutes from here. We're getting a color TV." Jan grabbed the guitar case in one hand and her remaining books in the other.

Hugh followed the rustle of her departure with his ears,

but not his eyes. He whittled slowly, letting the chips fall on the book till dusk. Then he made two more sandwiches and went to bed. Things were not right; he should leave.

The next afternoon Hugh found one of the traps sprung by a squirrel, almost unnaturally plump for spring. Quickly he returned to the house for a pair of work gloves from his duffel. He killed the squirrel with a quick wring of its neck. Excitedly he brought it back to the house, where he gathered enough stones for a circle and built a fire. He carved supports for a roasting spit and then located a good hard shaft of ironwood for the spit itself. This time he'd make dinner.

Hugh had just begun to prepare the squirrel when Jan arrived. "Hi."

She didn't answer. Slicing the thin membrane as it stretched between the loose folds of gray fur and the lump of red-white clay still warm with life, he skinned the squirrel. He draped the limp skin over a boulder, its head dangling into the leaves. "When I get enough I'll make you a fur collar, okay? But I'll need some salt."

Again she failed to answer. He didn't notice.

Jan quivered like the leaves of the birches by the stream. She struggled to speak. Looking on helplessly, unable to turn away, she at last whispered, "That's terrible."

Hugh looked up, his expression changing from surprise to hurt. "No it isn't! If we hadn't, something else would have gotten him in the long run anyhow." He returned to his task. His fingers slipped into the hollow of the squirrel's belly, separating out the entrails with a swift jerk. "Besides it's good for the other squirrels. You get too many in one place and they starve to death. Not enough food around for them, and not enough of their natural enemies left when they start building all those houses. They told us that in school. How come your Mr. Hagart never taught you that?" He rammed the well-sharpened spit thoughtfully through the squirrel's body and placed it over the fire. "You'll see, you'll like it real well."

"No I won't! I wouldn't eat that in a million million years!"

"Now that's nice!" He smiled, but it was a hard smile, harder than he would have liked had he seen himself in a mirror. "You're the one who wanted to play house. Now what kind of a husband . . . ?" He looked away and stirred the coals with a stick. "I mean I'm supposed to be the one who supplies the eats, aren't I?"

"Well, that's no way to do it." She consciously scuffed her black patent-leather school shoes against a rock. "Dad just brings home the money and gives it to Mom. She goes to the store. Why can't we do it that way?" Jan sniffed the air. Smoke and the smell of roasting meat filled the glen in front of their house. Hugh watched her expression change to one of hunger. Stirring the potatoes he had placed at the edge of the coals after the fire had taken properly, he turned the squirrel slowly.

"Honey, you know I don't have any money. Why, if I—"

"You could pretend, couldn't you? You have to pretend when you play house. It's not real. I mean, not really. You could pretend to give me money and I could get food from the icebox like always. And I get a dollar a week allowance."

"How much do you think we could buy with a dollar?" Hugh stirred the potatoes again. "Look at it this way, remember those chicken legs we had yesterday?"

"Sure."

"Well where do you think they came from?"

"A chicken, of course."

"Well somebody killed that chicken just like I killed this squirrel, and there ain't no difference, 'cept maybe I did a neater job of it. You ever see a chicken factory or—"

"They don't make chickens in factories."

"Course not, but that's what they call those places where they breed chickens. And if you think they're cruel, you ought to see what it's like in the stockyards."

"Stockyards?"

"That's the beginning of your hamburgers, or steaks. Boy I could tell you some things about them!" He salted the brown lump sizzling over the fire. "And the knackers, speaking of cruel bastards. They just pound those old horses on the head with a mallet until they die. Walk around in blood up to the ankles all the time, they do. You ought—"

"Stop it. Stop it!" Jan ran into the shelter of the house.

Hugh gave the meat one more turn and stood up. "I'm

sorry, honey, didn't mean to get you upset. Just wanted to show you I'm no meaner than anyone else, that's all." He stepped into the house, by her side where she sat, head down in the cradle of her arms on the table.

She didn't speak.

He stroked her hair slowly. It was soft. Hugh felt he had always wanted to stroke her hair. He took the coffee pot and left her sobbing lightly. By the door he turned, looking back at her youthful form in the dimness. He wanted to hold her close. "I'll be back in a minute. Just getting some water."

He wandered further down the creek than usual, stopping by the edge of a fair-sized pool to fill the pot. On his return up the leafy path he found some lime rock and threw it into the pot. Almost as good as eggshells. When he got back to the house, Jan was sitting by the fire, turning the meat.

"Think she's about done, Hugh?"

He smiled for a moment. "Well, I don't know. One thing you gotta learn is that wild animals like that have to be done to a crisp. They carry diseases. Same's with freshwater fish. Can't eat them raw like ocean fish. They got parasites and such." He went into the house for coffee, shouting, suddenly excited, through the woven walls as if they didn't exist, "Saw some sunnies down the pool. Maybe I can catch them for to-morrow."

"Can I help?"

"Sure thing."

But she didn't come the next day. Nor the day after. At first he thought she had forgotten to tell him something, that she had to go somewhere. But when she didn't show up the second day, Hugh's mind began to fill with schemes to combat his anxiety. He settled eventually on the idea of going to the shopping center he'd seen the first day, on the way to the glen. He needed food, but more than that, he hoped to bump into Jan, although he knew she'd be with someone else that would make it all impossible. Hugh ended up with a dozen eggs, marshmallows, bread and 39 cents' worth of oranges.

Back in the hollow, he paced and ate, staying within the confines of the house till late Friday afternoon, when he spotted a flash of red at the top of the hill and immediately took it for Jan. He raced out of the house. "Jan. Jan!"

She too came running. "Hugh!"

He picked her up in his arms, spinning around. "Where you been? What happened?"

They walked side by side, hand in hand.

"I had a fever and Aunt Edna made me stay in bed. Then yesterday Daddy came home and said I couldn't come out here anymore, that it was too cold and I'd get sick again."

By the house, where they'd roasted the squirrel. Hugh started a fire. They sat beside it, toasting marshmallows.

"Were you terribly hungry?" She pushed a marshmallow into his mouth.

"Nah, I caught some of the sunnies, and I went to the store."

"Where'd you get money?"

"I had a little stashed away for emergencies."

"I'm glad. I was so worried you'd be hungry."

"I was more lonely than anything else." Hugh kicked at a log protruding from the fire. "Loneliness is a strange thing. Don't suppose you've ever been lonely."

"Sure I have. When I'm all alone and there's only the TV in the house. The TV can't answer me. That's loneliness, isn't it?"

"In a way. But you can be just as lonely when there are people around to talk to. I guess I can't really explain it too well. But sometimes when you're with someone, or even something, when your whole body shakes inside and you just feel so good. That's when you're not lonely. All the other times you are. Get what I mean?"

Jan struggled with a yawn. She wanted to understand, but seemed suddenly so tired. "Not really, I guess."

"Oh."

They sat in silence, he stirring the coals with a stick so that glowing cinders leapt into the blackness of night. She leaned even closer on his shoulder, succumbing at last to her drowsiness, managing just to whisper "Gee, you smell nice. Sort of like a picnic, and my father, and the woods, all rolled into one."

"You're not lonely, and neither am I." He caught her drooping form, letting her head slip gently onto his lap.

"Your hair . . ." He stroked it slowly. "So beautiful, so soft."
He lifted Jan's head lightly in his hands and kissed her brow.

Hugh tensed. He heard shouting in the distance. He
couldn't distinguish the message, but he heard the voices
clearly. The shouting came closer. He heard her name. "Jan.
Jan."

Hugh slipped her pliant form from his lap, letting her rest
on the dry leaves. Quickly he entered the house and crushed
all his belongings and her book into his duffel. He pulled the
blanket back out. The voices grew even closer. Leaving the
almost completed carving on the table, he dashed out.

Her name shook the night. "Jan." She'd be all right. He
rested her head gently on part of the blanket, covering her
with the rest. What had he been thinking of? If they hadn't
come just then . . . What had gotten into him? Hugh knew,
but he wouldn't let the thought exist. Looking up through the
branches at the stars that somehow were not as bright as at
sea, Hugh began to jog away from the voices towards the
road.

DAVID SHETZLINE

Country of the Painted Freaks

(FROM THE PARIS REVIEW)

THE FIRST TIME AVRAM went over the bar, everywhere he looked emerald Pacific Ocean was working, except for the sky—firm above all that motion and the cast of blue he imagined one would see on a television set just before its tubes shattered. Hundreds of feet below the raft on which he squatted with Biggest Ron lay the continental shelf, another solidness where incredible things scuttled. Avram had already queried the local science center: cabezon and ling, hake, Irish lords, moray, wolf eel, great flat halibut the size of Volkswagens, variations of teeth and stomach enveloped in muscle and fin, all outrageously pigmented. In the middle waters cruised the commoner designs the fish markets consumed: salmon and the sole and snappers. But from time to time through the Oregon coast waters the true monsters surfaced: great whales and basking sharks, dolphin and sunfish and sea lions, all passing in their season, rare to landsmen, but respected by each generation of fishermen. On hands and knees Avram followed the sunlight downwards through zillions of plankton to where jellyfish wafted and minuscule lives glistened. He was at his very edge, having eaten one of Biggest Ron's smallest orange pills just before they lost control of the raft. Yet looking deep within the surge he felt himself drawn through terror and awe towards the peaceful understanding he could drop himself into that soup and after the initial pain of his bursting chest, sink on forever, disintegrating.

278

"Trouble with most those town people, they ain't got no sense of humor." Ron leaned over, offering sweet Ripple wine, the fifth dwarfed in his hand while his tendons bulged against the ocean chop. "Sorry about this rotgut, Av. I shouldn't have packed it along. But now we got it out here ..." He showed large white teeth in a wide mouth under a straight nose between two extremely large brown eyes. Biggest Ron's eyes were much like a deer's with swept eyelashes that often tangled in his shingle of blond hair. He had large, thin ears and tied his hair with tuna line in a queue hanging to the small of his back.

Avram was about to sip just to be polite, then realized he did not have to be polite, ever again, to Ron. If indeed they ever came down off this trip, why for a long time they'd have things very straight between them. Terror gurgled up through his center, blossoming over his face, itching. Ron distorted, limbs lengthening like cudgels, blondness radiating chestnut energy lines in which his wide brown eyes bulged, a Spanish Monk gazing through a Viking mask. Avram felt his teeth exposed to the saltry air as his flesh cramped upwards in an acidic grin. Of course, he realized, Ron was slightly mad, the fishermen in town also, all fishermen always had been somewhat mad. Snug little boats—lines all shipyshape and coppery bottoms drum tight for sailing the salty sea—seldom existed; such were landsmen's tales, the sort of treacle mothers fed into the porches of their sons' ears to insure their sons thought all the possible worlds dull space, and so went dutifully to fill the place behind fathers' dentist chairs. Of course—Avram understood, looking into Ron's wild wet eyes—Ron probably felt They and Us all his life. Walls shifted in his mind while distances yawned, distances on which thoughts spread faint as butter under time horizons raddled with galaxies of possibilities. The mystery of danger—the palpable danger in so much of man's work—glowed on Avram's landscape and his muscles stiffened to it. I must, he knew. *I must break my mold.*

Ron withdrew his bottle, staring as if he were about to fall into Avram. "It's sort of a sense of humor, you know? I mean if any those guys had lent us a boat for a percent of clamming ... but they're so used to renting them for money

. . . can't see . . . the shift. The humor." He turned his face at the beaches from which they floated southwest on a driftwood platform woven together by pieces of nylon rope.

They had bobbed along the shores of the bay higher than the gulls above them, paddling at the mud flats to dig clams, when the outgoing tide sucked them over the bar atop the Pacific surge. Now the ropes showed wear and a mile out they could see no boats except tiny dots far to sea or shore. *Full fathom five thy father lies; Of his bones are coral made* . . . Avram felt his mind shutting itself from panic so he looked again where Biggest Ron was studying his bottle, but not as if he was going to throw it away.

"Av, I watched that jetty going by with us in the rip and I never even thought of swimming. Shit, man, I could have made that swim. Never thought of it. I never should mix acid with wine."

"Maybe you just shouldn't take wine out over the bar."

"I been on many trips, Av. Wine's always a friend."

Some of Ron's trips eased through Avram's head: foster homes, reform schools, biking, pulling crab pots, taking his woman Jo from an Iron Horseman cycling out of Seattle. Not so untypical, Avram thought. Then most recently, taking in Avram as a boarder. That was not very typical; maybe it explained the Ripple wine somehow. For Avram, Ron's most impressive trip was at reform school when they were considering sending him on to the juvenile wing of the state penitentiary. One of the guards said: *They've some big guys up there'll tip up your ass and hide their sausage in it unless you swing on them . . . They like young stuff. It's switch or swing.* Ron had ripped off a butter knife and spent a full week sharpening its edge. But Jesus, Ron, Avram had asked, they weren't bigger than *you*, were they? *Yeah. You see, I grew up slow. Didn't put on much weight until* after *I made up my mind I wasn't going to switch for no one.* Of Ron's feats, that one lodged in Avram's head because he guessed it came closest to Ron as Ron saw himself: a skinny fawn-eyed kid with a weakness for sweet wine. And as long as Avram kept that in mind, they got along well, while the unenlightened could not see past Biggest Ron's bulk and if there was any real violence in them they tended to drive themselves up the wall scheming over what equipment they would need to control him.

Avram's own trips: Tremont Avenue, Bronx High School of Arts and Sciences, Harper College—certainly typical. Yet for Ron—that Avram could have lived such things and then split to the west coast of Oregon—truly remarkable. *Stoned,* Ron had said. *Far stoned out, man.* Ron sensed in Avram everything of the East: its street cunning, technical agility, its quick city way. And Avram recognized Ron from the movies: big, innocent, clean. Together they could make a huge success of something—whatever—and as much as this sent Avram up, its responsibility sometimes profoundly depressed. He was not sure he was ready yet for all that work.

Leaving the East had actually wasted him, the East being, after all, his home country where he could swing among the subways, surfacing here and there at one apartment or another, gathering up scenes like keys on a ring. But then Avram had seen his Purple Elephant. Purple Elephant grinned at Avram, Avram grinned back, and when he came down, he knew he could do just about anything to which he put his mind. Expansion was all. And Habit. He would expand his environments and change his habits. Besides, almost all his friends were either going into the Movement or splitting for the country, except for a few like his cousin, who had been a teen-age patient at Bellevue and was determined to practice psychiatry. So telling his parents he was off to query graduate schools, Avram hitched the southern route, moving steadily across the first half of the continent and finding that even outside Manhattan Island there seemed to be two Americas, each with a separate loyalty and language. He saw the war first in New Mexico where Spanish-Americans had turned against the head folk with predictable results: bracero nightriders shot down one in his own living room and raped a number of hippie ladies. A lot of the folk had split—except for the Texans, hog farmers and tree frog people, who sent home for their hunting rifles. The Jesus people remained, of course, digging the apocalyptic vibes. But much hair came off and many rings were eased from holes in noses and ears as many nice young couples backed off into the woodwork after painting their mailboxes battleship gray.

Still, Avram might have stayed in that harsh, dry, beautiful country but it was so anciently new worldly he felt it was not, after all, white man's land.

He suffered his first wound in Flagstaff, Arizona, where he was busted for hitchhiking one hundred feet inside city limits, spent three days in jail, was fined every cent of his visible money and had his hair and beard barbered. While he read a Gideon bible, trying very hard to stay mellow, he realized he might not be able to kill the cop who shaved his head and took his money, but neither would he lift his tongue to intercede if one of the brothern or sistern did. That sort of thing he decided to discuss with his cousin, who might understand. Flagstaff depressed him terribly, but he figured it had shown him the face of the enemy and he had good luck: they found neither his invisible money nor the old mangled beer can of New Mexico grass laying up the road from where he hitched. When he came out of the slammer he kicked that old can over the city line and let it lay until he scored a ride, whereupon he scooped it up and rolled a bomber to share with the students who drove through to Los Angeles.

There he saw his first rich folk: leathered acidheads chauffeured in a prewar Mercedes staff car, sending off show business karma. The rest of the town was not that much different from the Manhattan money trip so he split for San Francisco where Berkeley truly laid him back. Berkeley was dead. The revolution had blown out, there was probably more street action in Santa Barbara or Seattle or Boston, and Berkeley was getting bookish again. Avram had been on books for seventeen years, so he did the sights like any other tourist, avoiding the bad dope and the wasted ladies peddling clap. Then he hitched north through soft croplands that repelled him as had the Midwest; into the redwoods and ponderosa which were—somehow—too scenic, too precious. He came to rest halfway up the coast of Oregon, where he worked in a small cannery with a half-dozen other folk who were being used as cheap seasonal labor. Three of them, a kid from Illinois, an army deserter from Massachusetts, and Ron, a native, shared the same name, but Ron was unquestionably the Biggest.

"No sense of humor," Ron repeated, gazing peacefully at the shore.

"Who?" Avram was suddenly terrified Ron was astrally projecting, abandoning him to drown alone with the body of Biggest Ron as mate, but the head off and away to some place warm and private.

"Most people round here. Like they look at this ocean and they say: *Well, there's the ocean. Far out. I'm seeing the ocean.* What they don't see is the ocean looking at them. They're on the edge of the ocean's world. And not the other way round."

They were quiet for a long time as the Pacific went up and down, wet parts of it reaching between the logs while flotsam of a thousand dead lives drifted with them and around them. "We are sure out of our world," Avram said, his fear a tangible seizure. Fear was coming on like hiccups but if he breathed carefully—as, he had read, women in childbirth breathed to ride over their pain—he could feel fear subside.

Ron turned and looked at him very carefully. "Know what? I think we're going to come down and out of this. If this ocean wanted us, it would have taken us when we went over the bar in the rip. But it's too flat. Would take least an hour to get rough. And then if these sticks start to break up, we got another twenty minutes in the water before we get numb. And if we tie ourselves together over a log we got maybe another forty minutes . . . So add it all . . ."

"It spells *Another Chance.*"

They were both quiet, Avram thinking how very beautiful the ocean was and how certain people would migrate laterally across continents to get to the next ocean. All the while he breathed very carefully so Ron's words stayed in his head and his fear remained at the lip of his mind. Chances. Changes, he thought. Seasons. What had he read of Rilke? *You must change your life.* Poets, he realized for the umpteenth time, were really heavy. Being a poet had to be the heaviest thing a man could do, far more out of sight than being a saint, which had a bit too much of the locker room to it. Being a saint was a jock trip; saints were grown-up superjocks. But poets were heads. Biggest Ron was a saint, maybe, or on the way. But Avram was more the poet.

"I guess . . ." Ron pronounced, after an hour passed without a boat in sight while the chop picked up perceptibly, "I never quite been on the edge like this."

"Not with a motorcycle?"

"Not me. I mean I was never past the point I could ease up and step down off the goddamn thing . . . Have you, Av?"

"My mind, perhaps." He remembered once in his teens he had been so infuriated that for an entire week he felt himself literally unhinging, as if blocks of space time were swinging back and corridors were looming off into . . . he could not say. But he had felt such a plunge into himself would have crippled him horribly. Later he visited his cousin at Bellevue and saw in the eyes of the more helpless of his cousin's fellow patients that same pitiless terror. *I shall not hurl myself into myself like a suicide. I shall move on through like a scholar.* "The edge of the mind is a city thing," he explained. "Out there is more the edge of the body. Or both." Yes, he knew. *Both.*

They drifted. Talking. Occasionally Ron drank from his bottle, occasionally Avram sipped, occasionally one or the other raised himself to scan the swells, and always a gull or murre swam the air, the sea beside, above, while plankton streamed beneath and Avram's muscles stiffened with cold. Thinking of Socrates and water hemlock, he straightened at his turn, saw a salmon boat and sat again. A long moment went by while gates slammed in his head, fronts shifted and a grin split his face. Biggest Ron sensed it, muscled onto his feet and waved, but the boat held steady until quite a bit beyond them. Only then did it seem to shudder, slow, and turn, trolling slowly, growing bigger. Avram didn't watch it, for others moved in the waters, a presence was there and from time to time he saw life at the corners of his eye— small fish scattering, a silver thing leaping. Avram drew his knees to him, fascinated with feeding life beneath, surrounding the raft.

"They're all round us." He spoke carefully, as if he wanted to do nothing to frighten them, thinking even so: *This lowering the voice in the presence of food—I am doing something now a million years old.*

Biggest Ron looked into Avram's face and whispered: "What?"

"Fish. Feeding."

Ron studied the water, nodding, pointing to where anchovy skittered the surface and shapes like the backs of silvered knives split the waters. When the salmon troller was almost to them they heard his signal bells clatter high on his outrigger tips and they watched him leap to his gurdies to roll up the two main cables, plucking off the lines that held no fish, until he could draw a salmon in close to his boat. There he poised, hanging in some ancient position out over the deep water, gaff in hand while a salmon came alongside, drawn in by the line until the fisherman struck, sweeping the fish clear so they hung together against the seascape, the fish's body arched in death with steel through his head, the fisherman twisting against the weight of the fish to bring him up over the side and onto the deck. Thrice was this harvest repeated while the boat trolled by. Then the salmon were gone, Avram could sense it.

"Gone."

"Yeah. And our friend after them. But he'll be back." Ron sat and finished his bottle. "You see that? Big silvers. Like throwing a ten-dollar bill down on the deck each time. If I had that kind of boat I'd fish it every day of the season then buy a piece of property I got my eye on up there—" He pointed up the mountains above the receding bay. "Surround myself with friends, man. People to take care of me. Start up a goddamn commune. Freak farm."

Avram nodded, but saw only that frozen instant, the fisherman hanging far far out over the deep waters, the great silver fish arched with the curve of steel fastened to his body, fish and fisherman staring into each other atop the ancient sea. "Let's buy a boat."

"I'm your man." Ron showed his teeth. "I figured you had something up your sleeve. I know of a dory we can score, man. Outrigger's in already, all we need's a couple motors, lines, hand gurdies, tackle . . ."

"I'll send for my money tonight." They waved to the fisherman, who was moving at them, reeling in lines one by one so when he stopped they would not all tangle. *We've spoiled his fishing for the day*, Avram thought.

"Jesus." Ron studied the mountains. "Jo will really dig a

place of her own. Always been her trip ... How much bread you got, Av?"

"Couple hundred."

"WHAT?"

"But I know where we can raise the rest."

"Oh, shit, man. Don't do that to me. I don't like to kid about something like this. Where you gonna get the rest?"

"I'm going to sell your motorcycle—"

"ARE YOU OUT OF YOUR FUCKING MIND? MY CHOPPER? *MY* CHOPPER?"

"—Because you don't need it anymore. You're getting too old for that sort of thing. You need land and property and a place for your old lady—"

"You CRAzy FUCKing Jew BAStard east-coast nut! You college FREAK! Where'd they teach you to look a man in the face and even think such a thing?"

"—or else you're nothing but another big-bellied biker who'll lose his old lady one of these days and get himself drunk and stoned and wrap himself under a semi."

"If that troller hadn't spotted us you'd be over the side this thing. I never want to see you again. Never. I never want to hear your weird Bronx voice again. This is my town and you get the fuck out of it." Ron sunk to his heels—Indian fashion—and glared at the shoreline, eyes huge and blank.

Avram lay his hand on the pad of muscle over Ron's shoulder and watched the tendons moving along Ron's jaw and counted the strokes of blood entering Ron's temple while he spoke into one large thin ear: "We are not going to say anymore about this. We are simply going to go in there and do it. It's time for changes."

And so the second time Avram went over the bar it was in their own dory, a plywood double ender with a forty-horse outboard in the stern hole—strictly a calm seas and prosperous voyage affair designed for weekend sportsmen, but a hull they might have fished some thirty-odd days of the following two months had they gauged the bar very very carefully. Instead they chanced some fog, caught ground swell, bar swell and wind chop all in the same ribbon of water, and rolled, Avram drowning in the process. That is, Avram took very bad punishment, his worst trip, punishment he realized he survived only because his body was so young. Had it not been simply the youth of the fibers of his heart, none of Ron's muscle would have helped. For almost an hour, in the bitterest coldest water Avram's body had ever known, they clung to the overturned dory, drifting with agonizing slowness into the sound of breakers mindlessly battering the shore. Then with no warning they were seized from beneath, atop, going over and over and over with Ron's arm tearing him free of the wood into which his nails had locked while the water pressed into his mouth, his stomach, ear holes, crushing with such pain Avram screamed in the deepest crannies of his brain, driven by such a dying into animal rage. Finally on the beach—vomiting, his nose rushing blood, eyes streaming tears, teeth jumping in their bones as if every one had been tapped with a hammer, testicles drawn achingly up against his body, anus oozing warm liquids—he watched his torn shaking hands crawl the sand, while inside his head his own voice pleaded: *All right. Death by water, then. We need a bigger boat. Lady, believe me. Lady, I get your message . . .*

Next to him Ron's voice shook: "Man, that was a Mind-Fuck."

Of course he had been thinking steadily about another boat while his senses froze in the water, he had been pairing up dualities, taking stock of the past weeks. Biggest Ron, for one, had become Bigger Ron when Ron the Deserter from Massachusetts was picked up on some routine traffic violation and could produce very little identification. Massachusetts Ron had been jailed on suspicion and although the folk worked all night to raise bail and line him up a ride north over the border, the others, the gray people with their other language and loyalty, held him till the teletype came back from Washington and the MPs came down from Fort Lewis to take him away. Ron's old lady Jo led a bunch of women to the jail the last night where they serenaded Massachusetts Ron. Biggest Ron had gotten very drunk, howling mad animal drunk and wept—moons of water oozing from his brown eyes—standing in the yard of his shack in the Oregon woods yawping at the sky. Avram sat inside, head in his hands, shoulders rocking to and fro while his mind moved steadily backwards from one forwarding address to another, where, somewhere, even then, his own message from his own draft board was pursuing slowly as the laws would allow: *Greetings!*

Yes, that problem had to be handled. Also the problem of catching more fish. They were learning steadily, but fishermen were old, proud, loners. Avram would like to talk with the Russians; they lay off the coast netting fish for the factories in their mother ships, sneaking in under the fog to fish salmon with their illegal nets, playing their games with the Coast Guard. But there were not enough of the new people with them, either. Then there was money. Pressed against the dory, his mind numbing, he cast back across the continent—but for quick money could only think of driving for an outfit in Brooklyn making military truck bodies. Delivering to Them while He waited for Them to catch Him appealed, that was close enough to the edge, it might teach him something; lord knew he had tried all the conventional deferments. Even his psychiatrist cousin had denied him—thrice, Avram noted, bemused—explaining that he realized Avram sought neither to kill nor go to jail, but he could not lie and break a rotten law. *What* did *they do to you in Bellevue?* Avram had thought, looking at the son of his own father's brother.

Bigger Ron, on the other hand, stored tales of the less conventional deferments like a pack rat because his criminal record forever denied that adventure. Some of the farthest out people had pulled off deferments—it was becoming a test for genius. Ron's eyes would bulge shiny, his voice plunge grave as he spoke of friends who had wired, zonked, starved, wasted and strung themselves, sporting with death's monsters and grotesque self-animations, going far far, way way—painted and tattooed and blown escapees from unwritten sick poems—*and all the while the orange liquid marble eaters chewed through the walls old Ralphie laughed, sitting under that psychiatrist's desk naked in a puddle of piss and shit, so when the shrink reached to reason with him Ralphie grabs his hand and nearly bites off his finger. But that ain't all.* Then *the mushrooms hit and he starts to sweat all over and because of that other stuff Ralphie's sweating blue ink and ...* Avram's mind numbing in bitter Pacific slid that aside and thought only of money and fish. He would go back to the East Coast for money, back to books to learn fish. Yet death by water had brought such pain he allowed—briefly allowed—his mind to open and clamp about the prospect of self-mutilation. Why not suffer a hunting accident to the big toe? Could it possibly be worse than what the ocean had done to him in the surf?

He parted from Bigger Ron to drive the trails back and forth, delivering refrigerated locker wagons to various military motor pools, seeing in the eyes of those who accepted the ignition keys a shade of Bellevue. They would not get him; he had somehow drifted over a line. Died. Begun. They could kill him, roast and eat him, what did it matter? He looked into their faces and they could not meet his eye, turning from him in disgust and envy; making him feel so lonely, so alone. In his mind he always returned to the ocean, the fisherman leaning over the waters, the face of Bigger Ron saying OK., *we'll sell my chopper but if Jo asks, it was my idea.* Following long dark highways Avram found himself laughing aloud and alone out upon some piece of vast landscape. *Tiger! Tiger! burning bright.* Once he was so lonely he stopped on a Missouri shoulder, set his flashers blinking and stumbled towards a fence beyond which a landscape of wheat whispered under the stars. Hanging on the wire, the barbs between his fingers, he felt terror constricting his throat and he swallowed, swallowed, while his teeth shook and the tears came down into his beard and he wept, remembering Bigger Ron weeping in his clearing in the Oregon brush, throwing tear-struck eyes at the moon, howling for his namesake in the gray people's jail. *I'm not going to make it either,* Avram whispered inside himself. *There's too much work to it,* he said aloud. *I'm* LONELY. I'M ALL ALONE, he bayed at the stars. In the vacuum of his shout the landscape went still, no cars passed, the warning lights of his truck blinked silently, all life sounds ceased as his shout rushed everything into silence. Avram stood, mouth open, eyes dripping for a long empty moment. And then he heard it. A frog. A cricket, a creature. An answer. Another. Dozens. Hundreds, millions. Mouth open, he listened to a thousand zillion energies pouring out while an acidic grin lifted the corners of his eyes. *Oh yes I will.* You bet your sweet ass, he said, softly, so as not to disturb the others. *Silence has muscles,* he remembered from a poem. And went back to his work.

From time to time he would touch down with Ron, where he would sleep for days until Jo fixed him pots of tea to get him back to ten cents a mile plus expenses. She would touch his arm and laugh at him, saying he was getting heavy, the road was putting weight on him. Telling him about her sister who would be biking down from Seattle in the spring. And in the evening before he went back onto the road Ron would make him sip a little sweet Ripple wine while the rain beat down and Avram studied the plans for the boat they would build. Already they had its hull—a solid-timbered thirty-five footer—but all the rest must be built by hand. Ron looked upside-down at the plans, bored, blinking, fascinated by the words, numbers, the bookishness of the thing. *I ain't gonna be Bigger much more.* He grinned. *Illinois Ron's thinking of going south out of the rain. Guess he don't have anything together going for him.*

Very early next spring the wind began to warm into a chinook and the rain came with gray fronts as if tired. *Greetings!* had caught up with Avram, so he moved slowly, relearning to walk after a brief hunting accident to the great toe of his left foot. In a shed by the bay he and Bigger Ron pounded nails, cut timbers, drove bolts and fastened and braced. Some older fishermen watched, saying little but from time to time assisting as the wind died off, exhausted. By and by Illinois Ron came to sit and watch, looking wastedly at the lowering rains while their hammers beat the wheelhouse tight and worms of shaving and borings crept from the tools, carpeting the sanded deck. *Guess I'll go south,* Illinois Ron announced, hiding his hands in his pockets.

"Stay mellow, man," called Bigger Ron. "You ever get back this way and need a place to crash—why, hang out with us."

Avram looked up from a particularly nasty aching piece of labor, but Illinois Ron's eyes had already shied away so Avram went back at his job, fighting a mean warp in a piece of red cedar that had to fit just so. When he finally could allow himself a break for a joint, Illinois Ron had gone.

Days, weeks, two months. He knew something had happened, time had changed, when he read a letter from his cousin . . . *and so I was thinking of you out there . . . of moving myself. But everyone here finds it unwise. No one advises it. Moreover, I wanted to tell you I've contracted a touch of what seems to diagnose as mild sciatica. Annoying. But as these encumbrances sometimes run in families, you might want to watch* . . . Not in my family, Avram thought, using the letter to wedge a stud before he and Ron lay shiplap siding and walled the words up within their work.

Just before summer they painted the hull carefully, expensively, to seal it tight. But the wheelhouse was done in great swirls of color until they themselves were covered with paint. Then they braced scaffolding at the bow and fashioned two round eyes slowly, meticulously. On Ron's side the eye was round, brown and aimed slightly upwards into the mountains, while Avram's eye was blue, almost cold, aimed out where the ocean shrugged over the bar. And so, after months of work, Avram went out for the third time, their boat rising up, up upon a huge ground swell, then down between two walls of ocean, then up again easily and free of the shore, the rocks, the land.

I was wrong, Avram realized. There is not that much insanity to this. If you put your boat together, why then you know every piece. If you do the work yourself you know every weakness. *I was wrong, there is chance here and change here, but not madness. It is only a matter of doing the work.*

Atop the wheelhouse loosening the outrigger fastenings, Avram sensed the ocean stretching in unbelievable vastness until his eyes seemed to pull from his head, while down at his feet things in the water rose vertically like a jungle stretching upwards at the sun in its shattered blue sky. Setting his weight, he lowered the rigging and together he and Ron baited up and finally began to troll back and forth on the edge of those waters.

TENNESSEE WILLIAMS

Happy August the 10th

(FROM ESQUIRE)

THE DAY HAD BEGUN unpleasantly at breakfast, in fact it had gotten off on a definitely wrong foot before breakfast when Horne had popped her head into the narrow "study" which served as Elphinstone's bedroom for that month and the next of summer, and she, Horne, had shrieked at her, Happy August the Tenth! and then had popped out again and slammed the door shut, ripping off Elphinstone's sleep which was at best a shallow and difficult sleep and which was sometimes practically no sleep at all.

The problem was that Horne, by long understanding between the two ladies, had the air-conditioned master bedroom for the months of August and September, Elphinstone having it the other months of the year. Superficially this would appear to be an arrangement which was more than equitable to Elphinstone. It had been amicably arranged between the ladies when they had taken occupancy of the apartment ten years ago, but things that have been amicably arranged that long ago may become onerous to one or the other of the consenting parties as time goes on and, looking back now at this arrangement between them, Elphinstone suspected that Horne, being a New Yorker born and bred, must have known that she was going to enjoy the air conditioner during the really hot, hot part of the summer. In fact, if Elphinstone's recollection served her correctly, Horne had admitted that August was usually the hottest month in Manhattan and that September was rarely inclined to cool it, but

she, Horne, had reminded Elphinstone that she had her
mother's cool summer retreat, Shadow Glade, to visit whenever she wished and Horne had also reminded her that she
did not have to waken early in summer or in any season,
since she was self-employed, more or less, as a genealogical
consultant, specializing in F.F.V.'s, while she, Horne, had to
adhere to a rather strict office schedule.

During these ruminations, Elphinstone had gotten up and
gone to the bathroom and was now about to appear with ominous dignity (she hoped) in the living room at the back of
their little fifth-floor brownstone apartment on East Sixty-first
Street. Elphinstone knew that she was not looking well, for
she had glanced at the mirror. Middle age was not ap-
proaching on stealthy little cat feet this summer but was bursting upon her as peremptorily as Horne had shrieked her
into August the Tenth.

What is August the Tenth? she asked Horne in a decep-
tively casual tone as she came into the living room for coffee.

Horne chuckled and said, August the Tenth is just August
the Tenth.

Then you had no reason at all to wake me up at this hour?

I woke you up early because you told me last night to
wake you up as soon as I woke up because Doc Schrieber
had switched your hour to nine o'clock today in order to observe your state of mind in the morning.

Well, he is not going to observe it this morning after my
third consecutive night with no sleep.

You don't think he ought to observe your awful morning
depression?

My morning depressions are related only to prolonged loss
of sleep and not to any problems I'm working out with
Schreiber, and I am not about to pay him a dollar a minute
to occupy that couch when I'm too exhausted to speak a
mumbling word to the man.

You might be able to catch a few extra winks on the
couch, Horne suggested lightly. And you know, Elphinstone,
I'm more and more convinced that your chronic irritability
which has gotten much worse this summer is an unconscious
reaction to the Freudian insult. You are an Aries, dear, and
Aries people, especially with Capricorn rising, can only bene-

fit from Jung. I mean for Aries people it's practically Jung or nothing.

Elphinstone felt a retort of a fulminous nature boiling in her breast but she thought it best, in her exhausted state, to repress it, so she switched the subject to their Panamanian parrot, Lorita, having observed that Lorita was not in her indoor cage.

Where have you put Lorita? she demanded as sharply as if she suspected her friend of having wrung the bird's neck and thrown it into the garbage-disposal unit.

Lorita is on her travels, said Horne briskly.

I don't think Lorita ought to go on her travels till you have gone to your office, Elphinstone grumbled, since you move around so fast in the morning that you are likely to crush her underfoot.

I move rapidly but not blindly, dear, and anyhow Lorita's gone to sit in her summer palace.

Lorita's summer palace was a very spacious and fancy cage that had been set up for her on the little balcony outside the double French doors, and there she was, in it, sitting.

Someday, said Elphinstone darkly, that bird is going to discover that she can fly, and then good-bye, Lorita!

You're full of dire predictions this morning, said Horne. Old Doc Schreiber is going to catch an earful, I bet!

Both were now sipping their coffee, side by side on the little ivory-satin-covered love seat that faced the television and the balcony and the backs of brownstone buildings on East Sixtieth Street. It was a pleasant view with a great deal more foliage than you usually see in Manhattan outside the park. The TV was on. A public-health official was talking about the increased incidence of poliomyelitis in New York that summer.

When are you going for your polio shots? asked Horne.

Elphinstone declared that she had decided not to have the polio shots this summer.

Are you mad? asked Horne.

No, just over forty, said Elphinstone.

What's that got to do with it?

I'm out of the danger zone, Elphinstone boasted.

That's an exploded theory. The man just said that there is no real age limit for polio nowadays.

Horne, you will take any shot or pill in existence, Elphinstone said, but for a very odd reason. Not because you are really scared of illness or mortality, but because you have an unconscious death wish and feel so guilty about it that you are constantly trying to convince yourself that you are doing everything possible to improve your health and to prolong your life.

They were talking quietly but did not look at each other as they talked, which was not a good sign for August the Tenth nor for the flowers of friendship.

Yes, that *is* a "very odd reason," a very odd one, indeed! Why should I have a death wish?

Their voices had become low and shaky.

Yesterday evening, Horne, you looked out at the city from the balcony and you said, "My God, what a lot of big tombstones, a necropolis with brilliant illumination, the biggest tombstones in the world's biggest necropolis." I repeated this remark to Dr. Schreiber and told him it had upset me terribly. He said, "You are living with, you are sharing your life with, a very sick person. To see great architecture in a great city and call it tombstones in a necropolis is a symptom of a deep psychic disturbance, deeper than yours, and though I know how much you value this companion, I have to warn you that this degree of nihilism and this death wish is not what you should be continually exposing yourself to, during this effort you're making to climb back out of the shadows. I can only encourage you to go on with this relationship provided that this sick person will take psychotherapy, too. But I doubt that she will do this, since she doesn't want to climb up, she wants to move in the opposite direction. And this," he said, "is made very clear by what you've told me about her present choice of associates."

There was a little silence between them, then Horne said: Do you believe that I am an obstacle to your analysis? Because if you do, I want to assure you that the obstacle will remove itself gladly.

Schreiber is chiefly concerned, said Elphinstone, about

your new circle of friends because he feels they're instinctively destructive!

Well, said Horne, he hasn't met them and I think it's awfully presumptuous to judge any group of varied personalities without direct personal contact. Of course I have no idea what stories about my friends you may have fed Doc Schreiber.

None, none! Hardly any . . .

Then how does he know about them? By some sort of divination?

In deep analysis, said Elphinstone portentously, you have to hold nothing back.

But that doesn't mean that what you don't hold back is necessarily true. Does it? Shit, apparently you didn't mean a word of it when you told me you understood how I need to have my own little circle of friends since I'm not accepted by yours.

Elphinstone replied sorrowfully, I have no circle of friends unless you mean my group of old school chums from Sarah Lawrence whom I have lunch with once a month, and very, very occasionally entertain here for a buffet supper and bridge, occasions to which you're always invited, in fact urged to come, but you have declined, except for a single occasion.

Oh, yes, said Horne, you said a few days ago that you not only saw nothing wrong in our having our little separate circle of friends, but you said you thought it was psychologically healthy for us both. You said, if you'd try to remember, that it relieved the tensions between us for each to have her own little social circle, and as for my circle being hostile to you, I can only tell *you*—

Tell me *what?*

That *you* did not accept *them*, you bristled like a hedgehog on the one occasion you honored them with your presence, the single time that you condescended to meet them instead of running out to some dreary get-together of old Sarah Lawrence alumnae.

Another pause occurred in the conversation. Both of them made little noises in their throats and took little sips of coffee and didn't glance at each other: the warm air trembled between them. Even the parrot, Lorita, seemed to sense the domestic crisis and was making quiet clucking sounds and little musical whistles from her summer palace, as if to pacify the unhappy ladies.

You say I have a death wish, said Horne, resuming the talk between them. I think you are putting the shoe on the wrong foot, dear. My direction is outward toward widening and enriching my contacts with life, but you are obsessed with the slow death of your mother, as if you envied her for it. You hate what you call "my circle of Village hippies" because they're intellectually vital, intensely alive, and dedicated to living, in *here*, and in *here*, and in *here*.

(She touched her forehead, her chest, and her abdomen with her three *heres*.)

Oh, and all this remarkably diversified vitality is about to explode here again tonight, is it, Horne?

The social climate, said Horne, is likely to be somewhat more animated than you find things at Shadow Glade, but then the only thing less animated than your mother's is the social climate at your Sarah Lawrence bashes. Elphinstone, why don't you skip this weekend at your mother's and come to my little gathering here tonight and come with a different attitude than you brought to it before—I mean be sweet, natural, friendly, instead of charging the atmosphere with hostility and suspicion—and then I know they would understand you a little better and *you* would understand the excitement that I feel in contact with a group that has some kind of intellectual vitality going for them, and—

What you're implying is that Sarah Lawrence graduates are inevitably and exclusively dimwitted?

I wasn't thinking about Sarah Lawrence graduates; I am nothing to them and they are nothing to me. However, she continued, her voice gathering steam, I do feel it's somewhat ludicrous to make a religion, a fucking mystique, out of having once attended that snobbish institution of smugness!

Well, Horne, if you must know the truth, said Elphinstone, some of the ladies were a bit disconcerted by your lallocropia.

My *what*?

Lallocropia is the psychiatric term for a compulsion to use shocking language, even in the least suitable occasions.

Shit, if I shocked the ladies—

Horne stood up on this line, which was left incomplete because her movement was so abrupt that she spilled some coffee on the ivory-satin cover of the love seat.

Horne cried out wildly when this happened, releasing in her outcry an arsenal of tensions which had accumulated during this black beginning of August the Tenth, and, as if projected by the cry, she made like a bullet for the kitchen to grab a dishcloth and wet it at the faucet; then rushed back in to massage the coffee-stained spot on the elegant love seat with the wet cloth.

Oh, said Elphinstone in a tone more sorrowful than rancorous, I see now why this piece of furniture has been destroyed. You rub this ivory-satin cover, made out of my grandmother's wedding gown, with a wet dishcloth whenever you spill something on it, which you do with a very peculiar regularity because of hostility toward—

As a preliminary, yes! said Horne, having heard only the beginning of Elphinstone's rueful indictment. Then, of course, I go over the spot with Miracle Cleanser.

What is Miracle Cleanser?

Miracle Cleanser, said Horne in several breathless gasps, her respiration disturbed by their tension and its explosion, is a marvelous product advertised by Johnny Carson on his "Tonight Show."

I see you are mad, said Elphinstone. Well, I am going to send out this sofa to be covered with coffee-colored burlap.

Of course there's not much I can do to protect my china and glassware from the havoc which I know is impending *ce soir!* The breakage of my Wedgewood and Haviland is a small price to pay for your cultural regeneration these past few months, if six months is a few! And I can't see into the future, but if this place isn't a shambles in—

Why don't you put your goddamn Wedgewood and your Haviland in storage; who wants or needs your goddamn—

Horne, said Elphinstone with a warning vibration in her voice.

Horne replied with that scatological syllable which she

used so often in conversations lately, and Elphinstone repeated her friend's surname with even more emphasis.

Christ, Elphinstone, but I mean it. We are sharing a little apartment in which nearly all the space is preempted by family relics such as your Wedgewood and your crystal and your silver with your mother's crest on it, everything's mother's or mother's mother's mother's around here so that I feel like a squatter in your family plot in the boneyard, and oh, my God, the bookshelves! Imagine my embarrassment when doctors of letters and philosophy go up to check the books on those shelves and see nothing but all this genealogical crap and think it's my choice of reading matter, *Notable Southern Families Volume I, Notable Southern Families Volume II, Notable Southern Bullshit* up to the ceiling and down to your Aubusson carpet, shelves and shelves and—

Horne, I believe you know that I am a professional consultant in genealogy and must have my reference books and that I have to work in this room!

Shit, I thought you had it all in your head by this time! Who buggered Governor Dinwiddie in the cranberry bushes, by the Potomac; which tribe scalped Mistress Elphinstone, the Cherokees or the Choctaws, at the—

There's nothing to be ashamed of in a Colonial heritage, Horne!

Well, your Colonial heritage, Elphinstone, and your family relics have made this place untenable for me! I am going to check into the Chelsea Hotel for the weekend and you'll hear from me later about where to contact me for a reimbursement of my half of the rent money on this Elphinstone sanctuary!

She heard Horne slam the door of the master bedroom and, pricking her ears, she could hear her defecting companion being very busy in there. There was much banging about for ten minutes or so before Horne left for her office and then Elphinstone got up off the ruined love seat and went into the master bedroom for a bit of reconnaissance. It was productive of something in the nature of reassurance. Elphinstone discovered that Horne had packed a few things in a helter-skelter fashion in her Val-pac, had broken the zipper on it, and had left out her toilet articles, even her toothbrush, and so Elphinstone was reasonably certain the half-packed Val-pac was only one of Horne's little childish gestures.

At noon on August the Tenth, Elphinstone phoned the research department of the *National Journal of Social Commentary* which employed Horne and she got Horne on the phone.

Both voices were sad and subdued, so subdued that each had to ask the other to repeat certain things that were said in the long and hesitant phone conversation between them. The conversation was gentle and almost elegiac in tone. Only one controversial topic was brought up, the matter of the polio shots. Elphinstone said, Dear, if it will make you feel better, I'll go for a polio shot. There was a slight pause and a catch in Horne's voice when she replied to this offer.

Dear, she said, you know the horror I have of poliomyelitis since it struck my first cousin Alfie, who is still in the iron lung, just his head sticking out, wasted like a death's head, dear, and his lost blue eyes, oh, my God, the look in them when he tries to smile at me, oh, my God, that look!

Both of them started to weep at this point in the conversation and were barely able to utter audible good-byes . . .

But at four o'clock that hot August afternoon there was a sudden change in Elphinstone's mood. Having made an afternoon appointment with her analyst, she recounted with marvelous accuracy the whole morning talk with Horne.

When will you learn, he asked sadly, when a thing is washed up?

He rose from his chair behind the couch on which Elphinstone was stretched, holding a wad of Kleenex to her nostrils; he was terminating the session after only twenty-five minutes of it, thus cheating Elphinstone out of half she paid for it.

Gravely he held the door open for Elphinstone to go forth. She went sobbing into the hot afternoon. It was overcast but blazing.

Nothing, nothing, she thought. She meant she had nothing to do. But when she went home, an aggressive impulse seized her. She went into the master bedroom and completed Horne's packing, very thoroughly, very quickly and neatly, and placed all four pieces of luggage by the bedroom door. Then she went to her own room, packed a zipper bag of

weekend things, and cut out to Grand Central Station, taking
a train to Shadow Glade, where she intended to stay till
Horne had taken the radical hint and evacuated the East
Sixty-first Street premises for good.

When she arrived at Mama's, Elphinstone found her suffering again from cardiac asthma, having another crisis with a
nurse in attendance. She could feel nothing about it, except
the usual shameful speculation about Mama's last will and
testament: would the estate go mostly to the married sister
with three children or had Mama been fair about it and realized that Elphinstone was really the one who needed financial
protection over the years to come, or would it all go (oh,
God) to the Knowledgist Church and its missionary efforts in
New Zealand, which had been Mama's pet interest in recent
years. Elphinstone was sickened by this base consideration in
her heart, and when Mama's attack of cardiac asthma sub-
sided and Mama got out of bed and began to talk about the
Knowledgist faith again, Elphinstone was relieved, and she
suddenly told Mama that she thought she, Elphinstone, had
better go back to New York, since she had left without letting Horne know that she was leaving, which was not a kind
thing to do to such a nervous person as Horne.

I don't understand this everlasting business of Horne,
Horne, complained Mama. What the devil is Horne? I've
heard nothing but Horne out of you for ten years running.
Doesn't this Horne have a Christian name to be called by
you? Oh, my God, there's something peculiar about it, I've
always thought so. What's it *mean?* I don't know what to
imagine!

Oh, Mama, there's nothing for you to imagine, said Elphinstone. We are two unmarried professional women and unmarried professional women address each other by surnames.
It's a professional woman's practice in Manhattan; that's all
there is to it, Mama.

Oh, said Mama, hmmm, I don't know, well . . .

She gave Elphinstone a little darting glance but dropped
the subject of Horne and asked the nurse in attendance to
help her onto the potty.

Well, the old lady had pulled through another very serious
attack of cardiac ashma and was now inclined to be comfort-

ed by little ministrations and also by the successful cheese
soufflé which Elphinstone had prepared for their bedside supper.

Then Mama was further comforted and reassured by the
doctor's dismissal of the nurse in attendance.

The doctor must think I'm better, she observed to her
daughter.

Elphinstone said, Yes, Mama, your face was blue when I
got here but now it's almost returned to a normal color.

Blue? said Mama.

Yes, Mama, almost purple. It's a condition called cyanosis.

Oh, my God, Mama sighed, cyna—*what* did you call it?

Observing that her use of such clinical terminology had upset Mama again, Elphinstone made a number of more conventional remarks such as how becoming Mama's little pink
bed jacket looked on her now that her face had returned to a
normal shade, and she reminded Mama that she had given
Mama this bed jacket along with a pair of knitted booties
and an embroidered cover for the hot-water bottle on
Mama's eighty-fifth birthday.

After a little silence she could not suppress the spoken
recollection that Mama's other daughter, the married one,
Violet, had completely ignored Mama's birthday, as had the
grandchildren, Charlie and Clem and Eunice.

But Mama was no longer attentive, her sedation had begun
to work on her now, and the slow and comparatively placid
rise and fall of her huge old bosom suggested to Elphinstone
the swells and lapses of an ocean that was subsiding from the
violence of a typhoon.

It's wonderful how she keeps fighting off Mr. Black, said
Elphinstone to herself. (Mr. Black was her private name for
The Reaper.)

Lacey, said Elphinstone to her mama's housekeeper, has
Mama received any visits from her lawyer lately?

The old housekeeper had prepared a toddy of hot buttered
rum for Elphinstone and given her the schedule of morning
trains to Manhattan.

Sipping the toddy, Elphinstone felt reassured about
Mama's old housekeeper. She'd sometimes suspected Lacey

of having a sly intention of surviving Mama and so receiving some portion of Mama's estate, but now, this midnight, it was clearly apparent to Elphinstone that the ancient housekeeper was really unlikely to last as long as Mama. She had asthma, too, as well as rheumatoid arthritis with calcium deposits in the spine so that she walked bent over like a bow, in fact her physical condition struck Elphinstone as being worse than Mama's although she, Lacey, continued to work and move around with it, having that sort of animal tenacity to the habit of existence which Elphinstone was not quite certain that she respected either in Mama or in Mama's old housekeeper.

She can't hang on forever, Elphinstone murmured, half-aloud.

What's that, Miss? Inquired the housekeeper.

I said that Mama is still obsessed with the Knowledgist Church in spite of the fact it never got out of New Zealand where it originated a year before Mama's conversion, on her visit to Auckland with Papa when he failed to recuperate from the removal of his prostate in nineteen twelve . . .

What?

Nothing, she replied gently to the housekeeper's question. Then she raised her voice and said, *Will you please call me a cab now?*

What?

Cab! Call! Now!

Oh . . .

Yes, I've decided not to wait for the morning train to Manhattan but to return in a taxi. It will be expensive, but . . .

The sentence, uncompleted, would have been, if completed, to the effect that she intended to surprise Horne in the midst of a Babylonian revel with her N.Y.U. crowd, and she was thinking particularly of a remark she would make to the red-bearded philosophy prof.

Are you an advocate of women's lib? she would ask, for strictly personal reasons.

A slow smile grew on her face as she descended the stairs to the entrance hall of Mama's summer haven.

Hmmm, she reflected.

Her mood was so much improved by her masterly strat-
agem that she slipped a dollar bill into Lacey's old lizard-
chill fingers at the door.

The cab was there.

Told that the fare to Manhattan would probably amount
to about eighty dollars, Elphinstone angrily dismissed the
driver, but before he had turned onto the highway from the
drive she called him back in a voice like a clap of thunder.

It had occurred to Elphinstone that eighty dollars was less
than half the cost of two sessions with Schreiber and she suspected so strongly that she was nearly certain that on the
early morning of August the Eleventh her little home would
be exorcised forever of the demonology and other mischiefs
related to that circle from N.Y.U. as well as—

Yes, Horne will attempt to stick to me like a tar baby, but
we'll see about that!

When Elphinstone admitted herself by latchkey to the Sixty-
first Street apartment, she was confronted by a scene far different from that which she had anticipated all of the long
and costly way home.

No revel was in progress, no sign of disorder was to be
seen in the Horne-Elphinstone establishment.

Horne? Where *is* she? Oh, there!

Horne was seated in sleep on the ruinously stained love
seat. She was facing the idiot box. It was still turned on, although it was after "The Tonight Show" had been wrapped
up and even the "Late Late Movie." The screen was just a
crazy white glaze of light with little swirling black dots on it,
it was like a negative film clip of a blizzard in some desolate
country and it was accompanied, sound-wise, by a subdued
static roar. Why, my God, it was just like the conscious and
unconscious mental processes of Elphinstone were being
played back aloud from a sound track made silently during
that prodigal gesture of a cab ride home, Christ Jesus.

Elphinstone studied the small, drooping figure of Horne
asleep on the love seat, Horne's soft snoring interspersed with
her unintelligible murmurs. Before her, on the little cocktail
table, was half a bottle of Jack Daniel's Black Label and a
single tumbler.

Apparently Horne had drunk herself to sleep in front of
that idiot box, quite, quite alone . . .

Elphinstone was in the presence of a mystery:

She checked with their answering service, requesting all
messages for herself and Horne, too.

The single one which she had received was from a Sarah
Lawrence graduate who was canceling a luncheon appointment because of a touch of the flu. The single message for
Horne was more interesting. It said, with a brevity that
struck Elphinstone as insulting, Sorry, no show, Sandy Cut-
soe.

(The name was that of the red-bearded philosophy prof
from the poison-ivy-league school.)

Sympathy for the small and abandoned person on the love
seat entered Elphinstone's heart like the warm, peaceful
drunkenness that comes from wine. She turned off the TV
set, that negative film clip of the snowstorm at night in some
way-off empty country, and then it was quite dark in the
room and it was silent except for Horne's soft snores and
murmurings and the occasional sleepy clucks of the parrot,
still in her summer palace on the balcony where she might as
well stay the night through.

Ah me, said Elphinstone, we've gotten through August the
Tenth, that much is for sure anyhow . . .

She did, then, a curious thing, a thing which she would
remember with embarrassment and would report to Schreiber
on Monday in hope of obtaining some insight into the deeper
meaning that it must surely contain.

She crouched before the love seat and gently pressed a
cheek to Horne's bony kneecaps and encircled her thin calves
with an arm. In this position, not comfortable but comforting, she watched the city's profile creep with understandable
reluctance into morning, because, my God, yes, Horne's comment did fit those monolithic structures downtown; they truly
were like a lot of illuminated tombstones in a necropolis.

The morning light did not seem to care for the city, it
seemed to be creeping into it and around it with understandable aversion. The city and the morning were embracing each
other as if they'd been hired to perform an act of intimacy
that was equally abhorrent to them both.

Elphinstone whispered "Happy August the Eleventh" to Horne's kneecaps in a tone of condolence, and the day after tomorrow, no, after today, on Monday, she would begin her polio shots despite her childish dread of the prick of a needle.

BIOGRAPHICAL NOTES

Biographical Notes

DONALD BARTHELME was born in Philadelphia and raised in Houston. His stories have appeared in *The New Yorker, New American Review, Paris Review,* and other periodicals. Some of these stories were collected in *Come Back, Dr. Caligari,* which was published in 1964, and in two later collections, *Unspeakable Practices, Unnatural Acts* (1968) and *City Life* (1970). He has also written a short novel, *Snow White* (1967), and *The Slightly Irregular Fire Engine* (1971), a book for children that was awarded the 1972 National Book Award.

HENRY BROMELL was born in 1947 in New York City and attended Amherst College in Amherst, Massachusetts. He has written short stories which have appeared in *The New Yorker* and is currently at work on a novel in London, where he now lives.

JOHN CHEEVER was born in Quincy, Massachusetts, in 1912, received his only formal education at Thayer Academy, served four years in the army, and has published novels and collections of short stories. He lives with his wife and children in an old farmhouse in the Hudson Valley.

JOHN J. CLAYTON was born in New York City in 1935. A graduate of Columbia College, he holds a master's degree from New York University and a doctorate from Indiana

University. He has published one book, *Saul Bellow: In Defense of Man*, and many pieces of short fiction and criticism in magazines, including *American Review*, *Antioch Review*, and *Massachusetts Review*. Mr. Clayton lives in a house he helped build on a hillside in Montague, Massachusetts, and teaches at the University of Massachusetts.

JOHN WILLIAM CORRINGTON is from Shreveport, Louisiana. He holds a doctorate from the University of Sussex and is presently working toward a doctoral degree in law at Tulane University. His novels include *And Wait for the Night*, *The Upper Hand*, and *The Bombardier*. He has also published a collection of stories, *The Lonesome Traveler*, and four volumes of poetry, the last being *Lines to the South*. In collaboration with Joyce H. Corrington he has written five filmed screenplays, including *The Omega Man* and *The Battle for the Planet of the Apes*. He has published poetry, fiction, and criticism in some fifty journals, ranging from the *Kenyon Review* to *Recherches Anglaises et Nord Americaines* and the *James Joyce Quarterly*. In 1967 he won a National Endowment for the Arts fiction prize, and in 1968 was visiting professor of modern literature at the University of California, Berkeley.

GUY DAVENPORT was born in Anderson, South Carolina, in 1927. He was educated at Duke University; Merton College, Oxford; and Harvard. His books include *The Intelligence of Louis Agassiz*, *Carmina Archilochi*, *Sappho: Songs and Fragments*, and *Flowers and Leaves*. His articles, reviews, essays, and poems have appeared in the *Hudson Review*, *Life*, *Arion*, *National Review*, the *New York Times Book Review*, *Poetry*, and other journals. His poem "The Resurrection in Cookham Churchyard" won the Blumenthal-Leviton Prize in 1967. He has illustrated two books by Hugh Kenner, draws the covers for *Arion* and *Paideuma*, and divides his time among painting, writing, and teaching. He teaches English and comparative literature at the University of Kentucky.

WILLIAM EASTLAKE was born in New York City attended

school in New Jersey, and while in the army won four medals, including the Purple Heart and the Bronze Star. He has published five novels, sixty short stories, and ten anthologies, and has been translated into ten languages. He has received a Ford Foundation grant and a Rockefeller grant and has won the O. Henry Prize. Mr. Eastlake and his wife currently live on a small ranch in Arizona with two dogs and several horses.

ALVIN GREENBERG teaches at Macalester College in Saint Paul, Minnesota. He has recently published a novel, *Going Nowhere*.

JULIE HAYDEN grew up in Larchmont, a suburb of New York City. She attended a Catholic boarding school and was graduated from Radcliffe College in 1961. She has lived in San Francisco and Hawaii, where she was deselected from a Peace Corps training program, and now writes out of the latest of a series of Greenwich Village apartments. In recent summers she has been a Fellow of the MacDowell Colony in New Hampshire, a haven for artists. Other stories of hers have appeared in *The New Yorker*.

GEORGE V. HIGGINS celebrated his thirty-third birthday in greater Boston, where he has spent most of his life. A graduate of Boston College, Stanford University graduate school, and the Boston College Law School, he is a federal prosecutor. His novels are *The Friends of Eddie Coyle* and *The Digger's Game*. His stories and short pieces have appeared in the *Massachusetts Review, Arizona Quarterly Review, North American Review, Cimarron Review,* and *Esquire*.

WARD JUST was born in 1935 and raised in the suburbs of Chicago. For twelve years he worked in the United States and abroad for *Newsweek, The Reporter,* and the Washington *Post*. He is the author of a novel, *A Soldier of the Revolution*, and a collection of short stories, *The Congressman Who Loved Flaubert and Other Washington Stories,* from which "Burns" is taken. Mr. Just and his family recently moved from the District of Columbia to Vermont.

JAMES S. KENARY was born in Worcester, Massachusetts, in 1947. After four years in the Marine Corps, he is now attending the University of Massachusetts as an undergraduate. He lives in Amherst, Massachusetts, with his wife and daughter. "Going Home" is his first published short story.

WALLACE E. KNIGHT was born in West Virginia in 1926 and now lives in Ashland, Kentucky, where he is a public relations executive for an oil company. He began writing poetry for relaxation about four years ago and his work has appeared in *The Atlantic* and several anthologies. His short story, "The Way We Went," was the Atlantic *First* prizewinner for 1972, and he is now at work on a novel. He is a graduate of West Virginia Wesleyan College and holds an M.A. from Ohio University. He and his wife are the parents of three sons and a daughter.

KONSTANTINOS LARDAS was born in Ohio of parents who had emigrated from the Aegean island of Ikaria. He graduated from the University of Pittsburgh in 1950 and received his M.A. from Columbia in 1951 and a Ph.D. in comparative literature from the University of Michigan in 1966. His book of poems, *And in Him, Too; in Us* was published by *Generation,* the University of Michigan, 1964, and he has recently translated the complete songs of Sappho. He is married and the father of three sons and lives in New York, where he is a professor of English at the City College of New York.

JAMES ALAN MCPHERSON was born in Savannah, Georgia, in 1943. He has lived in the Midwest and in California. His stories have appeared in *The Atlantic Monthly* and several anthologies. He is presently at work on a novel.

BERNARD MALAMUD was born in Brooklyn and attended public schools there. He is a graduate of the City College of New York in Manhattan and holds an M.A. in English from Columbia University. In 1940, while working for the government, he began writing stories for the Washington *Post*. His short stories have appeared in *Harper's Bazaar, Partisan Review, Commentary, World Review* (London), *The New Yorker,* and *The Atlantic*. This is his fourth appearance in *Best American Short Stories*. His novels include: *The Natural* (1942), *The Assistant* (1957), *The Magic Barrel* (1958), *The Fixer* (1966), and *The Tenants* (1972).

JOYCE CAROL OATES, winner of the National Book Award for fiction in 1970, was born in 1938 and grew up in the country outside Lockport, New York. She was graduated from Syracuse University in 1960 and received her master's degree in English from the University of Wisconsin. She has won many literary awards and high critical acclaim for her essays and plays as well as for her fiction. Her works have been widely anthologized and have appeared in several magazines, including the *Southern Review,* the *Partisan Review, Harper's, The Atlantic,* and *Cosmopolitan*. Miss Oates, an associate professor of English at the University of Windsor, Ontario, is currently on sabbatical with her husband in England and has just completed a new novel entitled *Do with Me What You Will*.

SYLVIA PLATH was born in Boston in 1932. She graduated from Smith College and went on to Cambridge, England, as a Fullbright scholar, receiving her M. A. in 1957. She married the British poet Ted Hughes in 1956 and after a brief return to America settled permanently in England. Her first book, *The Colossus,* was published in 1960. Her novel *The Bell Jar* was published in England in 1963 and finally in the United States in 1971. She died in 1963 and three volumes of the poems she left have since been published: *Ariel* (1965), *Crossing the Water* (1971), and *Winter Trees* (1972). "Mothers" is the last story Sylvia Plath wrote. It is set in the small Devon village where she moved with her husband and daughters in 1961 and where her son was born in 1962.

ERIK SANDBERG-DIMENT was born in Sweden in 1940. Arriving in the United States at the age of ten with only the English word "Coke" at his command, he enrolled in kindergarten. His stories and articles have appeared in such magazines as *Family Circle, Kansas Quarterly, the quest, Redbook, South Dakota Review,* and *University Review* (Missouri). He is presently a contributing editor of *New York* magazine, and, along with what he feels to be approximately half the other residents of New York, is at work on a novel.

DAVID SHETZLINE was born in 1936 in New York and educated at Cornell and Columbia. For the last several years he has lived with his wife, the writer M. F. Beal, and family, on the Oregon coast and in the Sierra foothills. Two of his novels, *DeFord* and *Heckletooth Three,* have been published and a third, set in the country of the painted freaks, has just been completed.

TENNESSEE WILLIAMS (Thomas Lanier Williams) was born in Columbus, Mississippi, in 1912, and grew up there and in St Louis. His college education at the University of Mississippi was interrupted for financial reasons but he later received his B.S. from the University of Iowa. He started writing and publishing poetry when still very young while simultaneously holding a variety of jobs, and since that time many of his plays have been produced on TV and made into movies and ballets—*A Streetcar named Desire* (winner of the Pulitzer Prize and Drama Critics Award), *Summer and Smoke, Night of the Iguana,* and *Cat on a Hot Tin Roof* (also winner of the Pulitzer Prize and Drama Critics Award), to name a few. His latest work, *Small Craft Warnings,* was published in the fall of 1972 and he has recently finished *Out Cry,* to be published in the fall of 1973. Mr. Williams resides principally in Key West, Florida.

THE
YEARBOOK
OF THE
AMERICAN SHORT STORY

January 1 to December 31, 1972

Roll of Honor, 1972

I. *American Authors*

ATWOOD, MARGARET
Underglass. Harper's Magazine, February.

BABER, ASA
The Ambush. The Falcon, Spring.

BARTHELME, DONALD
The Sandman. Atlantic Monthly, September.
Edwards, Amelia. The New Yorker, September 9.

BAUM, THOMAS
Backward, Turn Backward. Playboy. August.

BRIGHAM, BESMILR
The Old Woman and the Garden. Southwest Review, Autumn.

BROWN, ROSELLEN
The Ceremonies. Prism International, Spring.
Re: Femme. Hudson Review, Winter.

BROMELL, HENRY
Photographs. The New Yorker, April 29.

BUMPUS, JERRY
A Lament to Wolves. Seneca Review, May.

BUSCH, FREDERICK
Is Anyone Left This Time of Year? Fiddlehead, Summer.
What's Left. North American Review, Winter.

CAIN, EMILY
The Day the Package Came. Redbook, December.

CARVER, RAYMOND
What Is It? Esquire, May.

CLEARMAN, MARY
The Reining Pattern. North American Review, Winter.

COLLIER, ZENA
Mrs. Gold. Literary Review, Winter.

CONNOLLY, EDWARD
A Better Good-by. Redbook, September.

CORFMAN, EUNICE LUCCOCK
Her Time Gone Out of Joint. Hudson Review, Winter.

CRICHTON, ROBERT
Gillon Cameron Poacher. Playboy, October.

CULLINAN, ELIZABETH
In the Summerhouse. The New Yorker, July 8.

317

DE LANUX, EYRE
Pulu. The New Yorker, June 17.

DRAKE, ALBERT
Making the Point. The Falcon, Spring.

EATON, CHARLES EDWARD
A Flight of Flamingoes. Kansas Quarterly, Summer.

EPSTEIN, LESLIE
Lessons. Yale Review, October.

FRIESEN, VICTOR CARL
The Two Sisters. Fiddlehead, Summer.

GANZ, EARL
Gull's Ransom. New Letters, Spring.

GODWIN, GAIL
The Legacy of the Motes. Iowa Review, Summer.

GOYEN, WILLIAM
Tenant in the Garden. Transatlantic Review, Winter-Spring.

GRIFFIN, EDITH
May's Boy. Arizona Quarterly, Winter.

GRIFFIN, SUSAN
There Are Already Too Many Candlemakers in Peru. Aphra, Summer.

HAGGARD, JAMES
But the Daddy Doesn't Get to Cry. Redbook, June.

HALL, DONALD
Widowers' Woods. Iowa Review, Summer.

HANSEN, JOSEPH
The Dog. South Dakota Review, Winter.

HARRIS, JOEL
The Box. Carleton Miscellany, Spring-Summer.

HAY, JOHN
High. Sewanee Review, Summer.

HENSON, ROBERT
The Relevance of Backparts Constable. Carleton Miscellany, Spring-Summer.

HERRMANN, JOHN
In a Terrible Season. South Dakota Review, Winter.

HOCHSTEIN, ROLAINE
What Kind of Man Cuts His Finger Off? Antioch Review, Spring-Summer.

HOOD, HUGH
A Near Miss. Fiddlehead, Summer.

HORNE, LEWIS B.
Dream-Visions. Ohio Review, Winter.

HUNT, HUGH ALLYN
Goodnight, Goodbye, Thank You. Transatlantic Review, Spring-Summer.

ISRAEL, PHILIP
Pelike. Carleton Miscellany, Winter.

JAMES, BETTY PAYNE
Set Free the Wild and Savage Heart. Southern Humanities Review, Spring.

JOHNSON, DENIS
There Comes after Here. Atlantic Monthly, April.

JUST, WARD
The Congressman Who Loved Flaubert. Atlantic Monthly, October.

KITTREDGE, WILLIAM
The Van Gogh Field. Iowa Review, Summer.
Silver and Gold. North American Review, Winter.

KRANES, DAVID
The Frame Lover. Michigan Quarterly Review, Winter.

KURTZ, MADALYNNE
A Victim of Rape. Redbook,
February.

LESTER, JULIUS
The Ram's Horn. Massachu-
setts Review, Summer.

LYONS, AUGUSTA WALLACE
No Chance for Justice. The
New Renaissance, Vol. II,
No. 2.

MALONEY, RALPH
One's Twenty-Fifth. Atlantic
Monthly, July.

MANSERGH, DANIEL ROBERT
The Human Touch. South-
west Review, Spring.

MAYHALL, JANE
The Enemy. Partisan Review,
Vol. XXXIV, No. 1.

MERWIN, W. S.
The Salt Peddler. Seneca Review. May.

MONROE, DONALD M.
Ransome at Sublimity. New
American Review, No. 14.

MOORE, HAROLD
The Bull. Western Humani-
ties Review, Autumn.

MOUNTZOURES, H. L.
The Lotus-Eater. The New
Yorker, February 12.
Silver in the Cold Twilight.
Atlantic Monthly, April.

OATES, JOYCE CAROL
Blindfold. Southern Review,
Spring.

OLIVER, CHARLES
Drunk and Singing on a
Southern Mountain. South-
west Review, Summer.

OZICK, CYNTHIA
An Education. Esquire, April.

PANSING, NANCY PELLETIER
Happy New Year, Lutie.
Ohio Review, Winter.

PECK, ROBERT NEWTON
A Day No Pigs Would Die.
Atlantic Monthly, Decem-
ber.

PINTARO, JOSEPH
Let's Make Believe There's
No Problem. Redbook, De-
cember.

PORTERFIELD, BILLY MACK
"Down in Egypt Land."
Southwest Review, Sum-
mer.

PUTNAM, CLAY
The Pavilion. Carleton Miscellany, Spring-Summer.

REID, BARBARA
The Meeting. Quartet, Summer-Fall.

REID, RANDALL
Detritus. New American Review, No. 14.

RESSNER, LYDIA
The Way to Ogden Park.
Aphra, Summer.

RICHARDS, DAVID ADAMS
The Fire. Fiddlehead, Fall.

RICHARDS, SUSAN
Ping Pong. Sewanee Review,
Winter.

ROOKE, LEON
Memoirs of a Cross-Country
Man. Prism International,
Spring.

ROTHSCHILD, MICHAEL
The Austringer. Paris Re-
view, Summer.

SCHULTZ, PHILIP
Billy's Older Brother Herbert.
Transatlantic Review,
Spring-Summer.

SILBERT, LAYLE
The Man from Harappa.
South Dakota Review,
Spring.

SINGER, ISAAC BASHEVIS
Neighbors. The New Yorker,
June 10.

STADELHOFEN, MARIE MILLER
How the Safari Ended. Yale Review, Summer.

STUART, JESSE
Sunday Morning on Sulphur Creek. Kansas Quarterly, Summer.

SULKIN, SIDNEY
The Living Season, Michigan Quarterly Review, Spring.

SWAN, GLADYS
Flight. Virginia Quarterly Review, Summer.

TARGAN, BARRY
Little Parameters. Salmagundi, Spring.

TERRY, MARSHALL
Endzone. Southwest Review, Autumn.

THEROUX, PAUL
A Deed Without a Name. Malahat Review, July.

TREFETHEN, FLORENCE
Waiting for Francesca. Virginia Quarterly Review, Summer.

TYLER, ANNE
The Bride in the Boatyard. McCall's, June.

WARD, ANDREW
The Regular. Audience, September-October.

WEST, THOMAS A., JR.
Gone Are the Men. Transatlantic Review, Winter-Spring.

WILLIAMS, JOY
Shorelines. Esquire, June.

WOLF, STEPHEN
The Visible Man. Shenandoah, Fall.

WOOD, SALLY
The Virginia Forest. Sewanee Review, Summer.

YGLESIAS, HELEN
Semi-Private. The New Yorker, September 5.

II. *Foreign Authors*

BERGMAN, INGMAR
Cries and Whispers. Trans. by Alan Blair. The New Yorker, October 21.

BRENNAN, MAEVE
The Springs of Affection. The New Yorker, March 18.

CLARKE, AUSTIN
Hammie and the Black Dean. New American Review, No. 14.

FRATER, ALEXANDER
The Scribe. The New Yorker, April 8.
The Bushman. The New Yorker, June 3.

JHABVALA, R. PRAWER
In the Mountains. The New Yorker, December 6.

KIELY, BENEDICT
Maiden's Leap. The New Yorker, July 1.
A Room in Linden. The New Yorker, September 9.

LESSING, DORIS
An Old Woman and Her Cat. New American Review, No. 14.

NORRIS, LESLIE
A Roman Spring. Atlantic Monthly, February.

O'CONNOR, FRANK
Ghosts. Atlantic Monthly, November.

O'FAOLAIN, SEAN
Falling Rocks, Narrow Road, Cul-de-Sac, Stop. Playboy, June.

PERERA, PADMA
Birthday, Deathday. Southern Review, Summer.

RAMOS, GRACILIANO
Father and Son. Sewanee Review, Summer.

ROWE, ALICK
The Good Dogs. Esquire, September.

STEAD, CHRISTINA
The Milk Run. The New Yorker, December 9.

TREVORD, WILLIAM
The Ballrooms of Romance. Transatlantic Review, Spring-Summer.

WALKER, TED
The Ariel. The New Yorker, March 28.
Discobolus. The New Yorker, May 27.
The Swan Man. The New Yorker, August 19.
In Kittywake. Virginia Quarterly Review, Winter.

WARNER, SYLVIA TOWNSEND
The Inside-Out. The New Yorker, April 15.

ZAMAYATIN, EUGENII
The Fisher of Men. Trans. by Marvin Kantor and John Conron. North American Review, Summer.

Distinctive Short Stories, 1972

I. *American Authors*

ALGREN, NELSON
The Last Carrousel. Playboy, February.

AMFT, M. J.
Creations. Seventeen, April.

ARKING, LINDA
Piombino's an Hour from Livorno. The New Yorker, June 24.

BARTHELME, DONALD
Over the Sea of Hesitation. The New Yorker, November 11.

BARTLETT, BRIAN
The Polar Passion. Fiddlehead, Fall.

BARUCH, FRANKLIN R.
The Brighton Line. Colorado Quarterly, Summer.

BATAGLIA, J. FRANCIS
Serpentina. Michigan Quarterly Review, Fall.

BIENEN, LEIGH
We Are All Africans. Mississippi Review, Vol. I, No. 2.

BINGHAM, SALLIE
The Mad Woman. Ms., November.

BLISH, JAMES
The Light to Fight By. Penthouse, June.

BONTLY, THOMAS
Eight Meetings. Esquire, March.

BOUCHER, SANDY
The Fifth Great Day of God. Michigan Quarterly Review, Winter.

BRADBURY, RAY
McGillahee's Brat. Fantasy and Science Fiction, January.

BRIAN, LEE
Commitments. Kansas Quarterly, Winter.

BRIGHAM, BESMILR
The Cathedral. North American Review, Fall.

BROWN, ARA
If He Goes. Family Circle, July.

BROWN, ROSELLEN
The Ceremonies. Prism International, Spring.

BRUNOT, JAMES
"Father—Unfinished." New Letters, Spring.

LE DEUX, DAVID G.
Yowk. Forum, Spring.

LEFFLAND, ELLA
The Famous Toboggan of Laughter. Cosmopolitan, February.

LEVIANT, CURT
Keep Clapping. Event, Vol. 1/3.

LIBERMAN, M. M.
Narragansett, Fare Thee Well. Mississippi Review, Vol. I, No. 2.

LITTKE, LAEL J.
A Puff of Orange Smoke. Ellery Queen's Mystery Magazine, December.

LOGAN, JOHN
The Success. New Letters, Spring.

LOURA, ANN
Rented Houses. Event, Vol. 1/3.

MCKEAN, ROBERT
You, Stanley, and Your Stockcar in a Dying Town. Chicago Review, Vol. XXIV, No. 4.

MCNAMARA, EUGENE
Beautiful Country, Burn Again. Canadian Fiction Magazine, Spring.

MCNEAR, SUZANNE
The Plum Is Back! Tell Your Friends! Redbook, November.

MAIOLO, JOSEPH
Brother, Father. Greensboro Review, Winter.

MALOON, RUNAWAY
The Lost Animal. South Dakota Review, Winter.

MATTHEWS, JACK
The Colonel's Birthday Party. Ohio Review, Spring.
The Stone in the Path. Sewanee Review, Summer.

MAYNARD, JOYCE
Country Music. Seventeen, January.

MITCHELL, KEN
Truckin'. Prism International, Spring.

MOLYNEUX, THOMAS W.
The Value of All You Can Know. Shenandoah, Fall.
Visitors. Greensboro Review, Winter.

MOUNTZOURES, H. L.
The Pornography of Violence. The New Yorker, September 23.
At the End of Love. Redbook, August.
Winter Scene. Redbook, December.

MUELLER, ELAINE
Love in the Hamptons. The New Yorker, July 29.

MURO, AMADO
Helping Hands. Arizona Quarterly, Autumn.

NABOKOV, VLADIMIR
The Circle. The New Yorker, January 29.

NEWMAN, C. J.
San Francisco—Hong Kong. Prism International, Spring.

NORMAN, PHILIP
Blues Next Door. Playboy, June.

NOZICK, ROBERT
R.S.V.P. Commentary, March.

OATES, JOYCE CAROL
A Girl at the Edge of the Ocean. The Falcon, Spring.
The Sacred Marriage. Southern Review, Summer.
Stalking. North American Review, Summer.

OBER, HAROLD
Real Roger. Prism International, Spring.

O'CALLAHAN, E. J.
Torrid Torts. Forum, Spring.

O'HARA, J. D.
Beginning to End. Western Humanities Review, Winter.

ORVIS, PATRICIA M.
The Emotions. South Dakota Review, Winter.

OSBORN, MARGOT
Last Will and Testament. The New Renaissance, Vol. II, No. 2.

OZICK, CYNTHIA
An Education. Esquire, April.

PETESCH, NATALIE
No Such Thing as Death. Contempora, August-December.

POMERANTZ, EDWARD
What You Don't Know, Can't Hurt You. Ms., October.

POSTELLE, YVONNE
At Sebastian's House. North American Review, Fall.

POWERS, ROBERT M.
Shadows. Western Review, Spring.

REED, KIT
In the Squalus. Transatlantic Review, Winter-Spring.

REID, BARBARA
The Meeting. Quartet, Summer-Fall.

REINBOLD, JAMES S.
Eels. Esquire, February.

ROBINSON, IAN
Their Balconies Are Made of Fur. Prism International, Fall.

ROGIN, GILBERT
Facing Reality. The New Yorker, September 2.

RORIPAUGH, ROBERT
The Legend of Billy Jenks.

South Dakota Review, Winter.

ROTH, HENRY J.
Epilogue of Poliakogg. Prism International, Spring.

ROUSE, MARY
The Red-Haired Orphan. Aphra, Fall.

SAROYAN, WILLIAM
There's One in Every School. Ladies' Home Journal, February.

SAVAGE, JOHN
Priscilla in the Pond. Ms., December.

SCHAFER, WILLIAM J.
Spudnut. Forum, Spring.
Gains & Losses. South Dakota Review, Winter.

SCHOR, SANDRA
It Takes One to Know One. Carleton Miscellany, Spring-Summer.

SEE, FRANK M.
The Logger's Tale. Carleton Miscellany, Winter.

SEGNAR, DIXIE LEE
The Grocery Bill. Literary Review, Winter.

SELZER, RICHARD
Ride. Esquire, April.

SEXTON, ANNE
The Letting Down of the Hair. Atlantic Monthly, March.

SIKES, SHIRLEY
The Death of Cousin Stanley. Kansas Quarterly, Summer.

SILBERT, LAYLE
I Pledge. Literary Review, Winter.

SMITH, APRIL
Sailing. Atlantic Monthly, December.

SMITH, R. B.
A Late Benediction for Fa-

ther's Day. Arizona Quarterly, Summer.

SPENCER, ELIZABETH
A Kiss at the Door. Southern Review, Summer.

STUART, JESSE
Uncle Sam Married an Angel. Forum, Summer.
He Saw the Sun Rise This Time. Arizona Quarterly, Autumn.

SWANSON, RICHARD
Dear Rachel. Wisconsin Review, Spring.

THOMPSON, KENT
I Live in Canada. Fiddlehead, Spring.
What Costume Shall the New Man Wear? Fiddlehead, Spring.
A Broken Bottle: A Suicide for Barbara Ann Shea. University of Windsor Review, Spring.

TRACY, STEPHEN
The Potato Baron and the Line. The New Yorker, February 26.

UPDIKE, JOHN
The Invention of the Horse Collar. Transatlantic Review, Spring-Summer.

VALGARDSON, W. D.
An Afternoon's Drive. University of Windsor Review, Fall.

VEDER, BOB
The War Dead. Literary Review, Winter.

VENN, TOMMY EDWIN
Church Mice. Roanoke Review, Spring.

WALKER, DON D.
Salamandra Salamandra. Western Humanities Review, Winter.

WEIR, ALLEN
Bob and the Other Man. Georgia Review, Spring.

WILLARD, NANCY
Sinner, Don't You Waste That Sunday. Chicago Review, Vol. XXIV, No. 4.

WILLIAMS, DAVID
Shades. Contempora, February.

WILLIAMS, JOY
Taking Care. Audience, January-February.
The Bridgetender. Transatlantic Review, Winter-Spring.
The Route. Antioch Review, Spring-Summer.
Woods. Audience, November-December.

YATES, J. MICHAEL
The Sinking of the Northwest Passage. Event, Vol. 1/3.

YOUNG, ROBERT F.
Chicken Itza. Playboy, February.

II. *Foreign Authors*

APRIMOZ, ALEXANDRE
Seeds for the Sonata of the Birds. Prism International, Fall.

ATHILL, DIANA
The Beady Eye. Transatlantic Review, Spring-Summer.

BECKETT, JENIFER
  The Trap. Cosmopolitan,
    July.
BORGES, JORGE LUIS
  Twice-Told Tales. The New
    Yorker, January 1.
BRENNAN, MAEVE
  Christmas Eve. The New
    Yorker, December 23.

CHVATAL, VACLÁV
  Déjà Vu. Prism International,
    Spring.
DÖBLIN, ALFRED
  Two Stories. Prism Interna-
    tional, Fall.

FARZAN, MASSUD
  Loh. Prism International,
    Fall.

GILLIATT, PENELOPE
  Staying in Bed. The New
    Yorker, April 22.
  Catering. The New Yorker,
    September 30.

ISHIHARA, SHINTARO
  Lying in Wait. Malahat Re-
    view, No. 21.

MACOUREK, MILOS
  Sketches. Trans. by L. Freund
    Marketa. Colorado Quar-
    terly, Autumn.
MÁRQUEZ, GABRIEL GARCIA
  Blacaman the Good, Vendor
    of Miracles. Trans. by
    Gregory Rabassa. Esquire,
    January.
MERIÇ, NEZIKE
  Blue Void. Trans. by Nermin
    Menemencioglu. Literary
    Review, Summer.

NOLLEDO, WILFRIDO D.
  Rice Wine. New Letters,
    Winter.

ROSS, MAGGIE
  Sea Story. Transatlantic Re-
    view, Winter-Spring.

SALIMOGLU, ZEYYAT
  Green Gold. Trans. by Nural
    Yasin. Literary Review,
    Summer.
SANSON, WILLIAM
  Ghost Town. Mademoiselle,
    February.
SARANG, VILAS
  Bajrang, the Great Indian
    Bustard. Malahat Review,
    No. 21.
STEAD, CHRISTINA
  A Nice Cake. Partisan Re-
    view, Vol. XXXIV, No. 1.

VIRGO, SEAN
  Haunt. Canadian Fiction
    Magazine, Spring.

WALKER, TED
  As May Be. The New York-
    er, April 29.
  The Third Person. The New
    Yorker, October 26.
  Man on a Hill. The New
    Yorker, November 11.
WARNER, SYLVIA TOWNSEND
  Something Entirely Different.
    The New Yorker, January
    22.
  The Listening Woman. The
    New Yorker, May 20.
  Afternoon in Summer. The
    New Yorker, August 26.

Addresses of American and Canadian Magazines Publishing Short Stories

American Review (formerly New American Review), 666 Fifth Avenue, New York, New York 10019

Americas, Organization of American States, Washington, D.C. 20006

Antioch Review, 212 Xenia Avenue, Yellow Springs, Ohio 45387

Aphra, R.F.D. Box 355, Springtown, Pennsylvania 18081

Ararat, 109 East 40th Street, New York, New York 10016

Argosy, 205 East 42nd Street, New York, New York 10017

Arizona Quarterly, University of Arizona, Tucson, Arizona 85721

Arlington Quarterly, Box 366, University Station, Arlington, Texas 76010

Atlantic Monthly, 8 Arlington Street, Boston, Massachusetts 02116

Canadian Fiction Magzine, 4248 Weisbrod Street, Prince George, British Columbia, Canada

Canadian Forum, 30 Front Street West, Toronto, Ontario, Canada

Carleton Miscellany, Carleton College, Northfield, Minnesota 55057

Carolina Quarterly, P.O. Box 117, Chapel Hill, North Carolina 27514

Chicago Review, University of Chicago, Chicago, Illinois 60637

Cimarron Review, 203B Morrill Hall, Oklahoma State University, Stillwater, Oklahoma 74074

Colorado Quarterly, University of Colorado, Boulder, Colorado 80303

Commentary, 165 East 56th Street, New York, New York 10022

Contempora, 74 Peachtree Street, N.W., Atlanta, Georgia 30301

Cosmopolitan, 1775 Broadway, New York, New York 10019

Ellery Queen's Mystery Magazine, 229 Park Avenue South, New York, New York 10003

Epoch, 252 Goldwin Smith Hall, Cornell University, Ithaca, New York 14850

Esquire, 488 Madison Avenue, New York, New York 10022

Event (Canadian), Douglas College, P.O. Box 2503, New Westminster, British Columbia, Canada

Event (U.S.A.), 422 South Fifth Street, Minneapolis, Minnesota 55415

Falcon, Mansfield State College, Mansfield, Pennsylvania 16933

Family Circle, 488 Madison Avenue, New York, New York 10022

Fantasy and Science Fiction, 347 East 53rd St., New York, New York 10022

Fiddlehead, Department of English, University of New Brunswick, Fredericton, New Brunswick, Canada

Florida Quarterly, University of Florida, 330 Reitz Union, Gainesville, Florida 32601

Forum, Ball State University, Muncie, Indiana 47302

Four Quarters, LaSalle College, Philadelphia, Pennsylvania 19143

Gallery, 936 North Michigan Avenue, Chicago, Illinois 60611

Georgia Review, University of Georgia, Athens, Georgia 30601

Good Housekeeping, 959 Eighth Avenue, New York, New York 10019

Green River Review, Box 594, Owensboro, Kentucky 42301

Greensboro Review, University of North Carolina, Box 96, McIver Building, Greensboro, North Carolina 27401

Harper's Bazaar, 717 Fifth Avenue, New York, New York 10022

Harper's Magazine, 2 Park Avenue, New York, New York 10016

Hudson Review, 65 East 55th Street, New York, New York 10022

Husk, Cornell College, Mount Vernon, Iowa 52314

Intro, Associated Writing Program, Brown University, Providence, Rhode Island 02912

Iowa Review, University of Iowa, Iowa City, Iowa 52240

Kansas Quarterly, Kansas State University, Manhattan, Kansas 66502

Ladies' Home Journal, 641 Lexington Avenue, New York, New York 10022

Laurel Review, West Virginia Wesleyan College, Buckhannon, West Virginia 26201

Literary Review, Fairleigh Dickinson University, Teaneck, New Jersey 07666

Lotus, Department of English, Ohio University, Athens, Ohio 45701

McCall's, 230 Park Avenue, New York, New York 10017

Mademoiselle, 420 Lexington Avenue, New York, New York 10017

Malahat Review, University of Victoria, Victoria, British Columbia, Canada

Manhattan Review, 229 East 12th Street, New York, New York 10003

Massachusetts Review, University of Massachusetts, Amherst, Massachusetts 01003

Michigan Quarterly Review, University of Michigan, Ann Arbor, Michigan 48104

Mississippi Review, Box 37, Southern Station, University of Southern Mississippi, Hattiesburg, Mississippi 39401

Modern Occasions, 5A Bigelow Street, Cambridge, Massachusetts 02139

New Letters, University of Missouri, Kansas City, Missouri 64110

New Orleans Review, Loyola University, New Orleans, Louisiana 70118

New Renaissance, 9 Heath Road, Arlington, Massachusetts 02174

New Yorker, 25 West 43rd Street, New York, New York 10036

North American Review, University of Northern Iowa, Cedar Falls, Iowa 50613

Northern Minnesota Review, Bemidji State College, Bemidji, Minnesota 56601

Northwest Review, Erb Memorial Union, University of Oregon, Eugene, Oregon 97403

Occident, Eshelman Hall, University of California, Berkeley, California 94720

Ohio Review, Athens, Ohio 45701

Old Hickory Review, P.O. Box 1178, Jackson, Tennessee 38301

Panache, 221 Nassau Street, Princeton, New Jersey 08540

Paris Review, 45-39 171st Place, Flushing, New York 11358

Partisan Review, Rutgers University, 1 Richardson Street, New Brunswick, New Jersey 08903

Pathway Magazine, P.O. Box 1483, Charleston, West Virginia 25325

Penthouse, 1560 Broadway, New York, New York 10036

Perspective, Washington University Post Office, St. Louis, Missouri 63130

Phylon, Atlanta University, Atlanta, Georgia 30314

Playboy, 919 N. Michigan Avenue, Chicago, Illinois 60611

Ploughshares, P.O. Box 529, Cambridge, Massachusetts 02139

Prarie Schooner, Andrews Hall, University of Nebraska, Lincoln, Nebraska 68508

Prism International, University of British Columbia, Vancouver, British Columbia, Canada

Quarry, College V, University of California, Santa Cruz, California 95060

Quarterly Review of Literature, 26 Haslet Avenue, Princeton, New Jersey 08540

Quartet, 1701 Puryear Drive (Apt. 232), College Station, Texas 77840

Queens Quarterly, Queens University, Kingston, Ontario, Canada

Redbook, 230 Park Avenue, New York, New York 10017

Remington Review, Kent Associates, 12 East 12th Street, New York, New York

Roanoke Review, P.O. Box 268, Roanoke College, Salem, Virginia 24153

St. Andrews Review, St. Andrews College, Laurinburg, North Carolina 28352

Salmagundi Magazine, Skidmore College, Saratoga Springs, New York 12866

San Francisco Review, P.O. Box 671, San Francisco, California 94100

Saturday Evening Post, 1100 Waterway Boulevard, Indianapolis, Indiana 46203

Seneca Review, Box 115, Hobart and William Smith Colleges, Geneva, New York 14456

Seventeen, 320 Park Avenue, New York, New York 10022

Sewanee Review, University of the South, Sewanee, Tennessee 37375

Shenandoah, P.O. Box 722, Lexington, Virginia 24450

South Carolina Review, P.O. Box 28661, Furman University, Greenville, South Carolina 29613

South Dakota Review, P.O. Box 111, University Exchange, University of South Dakota, Vermillion, South Dakota 57069

Southern Humanities Review, Auburn University, Auburn, Alabama 36820

Southern Review, Louisiana State University, Baton Rouge, Louisiana 70803

Southwest Review, Southern Methodist University, Dallas, Texas 75222

Sumus, P.O. Box 469, Chapel Hill, North Carolina 27514

Tamarack Review, P.O. Box 157, Postal Station K, Toronto, Ontario, Canada

Texas Quarterly, P.O. Box 7527, University Station, Austin, Texas 78712

Transpacific, P.O. Box 486, Laporte, Colorado 80535

TriQuarterly, Northern University, Evanston, Illinois 60201

Twigs, Hilltop Editions, Pikeville College Press, Pikeville, Kentucky 41501

University Review, University of Missouri, 5100 Rockhill Road, Kansas City, Missouri 64110

Virginia Quarterly Review, 1 West Range, Charlottesville, Virginia 22903

Wascana Review, Wascana Parkway, Regina, Saskatchewan, Canada

Western Humanities Review, Building 41, University of Utah, Salt Lake City, Utah 84112

Western Review, Western New Mexico University, Silver City, New Mexico 88061

Windsor Review, University of Windsor, Windsor, Ontario, Canada

Woman's Day, 1515 Broadway, New York, New York 10036

Yale Review, 451 College Street, New Haven, Connecticut 06520